ROUGH-HEWN

ROUGH-HEWN

BY

DOROTHY CANFIELD

"There's a divinity that shapes our ends,
Rough-hew them how we will."

NEW YORK

HARCOURT, BRACE AND COMPANY

PS
3511
I7416
R6

ANY LITTLE BOY

CHAPTER I

In the spring of 1893 Strindberg had just published "A Fool's Confession," D'Annunzio was employing all the multicolored glory of his style to prove "The Triumph of Death"; Hardy was somberly mixing on his palette the twilight grays and blacks and mourning purples of "Jude the Obscure"; Nordau, gnashing his teeth, was bellowing "Decadent" at his contemporaries who smirked a complacent acceptance of the epithet . . . and, all unconscious of the futility and sordidness of the world, Neale Crittenden swaggered along Central Avenue, brandishing his shinny stick.

It was a new yellow shinny stick, broad and heavy and almost as long as the boy who carried it. Ever since he had seen it in the window of Schwartz's Bazar, his soul had yearned for it. For days he had hoarded his pennies, foregoing ice-cream sodas, shutting his ears to the seductive ding-dong of the waffle-man's cart, and this very afternoon the immense sum of twenty-five cents had been completed and now he owned a genuine boughten stick, varnished and shiny. What couldn't he do with such a club! He beat it on the side-walk till the flag-stones rang; he swung it around his head. What stupendous long-distance goals he was going to make! How he would dribble the ball through the enemy!

Spring had turned the vacant lots into sticky red mud, but Central Avenue was hard if somewhat undulating macadam. It had stone curbs too, that bounced the ball back as if specially designed for side-boundaries by a philanthropic Board of Supervisors. Somewhere along it he was sure to find a game in progress. Yes, there they were in front of Number Two School. Neale broke into a run and coming up breathless plunged into the scrimmage.

Shinny as played on Union Hill in the nineties had none of the refinements of its dignified cousin, field-hockey. Roughly

3

divided into two sides, an indeterminate number of players tried with their sticks to knock a hard rubber ball to opposite ends of a block. Team work was elementary: the slowest runner on each side lay back to "tend gool"; the rest, following the fortunes of the ball, pelted to and fro in a seething mêlée of scuffling feet and clashing sticks. After each goal the ball was brought to the middle of the block, the two captains took their stand with sticks on either side of it. "One," they rapped their sticks on the pavement; "two," they rapped them together; "one, two, one, two." Then pandemonium broke out shrilly, sticks rapping against each other or against opposing shins, yells of "shinny on your own side," a welter of little boys battling around the ball as it shot up and down, sometimes advancing rapidly, sometimes stationary among a vortex of locked sticks until finally a lucky knock drove it past one or the other side street.

Once as they were walking back after a goal, Fatty Schmidt noticed Neale's new weapon. "Oh, you gotta new shinny. Where'd you get it? Schwartz? Huh, them kind ain't no good; they split." Neale was silent as an Iroquois, but he had already begun to doubt. The heavy new stick didn't seem to be turning out what he had expected. It tripped him up occasionally and he never got it on the ball as quickly as he had his old home-made locust-shoot with the knob of root at the end. But he kept his doubts to himself, let out another notch of speed, and tried harder. It began to go better. He stopped a dangerous rush by hooking Franz Uhler's stick just as he was about to shoot for goal. Another time unaided he took the ball away from Don Roberts, lost it, but Marty Ryan retrieved it, and Neale and Marty raced down almost on top of the opposing goal keeper. Marty hit the ball a terrific crack. "Gool!" they cried exultingly, then on another note, indignantly, "Hi there, drop that!" For as the ball bounded along the street, a ragged little boy who had sprung up from nowhere grabbed it and made off. The pack gave chase. The little gamin had a good start but the bigger boys ahead of Neale were gaining on him. He turned off eastward. As Neale tore along he saw Marty and

Franz catch up with the little kid, and then . . . what was this? Where did all those other boys come from?

With a whoop of joyous exultation he recognized the familiar ambush, the welcome invitation to battle. "Come on, fellers!" he yelled back to his own crowd. "Hoboken micks!" And with the rest of the Union Hill crowd charged through a fire of stones at the invaders.

Then it was that the new shinny stick vindicated itself. Swinging it like a crusader's two-handed sword, Neale hacked and hewed. He landed on the funny-bone of a boy struggling with Marty for the ball. He landed on another mick's ribs. He heaved the stick up and was going to smash a hostile head when the enemy broke and ran. Triumphant, the Union Hill boys chased them to the edge of the hill, and sent a volley of stones after them as they scrambled down the steep path among the rocks, but pursued them no further. Below was the enemy's country. The Union Hill crowd never ventured down the rocks to the level cinder-filled flats beside the railroad tracks. That was Hoboken and a foreign land.

It was supper time now. The victors said "So long" to each other and dispersed. Neale, somewhat lame but elated, went up the wooden steps of the porch. He stood his stick up in the umbrella-stand, went to the bath-room, washed his hands, brushed his hair, at least the top layer of it, and went quietly down to the dining-room. There he ate his buttered toast and creamed potatoes and drank his cocoa silently, while his father and mother talked. He paid no attention to what they said. He was living over again the fight of the afternoon, and forecasting fresh conquests for the future. His mother passed him a sauce-dish of preserved cherries and a piece of cake. After he had eaten this, he got up silently and went back to his room. His mother looked after him tenderly. "Neale is a *good* boy," she said. Although he was no longer there, she still saw his honest round face, clear eyes, fresh color. She smiled to herself lovingly.

Her husband nodded, "Yes, he's a good boy." After a thoughtful pause, he added, "Seems an awfully *quiet* kid, though. I mean he keeps things to himself. You haven't any idea whether he's having a real boy's fun or not. He makes so little noise about it."

As he passed through the hall Neale lingered a moment to handle the shinny stick again. He looked at it carefully to see if perhaps there was not a little blood on it.

CHAPTER II

UNION HILL had been created by two very different classes of home-makers, a fact which was obvious from its aspect. Its undistinguished frame buildings for the most part sheltered families who, having to live somewhere, had settled there where inadequate communication with the rest of the world kept rents down. Side by side with this drab majority, but mingling with it little, a few well-to-do business men had built comfortable, roomy homes in an uninspired compromise between their business connections in the city and their preference for open-air life for their families. This narrow ridge of trap rock continuing the Palisades southward between the partly reclaimed backlots of Hoboken and the immense, irreclaimable salt marshes of the Hackensack Valley, had a certain picturesqueness, had seemed to promise freedom from malaria (supposed at that time to result from the breathing the "miasma" hanging low about swamp land), and certainly offered fresher air than a flat on a New York street or a town beside a New Jersey marsh. It was a one-sided sort of compromise in which the families came out rather badly. Whatever natural beauty might be inherent in the site was largely nullified by the tawdry imaginings of small architects and building contractors, and despite popular medical theories, the malaria was about the same on the hill as on the flats. But though the advance of the suburban idea was already developing more attractive sites at no very great distance, few families moved away. With the massive immobility characteristic of humanity, the scattered well-to-do families of Union Hill stuck it out, grim and disillusioned, taking the consequences of their error of judgment rather than lose the sensation of stability, which means home.

Little Neale was quite unconscious of all this. To his ten-year-old thoughts "the Hill" was home, and where could you

live except at home? It never occurred to him that there might
be other or better homes—the Hill was where he lived.
He accepted it as uncritically as he accepted life, school, his
parents. Being, for that region where every one took quinine
as a matter of course, rather a healthy boy, he accepted the
initial facts of nature without criticism or much interest, working off the surplus of his young energy in baseball, shinny
and guerilla skirmishes with the boys from other localities.

His unconcern with the world around him, except for the
details of boy-life, was complete. Home was warm and
secure; he did not inquire whether other homes might be less
warm or more elegant. Food was good to eat, though meals
with adult conversation between his father and mother were
tedious and occupied far too much time that might have been
spent in play. His father was kind and remote. Neale
thought very little about his father. He went away in the
morning after breakfast and came in just before supper. He
was in the lumber business, and when he went away, it was
to the "office." Neale never went to the office; but once in a
while, on Saturdays, Father took him walking down the long
flight of wooden steps, down to the enemy's country where,
thanks to the size of his father's protecting figure, never a
Hoboken mick dared to throw a mudball; across the railroad
track and a long, long way on paved sidewalks till they
came out on a wide, noisy, muddy street filled with trucks
drawn by horses with gleaming round haunches. And on
the other side of the street there wasn't any more land,
but long sheds that stuck out into the oily, green Hudson
River. These sheds had huge doors through which the big,
dappled horses kept hauling trucks, in and out. Some of
the wharves had ships tied beside them. Occasionally
these were sailing ships with bow-sprits slanting forward
over the street, but more often steamers, black except for
a band of red down near the water. As Neale walked along,
although he never ventured to ask his busy father to stop
and let him stare his fill, he could catch glimpses through
the doorways of what went on inside the sheds. There were
steep gang-ways, sloping from the plank floor of the pier to

the ships, and up and down these, big men in blue jumpers wheeled hand-carts, always moving at a dog-trot. Through other openings, bundles of boxes tied together with rope slid down sloping boards, and other men with sharp hooks were always loading them on trucks or unloading them from trucks; or huge bales descended from the air, dangling at the end of a clinking chain. This bustle and noise, the strange tarry smells and the clatter of steam winches exhilarated Neale, excited him, made something quiver and glow within him. He longed to go in and be part of it.

But Father never went inside, and it never occurred to Neale to explain how he felt, and to ask Father please to take him in. Silent as an Iroquois, he walked beside his father, who often glanced down, baffled, at the healthy, personable little boy beside him, looking so exactly like any other well-dressed, middle-class little boy.

And yet, often before he fell asleep at night, Neale heard again the clanking clatter of the great unloading cranes, smelled again the intoxicating tarry salty ocean smells and felt again something quiver and glow within him.

There was neither quiver nor glow about the place where Father finally stopped of his own accord. In a wide part of the street, huge piles of lumber were stacked. Father would walk slowly along these, looking at them very hard, and then he would go into a tiny, stuffy little wooden clap-boarded house —just one room, with men in shirt sleeves writing at desks —and there he would talk incomprehensible grown-up talk with one of the men, and the man would write at his desk, and Father standing up, would write in a note-book with a fountain pen . . . and that was all the fun there was to the lumber business!

Left to himself, Neale sat on the door-step and watched the fascinating life on the docks. Once he slipped across the street and tried to follow a truck in, but a big man with a red face yelled at him so loudly to "get out of there" that Neale ran back again, furiously angry but not knowing how to get around the big watchman. All he could do was to sit just inside the door, hating the watchman, and stare at the tantalizing activity so far away, and wish with all his heart that Father's business were more romantic.

Mother meant more to Neale than Father did. He knew her better . . . a little better. He had even some abstract ideas about her, that she was beautiful when she dressed up to go out in the afternoon. Mother fussed about his clothes more than was convenient, and insisted on baths, and washing hands before meals, but when he was sick, Mother read him stories, and let him leave the gas turned on in his room when he went to bed. Mother gave him pennies, too, and when Father was away on a business trip, he and Mother would eat alone together, and she would talk to him and ask him questions about school and play, and his boy friends. Neale didn't mind telling her things . . . he liked Mother . . . but he couldn't seem to manage to think of a great deal to tell her. It sounded foolish to talk about games to grown-ups.

And games were really all that Neale cared about, almost all that he ever thought about. As to telling Mother other things, the few other things he did occasionally think about, why, there didn't seem to be anywhere to start. He'd have to begin "way back at the beginning" and now that Neale was ten years old, the beginning was too far back for him to lay hold of.

As a matter of fact, she did not often ask about any of it, even in her distant careful way of asking. She just took good care of him, and had what he liked for supper, and put the kind of books he liked up in his room, and kept his buttons sewed on, and every night, till he was a big, big boy came into his room to kiss him good-night in his bed. She didn't say anything much then; just, "Have you enough covers?" maybe; or, "I believe I'd better open that window wider," and then, with the kiss, "Good-night, Neale."

"Good-night, Mother."

Then he turned over and nearly always went instantly to sleep.

When Father was at home, mostly Father and Mother talked together at table, and read together after supper in the sitting-room, while Neale "did" his lessons upstairs. Or

else Mother would dress up in one of her pretty dresses and
Father would put on a clean shirt and his dark suit and they
would go across the river to a theater in New York, leaving
Neale to Katie, the good-natured, middle-aged Irish cook
who had been with them since before Neale's birth. Or some-
,times they had "company"; other ladies in pretty dresses and
other husbands in clean shirts and dark suits. Then they had
a specially good supper, the sort of expensive things that were
usually reserved for Sunday dinner, planked shad and roast
chicken and ice-cream, and coffee in the little gold-lined cups
that Mother always washed herself. Neale didn't mind company since nobody paid much attention to him, and he liked
the extra Sunday eatables on a week-day, but one of his
few impressions about his father and mother was that, although
they always talked and laughed a great deal more when there
was company, and seemed to have a lively time, they really
liked it better when there were only the two of them talking
over Neale's head at the table, and settling down afterwards
to read and talk to one another around the drop-light.

Another of those impressions was the tone of his father's
voice when looking up from his book, he said, "Oh, Mary!"
Neale always knew just the look there would be in Mother's
eyes as she laid down her own book and asked, "Yes, what is
it, dear?"

CHAPTER III

AMONG the many things which Neale never thought of questioning was the fact that he did not go to a public school as all his play-mates did. If he had asked, he would have found that his father and mother had an answer all ready for him, the completeness and thoroughness of which might have indicated that they had perhaps silenced some questionings of their own with it. He would have heard that of course they approved of public schools, and that if they had continued to live in Massachusetts, even if they had gone to live in a nice part of New York City, they would certainly have sent their son to a public school. But here at Union Hill, with the public schools so thickly populated by foreign children, the conditions were really different. What could a little American boy learn in a class-room with forty foreign children, whose constant study must needs be English?

There was no flaw in the reasoning they were prepared to present to their son when he should ask the natural question about his schooling. But Neale never asked it. By the time he was old enough to think of it, habit had made him incapable of conceiving it. He no more wondered why he went every morning to the Taylors' house on Bower Street, instead of to Public School Number Two, than why he had two eyes instead of one. That was the way things were. Neale was slow to question the way things were.

Dr. Taylor was another transplanted New Englander like Neale's father, with another college-graduate wife (rarer in those days than now), like Neale's mother. His ideas on children and the public schools would have been exactly like those of the Crittendens, even if they had not been fortified by the lameness of his only son. Jimmy's crutches made Public School definitely out of the question, and since Jimmy must have instruction at home, why, his two sisters, Elsie and

12

Myrtle, might as well profit by it. Dr. Taylor was glad enough
to have the expense of paying Miss Vanderwater shared by
Mr. Crittenden, and to let Neale share in the benefits of Miss
Vanderwater's instruction.

Hence it happened that every morning Neale rang at the
Taylors' front door, and when the maid let him in, went upstairs to the big front room on the top floor and there did
whatever Miss Vanderwater told him to do. He was under
her command from nine in the morning till noon, when he
went home and had lunch with Mother, who always asked
how school had gone, to which question Neale always made the
same truthful answer that he guessed it was all right. At one
he returned for two more hours with Miss Vanderwater. In
this way he went through a series of Appleton's Readers, filled
copy-books with thin Spencerian script, copied maps in colored
ink with the coast-line shaded with scallops, did arithmetic
on a slate and made very fair progress in learning German.
German was much in the air in that locality.

Of course he did not spend all those years of his life, side
by side with three other children without becoming intimately
acquainted with them. But one of the instinctive water-
tight compartments in Neale's Anglo-Saxon mind was the one
in which he kept his school separate from his life. He studied
with the Taylor children, but he never dreamed of staying
after hours to play with them. And yet he knew them infinitely better than any of the innumerable chance street-ac-
quaintances with whom he flew kites or played one-old-cat.
He knew instinctively, knew without thinking of it, knew to
the marrow of his brutally normal bones that Jimmy Taylor
was lame not only in his legs but in his character. Jimmy's
delicacy, the great care taken of him, the fact that he always
played in the house or back-yard with his sisters, made a sissy
of him. That was the plain fact, and Neale was not one to
refuse to admit plain facts. He was always kind to Jimmy,
at least not unkind, but he was always secretly relieved when
the front door shut behind him, hiding from him Jimmy's
too-white hands, thin neck and querulous invalid's voice.

Of the two girls, Elsie was only a little kid, so much younger than Jimmy and Neale that they were barely aware of her existence. Myrtle, on the contrary, was very much there, a little girl whose comments on things never failed to arouse in Neale the profoundest astonishment. How could anybody think of such dotty things to say? You never had the least idea how anything was going to strike her, except that it was likely to strike her so hard that she made an awful fuss about it.

Myrtle lived in mortal terror of any little dirt, it seemed to Neale. One day in May, when they had had a picnic-lunch out in the back-yard of the Taylors' house, Myrtle carried on perfectly wild about a little flying white thing that had fallen into her glass of lemonade. Holy smoke! thought Neale, if she was afraid to get it out, *he* wasn't. So he fished it out with a spoon, and handed her back the glass. And what did she do? She made up an awful face and threw the lemonade on the ground! Neale was horrified at the waste.

And the day when Miss Vanderwater in their "natural history lesson" told them about angle-worms and how they keep the ground light and open, didn't Myrtle go off in another fit, with her eyes goggling and her fingers all stretched apart as though she felt angle-worms everywhere. She insisted that Miss Vanderwater must be wrong, that such an awful thing could not be true.

"Why, what do you mean?" asked Miss Vanderwater, for once, Neale noticed with satisfaction, as much at a loss as he.

"Ugh! *Nasty!*" cried Myrtle. "So all we eat has grown out of what angle-worms have vomited up! And so they're wriggling around, *every*where, touching everything that grows! I never dreamed of such a nasty thing! I'll never eat a radish again! It makes me sick to think of it—to put my mouth where a horrible old angle-worm has been rubbing all its slime off!"

"Now what do you think of that?" Neale asked himself.

Mostly, Myrtle was just the worst dead loss you ever saw; but once in a while you got some good out of her foolishness, like the time when she bit into a lovely-looking apple and laid it down, looking very white and sick at her stomach. She had bitten into a rotten place, and although Neale pointed out honestly to her that it was the only bad spot, and that the rest of the apple was a corker, she refused to touch it, or even to look at it. She said she never wanted to see another apple again as long as she lived! So Neale ate it to save it, sinking his strong teeth through the taut red skin, reveling in the craunchy, juicy white flesh, chewing away on huge crisp delicious mouthfuls. It was perhaps as well, too, that Myrtle hadn't tried to go on eating it, for Neale found another rotten spot. But he spit out the cottony-feeling, brown, bad-tasting stuff into the waste basket, and having got rid of it, went on with the apple, his zest undiminished to the last mouthful gnawed off the core. The idea of going back on apples because you struck a rotten place! Nobody asked you to *eat* the rotten places! It was perfectly easy to spit them out, or, if you saw them before-hand, to eat your way around them. He couldn't make anything out of Myrtle, at all.

But he didn't allow himself to be bothered by her, any more than by rotten spots in apples, and he escaped from her and from the whole genteel atmosphere of the Taylor household, the moment three o'clock came. The instant Miss Vanderwater said, "dismissed," he hurried home, left his books and hurried out again to hang around Number Two School, till four o'clock sent all its mingled conglomeration, ranging from tattered ragamuffins to little boys in white sailor-suits, yelling and whooping out to the vacant lots.

For, although the Crittendens' New England Americanism was not quite resolute enough to make them send Neale to a public school full of foreigners, it was more than enough to make them incapable of conceiving so odious an act of tyranny as forbidding a little boy to play freely with other little boys, whether any one knew their parents or not. They would have detested the idea of keeping Neale alone in their safe, sheltered back-yard, and would have been horrified to detect in him any trace of feeling himself better than the public-school children—which he certainly did not.

Sundays had a special color of their own, not at all the tra-

ditional one. The Crittendens were Unitarians, not much
given to church-going anywhere, and the nearest Unitarian
church was across the river in New York. Mr. Crittenden
had enough of New York on week-days. So they never went.
Few of the Union Hill families did. Union Hill was anything
but a stronghold of Sabbatarianism. It considered Sunday
rather as a heaven-sent opportunity for much comfortable
beer-drinking, attendance on a Turn-verein, and for enormous
family gatherings around a big dinner.

For Neale, with no other children in the family, the day
was always solitary; not unpleasantly so. It was a day for long
imaginings, stirring, warlike imaginings, realized through lead
soldiers. Lead soldiers were a passion of his little boyhood.
He had two hundred and ten, counting the ones with their
legs broken, that he had mounted on half corks. He did
not move them around much. He did not knock them down.
When he got them set up in the order he wished, he fell into
a trance, imagining stories and incidents. It took a long time
to get them arranged to his satisfaction, with stiff marching
columns, at shoulder-arms in the middle, some Indian sharp-
shooters prone or kneeling behind painted lead shrubbery
out in front, a squadron of parade cavalry on one wing, a
troop of galloping Arabs on the other. Always he had a pile
of blocks behind which a coal-black charger was tethered,
and on top, leaning against a spool of thread, stood the general surveying his army. By uniform and whiskers the toy-
maker had intended the figure for Kaiser Wilhelm I; but
to the boy's eyes it was no Prussian king, but Neale—
Neale commanding his victorious troops. It was all arranged
with a careful hand and a loving heart, and it took a long,
long time.

Very often the dinner-bell rang before he had even finished
setting them up. At Sunday dinner there was generally "company," men friends of Father's mostly, but sometimes husbands and wives. Neale knew all their names, and shook
hands without self-consciousness. He grinned silently if they
spoke to him, and retired to his shell, busying himself with
his own thoughts, all concentrated on the impending battle.

He liked the things you had to eat on Sunday and had found that on Sunday he could eat the soft parts out of his bread and hide the crusts under the edge of his plate. Mother always caught him if he tried that on week-days, but on Sundays, with company there, she never said a word.

But no matter how slowly he ate, he was always through, wriggling uncomfortably on his chair and horribly bored, while those tedious grown-up people were still gabbling on. Mother always saw this, took pity, and smiled a permission to him to be off. He slipped from his chair and tiptoed silently into the kitchen where Katie was dressing the salad. But she stopped long enough to open the pasteboard ice-cream box from Schlauchter's candy-store and give him a saucer-full from the soft part on top.

Then he hurried upstairs again to act out with his army the glorious scenes he had been imagining during dinner. Sometimes it was a surprise attack on the march, with cavalry sweeping down on limbered guns, sometimes it was artillery formed in triangles, a muzzle at each apex, blowing the advancing cavalry to flinders. Sometimes it was a magnificent parade of triumph through a city gate with Kaiser Wilhelm (Neale) at their head.

But at any moment, especially as he came on to be ten years old, quite suddenly and inexplicably he grew tired of it. The illusion would. pass . . . they would be just lifeless stupid dead soldiers, with broken legs and rifles, and the paint flaking off . . . impossible to imagine anything with them. Also his arms and legs would feel numb with sitting still on the floor so long. Then Neale would slide noiselessly down the banisters, using his hands and legs as a brake to keep from crashing into the newel-post, slip by the dining-room door with its clinking coffee-cups and blue haze of cigar smoke, grab his cap and go quietly outdoors.

Nobody would have stopped him, he knew that, but it was more fun to keep it quiet. Free from the house he would act out his drama of escape by running for a block or so, and then drop into the roaming boy's slow, zig-zag ramble.

You can walk south or north on Union Hill for miles beyond

a boy's endurance, without finding a single feature to quicken
the imagination; but if you go east or west from anywhere
on the Hill, you come at once to a jumping-off place where
below you stretches the flat, marshy river or the flats. Neale
preferred the western edge, even though it had no steep rocks.
He was far from having any conscious love for landscape, but
he found a certain satisfaction in looking over the yellow and
brown expanse of the marsh-grass and cat-tails, hazy in the
afternoon sun, cut with straight black lines of railroads (he
named them over to himself, identifying every one, the Jersey
Central, Pennsylvania, Erie, Lackawanna, and Jersey Northern), each with little toy-trains, each tiny locomotive sending
up little balls of cotton-wool to hang motionless in the still
afternoon air. To the southwest a hazy blur that was Newark, and right in front, like a doomed mountain, bogged and
sinking into the marsh, the sinister bulk of Snake Hill. Neale
used to stand and brood over it, sometimes till the sun went
down, all red and orange. He did not stir till the cold roused
him to think of home and supper.

But his feet did not always turn westward. Sometimes he
walked to the eastern edge. The rocks were steeper here,
steep enough to be the impregnable fortress he always imagined
them. When he came here, after reconnoitering the ground
(for his tribal enemy did not observe the Truce of God on
Sundays), Neale would go out to the edge of the sheerest
promontory and dangle his legs down. Under his feet were
railroad tracks again, then a belt of vacant lots, some of
them black with cinder-filling, others green with the scum
of stagnant water, then a belt of frame houses where the enemy
lived, then a zone of city brick and flat tin roofs. Beyond
it all was Castle Point, high and green (healthy green this,
not scum), jutting out into the Hudson. Indistinctly he could
make out the other side of the river, the line of ships at
the wharves and more city . . . New York.

Occasionally Neale thought of New York, an almost myth-
ical spot, though he went there once in a while with Mother
on tiresome quests for clothes, as well as to matinées; sometimes he thought of the ships and the wharves, and how

much he wished he could see more of them. But mostly he forgot the actual world. He was in command of the fort. All around him his brave men were working the guns. Bang! Bang! The enemy were marching along those straight paved streets. Their cannon balls were bursting all around, but the garrison did not quail. Their sharp-shooters were starting to climb the rocks. Ah, this was serious! No time for delay. The commander seized the rifle from the hand of a dying soldier . . . how plainly Neale saw that dying soldier there at his feet . . . bang! bang! bang! . . . with every shot one of the foremost scalers dropped headlong.

The engagement was a decisive victory.

CHAPTER IV

INEVITABLY Saturdays were all devoted to play. Neither
Neale's parents nor he himself could have conceived of any
other way of spending Saturdays. What were Saturdays for?

It is true that in some of the more prosperous German-Amer-
ican families, Saturday was music-lesson day, just as four
o'clock instead of ushering in roller-skating or marbles meant
sitting in front of a piano, or stooping over a 'cello. But
Neale felt for play-mates thus victimized the same slightly
contemptuous pity he felt for Jimmy Taylor's lameness, and
the same unsurprised acceptance of his own good luck in being
free from such limitations.

Once in a while, too, Mother took him over to New York
to a matinée, and that was all right, too, if it didn't happen
too often. Neale liked going out with Mother pretty well,
and if there was fighting in the play he liked it fine. But
all that was having something done to you, a sensation of
which school gave Neale more than enough, and which he
didn't like half so well—oh, not a quarter as well—oh,
really not at all, compared to the sensation of starting something and running it yourself. If it really came right down
to a comparison, there wasn't any fun at all in seeing Irving
pretend to be a crazy man, compared to the fun of starting out Saturday morning, with no idea what you were going
to do, and rustling around till you got enough fellows together
for the game of the season.

To stand in your old play-clothes on your front-step, of a
Saturday morning, all the world before you, unfettered by
obligations, a long, long, rich day of play before you that was
yours . . . how could anybody be expected to prefer to dress
up in things you had to try to keep clean, sit in a dark,
hot theater and watch painted-up men and women carry
on like all possessed about things that weren't really so. But

that was all right enough for a change, and was as good a way as any to spend a rainy afternoon. Also, you could occasionally get ideas about fights, out of a play.

But the real occupation of life was the playing of games. He nourished his soul and grew strong on the emotional thrills of games. They were the rich, fertile, substantial soil out of which he shot up into boyhood from childhood. They were his religion, and his business-in-life, the wide field where, un-hampered, free as any naked savage, for all his decent knicker-bockers and sweater, he raced to and fro, elastic, exultant, wild with the intoxication of the heady young strength poured into him by every new day.

The astounding volume of sound, bursting up like flame and lava from a volcano, which rose from every group of boys at play bore witness to the extravagant and superabundant splendor of the intensity with which they lived, a splendor not at all recognized by suffering householders near whose decent and quiet homes a gang of boys settled down to play and yell and shriek and quarrel and run and yell again.

It was the boys' world, not only untouched by grown-ups but blessedly even unsuspected by parents. Since it was theirs, since they created it anew every day, it exactly fitted their needs, and it grew and changed with their inner growth as their school never did. They were far from any self-conscious notion that they created it. Rather they seemed to them-selves to accept it from the outside, as they accepted the weather. What had they to do with the succession of the seasons, either of games or temperature? In the nature of things you could no more play marbles in the autumn than pick wild strawberries in December.

In the autumn, they played football, a sort of association-football with no limit to the number on each side, played with a heavy black rubber ball, blown up with a brass tube. The tube always got lost, and the valve always leaked. After a few games it became deflated, with the resiliency of a soggy sponge. But it was kicked to and fro just the same.

When snow came, there was snow-balling, with forts of a rich, chocolate color, from the street-dirt mixed with the snow. About these raged feudal chivalry, loyalty and pride of place, one street against another. Sometimes all the district united against invading Huns from Hoboken or Jersey City Heights. Only a few boys skated, and Neale was not one of them, but everybody made slides in the slush.

With spring came roller-skates, marbles (utilizing the cracks between sidewalk slabs), tops, kites, cat (a game for two), and, ah! baseball in the vacant lots!

Neale was neither a star nor a dub at any game, but craving proficiency more than anything else in the world, he learned to do pretty well at all of them. At baseball, the major sport of the year, he toiled incessantly, and when he was ten years old, he was pretty sure of his job at second base on the Hancock Avenue Orioles. On ground balls he was erratic, but so was everybody on those rough, vacant-lot diamonds, where the ball ricocheted zigzag from one stone to another. Long practice catching fungoes gave him a death-like certainty on pop flies. His "wing was poor," as he expressed it; strong enough in the arm, he had never mastered the wrist snap that gives velocity. As a batsman he was temperamental; one day he would feel right, and hit everything, another day his batting eye would inexplicably be gone, and he would fan at the widest dew-drops.

One Saturday afternoon they were playing the Crescent Juniors, a glorious swat-fest of a game in which Neale had run wild all the afternoon. It was in the ninth, the score was 17 to 15, with the Crescents ahead. One was down, Neale at the bat, Marty Ryan, the captain, was dancing on the base line, ready to dart in from third, Franz Uhler was taking a dangerous lead off second. Neale rapped his bat professionally on the plate and glared at the pitcher.

"Hit it out, Crit, old man!" yelled Fatty Schwartz, with a perfectly unnecessary steam-calliope volume of tone, "Hit it out! Save me a lick!"

"Much good you'd do with a lick," thought Neale to himself. "You couldn't hit a basket-ball with a telegraph pole." Yes, it was up to him, to him alone. It was like a scene from one of his favorite stories about himself, actually happening;

and it went on actually happening. A wide one, another wide. They didn't call balls in Neale's league. He rapped the plate, "Aw! put it over, if you know how!" he taunted. A foul tip caught, another wide one haughtily ignored, a strike. The catcher put on his mask and moved up close behind the bat. Neale felt himself nerved to great things. He glued his eyes to the pitcher. By the motion it should be a slow out. It wasn't breaking. Neale stabbed at it, sliced it and landed a Texas leaguer back of short.

He didn't see what happened. He ran. He flew. As he rounded second he caught a glimpse of the left fielder and short-stop falling over their feet, both trying to pick up the ball. As he turned the corner at third he saw the pitcher starting to run in to cover the plate and guessing that the catcher was chasing a wild throw, Neale put his head down and sprinted for dear life. Fifteen feet from the plate he dove, and shot over in a cloud of dust.

Neale, the ball, and the pitcher all arrived there at the same moment, but a partial umpire called it "safe." Don Roberts fouled to the catcher, Fatty Schwartz fanned. But the game was won.

With his chest a couple of inches bigger than normal, Neale started for home, and there on the sidewalk watching him, stood his father, looking right at him, instead of over his head as Father was apt to do. Father patted him on the shoulder. "That was a good swat, Neale," he said.

Neale wriggled. "Well, we had to have a hit," he explained, "and I knew Don and Fatty wouldn't do much."

His father found no other comment to make. Neale had said his say. Silent as Iroquois, they walked home to supper.

The next afternoon Father brought him a Louisville Slugger bat and Neale was in the seventh heaven.

And yet, at the next game, he fanned the first three times up and Marty waved him to the bench. This was terrible.

But the sting did not last because two days later Miss Vanderwater gave each of them a present of a little book in German, and said auf wiedersehn for the summer.

CHAPTER V

THE end of school always meant the beginning of the yearly romance, the beginning of the two months when Neale really lived all the time, not just after four o'clock, and on Saturdays. And yet it was not all made up of games! In fact there weren't any games at all. Queer!

Neale's life was largely made up of things that happened over and over the same way, and so did this. The last day of school he always went home and found the house smelling trunky and Mother with piles of clothes folded on all the chairs, packing a Saratoga trunk. All the afternoon she would pack it, putting things in and taking things out to make room for other things, and when Father came home, things would be all unfinished. It happened just that way, always. When Father came home things *were* all unfinished, and Father took out his watch, and said the expressman had said he'd come at five-thirty, and Mother answered, "You know they're always two hours late."

Nevertheless she stopped taking things out, and there was a scramble and things put in any old way, with a good deal of laughing and funning from Father and Mother, and finally with Mother and Neale sitting on the lid, Father in his shirt sleeves strapped and locked it. Then while they were eating supper, the expressman drove up (only an hour late, no, not even quite an hour late, Neale thought), and took the trunk away, and now Neale felt they were going.

He lay awake that night thinking of the coming adventure, his heart beating faster, and then it was morning, and Mother was shaking him and getting him into his clothes. A hurried breakfast on lukewarm oatmeal. They went outside and got into a coupé standing there. Father and Mother sat on the back seat, and Neale on the little front seat you had to unfold. Then jog, jog, they went along Griffith Street down the curlycue road, the horse's feet going clatter on the cobble-stones. Then jog, jog, jog again till at last they stopped and got out. They had come to the ferry.

After they were on the ferry-boat, Father and Mother always waited so that Neale could see the deck-hand pull down the gates that closed the end of the boat and take out the iron hooks that held her fast to the dock. Then the whistle blew, and the boat started, leaving the dock looking as though a giant had bitten a half-circle out of it. Father walked with him out to the front deck, where, holding to his wide-brimmed sailor hat, Neale watched the waves and tug boats, and the gulls flapping about. Father made him look at the city ahead, and pointing out a building with a gold dome, told him that it was the World Building, and the highest in the city. Neale looked, found it of no interest and went back to his waves and gulls, which stirred something of the quiver and wonder the wharves made him feel.

When the boat got across, it went smash into the piles and slid along into the dock, where men hitched it fast with iron hooks and pulled the hooks tight by turning a wheel around. Neale always noticed just how such things were managed, and Father always gave him plenty of time to look.

Then up went the gates and off went everybody. Outside they got into a horse-car. After a while the horse-car began to run through a long, white-washed cellar, and Father explained (just as he had last year and the year before that), that *he* could remember when the trains used to be pulled through that tunnel by horses. At the other end of the tunnel they all got out once more, and now, at last, you were really getting quite "warm," for this was the railway station.

After Father had bought the tickets and checked the baggage, they got on the train, and Father and Mother talked for a while, till Father said, with a long breath, "Well, it might as well be soon as late," and kissed Mother and she kissed him.

Until Neale was a pretty big boy, Father always stooped and kissed him too. But Neale felt that this was quite a different sort of kiss, and he noticed too, that after it, Father always kissed Mother again, and held his cheek for an instant close to hers. But after this he always walked right away, quietly, turning around once or twice to wave his hat at them, his face as composed as that of any man in the crowd coming and going beside the train.

Mother let Neale settle things in the train, making no comment as he fussed over it, putting the satchel up in the rack, and then deciding that it would be better to have it down where he could put his feet on it, arranging his coat and her golf-cape over the back of the seat and then remembering the hook between the windows. Then the train started. A smoky tunnel, a scraggly belt of half-city—and then the real country. Neale never called anything the real country unless there were cows in the fields.

He was always astonishingly glad to see it, and stared and stared till his eyes ached, and drooped shut, and he had a nap, hunched up with his feet on the seat. When he woke up there was more real country, and finally they got there.

There was Grandfather Crittenden waiting for them, with the team and the three-seater, only the two back seats were out to make room for the big trunk. This was something like living! Grandfather Crittenden let him hold the lines. He remembered—*how* he remembered—every step of the eight miles, every hill, every house and barn and big rock, till finally they drove into the yard, got out, were kissed, and went up to the same room as last year, with its rag-carpet and painted yellow bed. Mother washed his face very hard in the cold water from the big white pitcher, there was supper of fried ham and scrambled eggs and *soft* rolls, and cherry pie—and that was all a tired little boy could remember that night.

Next morning vacation really began with a rush outdoors to see the mill, the saw-mill, the center of Neale's life in the country. There it was, just as it ought to be, the big saw snarling its way through a pine log, and old Silas with the lever in his hand, standing as though he hadn't moved since the day Neale had gone away last September. Neale ran around to the back, climbed on the carriage and rode back and forth as Silas fed the log methodically down on the saw, and raced it back to set a fresh cut. Silas only nodded without speaking. He didn't like wasting words, and speaking was mostly wasted when the saw was screaming, the belts slapping, and down below was the pound! pound! pound! of the mill-wheel.

After a time Neale went down to the far end of the mill where the fresh sawed boards fell off from the logs. A new lad he didn't know was "taking away." He wasn't keeping up with the work very well, and to help him Neale picked up a slab and started to cut it into stove lengths on the cut-off saw.

"Hey there! Whacher doin'? You'll saw your arm off, boy!" yelled the lad. But Silas, stopping the saw so that his voice could be heard, saved Neale's face, "Let be, Nat. He won't get hurt. He knows more about the mill now than you do, or ever will."

Neale felt his heart swell with pride. He sawed pine slabs till his back ached from lifting and his shirt and hands were black from the dried resin.

There were other things to do at Grandfather Crittenden's, all the other things that boys do in the country, and Neale did them all. But none of them came up to the mill. Day in and day out it was around the mill that he spent his time, lying on the piles of fresh sawed boards in the sunlight, watching teamsters roll huge logs on the skidway with cant-hooks. Or he went below where you could look through the doorway at the flapping belts, and watch the sawdust raining down and making a great yellow pyramid. Even such an experienced millhand as Neale was not allowed to go into the cellar while the mill was running, under pain of all sorts of violent and disagreeable deaths. Getting your coat caught by the shafting and being whirled round and round and beaten to a pulp against the beams was one of the mildest.

But after supper, when the mill was shut down, he used to saunter out to it, in the long soft twilight, and then tiptoe down into the cellar and play uneasily in the sawdust, casting scared looks now and then at the shining semi-circle of the saw, with its wicked hooked teeth just over his head.

One day, as he played thus about the mill, his destiny

came and tapped him on the shoulder, and he knew not that
day from any other day.

As he was watching Silas take up the slack in a belt, a
strange man, an elderly, powerful, bent, old countryman came
into the mill, and asked, without salutations to any one,
"Where's Jo?"

"Gone to town for feed," said Silas. He added with a grin,
"Mr. Burton, make you acquainted with a relation of yours,
Dan'el's boy." He jerked his head at Neale.

The stranger looked hard at the boy, out of sharp gray eyes,
and the harder he looked the sharper grew his eyes.

"What's he doin' here?" he asked Silas.

"Oh, he's always hangin' round. He knows the trade as well
as some folks twice his size," said Silas.

"Well, what do you think of the sawyer's trade?" asked the
old man suddenly of Neale.

Neale could not think of anything to answer except that
he guessed he liked it all right.

The stranger seemed to dismiss him from his mind, fingered
his gray goatee, and looked all around as if seeing the establishment for the first time. "Mebbe. Mebbe. All right for
Massachusetts pine and saft maple. But if you want to see
a real mill, that'll handle tough Vermont yellow birch and
rock-maple, you come back to Ashley with me."

The stranger stayed to supper, and Neale learned that he
was his great-uncle Burton Crittenden. He asked many sharp-
sounding questions that made his brother, Neale's grandfather,
snort and say hotly, "Oh, we all know there ain't any proper
mill practice outside Vermont, but the Commonwealth of
Massachusetts is managing to worry along somehow, in her
shiftless fashion."

But when the old man spoke to Neale there was a gentler
note in his voice. He talked of sugaring-off, and twenty-two-
foot snowdrifts, and asked Neale's mother if she wouldn't send
the boy to Ashley some time, to visit his great-uncle.

His mother agreed to do it—"some time."

CULTURE IN THE AIR

CHAPTER VI

April 10, 1898.

OLD Jeanne Amigorena was on her way to Bayonne to complain to her niece of her rheumatism and her daughter-in-law. She detested the railroad, as she did everything new and not Basque, but at her age it was not easy to foot it along the fourteen kilometres of white road between Midassoa and Bayonne. So, grimly disapproving, she hoisted her square, stalwart, black-clad body into the third-class compartment of the slow way-train which comes shuffling up from the Spanish frontier about noon.

Even for a Basque of the oldest rock, there is one satisfaction to be had out of the forty-minute trip by rail to Bayonne. This is at the station of La Negresse where your way-train meets the down express from Paris. The chic people from the first-class compartments are there summoned to get out and change to the little local line which jolts them the three kilometres to Biarritz. This change of cars is never announced at Paris, it is always furiously exasperating to tourists, and in consequence they afford an entertaining spectacle to any one with a low opinion of human nature. Jeanne, who had less than no regard for any human nature outside the Basque race, always enjoyed the contempt she felt for these fashionably-dressed, ineffectual French weaklings. She took advantage of the leisurely wait at La Negresse, while the luggage was noisily transferred from one train to the other, to lean her head and shoulders out of the window, and to indulge herself in a hearty bout of derision for the uncomely fashionable Parisians, city-pale and flabby. She drew a long breath of satisfaction in her own untrammeled ribs, to see their rigid bodies like badly carved pieces of wood in the steel armor of their corsets, their

shoulders grotesquely widened by their high puffed sleeves.
Used to stepping out for a daily ten-mile walk over mountain
paths, free and rhythmic in her flexible cord-and-canvas sandals,
she laughed inwardly at these fine ladies, tottering on their
high-heeled leather shoes.

Some of them were dragging along tired, over-dressed, pasty-
faced children. Jeanne had a passion for children, and she
now cried to herself, for the thousandth time, "What can the
Blessed Virgin be thinking of, to trust babies to such creatures!" Straight as a lance, with more vigor in her body
at seventy than any of them at twenty, with more glistening black hair of her own under her close black coif than any
of them could afford to buy, Jeanne who never altered her
costume by a hair or a line from one year's end to another,
who looked forward confidently to fifteen or twenty years of
iron health, felt a cheerful glow of contempt as she watched
them, running here and there, screaming nervously that one
of their innumerable bags or valises was lost, their faces distorted with apprehension for some part of their superfluities.

She did not altogether approve of the hatted, conventionally
dressed women she passed half an hour later in the sunny
streets of the little city on her way to the home of Anna
Etchergary. Anna was concierge of one of the apartment
houses on the Rue Thiers, opposite the Old Castle, and to reach
it, Jeanne had to pass through the new quarter of Bayonne, the
big open square where the fine shops are and the Frenchified
madames walking about. Bayonne was a poor enough apology
for a Basque city, thought Jeanne, but its somewhat back-
sliding and partly Gascon and Spanish inhabitants were at
least not such grimacing monkeys as those Parisians.

She strode along with the swift, sure, poised gait of sandal-
wearing people, her mind full of the grievances she wanted to
pour out to Anna; the disrespect of her son's wife, and the
scandalous extravagances of her expenditures. "Consider,
Anna," she rehearsed her story beforehand. "She uses the
eggs herself, instead of sending them to market. She serves
omelettes, as though Michel's house were a hotel! And she

will not spin! She uses Michel's money to *buy yarn!* To think that money from the Amigorena farm should go to buy yarn, with a distaff hanging on the wall and ten idle, good-for-nothing fingers at the end of her arms."

On the terrible subject of lack of children in that house Jeanne could not trust herself to speak. It was too sore a spot that with all Jeanne's five grown sons, she had not a grandchild to hold in her arms. The two, Americans now, who were in the Argentine making their fortunes, were married and had families, but what were grandchildren on the other side of the globe to Jeanne? The two younger ones, who were sailors, were not married, and Michel, who had promised to be the mainstay of her life and had stayed at home to run the farm, here he had been caught by that impudent little French girl, one of the chamber-maids in a Biarritz hotel, a girl who did not know how to spin, who laughed at the decent Basque ways, and who had no shame for her sterility, refusing to go to Lourdes to pray for children.

Jeanne had never had any romantic feeling for her shiftless, hard-drinking husband, whose irregular earnings as a fisher she had been forced to piece out with much domestic service in the houses of others; and now he was dead, she never thought of him. She had never been to a theater in her life, nor read a novel, for she could not read at all. None of her native capacity for emotion had been used in her youth, nor frittered away later in the second-hand make-believes of modern life. It had all been poured out upon children; on her five sons, and on the one little dark-eyed, black-haired daughter, the little Marie—who had died at eleven, so many years ago, just after her first communion—the blessed saint Marise had looked, slim and straight in her white dress! The Blessed Virgin had found her namesake too sweet to wait for, and had taken her at once.

And now those strong, yearning old arms were empty of young life, and Jeanne's heart was bitter. She might scold her loudest over the waste of butter and eggs at the farm, she might gossip her head off about the faults of the neighbors,

and shriek out maledictions on the stingy bourgeoise who
wanted to buy her vegetables for nothing, she could not drown
out the forlorn echo of emptiness and loneliness within.

She turned up the Rue Thiers, glanced frowningly at the
Paris-like department store on the other side of the street with
its gaudy plate-glass show-windows, the pride of the younger
generation in Bayonne, and looked up with approval at the
huge, thick, battlemented walls of the Old Castle, substantial
enough that, and plain enough and old enough to please even
a Basque.

As she turned in at the door of Anna's apartment house,
her mouth was open to begin her litany of grievances; but when
she entered Anna's one-room, brick-paved lodging, she found
her niece with a budget of exciting news of her own, "Oh,
Tante Jeanne, what do you think . . ." she burst out as the
old woman swung lightly in; but before she would go on, she
went to close the door, bearing herself so secretly, with such
self-importance that Jeanne was between exasperation and
greediness to hear. Like all illiterates who cannot glut on the
newspapers their appetite for gossip, she was insatiable for it
in talk. She sat down on the front of her chair, her ear
cocked eagerly. Anna drew her own chair up close and began
to speak in Basque very rapidly. "I'm so glad you've come,
Tante Jeanne, you've had so much experience in working out
in families, you know about things. You know about those
American farm machines, that they're beginning to use on the
big farms, painted red, you know. Well, the American agent
for that company, he has come here to live, here in this house,
the grand second-floor apartments, the ones old Père Lapagorry rents furnished, on *both* sides of the landing, yes,
the two of them, because his wife, a very chic madame,
didn't think one was big enough, and what can one family do
with two kitchens, tell me that, and they with only one child
to their name, a little girl, who doesn't take up any more
room than a flea, so to speak, and the lady has asked me to
find her a cook and a maid, and listen, Tante, she says she
will pay sixty francs a month *each*, and fed and lodged!"

She paused to underline this and looked triumphantly at

her aunt, who for years had worked as cook in families for forty francs a month and lodged herself. Jeanne looked back at her hard, a new possibility lifting a corner of its veil in her mind.

"What are they like, these Americans?" she asked, "Spanish-Basque or French-Basque?" (To a Basque, the term *"American"* means one of his own race who has emigrated to South America, made his pile, and returned to his own country to spend it.)

"They're not Basques at all," said Anna.

"What, French?" said Jeanne instantly incredulous of Anna's story. There was no use trying to tell *her* that any French family was willing to pay twice the usual wage for servants.

"No, they don't even understand French, but the madame can read it a little."

"Oh, Spanish, then."

"No, I had Pedro Gallon go up to see them and they don't speak a word of Spanish. They're not even Catholics!"

The two women stared at each other. What could people be who were not Spanish or French or Basque, or even Catholics?

Anna went on, "Tante Jeanne, come upstairs and see for yourself what they are like. You have seen so many bourgeois families, you can tell better than I. I'll only say you have come to help me find servants for them."

Anna followed her aunt out into the hall and locked the door behind her. The key to the door hung with a dozen others, large and clanking at the belt of her blue jeans apron. Anna's philosophy of life consisted in having plenty of keys and keeping them in constant use. The only things you could be sure of were the things you yourself had locked up.

They climbed the shining, well-waxed, oaken stairway, Anna's special care and pride, turning itself around and around in the circular white-washed well, lighted by small pointed windows, which showed the three-foot thickness of the stone walls. They stood before the dark paneled door, its highly polished brass knob in the middle, and pulled hard at the thick, tasseled bell-rope. A bell jangled nervously, light uneven footsteps sounded on the bare floor inside, and a small, pretty, fair-haired woman stood before them, dressed in a pale blue house-gown elaborately trimmed with white silk. She smiled a pleasant recognition at Anna, and gave a friendly nod to the older woman. . . . Jeanne disliked her on sight.

The old peasant assumed a respectful, decorous, submissive attitude as became her social position, and made a quick estimate at the age of the other woman. She made it thirty-six at a guess although she reflected that probably any man would guess not more than twenty-eight. Jeanne knew by the sixth sense which comes from many years of unbiased observation of life, that the other woman was the sort who looks much younger than she is. She also was aware as by an emanation, that the other woman was not French. That was apparent from every inch of her, the way she stood and smiled and wore her gown; and yet she was dressed like any French lady, with a high, boned collar up to her ears, sleeves with a stiff puff at the shoulders, and a full, long, heavy skirt that hung in ripples and lay on the floor behind. Also her fair hair was tousled up into a pompadour, with a big, shining knot on top. Jeanne, her head a little to one side and bent forward in a patient pose of silent respect, wondered if that fair hair were her own or were false, and made a guess that a good deal of it was false.

All this Jeanne took in and pondered while Anna was trying to explain by dumb-show who her aunt was and why she had come. The foreign lady listened intently, but it was evident that she did not understand at all.

Jeanne took advantage of her absorption with Anna to look at her intently, with the ruthless peasant scrutiny, going straight through all the finer distinctions of character, deep down to the one fundamental, the one question essential to the peasant mind in all human relationships, "Is she stronger than I?"

Jeanne saw at once that the lady before her was not stronger than she, was not indeed strong at all, although she looked as though she might have an irritable temper. She was one you could always get around, thought Jeanne, her strong hands folded meekly before her, her powerful body a little stooped to make herself look politely mild. She was one who didn't know what she wanted enough to go after it and get it, thought Jeanne, casting her black eyes down, the picture of a well-trained, European servant, with a proper respect for the upper classes she served.

The lady, laughing and fluttering, now motioned them into the salon. Some of the furnishings had been taken away, thought Jeanne, looking about out of the corner of her eye—no lace over the windows! In this room sat the monsieur of the family, a large man, smoking a large cigar, and reading an enormous newspaper.

On encountering a new member of the male sex, Jeanne, although she had long passed the age when she needed personally to make the distinction, always made a first, sweeping division of them into two classes: those who were dangerous to women and those who were not. She instantly put down the monsieur of the new family among those who were not, although he was not bad looking, not more than forty-five, with all his teeth still in his mouth and all his thick, dark hair still on his head. But a woman of Jeanne's disillusioned experience of human nature knew from the expression of his listless brown eyes, from his careless attitude in his chair, from the indifferent way he looked at the three women before him, from the roughness of his hair, evidently combed but once a day, with no perfumed dressing on it, that he was not now and never had been a man who cared for conquests among women, or who had had many. She immediately felt for him a slight contempt as for somebody not all there mentally, and wondered if his wife were not occasionally unfaithful to him. She looked as though she might be that kind, a rattling, bird-headed little thing like that, reflected Jeanne behind her downcast eyes, changing imperceptibly from one humble, self-effacing pose to another.

Anna now turned to her aunt with a long breath, "I cannot make her understand," she said in Basque. "Think of a nice, pretty-looking lady like that not being able to talk! I cannot make her think anything but that you have come to be the cook yourself."

"Well, I might do worse," said Jeanne unexpectedly, her mouth watering at the chance for pickings. She spoke in Basque. Her face remained as unmoved as though it were the wood-carving it seemed.

Her niece stared for a moment, horizons opening before her. "Oh, Tante Jeanne, if you only would! With you here and me in the concierge's loge, what a chance for commissions off everybody from the grocer to the wash-woman!"

Jeanne agreed although with no enthusiasm. "But I'm not young. I don't need the money, if only Michel's wife would. . . ." She gave a quick look at the man and woman before her, who were now exchanging some words in their queer-sounding tongue. "They seem such odd people. Who knows what they are like? Their not being able to talk, and all—and not even Catholics!" She hesitated, feeling a distaste for their foreignness, and for the fussy, effusive smilingness of the madame. Jeanne always distrusted ladies who smiled at their servants. There could only be war to the knife between servants and their employer. Why pretend anything else?

A little girl in a white dress came swiftly into the room now, a long-legged, slim child of eleven. She darted in as though she was looking for something, and in a hurry to find it. When she saw the two Basque women, she paused, suddenly motionless, and gave them a steady inquiring gaze out of clear dark eyes.

Jeanne stared at her, startled. The child had thick black hair, glossy and straight, a cream-like skin, and long eyes with arching eyebrows as black as her hair, which made a finely-drawn curving line on her forehead and ran back at the sides upon her temples.

Anna noticed the older woman's surprise and said casually, "Yes, isn't it queer how the little girl looks like one of us, a real little Basque? She seems nice enough, only with no manners. See how she comes bursting into a room and then only stares; but none of the family have any manners, if it comes to that."

The child made a quick move now and still moving swiftly stepped to Jeanne's side. To Jeanne's astonishment she put out her small white fingers and took Jeanne's gnarly old hand in a firm grip. "Bonjour, Madame," she said, smiling faintly at her attempt to speak the foreign language, although her eyes were grave.

Jeanne had for an instant a strange impression that the child seemed to think that she had found what she was looking for. At the sight of the little girl, at the living touch of that small, warm hand, Jeanne forgot the chic madame with the shallow eyes, and the dull monsieur with the tired eyes. She looked down at the child who had eyes that were looking for something. The old woman and the little girl exchanged a long serious gaze, one of those deep, inarticulate contacts of human souls which come and go like a breath taken, and leave human lives altered for always.

Jeanne drew a long breath. She said in a low tone to the child, forgetting that she could not understand, "What do you call yourself, dear?"

The child answered in French haltingly, but with a pure accent, "I call myself Mary."

"Oh, yes," explained Anna, "the little girl is picking up French fast. I can make her mother understand now, through her. She does the ordering for them at the Bouyenval pension already. They are taking their meals there, till they get servants to begin house-keeping. Madame Bouyenval was telling me this morning . . ."

Jeanne interrupted her niece, speaking in Basque, "Well, if you think you can make that featherhead of her mother understand anything, you can tell them that I'll come to-morrow to stay, and I'll bring a chamber-maid with me."

To the foreign lady she said respectfully in French, with a deferential inclination of her tall strong body, "À votre service, Madame."

CHAPTER VII

May 10, 1898.

MARISE sat in her room, in front of her table, a copy-book opening blank pages of coarse paper before her, a thin, mean-looking, pale-blue book marked "Mots Usuels" on her lap. It was her own impression that she had stopped for a minute's rest from study (although she had not yet begun), and that she was thinking hard. But she was not thinking. She was feeling.

She sat with her elbows on the table, her chin in her two hands, braced so that she was quite motionless. Her eyes were fixed on the candle flame, burning bright, fluttering and throbbing in the draughts which came into the old room, around the decrepit window-casing, under the door, through the worm-eaten base-board. There seemed to be a thousand wandering puffs from every direction. What Marise called her "thoughts" were burning bright, fluttering and throbbing like the tiny flame at which she stared. They too were blown upon by a thousand breaths from every direction. If they would only hold still for a moment, Marise thought, and give out a steady light that she could see something by! If she only had some shade to put around those flickering thoughts so they wouldn't quiver so! It upset her, jerking around so, from one way of seeing things to another. What she wanted to know was, how did things *really* look?

Of course it was worse here in France, where everything was so uncertain, but it had started back home in America, it had always been going on ever since she could remember. It had always made her feel queer, as though she were holding an envelope up to a mirror to read the address and saw it wrong end to, the way everything looked different at Ashley the moment Maman came up to Vermont to take her home after vacations with Cousin Hetty. Marise loved it so there at Ashley, the dear darling old house in the mountains, with its nice atticky smell that no other house in the world had! It just fitted all around you, when you went in the door, the way Cousin Hetty's arms fitted around you, when she took you up on her lap, and rocked and sang, "We hunted and we hallooed."

At the memory, Marise's heart gave a great homesick throb. How far away she was from Cousin Hetty and Ashley now! How long since she had sat on anybody's lap.

And yet when Maman came to take you away, from the first minute she went in and looked around her, you could see right through her eyes and what you saw was something different. After all it was just a homely old house with ugly crocheted tidies on the chairs, and splashers done in outline stitch back of the wash-stands, and old red figured carpets on the floors, the way *no*body did at home in Belton. And Cousin Hetty talking so queer and Vermonty, her white hair smoothed down flat over her ears instead of all roughed up, fluffy, over a rat the pretty way other ladies did, with her funny clothes, her big cameo pin holding down her little flat round collar, and all other ladies so stylish with high collars under their ears. Yes, of course, the minute Maman looked at her, you saw how ashamed you'd be of Cousin Hetty if she came to visit your school at Belton. And yet there *was* the other Cousin Hetty you'd been having such a good time with. You just flickered away from Maman's way of seeing it to yours and never could make up your mind which was the real way.

Marise shook her head, drew a long breath and looked down again at her spelling lesson. It was a list of the names of furniture and household utensils, all very familiar to her from old Jeanne's thinking them so terribly important. My! How much more Jeanne cared about her work than any girl they'd ever had in Belton.

"*Lit . . . sommier . . . traversin . . .*" all the names of the complicated parts of a bed, a sacred French bed. As Marise looked at them on the page she could see Jeanne in the mornings, taking poor stupid little Isabelle's head right off because she didn't make the bed up smoothly enough; and all the time it was about a million times smoother than any bed ever was in America! Marise didn't believe the President of the United States had his bed-clothes pulled so tight and smooth. And she wondered if Jeanne worked in the White House, if she would let even the President's little girl sit down on the bed in the daytime. How *particular* they were about things in France! About everything. When you bought anything in a store how they did drive you wild with their slowness in getting it put up in the package just *so,* as if it mattered, when you were going to take it out of the package three minutes later, as soon as you got home. And at school how they did fuss about neatness! The lessons were easy enough to learn. Marise never had any trouble with lessons, but how could anybody ever do things as neatly as they wanted you to. And how the teacher jumped on you if you didn't, ever so much worse than if you got the answer to an arithmetic problem wrong. Mercy! How she did scold! There wasn't anybody in America knew *how* to scold like that even if they wanted to, and they didn't. It had scared Marise at first, and made her feel like crying, and she never had got entirely used to it although she saw how all the other girls did, just took it and didn't care and did whatever they liked behind her back.

Marise couldn't get used to Jeanne that way either, to her yelling so when she scolded. Marise hated to have people get mad and excited. And how Jeanne did carry on about the house being neat, the part that is, where company could come; (under her kitchen sink it smelled awfully and was full of greasy rags) and yet she'd shine up the salon floor over and over when it was already shiny, and never think of those rags. The least little bit of clutter left around in the dining-room, or even your own room, and how she would scold! And yet she was so awfully good to you, and was always giving you big, smacking kisses, and hugging you, and she always saved over the best things to eat when Maman had a lunch party, and you were at school. Even when

Maman had said you couldn't have any of something Jeanne always brought it to your room, under her apron, after you'd gone to bed. It wasn't very nice to do things behind Maman's back, but everybody seemed to be doing things behind everybody else's back. Maman did behind Father's, lots of times, and it was perfectly understood between them that Marise was never to tell Father on her. And it would be telling on Jeanne if you told Mother. And anyhow Marise didn't see Maman so very much any more, to tell her things; it was mostly Jeanne who did things for her.

Marise laid down her book again, lost in one of her recurrent attacks of amazement at there being so many different Jeannes inside that one leathery skin. There was the Jeanne who came every morning to take orders, and folded her hands on her apron, and sort of stooped herself over and said, "Oui, Madame," to everything Maman said. You'd think she was scared to death of Maman, and yet she went away to the kitchen on the other side of the landing and became another Jeanne who never paid the least attention to what Maman had said, but ran the house just the way she thought it ought to be.

There were two Jeannes right there, and there was another one, the outdoor Jeanne, who took her to school every morning—how funny that in France a great girl of eleven had to have somebody tagging along every time she stepped outside the house! This was the most interesting Jeanne of all. She told stories every single minute. Lots of them were about when she had been a little girl—gracious! think of Jeanne ever having been a little girl! That was ever so long ago, before the Emperor and the Empress had made Biarritz the fashion. Jeanne said those were the good days, when the Basques had their country to themselves, and you never saw a hat on any woman's head; they all wore the black kerchief for everyday and mantillas on Sunday for Mass, and lived like Christians. Jeanne could remember when Biarritz was just a little fishing village, a decent place, and *now* look at it! She could remember just as well when Napoleon and his Spanish wife first began to come down there so the Empress could get as near to Spain as possible. Many and many's the time Jeanne had seen them in their springy barouche, driving right along this very street, he with his eyes as dead as a three-days-caught fish's, and she as handsome as any Basque girl!

They weren't all stories of Jeanne when she was a little girl. Lots of them were of what had happened hundreds and hundreds of years ago around here. There were ever so many stories of witches and ghosts and sorcerers. There were plenty of those still in the Basque country. There was a sorcerer living in that little tumble-down house near the river on the road to St. Barthélemy. Why, Jeanne's own mother, years ago, one day looked up from her spinning and saw a monstrous pig, big and black. She jumped up and ran out to try to catch it. Her grandmother went out too, and there were a lot of the neighbors who were trying to drive the pig away. But it didn't pay a bit of attention, butted at them so fierce when they came near they were afraid, for he was as tall as a calf, and whoever saw a pig as big as that? And then the grandmother made the sign of the cross, Spanish fashion . . . and like snapping your fingers, didn't the pig change, right before their eyes, into a little wee woman they'd never seen, and she went up in the air as thin and light as a loose spider's thread, and drifted away and there was nothing there.

The little American girl knew enough to know that this story couldn't be true, of course. And yet Jeanne's mother and all those people had seen it. They saw a pig and it turned into a wee witch woman.

Marise stopped thinking about that, leaned forward and began kneading the softened tallow at the upper end of the candle. Father could say all he liked about candles being a bother, they were lots of fun. This part up next the flame got just right so you could poke it and it stayed put, any way you wanted it. And it was fun to lean the candle over and drop the melted tallow on your hands in little drops that got hard and you could peel them off.

As she poked at it, a dozen pictures flickered through her mind; the bridge over the Adour with the river flowing yellow and strong under it, and the bright painted vessels loading and unloading; the Sister who opened the door at school, always so calm and silent; the playground at school with the black-aproned girls, their faces twisted up with running and screaming and catching each other; and the same girls at their desks, with their faces all smoothed and empty, looking up at Mademoiselle as though they had never thought of doing anything she told them not to; the school-room itself, battered and gray with age, the old black desks with the slant lids that lifted up; Reverend Mother stopping in to hear a lesson, with her old, old quiet face; Maman so pretty and stylish, looking so sweet when she made mistakes in French that nobody minded, or thought of laughing at her.

Marise tipped the candle over carefully and let some melted tallow fall on the back of her hand. As she set it back and waited for the tallow to harden, she was thinking how very different from home Bayonne was; the Basque fishwomen, with the shiny fish in the round flat baskets on their heads; the white oxen with the sheep-skin on their horns, and their red-striped white canvas covering, pulling those two-wheeled carts; everybody streaking it along in canvas sandals and bérets, talking French and Basque and Spanish and never a word of English. And yet, Marise reflected as she slowly peeled off the hardened tallow drops, none of that was the *real* difference. And there was a real difference. The real difference was something inside you. You felt different, as if you'd looked in the glass and seen somebody not quite you. It was . . .

Somebody was walking slowly down the brick-floored hall to her room. It was Father's heavy step. That was nice! She hadn't thought she would see either Father or Maman, because there had been company to dinner again. She gathered the tallow drops together and dropped them in the base of the brass candle-stick. Then she remembered that Jeanne would scold if she did that. These candle-sticks like everything else in the house had to be just *so*, or everybody caught it. She swept them out again with her fingers, and stood holding them in her hand, looking around her for some place to put them.

The waste-paper basket was too open, they would fall right through on the floor, and what a fuss there would be over that! Oh, there was the fireplace, if you put things way back of the sticks, Jeanne didn't see them.

She was just straightening up from reaching back of the wood, when Father came in. He said, "Hello, kid," and she answered, "Hello, Poppa." They did this for a kind of a joke, to be extra American when Maman couldn't hear them.

Father sat down on the edge of the bed, making a big dent in the fluffed-up crimson, eider-down quilt, which Jeanne rounded so carefully each morning, and which she never let anybody disturb. Not, of course, that Jeanne would dare to say anything to Father, le patron. She would only grumble in Basque, under her breath, and Marise would feel her opinion of Americans going down even lower than it was. Marise could always feel everybody's opinions as they went up and down. And how she did hate to feel them going down, anybody's about anything! She always tried to fix it so they would go up. She now planned to fluff the édredon to a puff again, after Father had gone back. She didn't say anything about it to Father. You never did, about that sort of thing, even Maman didn't, although it made her awfully provoked not to have Father care, and she always said a lot afterwards. Marise didn't even say anything to him about the white down that would be sure to work through the cover of the édredon and get on his clothes. Father wouldn't care if it did. There were such lots of things Father didn't care about. But Maman would. She must remember to brush him off before he went to the salon.

"Having a good time?" asked Father slowly, the way he did, that let you see how he knew perfectly well you weren't.

"Not so very," she answered.

"Neither am I," he returned, "though you needn't mention it to Momma." There were always a great many things that were not to be mentioned to Maman, and a lot of quite other things that were not to be mentioned to Father, and Isabelle told her things she didn't want Jeanne to know, and *everything* that Jeanne said was not to be mentioned either to Father or

Maman. Marise, coming back from school, used to feel when she opened the door of the apartment, as though she were walking into cobwebs spread around in the dark, and you mustn't on any account brush into any one of them.

Father now went on, "What are you doing with yourself?"

Marise looked down at the cahier, its pages as blank as when she had sat down. Her father looked with her. "That's lovely paper, I must say," he commented, always with his way of showing that he meant just the opposite. "Are you supposed to write on it in ink?"

"Oh, yes," cried Marise, flashing up to seize the chance of sympathy for one of her grievances, "they *never* let you use lead-pencils because in lead-pencil there's a chance to rub out your mistakes. You're not supposed to *make* any mistakes."

"Doesn't your pen get stuck in it—it must be like writing on mosquito-netting," said Father.

"Yes, it does," complained Marise, "and you spatter the ink all over and break off the tips of the pen, and everything. And the teachers just kill you if it's not perfectly neat."

Father took up the cahier and looked at the paper hard, scratching it a little with his finger-nail. "Well, there's culture in the air, anyhow," he said without smiling, although Marise knew he was quoting Maman. He looked around the room now without saying anything more. Marise followed his eyes and saw with him the dingy, high-ceilinged room, dimly lighted by the one weak candle-flame, the heavy, figured tapestry curtains drawn over the window, the draught, although the window was closed, making them suck in and out; the ugly, ugly wall-paper, dark and scriggly; the stuffed red chair, the only comfortable one, where Jeanne would never let her curl up with her feet under her, because she said the place for shoes was on the floor; the marble-topped washstand with its little chipped white earthen-ware basin and pitcher like the old things at Cousin Hetty's; the clock on the chimney-piece that looked as though it were carved out of greasy, dark-green soap with a greasy dark-green man in a Roman toga on top of it; the shabby, dingy, red-and-white checked curtains hanging over the hooks where Marise hung up her

dresses, the tall dark armoire whose slightly greenish mirror
reflected all these things as if you were looking at them through
water; and finally over the bed, the big, shiny lithograph of
Our Lady of Lourdes in her bright blue cloak, standing in
front of her grotto.

"Well, maybe it's in the *air*," said Father. He spoke in his
usual tired, slow voice, sagging down on the bed the way he
always sat.

But then he surprised Marise very much and said something she never forgot. It gave her such a jump of astonishment to have Father say something as though he really
meant it, that she sat up straight at his first words, staring
at him. He said in a strong voice, "But look here, Molly,
there *is* something in the air here, by heck, and I wish you'd
get it. I mean the way every one of them in this country
keeps right after what he's doing, till he's got it just right.
That's the way to do, and we're all off the track with our
'that'll do,' the way we say back in America. It's the only
thing in their whole darned country *I* can see, that don't
make you sick. Now, look here, kid, you go after it and get
it. Start right in now. Learn how to make that infernal
note-book perfectly all right in spite of the bad paper. I
wish to the Lord *I* had been taught that."

And then, while Marise was still staring, the words echoing
loudly in her ears because of the strangeness of hearing them
from Father, he went on in his usual voice, "It might be *something* to hold on to, and I don't see much else."

Marise had never before known Father in any way to try
to "bring her up!" He made Maman so much provoked
because he always said that he didn't know, any more than
Marise, how she ought to be brought up, and he didn't
see that it made so much difference what you did, everything
turned out about the same in the long run. Now her little
room seemed full of the oddness of his thinking that something did matter, of his telling her so hard that he wished
she'd do something. In the loud silence which followed, she
could hear his voice and what it said, sinking deeper and deeper
into her mind.

After a while Father yawned very wide and rubbed his hair forward and back so that it was all rumpled up the way Maman didn't like to see it. "What did you say you were doing?" he asked again.

"I'm writing down my leçon d'orthographe," said Marise.

"Your *what!*" said Father.

"My spelling lesson," Marise corrected herself with a jerk. She knew how Father hated to have people mix up their languages.

"Well, I don't know that you're any worse off at that than we are in the sitting-room," said Father. He always called the *salon* the sitting-room. He added, glancing at her blank note-book, "You haven't got very far, I see." He paused, and smiled a little with one corner of his mouth, "But then neither have we in the sitting-room."

It came into Marise's mind that perhaps Father, seeing he was so specially serious to-night, might tell her some way to keep her thoughts from jiggling around so, from one way of feeling to another, according to what other people thought of things, instead of knowing what she thought of things. But she had no chance to ask him, for when she began, "Well, I sort of forgot about my spelling. I got to thinking," Father broke in, as he got up heavily to go, "I wouldn't advise you to do *that*, either. It never gets anybody anywhere."

Marise forgot till after he had got clear back to the salon that she had not brushed off the down from the édredon. Maman wouldn't like that a bit, to have him look untidy when company was there! Oh, dear!

But she forgot this as she thought again about the queerness of Father's seeming to care so much about her doing one thing rather than another. It was still there, this wonder at him, when she turned to her book finally to study that spelling lesson. "Lit . . . sommier . . . traversin. . . ." She wrote the words down on the coarse paper, with infinite care, drawing on some deep, unfamiliar store of patience when the pen sputtered and caught its point and stuck. She was going to try to do as Father said. She would take as much trouble with writing those words about a bed, as old Jeanne took in making the bed every morning; and that was more trouble than anybody in America ever took about anything.

Her dark, shining hair fell forward about her cheeks as she leaned over the copy-book, writing slowly, chewing her tongue, frowning in her concentration on the formation of those letters.

She forgot all about her uncertainties as to how things really were; she forgot her loneliness. All her flickering thoughts steadied themselves and grew quiet as she worked. A stillness came over her. She felt happier than she had since they came to France to live.

Later, ever so much later, after she had undressed, washed in the cold water in the little earthen-ware basin, gone to bed and to sleep, the night-time Jeanne tiptoed in to see that she was all right. This Jeanne was very different from all the others, because she was so quiet. Marise half-waked up when she felt the energetic French kiss on her cheek (Jeanne always kissed you so hard), and as she dozed off again, she heard Jeanne saying a prayer over her, half in Basque and half in Latin. Marise couldn't understand either Latin or Basque, but she understood the intention of that nightly prayer at her bed, and she caught sleepily at old Jeanne to return her kiss. It wasn't as good as Cousin Hetty's taking you on her lap and putting her arms around you, but it was enough sight better than nothing. Also she heard Jeanne carefully close the window. Jeanne always did this every night, although Maman said to leave it open. Jeanne was the last one in there always so she had it her way. She didn't think it healthy to let night air into rooms. Marise was too sleepy to get up and open it again. Anyhow Jeanne often told her about the evil spirits, that come in through open bedroom windows, and sit on your chest and suck your life into their black bodies, as you sleep. Marise did not believe this, in the least, of course, and yet . . .

CHAPTER VIII

I

May 12, 1898.

Two plump ladies with large busts and very small waists were sitting in the salon of the Allen apartment, waiting for the mistress of the house. They wore very tight-fitting dresses of excellent silk, obviously not new, obviously made by the sort of "little dressmaker" who goes from house to house. Their shoes were stout and clumsy, their hats somewhat heavy in line, their gloves exquisitely fitting, perfectly fresh, made of the finest-grained leather. Although the sky was blue, each lady carried a small silk umbrella of the very best quality, tightly rolled with a masterly smoothness, as smoothly tubular as the day it was bought.

The two women held their cruelly corseted bodies very erect, and sat squarely on their chairs, both feet on the floor, their knees close together, their backbones very straight. Under the brims of their heavy, much-ornamented hats, their fresh, healthy faces wore an expression of perfect stability. They knew that they produced exactly the impression they meant to produce, and that they looked exactly like what they were. From every inch of them was proclaimed the fact that they were fine housekeepers and economical managers of their husbands' incomes, that they were of the well-to-do bourgeoisie and proud of it, as of everything else they were and did. They looked out on their lives and found them good in every detail, from their slightly and purposely behind-the-fashion dresses to their stout shoes, evidence of their respectability; from their fixed ideas to their excellent gloves.

They glanced about them now, keenly, with the penetrating survey of the professional good housekeeper, and found much to comment on.

51

"How strange to have no lace curtains over the windows, only the heavy ones at the side. Why, people outside must be able to *look right in!* Do you suppose they have taken them out to be washed? Or don't they know about curtains in America?"

They murmured their remarks in a low tone, keeping a weather-ear cocked to the hall.

"That wall-paper is disgraceful. It was on when the Charpentiers lived here."

"M. Lapagorry had expected, you know, of course, to do this apartment over after the Charpentiers moved out. But these new people never made a single comment, or complaint. Just accepted it."

"I daresay they are used to log-cabins at home, with Indians at the door."

"Oh, no, Madame Garnier, my Henri says that the Indians are quite civilized in America now."

Madame Garnier frowned slightly at the mention of Henri.

The other woman went on, "Apparently they thought it was all right to have faded paper and those awful old curtains. M. Lapagorry was so astonished he almost fell over backward. And when he saw they didn't find fault with anything, he asked a higher rent, ever so much higher than the Charpentiers had paid, and they took *that* too without a word. People say M. Lapagorry can't sleep nights now because he didn't ask more."

Madame Garnier observed, as one mentioning an obvious fact, "Oh, well, Madame Fortier, he will, of course, next time."

Madame Fortier saw nothing to smile at in this. "Yes, of course," she said seriously.

Madame Garnier now said, "They must be *very* rich. Where is it they are from, Buenos Aires?"

"Oh, no, Madame Garnier. I think it is somewhere in North America. My Henri says that . . ."

Madame Garnier broke in, irritated, to say with suppressed heat, "Oh, North America or South America, what's the difference? They are all foreigners, and who knows what strange, immoral ideas they have? They don't come to Mass, you know. It wouldn't surprise me to learn that the man is a Free-Mason. I wish M. Garnier had not asked me to call on them."

The other shrugged her shoulders resignedly, "Yes, it's a very strange thing to do, make the first call, and on people you know nothing about. But M. Fortier says the man, M. Allen, is very important in a business way, and he specially asked all the business men to have their wives call on his wife. He almost seemed to make it a sort of condition, so M. Fortier said, almost made them promise before he would talk business with them. It may be in America, they do. And of course anything M. Fortier thinks may be good for his business. . . ."

Madame Garnier's nod signified that of course that principle went without saying for any good wife; the expression of her face adding that this was an application of it which might count as one of a good wife's sacrifices. But she said hopefully, "Well, they won't stay very long, foreigners never do."

Madame Fortier now murmured, "They say she's very free with the gentlemen. M. Fortier and his friends are laughing about her. They say they really don't know how much of what she says is due to her bad French; or how far she really does expect them to go."

This did not surprise Madame Garnier. "What can you expect? I shall see to it that our Jean-Pierre has nothing to do with them."

This apparently started a new train of thought for Madame Fortier, for she now said with the cheery warmth of one who brings out something which will be a bitter pill to her interlocutor. "It seems the American, M. Allen, has taken quite a fancy to our Henri. We think we can get a position for Henri, through him, in America, where Henri can learn English, and study the American market. It would be a great help in the business if Henri knew English and all about American imports. And of course the salaries paid in America are enormous."

Madame Garnier's eyes opened wide. She fell into a trance-like meditation, and presently murmured, "Our Jean-Pierre

made quite a specialty of English in the lycée. I should
think. . . ."

The mother of Henri shook her head decidedly, "I don't
think America would suit your Jean-Pierre's temperament,"
she said. "He's not at all practical. And you get skinned
alive by American business men if you're not as sharp as
they. No, you'd better keep Jean-Pierre away from them."

The two looked at each other hard. A brilliant light of
rivalry came into their eyes. It brought an animation, a zest
into their faces, which made them look years younger. A
main-spring had been touched, and all their wheels began
visibly to turn.

Steps were heard in the hall.

They composed their faces, and turned towards the door.
The American lady now came in, and they rose to greet her.
They were extremely cordial, a competitive friendliness in their
manner.

They went down the well-polished oaken stairs in silence,
each holding up her long heavy skirt with one gloved hand and
letting the other rest on the railing. At the bottom, each with
an automatic gesture like a reflex action, looked at the palm
of her glove to see if it had been soiled by the railing, and
with a similar mechanical action, shook their heads disapprovingly, although there was not a grain of dust on the smooth,
tightly-stretched, pale kid.

They shook out the trains of their skirts and swept into
the street, conscious of the pouncing inspection of Anna
Etchergary, gazing at them from the loge of the concierge, and
proudly aware that there was nothing to criticize in any detail
of their backs or anywhere else about them. They turned to
the left and began to climb the steep street which led towards
the Cathedral. Madame Fortier remarked presently, "Very
bad taste, that dress, like an actress. All that white silk and
lace. And slippers like a dancing girl's. It must be she never
puts her hand to anything in the house."

"No, she doesn't," returned the other disapprovingly. "My
Marguerite meets her Jeanne every morning at market. She

says that Jeanne says the American lady never does anything about the house, and doesn't even verify her accounts. You can just imagine what Jeanne is getting out of it. It quite upsets Marguerite, and I have to be specially careful with my own accounts. Everybody near them is getting a rake-off on everything." She made these revelations with a satisfied look as though the words had a pleasant taste in her mouth.

Madame Fortier's comment was made with the accent of mature, worldly experience, "Mark my words, money spent in a loose careless way like that *must have been ill come by*. That's the way disreputable women spend money."

"It's very hard on the rest of us, at any rate. And Jeanne tells our Margot that she is a very poor housekeeper, as heedless as a child, wears her best tailored street dress in the house as like as not, lies down on the bed when she is not sick at all, and doesn't do a thing but read novels all the time; or fool away a whole afternoon in the Museum. Very suspicious, that, too. Why should anybody go to the Museum so much? I'd just like to know whom she meets there. A regular place of rendezvous, the Museum. I wonder if her husband knows."

They were enjoying the conversation so much that their faces looked quite sunny and bright. The other shook her head forebodingly. There was a silence as they climbed steadily up the steep, narrow, stone-flagged street.

Then Madame Garnier remarked, "The little girl is quite pretty, though so mannerless."

"Her dress was covered with grease spots, and had a hook off the back," reported Madame Fortier.

"I didn't see but *three* grease spots," demurred Madame Garnier, "and she really has lovely eyes and hair."

"How badly that woman speaks French. Without the little girl to interpret, it would actually have been hard to know what she was saying. Strange they don't know French better. But perhaps they don't have regular schools like ours."

Madame Garnier made no answer to this conjecture, but asked, looking sideways at her neighbor, "Shall you ask them to dinner?"

Madame Fortier all but groaned, and said in a martyr's tone, "Oh, I suppose so, for Henri's sake."

The other digested this thrust in silence, and then changed the subject. "What was that she was saying about De Maupassant? Was she quoting him, to *us?* What did she take us for?"

"Yes, she didn't realize what we might think of her. It was that indecent Boule-de-Suif, too. But she knows so little French most likely she didn't understand what it was all about."

"Have you read that?" asked Madame Garnier.

"Yes, I thought it my duty to, as a mother, to know what it is. But I burned the book, and you may be sure *I* don't go around letting everybody know I've read it. Did you find her pretty?"

Madame Garnier answered obliquely, but quite understandably. "I daresay a man would think so. I couldn't think of anything but her manners. How she lolled in her chair, and crossed her legs. I wouldn't want my Gabrielle to see her. And to my eyes she had a faded look. Queer, her being so fair. I don't see any trace of Indian blood. I thought all Americans had Indian blood."

"Oh, no, Madame Garnier, my Henri says that. . . ."

Madame Garnier made a gesture of one thoroughly out of patience with Henri, and ended the conversation abruptly, "Oh, here we are at the corner. I must turn down here. Goodday, Madame Fortier."

II

May 15, 1898.

The rosy, wrinkled face of the Sister of Charity shone out from the white quilled band over which the black veil was draped. Beside her the distinguished old lady showed, under her long crape veil, a face as quiet as that of the nun. The two elderly women sat at ease, their hands folded in their laps, chatting in a pleasant low tone.

"Yes, so every one says, a great deal of money, Madame la Marquise," said the nun in her murmuring monotone, "as all Americans have."

The other breathed out with a great wistful sigh, "Oh, Sœur Ste. Lucie, if only the good God has sent us at last the opportunity to get our chapel."

"Yes, yes indeed," assented the nun, drawing in her breath sharply between her teeth. She raised her eyes, singularly bright and personal in her professionally passive face. "They say there is a child, too. Perhaps a soul to save. Our Mother Superior always so zealous for the honor of our Order has asked us specially, specially . . . the Bishop has so much to say about one of the Sisters of the St. Francis Order because of the conversion of a Swedish sailor, whom she nursed in their hospital. The Mother Superior hopes very much that some one in *our* Order. . . ."

"Yes, yes, I understand," said the great lady, nodding.

The nun went on, deferentially, "Madame la Marquise is so good to be willing to come to call on the foreign lady! I shall see to it that the foreign lady understands the honor done her."

The other made a graceful deprecatory gesture with a shapely black-gloved hand, and explained with great simplicity and gentleness, "Oh, no, ma sœur, it is nothing, nothing to praise. I would make a far greater sacrifice for the sake of our beloved work. But in this case, there is no risk of being misunderstood. It is not as though they were French bourgeois, who might have their heads turned. There can be no question of social equality with transient foreigners." She smiled, bowed her head with humility and said, "So you see, dear Sœur Ste. Lucie, that I deserve no praise for making a sacrifice."

The nun nodded her understanding. It was evident that they understood each other to perfection. "Yes, yes, of course, I see. No social equality possible," she murmured, drawing in a sharply taken breath again.

They looked about them in silence now, the restrained calm of their faces uncolored by their thoughts. Hearing steps in the hall, Sœur Ste. Lucie shook out her long black sleeves to cover her hands more completely, and cast down her eyes so that her sweet, rosy, wrinkled old face was once more blank and impassive.

Anna Etchergary was waiting at the door of her loge as they descended the stairs, and she ran before them out to the old closed carriage, which stood at the curb. Bowing deferentially and murmuring under her breath, ". . . Madame la Marquise . . ." she held the door open for them. The lady smiled her thanks at her, a pre-occupied, well-modulated smile which took for granted the deference and the service.

As the nun stepped into the carriage she said with unction, "Now I see how lives in the world can be as useful to Our Lady as those of the convent. No one could have resisted Madame this afternoon. To have a great name and all worldly graces, and to use them only for the greater glory of Our Lady!"

The other sighed and said sadly, "Dear Ste. Lucie, since the death of my dear one, there is nothing for me in the life of the world, except an opportunity to serve our good work." She went on more cheerfully, with a little animation, "Yes, I must say, it seemed like fruitful ground this afternoon, fruitful ground. I think we may say we made a good beginning."

The old coachman came to the door for his orders. "To 4 rue Marengo, in the Petit Bayonne," said his mistress, and as he stepped to his seat, she explained to the nun, "I feel so much encouraged that I am going straight to an architect to have him make an estimate of what the chapel would cost."

The carriage proceeded very slowly and rackingly over the rounded boulders of the pavement. Inside it, the two women, accustomed to such joltings, thrust their arms through the broad, hanging loops, and went on talking.

"Not a disagreeable person," said the great lady in a kind tone of tolerance. "A very middle-class little woman, but no harm in her, I should say. I was afraid to find some one not quite—not quite—you know it is said that American women are not very moral—so many divorces in America."

"And still you went . . . !" breathed the nun, lost in admiration of the other's heroic devotion, "when you ran the risk of meeting a *divorced* woman!"

The Marquise made another gentle, fatigued gesture of warding off praise. It was a practised gesture as though she had occasion to make it often.

After a time she said, "Odd she should be so interested in the Cathedral here, and yet a free-thinker. What made her talk so much about the South Portal? I never heard of anything unusual about it, did you? Except that that disagreeable, anti-clerical fountain is somewhere near there, to the memory of those wicked revolutionists."

The nun shook her head, indifferently. "I always enter by the North Portal," she said. "I don't believe I ever happened to see the south one."

After reflection, the marquise said, "I don't believe I ever saw it either. Why should any one? You never enter from that side. Nobody lives on the rue d'Espagne, that anybody would ever have occasion to visit."

III

May 20, 1898.

ANNA ETCHERGARY measured accurately the social status of the two ladies who asked for Madame Allen's apartment, and without getting up, or stopping her sewing, she answered in the careless tone suitable for people who wore home-made hats and cotton gloves, that Madame Allen was at the top of the first flight. After they had passed, she thought to herself that she believed she knew them, Mlle. Hasparren, the school-teacher and her married sister. They were Basques, like Anna, but of the small government employee class, who put on airs of gentility, and wore hats and leather shoes. Mlle. Hasparren gave music lessons, as well as teaching school. Probably she had come to try to be taken on as Marise's music-teacher.

The two ladies were mounting the stairs in silence and very slowly, because the school-teacher had taken off her cotton gloves and was putting on a pair of kid ones, which she had pulled from her hand-bag. She explained half-apologetically, to her sister, who had only cotton gloves, "It's to do honor to America!" and then with a long breath, "The first American I ever saw."

"What do you care if it is, Rachel?" asked her sister languidly. She added with more animation, "Your hat is over one ear again."

The other stopped short on a stair. "America! . . . free America!" she said passionately, "don't you remember what Voltaire said, 'Europe can never be wholly a prison so long as it has America for open window?'" She knocked her hat back into place with the effect of using the gesture to emphasize violently what she said.

"I wouldn't quote Voltaire, if I were you," advised her sister, mildly. "You never know who may be listening. People think badly enough of you for being a school-teacher in a lay-school as it is."

"There you are!" Rachel caught this up as a point for her side. "There it is, our airless, stagnant European prison-house of prejudice!" She struck a hand, gloved in kid now, on her breast, with the gesture of one suffocating.

Her sister shrugged her shoulders resignedly and said, "Which door do you suppose it is? We forgot to ask which side."

They were now on the landing, hesitating between the two exactly similar doors. Rachel made a quick decision at random, crossed to the right-hand side, and pulled the bell-rope.

The door opened, and showed the upright frame of Jeanne Amigorena. There was a moment of mutual surprise, and exclamations of greeting and inquiry. "Why, Jeanne, you here? I thought you were on the farm at Midassoa!"

Jeanne broke out upon them with a great rush of Basque, enchanted to see familiar faces, enchanted to have a new audience. "Oh, good-day, Madame Hardoye. Good-day, Mlle. Hasparren. Who ever would think to see you here? Yes, here I am in a family of the queerest foreigners you ever saw. But they pay very well. They have both apartments on this floor. Yes, they must be *made* of money, and I have little Isabelle from Midassoa with me, as femme de chambre, and what do you think, we have each a room, a real furnished bedroom, just as though we were guests. The madame took one look at the maids' rooms, under the roof, on the fifth floor, you know, and when she saw they are all dark except that little sky-light, with no furniture to speak of, she said she wouldn't let a dog sleep there. The idea! It would have been plenty good enough for Isabelle and enough sight better than what she ever had at home. She is getting beyond herself all the time, Isabelle is. I have an awful time keeping her in her place. The lady hasn't the least idea of doing it. They are such queer people, I can't tell you! She knows no more about taking care of a child, our madame! She started to let our little mademoiselle go *alone* to school, through the *streets!* And the poor child was so disgraceful with spots and dirt on her dresses that I was ashamed to have people see her and had Madame buy her some aprons and now I keep her in order myself. She is a sweet child, only brought up the way you'd expect a little savage to be, puts her *feet* on the *chairs!* Or else sits on the *floor!* And *runs* on the street, or else loiters along looking at shop-windows. But she is learning fast. I don't complain, oh, no. I know well enough that when you are a servant, you must take what comes to you, and make the best of it. But I never thought I would work in a family of free-thinkers! Still, they sleep over there on that side of the landing, and Isabelle and I sleep here. I keep the holy-water shell well filled, and we brought the branch of box from home that had been blessed last Palm Sunday, and we sprinkle a few drops of Lourdes water on the table before we eat. I hope we are safe. M. le Curé says that is enough. I often think that . . ."

Madame Hardoye had been listening to this flood of talk, her lively interest in the matter struggling with her distaste for Jeanne's familiar manner.

She now broke in with an accent which she meant to ex-

press, "There you've talked quite enough. After all, though
my sister has queer ideas, we are not in your class. We are
not peasants. And it's high time you remembered that."
What she actually said in a curt tone was, "Where do we
ring to make a call on your mistress?"

Jeanne understood the implication perfectly. It was one
quite familiar to her. With a change of manner she motioned
them silently across the hall. "There," she said laconically,
her face suddenly hard and somber.

Rachel Hasparren also understood the implication and
flushed an even more vivid color than that habitually on her
dark cheeks. She held out her hand, her kid-gloved hand, to
Jeanne, with a defiant gesture of equality, "Good-by, Jeanne.
I'm glad we had a glimpse of you."

Jeanne took the hand awkwardly, with a sort of rancorous
reluctance to have her grievance appeased, and turning back,
shut the door behind her.

"Now, Rachel!" expostulated her sister.

Rachel breathed ragingly and stared at her sister in an old
resentment, which the other took calmly, looking inside her
card-case.

Rachel advanced provocatively, "Did you hear what old
Jeanne said, how the American lady would not put a dog
to sleep in lodgings in which we French expect to house our
servants?"

The married sister resented this spiritedly. "Spoiling servants for the rest of us, that's what it is!" she said impatiently.
"And what good does it do? You saw how old Jeanne only
thinks the less of her for it. The more you try to do for
that class, the less they think of you."

"That's because Jeanne's whole nature has been degraded
by our caste ideals!" shouted Rachel. "She's a poor, super-
stitious, medieval old thing, incapable of ordinary decent
human relations. If she'd lived in America. . . !"

Angèle pulled the other bell-cord here with an air of cutting
short another outburst, and they both stood silently looking
at the closed door, which presently was opened by little Isabelle.

As they went down the stairs, Angèle remarked, "Well, she seems to be all right. Like everybody else, as far as I can see. I expected to see her with a Liberty cap on her head and swinging a lighted bomb, to hear you going on."

Rachel was taking off her kid gloves and putting on cotton ones. She said dreamily, her black eyes deep and glowing, "When I asked her how the peasants lived in America, she said . . . the dear American . . . 'there aren't any peasants in America.' "

Her dark flushed face was shining as they came out on the rue Thiers and stood for an instant, glancing up at the battlemented walls of the dark old Castle.

Rachel suddenly shook her fist at it, her cotton-gloved fist, and cried out, "You needn't glower down like that, you hideous old relic of an evil past! There's a great, wide, rich country across the seas, that never heard of such as you, that never had a feudal castle in it, that isn't darkened by a single hateful shadow such as you still throw down on us here."

"Hush, Rachel," said her sister, patiently attempting to quiet her, "Anna Etchergary is looking out of the window at us."

Rachel instantly lowered her voice, with an instinctive response of caution to this warning, but she was furious that she had done so. "That's Europe, that's Europe for you! she said hotly, under her breath. "Spied upon every minute by suspicious, mean, malicious eyes."

Angèle broke in on her to say reasonably, "Well, anyhow, your hat is on one side again."

CHAPTER IX

Round-robin Letter to Mrs. Horace Allen's Neighbors and Friends in Belton, New Jersey

Bayonne, France, May 25, 1898.

Mes Chére Amies:

Je vous demande pardon for being so late with this letter, I know I promised to write just as soon as we got here. But, chére amies, I know you would forgive me if you knew how *marvelous* our new life is here in this old, beautiful, *civilized* world. I have just been letting myself go in it, just *grabbing* at its charm and wonder, and all I can tell you is that Europe is even more *wonderful* than I thought. I just wish every one of you could persuade your husbands, as I did, to take a position that will bring you across the seas to this "fabled old land of story and art." *You owe it to your children* to give them the culture which they would get here.

But let me begin first with the material things. Mr. Allen, you know, felt sort of badly because the position here didn't seem to be as important and have as big a salary as the job the Company offered him in Chicago—*Chicago!* Well, you cannot imagine anything like the cheapness of the life here. We have two flats of six rooms each, on the same floor, just the landing between them, twelve rooms in all, furnished elaborately down to the last little things in the kitchen even, and we pay about half the rent we paid in Belton for our unfurnished house. There is perhaps a little old-world dinginess about the wall-paper and the curtains and things, but that only adds to the delightful *atmosphere* and makes you realize that you are really in old Europe and not raw young America.

We have two maids for *less than three dollars a week* each,

64

and such maids! In America we haven't any idea what it is to have good servants. I am not expected to lift my hand or think about the housekeeping. My old cook, the most *fascinating* creature, in a quaint peasant's costume, takes *all* the responsibility on her own shoulders. She gets up frightfully early in the morning, and goes off to market with a big, flat basket, and comes bringing it in *on her head* all filled with the loveliest things to eat you ever saw, and bought for almost nothing! But she buys just as closely for me as she would for herself. Servants identify themselves with the family of their masters here, and are glad to! I know the word "masters" sounds very un-American; but one so soon gets used to the vocabulary of the country. Pardonnez moi!

Jeanne—that is our cook—brings our breakfast to us *in bed*, all except of course for Mr. Allen, who can't seem to adapt himself to other ways of living. The first morning when she started to, he just jumped out of bed as though the house were on fire, and slammed the door shut in her face. He can't get over his Anglo-Saxon prudishness. But we have separate rooms now, and I have my tray in bed, and read my mail there, and between you and me, it makes me feel just like a heroine in a novel, to lie there in my pretty negligée—you know in America we don't realize what negligées are for. When do you ever have a chance to wear one except when you are sick? And then you don't care. Marise has hers—her breakfast I mean—in her room, too, as she dresses, and Jeanne always expects to help her dress, so I don't have to think at all about getting her off to school! Oh, mes amies, *what* a rest to one's nerves that is! Not to have that horrid, hurried hour trying to find clothes and books and get Marise off in time. I just lie in bed reading the mail or a book and Marise comes in, all fresh and combed (Jeanne is wonderful with her hair), and kisses me and says, "Au revoir, Maman." We always try to speak French together for the practice.

Then, as I am getting dressed, Jeanne comes in, with a clean apron to "take her orders," in the good old European way. And from that minute on, I have no more bother about it. Everything is set on the table at the right time, beautifully cooked, the house is kept clean and in the most *perfect* order.

Perhaps you are wondering why I call Mary, "Marise?" It is a quaint nickname for her that the servants have, and I have picked it up from them. Isn't it delightful? I never liked Mary, and I detest "Molly." Both the maids are devoted to Marise, and it is the European custom for the servants to do a great deal more for the children of the house than our girls ever dream of doing. Without a word, Jeanne has simply taken over the care of Marise's clothes as a part of her regular work, and she is always ready to go out with her, for it seems that no nice children go alone on the streets here. Every morning, Jeanne takes Marise to her school, and goes for her in the afternoon and brings her back. Marise is perfectly happy here, in a splendid school, and having wonderful opportunities. I am so happy about her advantages. It is not a public school (the "lay" schools as they say, because all the others are run by Catholic nuns). It seems the public schools are something quite new in France, and nobody sends children to them except the poor, or people who are queer in some way, with unbalanced ideas. I can easily believe this, since I had a call the other day from a school-teacher in the public schools, who also gives music lessons. She is a very queer and dowdy person, with the most awful hat you ever saw. Didn't you think that all Frenchwomen wore pretty, stylish hats? Not in the least. Quite the contrary. Her sister was with her, quite middle-class, both of them, and not at all like the other ladies who have called on me.

For they *have* called! Do you remember that little old French teacher who came to see me about getting a job in our High School, how discouraging she was about our coming to live in France, and how she said nobody would come to see me, at all? Well, if you ever see her, just tell her she is *entirely mistaken*. People are just as cordial as *they can be*, with the most beautiful manners you ever saw.

Do you wonder how I manage about the language? It is *much* easier to get along than I expected. Of course my thorough reading and writing knowledge of the language is a great help. And I have been making *won*derful progress in speaking it. Being right in the midst of the language all the time it just soaks into you. No one here speaks any English; not from provincial ignorance, the sort we have in America, but from choice, because of their concentration on their own perfect language. They are all deeply cultured. It is *won*derful to be in the midst of cultured people, to be able in casual afternoon calls to discuss De Maupassant with one lady and Gothic architecture with another.

For we have here in Bayonne—you notice that I already say "We,"—a simply splendid Gothic cathedral, the first one of my life. It is right up the street from where we live, and it is *won*derful. Chére amies, think what it means for a town to have in its midst such a marvelous thing! Think what people must be like who live right close to it, go in and out of it every day, and feel its "beauty and puissant power" (as Matthew Arnold says). The South Portal is especially fine, *starred by Baedeker,* which means a great deal, as you know. I make a pilgrimage there every day, to just *gaze* at that South Portal. *I* have a life-time of arrears to make up, not having lived with it from childhood, as these fortunate people have. It is no wonder that you meet here people absolutely *won*derful in their polish, like a lady who called on me the other day, the Marquise de Charmières. Her husband's family dates back to the days of Louis XII. I am ashamed to say I had to go and look up who Louis XII was, after she had gone. She had with her a nun, who lives with her, by special permission, the dearest old thing with her sweeping black robes and the quaint, quilled, picturesque head-dress. I suppose they used, in the old days, the Charmières did, to live in the *won*derful old castle, just across the street from us, which is another of my great admirations. Think of living across the street from a real castle! It was constructed in 1100, on the remains of the *old Roman wall,* if you please, for Bayonne is very, very old. And it is right there, just the way it always was, with battlements and a real drawbridge and everything, just as it was in feudal times. Many famous people have lived there, Richard Cœur de Lion, Louis Quatorze, and others. It was there that Catherine de Medicis planned the St. Bartholomew massacre,

and in a house on this very street that Napoleon took the
Spanish crown away from the King, and gave it to his brother.
Isn't it marvelous to think of?

I have had some of the curtains taken down in our *salon*
(the French simply swathe their windows in curtains, simply
swathe them!) and I often stand at the window and just gaze
out at those old castle walls and try to imagine the splendid
life that went on here then, the streets full of people in costumes
and knights in armor and everything. I see the modern crowds
coming and going under those massive walls, and I keep thinking how proud they must be of such an inheritance from the
past, and how they must often wish the good old feudal days
back again, when "life had color," as a writer said in a book I
was reading the other day. No such inspiriting reminders of
past glories in America! No such past glories! Nothing but
what Ruskin calls the drab, dead level of democracy.

There is a fine Museum here too, with perfectly splendid
works of art in it, pictures by Van Dyck, Rembrandt, Raphael,
Rubens, Ribera, Murillo, Poussin, Delacroix, Ingres, Troyon,
Meisonnier, Corot, Isabey, Bonnat, Bouguereau, Gervex, and
many others. I am simply *studying* them, absorbing them, I
go every day with a handbook on art which I bought here (in
French, of course), and just gaze at them till their very spirit
enters into me. I must tell you that Bouguereau is considered
very much out of fashion here, and not at all admired any
more. The Meissonier are simply *mar*velous. You could take
a microscope to them, and still not see any brush-marks. Indeed it is said that he painted with a microscope. There is
a *perfect* copy here of the Mona Lisa, which people who know
say is just as good as the original. Mes chére amies, think
what a privilege it is to sit there, right before her, with the
book in my hand, looking up into that mysterious face, and
reading those wonderful words of Pater's, which I have studied
with you so often. "Here is the head upon which all the ends
of the world are come, and the eyelids are a little weary. She
is older than the rocks among which she sits; like the vampire,
she has been dead many times and learned the secrets of the
grave; and has been a diver in deep seas, and keeps their fallen

'day about her; and trafficked for strange webs with Eastern
merchants; and as Leda, was the mother of Helen of Troy,
and as Ste. Anne, the mother of Mary; and all this has been
to her but as the sound of lyres and flutes, and lives only in
the delicacy with which it has molded the changing lineaments
and tinged the eyelids and the hands."

Mes amies, we have often read and studied this marvelous
passage together, and now I can only say to you *that it is true!*
But every bit of culture means so much more to me than it ever
did before and now that I know what European life is, I
can understand why they are more cultured than we are. It
is because they have *leisure*. Here the working classes *expect
to work*, as our American working class does not. And the
material cares are just taken right off the shoulders of the
upper classes. *We* are *expected* to occupy ourselves with
higher things. I am reading, reading, reading as never before,
and getting a closer knowledge of French literature, even than
our studies together gave me. It all *means* so much more to
me, now that I am right among the very people who are described in it. Think of looking up from a volume of Zola,
and having a caller come in, who might be a character right
out of the book. I often tell Mr. Allen, that the life around
me illustrates and explains the literature, and the literature
illustrates and explains the life. It is a wonderful, *won*derful
experience!

I have just finished De Maupassant's "Notre Cœur," and I
am not surprised that we found it impossible to get hold of
the French edition in America. Our strait-laced, old-fashioned,
Puritanic America doesn't know enough to appreciate such
a picture of this *free* European world, where relations between
men and women are different from those between high school
boys and girls. At home the girls rule the roost, if you will
excuse a vulgar expression. But not here. Here they are put
off in a corner, till they get a husband, and *then* they are allowed to blossom out. A woman of my age, so a French gentleman told me the other day, is considered *just at the right age*
for being fascinating. And he assured me he didn't say that
because it might apply to me, but *because it is so*. The men

have temperament here. They really look at you, and are just as different as can be from the American business-man who never thinks of any woman but his wife, and never pays any attention to *her!* Here the men positively sparkle in conversation, and they all say they would hardly know I am an American, I have acquired the French manner so entirely. Here a woman is not expected to have become a mummy, because she puts on a wedding-ring. *Quite the contrary*, I assure you!

But this is a terribly long letter. I have poured out my heart to you in untrammeled spontaneity, such as comes to you in the free intellectuality of this finished civilization.

May you all be able some day to enjoy it!

Your devouée friend,

FLORA ALLEN.

P.S.—Mr. Allen says the business part seems to be all right.

CHAPTER X

As happens to us all, there were certain moments which stayed alive in Marise's memory for years; and as is always the case, those moments did not at all correspond with apparently important events. Such events come, seem of great consequence, happen, and therewith sink down into the featureless mass of things which happen only once and then are in the past forever. The other moments, those queerly, heterogeneously tumbled-together impressions, are the things which happen over again every time one thinks of them.

One of Marise's fantastic notions was that the things which had happened were piled up in a big junk-heap in your memory in front of a great black curtain. But there were pinholes in the curtain, and if you put your eye to one, there, right before you, one of the things that had happened was alive again, and your heart knocked and your throat felt queer just as it did the first time. This notion may have come to her in this form because it was generally in the night that she experienced the vivid living-over of some long past moment. Wakened from a sound sleep by the hoarse whistle of one of the steamers in the Adour, taking advantage of a favorable tide to weigh anchor and be off, she saw in the instant while she drew a long breath and turned over in bed, one of those living scenes again, as actual, as piercingly real to her as though it were happening for the first time. Some of these she greatly dreaded, some set her to ringing all through with happiness, others she never understood at all.

I

One of the very happy ones was the moment when she had first really heard music. She had been "taking lessons" of Mlle. Hasparren for weeks and months. Mlle. Hasparren taught as Marise thought all the teachers in France taught, the hardest possible way; scales, scales, scales and then thumping, monotonous exercises, played over forty, fifty, sixty times, till Marise felt as though there wasn't anything left of her except that exercise, pound, pound, pound all over her. Marise saw nothing in music except hatefully numerous little black dots on white paper, and heard nothing in it beyond a combination of sounds as interesting to hear as a problem in arithmetic is to look at.

She rather liked Mlle. Hasparren, although Maman thought she didn't have a bit of style; but she certainly did hate the three-times-a-week music lesson. She never could have kept on with it in America, but here everything was hard work, and if you weren't working at your music lesson, they'd expect you to be working at something else. And then, too, there was what Father had said about keeping at what you were doing until you got it just right. Marise's bed-room seemed to have taken up the sound of Father's voice as he said that, so that many times, as she sat there doing her lessons and not thinking of it, all of a sudden, the very curtains and walls and chairs seemed to be reminding her of it. That was really what kept her going, as day by day she sat down heavily before the piano, prodding her mind up to keep it fixed on the little black dots.

That at least was what had kept her at it till the evening which came back to Marise so clearly. Father and Maman had gone out to dinner; she had eaten alone, with Jeanne's chatter for company, and then on her way back to her room, had wandered into the salon, candlestick in hand, sort of hoping she could think of something nice to do before she settled down to study.

But there was certainly nothing nice to do in the salon. It was awfully lonely in there, the chairs all empty and stiff, standing around heavily, the thick curtains drawn close over the tall windows, and in front of the alcove where Maman's writing-desk stood, the polished floor shining hard and bright, the stands, the table with one of Maman's yellow-covered books on it, the dark little cave of a fireplace. Marise set her candle down on a stand, and herself sank down on the piano stool, her back towards the keys, staring at the lonesome looking room. How perfectly dead it did look. Marise could hear faintly in the distance an echo of the brisk voice of Jeanne and Isabelle, laughing and carrying on over the dishes. But in here, in the empty salon, there wasn't a sound. Her ears fairly rang with the nothingness all around her. Her heart was big and heavy.

At school that day, the girls had started up a new fad, the "wishbook." You got a little blank book, and then went around asking everybody to write down in it what she most wished to be. Marise was astonished at what the other girls wrote; one, "I wish I could be a great actress," another, "I wish I could marry a millionaire," another, "I wish I could be a great and holy saint." Marise had not been able to understand why everybody did not write what she did, instantly, instantly, something she had always known she wanted. What she had written in everybody's book was, "I wish I could be happy." She thought of this now, and in the empty, cold, echoing room cried it aloud, "I wish I could be happy."

There was no answer from the stiff stuffed chairs, from the well-polished tables, from the black hole of the fireplace. Marise had expected no answer, would not have expected one if her parents had been there, never expected one. What answer could Father give, Father who apparently never thought of such a thing as being happy, and never hoped for anything more than to be a little less tired and bored. And if Maman had been there, she wouldn't even have heard what Marise said, busy as she always was with thinking something of her own. Maman wasn't nearly so cheerful as she had been. What *was* it Maman was thinking about when she sat so still and her face got dark and drawn? Certainly not about Marise.

The little girl sat on the piano stool, dangling her long legs and looking straight ahead into the empty room, which looked back at her, she thought, as though it had a low opinion of her and a very high opinion of its own importance and elegance. She knew she ought to get up and go into her own room and study a very long lesson on the reign of Henri IV. But she couldn't seem to get up the strength to do this, sitting fallen together on the piano stool, her heart heavier and heavier.

She looked hard at the empty chairs, and thought to herself that it wasn't any worse to see them empty, than to see the people that usually sat on them—not one who could help a little girl to be more happy. There wasn't a single person she knew, whom she'd wish sitting there now, unless it might be Cousin Hetty! Marise felt a knot come in her throat, and the corners of her mouth began to tremble. She would *like* to get up in Cousin Hetty's lap again.

But Cousin Hetty was not there. There was nothing there but the circle of unfriendly chairs and tables and the empty, silent room. The trembling of her lips got worse; Marise was afraid she was going to cry. She turned round on the piano stool, put one bent arm up on the music which stood there, and hid her face in it. She was not crying; though she wished she could, because the ache in her heart and the knot in her throat hurt too much.

The silent, motionless room stood aloof and meaningless about the silent, motionless child. Marise pressed her face closer against her arm. She was trembling now, all over her body.

The silence was intense.

And then it seemed to her that the silence had been broken by a voice, a beautiful, quivering voice, deep and true, which went straight to her heart, as though some one had spoken a strong, loving word. At the sound she stopped trembling and sat motionless.

Before she could draw her breath in wonder, she knew what it had been . . . only a note of music. Her own hand falling on a key of the piano had struck a note, which was even then echoing in her ears.

But the first impression was ineffaceable. That, too, rang in her ears. It seemed as though it was the first time she had ever heard a note of music. Really, really that was so. She had never been *still* enough before to hear how a note sounded. How it rang and rang in the stillness, its deep vibration stirring echoes deep within Marise's heart! She had thought it was a voice. Why, it was like a voice, a voice speaking to her, just when she had been so sure that there wasn't any voice she could possibly expect to hear.

She sat up marveling, and struck another note. Into the dead, stagnant air of the room, and into her loneliness, it sang out bravely, the same living voice, thrilling and speaking to her. She struck a chord, astonished at what she heard in it— all those separate voices, each one rich and true and strong and different from the others, and all shouting together in glorious friendliness. "That's the way things *ought* to be," thought Marise, "that's the way *people* ought to be." But, oh, how little they were like that! But here was a world where she could always make it come true, where she could have that singing-together any time she wished to make it for herself.

She struck more chords, her fingers finding the keys with the second-nature sureness, learned in her months of dreary practice.

She listened to the sounds, shaken and transported to hear how they flooded the barren emptiness of the room with glory, how they filled her heart full, full of happiness . . . only if she were happy, why was she crying, the tears running as fast as they could down her cheeks?

This was one of the remembered moments which brought nothing but a pang of joy to Marise. When it came, the world about her brightened.

II

There was another, one of those which came very seldom, which brought something deeper than pain or joy. This was the recollection of an instant, just one instant, of the day when Maman let Sœur Ste. Lucie take her to Lourdes. It was the feast of St. Louis, and Sœur Ste. Lucie always went every year then. She had been awfully nice and jolly, the way she always was with Marise, and it was fun to start off with her early in the morning, at dawn, in the special excursion train. At Lourdes it was fun, too, really exciting to be in such a monstrously big crowd, oh, *what* a crowd! She heard somebody tell Sœur Ste. Lucie that there were thirty thousand pilgrims there that day. It amused Marise very much to hear them called pilgrims and to think that she and Sœur Ste. Lucie were counted as pilgrims, too. She had always thought of "pilgrims" as people who landed on a stern and rock-bound coast and began to fight with Indians; and nothing could be more unlike that than the crowd at Lourdes, swimming in the dusty, yellow sunshine, everybody dressed up in his best, walking around in groups, talking and singing. Marise held on to the Sister's nice, soft, old hand and followed her around from one thing to another, taking a good big drink of the water, and kneeling down whenever Sœur Ste. Lucie stopped to pray before a shrine. Marise didn't pray much, but watched the crowd, the endless crowd shuffling slowly past. She was proud to be kneeling there beside a Sister, who had the right of entrance everywhere, who opened any gate in any railing she liked, and walked right in to say a prayer where the common run of people didn't dare go.

At noon, after three hours of this, Sœur Ste. Lucie took her charge off up along the bright, quick-flowing stream, off into the real country, till finally they came to a field that wasn't too thick with people. There they sat down on the grass, under a tree. Sœur Ste. Lucie got out the pasteboard shoe-box they had taken turns carrying around all the morning and they ate their lunch. Marise was simply starving by that time and anything would have tasted good. But that lunch would have made a stone statue eat, it was so good. Cold roast chicken, plenty of it, big slices cut recklessly right off the breast, tender and juicy and *flavored;* and crispy, crunchy rolls and fresh butter; and little radishes and green onions and salt, and a half bottle of the best white wine, which they watered down in their cups with Lourdes water. Sœur Ste. Lucie laughed over this as she poured it out and said they ought to be saints at least for a day or so, after drinking Lourdes water with their lunch, oughtn't they? She was as jolly as could be, anyhow, and was enjoying herself so much that she kept Marise laughing at her jokes all the time. One of those numerous friends of hers turned up here too, a stout, red-faced farmer's wife, who shouted with pleasure at seeing Sœur Ste. Lucie, and came over from the other side of the field to bring her lunch and eat with them. She and Sœur Ste. Lucie got into gales of laughter in which Marise joined with all her heart although she didn't always quite see what the joke was. Then they had their dessert, a triangle of creamy Camembert cheese, spread on the crust end of their roll, and after this a great golden pear apiece, so full of sweet juice that you couldn't take a bite of it without its running down your chin, so you had to lean way forward, to the tune of everybody laughing at you, and doing the same thing themselves.

After they had packed up what was left, and the farmer woman had gone back to her family, Sœur Ste. Lucie got very quiet and still, pulled out her rosary and began to murmur her prayers in a very fast, low tone, her eyes almost shut up. Marise sat beside her in the grass, watched the crowds beginning to turn back towards the Basilica, and a couple of little gnats dancing round and round each other in the air. The murmur of the prayers was like a bee-hum in her ears. She leaned back against the tree and drew a long breath, and the next thing she knew it was hours later, and Sœur Ste. Lucie was shaking her gently and saying she'd better wake up because it was time to go back if they were going to get a place to see the blessing of the sick.

After that ceremony was over, everybody was perfectly worn out and almost starved. Sœur Ste. Lucie went to one of the convents for supper, where the good Sisters took care of hundreds of the pilgrims, and looked as tired as Marise felt, and walked as though their feet hurt as hers did. But there was still one more Lourdes sight to see, the procession of the lights in the evening. When they came out of the convent, they found the weather changed, the wind blowing hard and a light rain falling and not a bit of light coming from the black, black sky. The damp was bad for rheumatism, and Sœur Ste. Lucie's knee began to pain her, so that she said they would not march in the procession but go up along the side of the high horse-shoe staircase, where they could see on both sides and

along the esplanade. How black and empty that looked, that
enormous stretch of pavement, like a great empty hole, out-
lined by the street lights on all four sides of it. Back of it,
down towards the Grotto, there seemed to be millions of people,
judging by the lights which danced around, every way at once;
and through the wind and the rain and the darkness, Marise
and Sœur Ste. Lucie could hear snatches of singing, the chant
which fairly rings from the stones and walls of Lourdes.

A-ve! A-ve! A-ve Ma-ri-a! A-ve! A-ve! A-ve Ma-ri-a!

Then as Marise stuck her head through the railing to watch
what went on there, far, far below them, she saw the lights begin to straighten out into two long lines and start streaming up
the lower part of the horse-shoe staircase where she and Sœur
Ste. Lucie stood. The procession had started; two by two they
were marching up towards the blaze of light at the top where
the door of the upper church stood open. The sound of their
voices grew louder and louder and there they were! The first
ones were a mother and her little girl; after them a couple of
working men; after them a man and his wife; after them a
priest and a soldier; after them—after them—Marise lost
count, she felt her head whirl, she couldn't see the people
any more, only the little dancing, quivering lights they were
carrying, candle-flames, scarcely at all protected from the
wind by a bit of card-board, or a hand curved about them.

They kept going by and going by, those little flames, until
Marise's eyes ached. And yet she couldn't look at anything
else, she couldn't stop staring at those flickering, swaying little
flames.

After a long time she was able to pull her eyes away from
them, to look past them down at the great esplanade—and
oh! now it was not a black and empty hole; it was all full, full
of lights, a million little marching and singing flames, in
endless lines, ordered, purposeful, marching to and fro. So
small, so tiny and feeble each one, but enough all together

to make a great light in the blackness, to fill all the emptiness with glory.

It was then that the terrible great moment came to Marise, something that she could never think about long enough to try to understand, because when she tried to think about it, she began to shake all over just as she had then, when, across the line of chanting pilgrims, she looked down at all those little, marching, singing flames. What was it that came to her then? The most aching sorrow; and yet an exaltation as though broad wings were lifting her up in a solemn beat of power.

It was all over in an instant. Whenever it came after that, it always came and went between heart-beats. But after it had come and gone, everything looked different. It was as though, plodding along on foot, a great wind had snatched her up, and blowing mightily for an instant so that all the world was filled with it, had set her down, ever so much farther along the road she had to go. And always after this moment, she had an hour or so when she liked people better, everybody, the dirty old flower-vendor, the street-sweeper, Jeanne, the teachers at school, Father and Maman. It was as though she saw them all in a procession, each trying to keep alive a precious, flickering flame.

III

There was another, a horrid one from which Marise always looked away the instant she knew it was coming because she couldn't bear it. And yet she never could be quick enough. She always saw it, as though in her, as in a camera, a lens had whirringly clicked open and shut.

And yet there was nothing to it. She had come from school with Jeanne, who had gone to the kitchen. Marise had crossed the landing and started to pull the bell-rope, and then noticed that the door happened to be a little ajar. So she pushed it open and walked in. As she walked past the salon door she had glanced in, and saw M. Fortier there, just going away

from making a call, the father of Elise Fortier, her class-mate
at school. He had his broad, fat back turned to her and was
stooping to kiss Maman's hand. There was nothing surprising
in this; everybody knew that gentlemen who kept on with the
old ways of doing things, always kissed ladies' hands. She had
seen the father of one of the girls kiss the bony hand of Mlle.
Ballot, the head teacher at school. What was registered indelibly on Marise's mind was the expression on Maman's face.
Maman was looking—oh, it was horrid to think such a thing,
to say such a thing, to have looked at her and seen such
a thing. . . . Maman was looking sort of . . . Marise could
never, try as she might, shut down on this moment quickly
enough to shut out the ugly thought she hated so. . . . Maman
was looking sort of foolish and silly, as though, as though . . .
But here Marise was always able to snap the shutter shut and
put it all out of her mind, except the dull heaviness it left.

IV

But the worst, the very worst and most awful of all those
remembered parts of the past, was what happened about the
gray cat. No, that wasn't the way to put it, because you
couldn't say that anything had *happened* . . . and yet how
sick it had made Marise, and did every time something reminded her of it!

One day when Marise came home from school, Jeanne gave
her a big, pretty, gray, yellow-eyed cat and said she thought
it might be company for her. Marise was awfully pleased,
took the cat in her arms, bending her cheek down to rest it
against the soft fur, and carried her off to her room to try
to get acquainted with her.

But there seemed to be something the matter. She didn't
act like Cousin Hetty's Tommy, up in Ashley, nice and cuddle-
some; she seemed to have something on her mind. She
wouldn't sit still on Marise's lap and be petted, she wouldn't
play with a string nor drink the milk Marise put in a saucer
for her, nor lie down and go to sleep the cozy way cats usually
do. She tramped around and around the room, and every

once in a while she'd give a loud miauw, in an anxious voice.

Marise thought it was because she was with strangers in a strange place, and that as she grew wonted, she would be happier. But she kept this up all that day, and at night when Marise shut her up in the extra kitchen they didn't use, she yowled so that Maman complained. And the next day she was even worse, acting so queer, doing such funny things, stooping her front paws down, and tramping hard with her back paws. And as she did this, she would look up at Marise and miauw in a loud, anxious way as though she were asking Marise to do something for her. At the end of that second day, Marise was too worried to keep it to herself, although she had resolved not to bother either Maman or Jeanne because they didn't like cats. She went across the landing to ask Jeanne to come. Jeanne came and Isabelle too, instantly sure of the worst as usual, and declaring that the man who had sold them the cat was a thief and a robber and had palmed off on them a sick cat that nobody wanted. They added emphatic precautions to Marise about not touching her if she was sick, because a sick cat's bite meant poison.

They went into the room. The cat got up and came towards them that same queer way, stooping and treading and switching her tail. And she gave again that strange, anxious cry.

"There, that's the way she does all the time," said Marise, troubled and concerned. She came round in front of the two women, so that she could look full up into their two faces, to see what they thought.

Not a turn, or color, or tone, or line of what they looked and said and did ever faded from her mind. Her first feeling as she looked up into their faces was of utter amazement; and after this an instant cold premonition of something evil. She stood perfectly still gazing at them. . . . What could it mean? . . . What made them look so . . . ?

Jeanne and Isabelle looked down at the cat; the anger went out of their faces, and in its place came a singular, secret expression, half amused . . . half *horrid*. . . . Marise could never think of any other name for it.

Then they looked at each other, their eyes meeting, their eye-brows arched high, and they laughed.

At the sort of laugh they gave, Marise burned hot all over, although she had no idea of what there could be to laugh at. But every line of the two women's bodies and faces, the tone of their laugh, the look of their glistening, amused eyes told her that it was something they thought shameful. And she was ashamed.

Then, as she stood there, cold and burning hot, they had both as by a common impulse glanced at her as if something about her also seemed very funny to them. That glance was the worst of all—like a smear she could never wipe off.

She felt very sick, her knees shook under her. But something furious and strong inside her told her that whatever else she did, she must not let them see how sick they made her. She stood her ground, her eyes burning, utterly at a loss. What could it be? What was this awful joke they laughed at and she couldn't see?

Jeanne said, as they looked at the cat with a greedy amusement in their eyes, "Oh, she's not *sick*. She's looking for a husband, that's all."

Isabelle laughed again at this, and said something to Jeanne in Basque. Marise could not understand a word of this, but her hot, straining eyes, fixed on their two faces, with a help-less fascination, received another deep and indelible impression of conscious shamefulness.

Jeanne nodded and said to Marise, "I'll take her back to M. Bergeret's brother-in-law for a few days, where there are other cats, and then she'll be all right again."

She picked the cat up by the middle and held her so, while she listened to Isabelle, who now said something else in Basque, half-grinning, her lips curled in an embarrassed, half-pleased way. Jeanne glanced sharply at Marise, as if to see whether she had understood this, in spite of its being said in Basque.

Then they both went out of the room, Jeanne carrying the cat by a hard, careless grasp about her middle. Outside the door they both burst into giggles, as though they had been restraining themselves before Marise. The little girl heard them giggling all the way down the hall, the sound broken once by the loud anxious miauw of the cat.

Marise stood perfectly still till she heard the outer door open and close. Then she looked about her wildly. She wanted to run somewhere and hide her face. She wanted to sink down on the floor; she wanted somebody to help her, to make it up to her, some one to wipe it away and put her back where she had been three minutes before, when Jeanne and Isabelle had come in the door. She *couldn't* go on, living the way she felt now, as though she were dirty inside and couldn't wash herself clean. What was it all about? What had it meant? What was there about having a husband that people thought was so . . . ?

At this it came over her in a wave again, so that she started as though she had been struck a slashing blow, and ran, ran breathlessly out to get help.

In the dark hall she stood still, the thump, thump of her heart loud in her ears. A murmur of voices came from the salon. Maman had callers. . . . But even if she hadn't, Marise now knew she could not have spoken to Maman about it. Something came and stood between her and Maman so that she knew she could not tell her. She had a horrible fear that Maman would look that way, too, perhaps she might laugh that way . . . perhaps everybody would. Perhaps that was one of the things they *did*. Not Father, either . . . no, she'd be ashamed of . . . not . . . why, there was *nobody* she could tell; there was nowhere to run for help.

She went slowly back to her room. The sight of it brought up before her again the glistening eyes of the two women as they had looked at the cat and laughed. A terrible burning came up all over her so that she was almost suffocated. She wanted to hide her face. She found herself leaning against the dingy, checked red-and-white curtains. They smelled of dust as she buried her face in them, burrowing deeper and deeper among them as though she must hide herself, hide herself from . . . but she couldn't hide herself from what was inside her own mind.

She stood there a long time, her face pressed into the dusty curtains, her body buried in them. She was sick, sick from head to foot.

And then . . . nobody came to help her, since there was nobody to come; nothing happened . . . nothing could happen. She had thought she *couldn't* live, feeling like this. But she would have to, since there wasn't anything else to do.

This came to her slowly, and slowly sank into her, like still, deep cold.

Two days after this, as Jeanne was brushing her hair, she said to Marise, "Our cat will be brought back to us to-morrow. She is all right now, M. Bergeret says."

Marise waited until the wave of sickness passed and she felt she could make her voice sound as usual. Then she said casually, "I've changed my mind. I don't want a cat now. It would bother Maman too much."

Jeanne was relieved. "Oh, very well. I don't ask anything better. I hate cats around the house anyhow." She went on brushing Marise's hair, with careful, loving skill, proud of its thickness, its sheen, its silky blackness. She thought to herself, "What a beautiful child our Marise is. And how I love her! There isn't anything I wouldn't do for her! May the Holy Virgin guard her and keep her safe always, Amen." She never thought again of the cat.

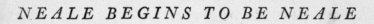

NEALE BEGINS TO BE NEALE

CHAPTER XI

ON Neale's thirteenth birthday, his mother gave him a little silver watch and his father, a bicycle. In addition to the excitement of getting into his teens and of owning these visible and outward symbols of advancement, he was told that he would now be sent to a real school, with no girls in the classes, where he would really learn something; that is to say where he would be prepared for college.

Hadley Prep. was an excellent school, a sort of model school, an information factory. You fed a small boy into it and at the end of four years the school turned him out completely filled with classified information. Boys entered with all sorts of hazy disorders of learning; they were ground out, possessed of a chain of facts, every link shining, polished and joined by flawless welding to the preceding and consequent facts. The curriculum took no count of modern educational fads; "spiritual awakening, character building, intellectual growth" had no place there. What would you have? Four years is a short enough time to prepare boys for their college entrance examinations. The non-essentials had to be cut out. The great point was that when the Principal signed a certificate of graduation he knew that the boy in question could produce any piece of information required of him, from the preterit of recevoir to the formula for accelerated motion of falling bodies, at any college entrance examination in the United States.

Into the hopper of this mental polishing-machine, Neale was poured with fifty other little boys and began painfully to adapt himself to its rigorous codes. It was a process trying to the most robust among them, and devastating to the weaker ones. The devastating quality was not only recognized and admitted but sedulously fostered by the faculty and Principal. It was part of their business to see that the weaklings fell by the wayside long before the flock was led up to the narrow gate of the college entrance examinations. And as some hospitals achieve a miraculously low death-rate by the simple process of never admitting a patient whom they are not sure they can cure, so Hadley Prep. achieved the miraculously low rate of examination mortality for which it was famous the country over, by the simple process of knocking on the head and throwing out on the scrap-heap any boy whose brains seemed reluctant to admit college-entrance examination facts.

Those whose heads were hard enough to resist the knocking, found themselves completely absorbed by the mental gymnastics which filled their days. The first two years of his life at Hadley Prep. had almost nothing in them for Neale except his over-time struggle to make up for the omissions of Miss Vanderwater's haphazard tuition. Everything else, even the assuming of long trousers, even the summers in the country, *even games,* were banished to the fringe of consciousness, like things seen out of the corner of your eye while you are gazing with all your might at something else. The life of his personality, his inner self, during those two years, realized the ideal of the eighteenth century educator who felt that the only safe up-bringing for boys would be to shut them up in a barrel, between the ages of twelve and eighteen, and feed them through the bung-hole. The record of what was fed through the Hadley bung-hole was set down on Neale's report cards, which he dutifully brought home to his parents. They glanced up from their absorption in each other, read, and smiled over the mathematical accuracy of the Hadley information about the state of Neale's mind (the Hadley professor often marked a boy as 87.75 proficient in American history, or 90.3 learned in German). At times they wondered if Hadley were the best place for him. But they were exactly like all other parents: they really had no idea what else to do with Neale. His health continued good and he did not seem rebellious, so they confined their supervision of his education to paying his rather expensive tuition, signing his report cards, and handing them back to him.

Towards the end of the second year Neale began to master ·

the new technique. He memorized the magic pass-words which are accepted as a proof of understanding many subjects. He began to draw breath, to tread water less frantically and still not to fear the closing over his head of smothering floods. The third year he felt earth beneath his feet again, and relaxed enough from his mental concentration to spend occasionally an hour or two on the school athletic field. He was fifteen years old now, wore long trousers and suits with vests, a stand-up collar, ties he tied himself, and carried a fountain pen. Underneath all this grown-up bravery of exterior, there was a brain that had learned to acquire and pigeon-hole information, and a perfectly dormant personality.

Life at the Crittenden home was, as far as he was concerned, exactly the same life he had always known, except that instead of playing on the streets, he went out on the school athletic-field, and instead of playing with his tin soldiers, he usually went up to his room to grind over his lessons. At breakfast and supper his father and mother talked peaceably to one another just as they always had, and although Neale was able now to understand the subjects of their chat, their talk was, as a matter of fact, often quite as incomprehensible to him as it had been when he was a small boy. They had grown so much together, had so shared life with each other and no one else, that they possessed almost a language of their own, made up of references, only half-expressed, to things they had said long ago, or to experiences they had had together, or to opinions they both knew so well there was no need to formulate them in words. Neale was not surprised at this, nor yet resentful. On his side he was absorbed in his studies and the life at school. It was true that every once in a while they talked directly to Neale; asked him questions— what studies he liked best—how the teachers treated him— what he had to eat at lunch. Whatever they asked Neale always tried to answer in accordance with the facts; that he was getting along all right he guessed, that everything was satisfactory as far as he could see, that he hadn't any idea what he should like to do later on to earn his living.

Occasionally, instead of taking the trolley cars, Father

and Neale walked together down the long steps to Hoboken and along 6th Street to Hudson, where his father turned south and Neale went to the school. Then talk was harder to dodge —not that Neale ever consciously dodged. They would walk a dozen blocks. Father would ask a question, Neale would answer it. Another dozen blocks, and another question. Once Father asked if Neale wasn't sticking indoors too much. Couldn't he manage to get a little more exercise? Neale explained the seriousness of his studies and pointed out that he still rode his wheel on Saturdays. But the suggestion took root. Neale bought a pair of Indian clubs and an instruction book, and took to swinging the clubs fifteen minutes night and morning with the windows open.

Another time Father said, "Look here, Neale, haven't you any friends?"

Neale was astonished, "Why, yes, I'm friends with the whole class."

"Yes, I suppose so, but you never seem to be with them outside of school. When I went to school we were always playing around in each other's yards and barns."

"You went to school in the country," Neale reminded him. "We haven't any yards or barns here. We have the athletic field at school."

"Yes, that's so," his father admitted. After a time he made a further admission, "Athletics are all right, too." But something in his tone intimated that he was baffled rather than convinced. Since Neale considered that athletics were not only all right, but all there was to life, he found no comment to make.

A moment later, "But, great Scott," began his father with some heat as though struck afresh with some aspect of Neale's life. He seemed to hear the too-great vivacity of his accent and to wait until he could ask quite casually, "Aren't there any of your school-mates you'd like to have visit you?"

Neale considered. It hadn't struck him before, but it was a fact that after school and athletic practice, all the boys vanished to their various homes. Never having known any other than this city relation with school-mates it seemed to him obvious and natural. "Visit me?" he said, trying to imagine one of his classmates sitting at the Crittenden dinner-table, and then, "No, I don't believe I do. There wouldn't be anything special to do at home, would there?"

His father drew on his cigar thoughtfully, and walked on in silence.

But he had a long talk with Neale's mother that evening, the two country and village-bred parents putting their heads together, earnestly though helplessly. The only course which occurred to them was proposed to Neale, a week later, when Mother asked him if he would do something to please her. Incautiously Neale said, of course, yes, he would. He was always willing enough to please Mother, and he had never made the slightest objection to anything his parents planned for him. But this plan turned out to be something very alarming. It was all arranged, Mother told him, that he was to go to dancing-school in the Germania Club ball-room on Tuesday afternoons. Mother pointed out that, now he was fifteen years old, and half-way through prep.-school, he ought to learn to dance. Neale had no theoretic objections to offer and had given his word that he would not object. So hiding, except for his first wild look of dismay, the terror and repugnance which filled him, he wrapped up the newly bought patent-leather oxfords and started. There were limits even to the Iroquois stoicism of his acceptance of what Fate brought him. No power on earth could have made him walk through the streets in those patent-leather shoes. But Mother never pushed him anywhere near one of those limits. She did not even suggest that he wear his dancing shoes. She helped him find the paper and string to wrap them up. Also she did not fuss over him . . . not much. She looked at him hard, picked a thread off the sleeve of the blue serge which was his dress-up costume, and called his attention to the fact that a button of his vest was unbuttoned. She did not offer to button it herself, or handle him in any way. Mother was all right, if she did want him to go to dancing-school.

So he went. And it was not so bad, not nearly so bad as he feared, the reassuring factor being that everybody else there was in the same boat. You could see how they all despised it. Except, of course, the girls. While he was changing his shoes in silent alarm and disgust in the cloak-room, who should come in but Jenkins, a "Lower Middle" at school. Neale didn't know Jenkins except by name, but at least he was some one to lean on. Neale was at once very cordial and Jenkins, surprised and flattered by this attention from an upper-class man, promised to show him how everything was done. They went into the ball-room, Neale clinging morally for dear life to Jenkins. A number of other young men of fifteen and sixteen, and girls who looked almost like young ladies, were sitting on opposite sides of the room. A bald-headed man to whom Jenkins referred as "One Lung" sat at the piano. The dancing master was young, German, energetic and thorough. He called the class to their feet, explained and illustrated the step and made them all practice it en masse, *"One* and *two! One* and *two!"* Then after a few minutes the music struck up and he left them to choose partners and dance. Neale, of course, did nothing of the kind, but pretended he couldn't find a partner (there were twice as many girls as boys), and went back to his seat. This was a tactical error. The Master spotted him at once. "Couldn't find a partner? Oh, dance with me, then." He whirled Neale about the room till his soul sickened, led him up to the other side of the room and sent him off with a bony, red-haired girl with freckles. Neale was caught that way twice, but no more after that. He had at least ordinary sense, he told himself. Next time the music started, he gulped down his objections to the whole proceeding and bowed to the prettiest girl in the room.

The course was very thorough, covering much that was obsolescent, and a good deal that was definitely dead. In that and succeeding lessons Neale received instruction in the steps of the Polka, the Schottische, the Varsovienne. The two-step he really learned, managing to "Yale" down the length of the hall without stepping on his partner's feet; and although he hated the waltz, he was forced by infinite repetition into mastering it. Oh, the misery of the hour-long waltz-lesson, with the Master's constant exhortation, "Don't hop! *Slide!*"

Neale carried into his dancing the same minute earnestness that won him success at his games and studies. He did not see the use of dancing, any more than he saw the use of learning German. But as the jobs seemed to have to be done, he tackled both of them conscientiously. He remembered to reverse in waltzing just as he remembered to put the auxiliary at the end of a sentence after "als." He came to be considered a good dancer. The girls did not claim to be tired when he asked them to dance with him. But he went no further. Even after he had mastered the steps and "leading," he did not talk as he spun methodically around. What was there to say? And even when he waltzed with Flossie Winters, the admitted belle, his heart beat no faster. It was nothing to him to put his arm around her waist. In spite of his long trousers and stick-up collar, the spirit of the thing escaped him; his time had not come.

After some months (they seemed very long months to Neale), the conscientious and thorough instructor gave him a printed testimonial of efficiency; there was no more he could teach Neale.

Over this his mother looked at him, "Wouldn't you like to go on, for the fun of it, Neale?" she asked him rather urgently. Neale's father took his cigar out of his mouth to hear Neale's answer.

"For the *fun* of it!" said Neale, stupefied at the idea. His parents exchanged glances and shook their heads, beaten.

"Oh, of course you don't *have* to!" his mother assured him hastily. His father put his cigar back in his mouth.

CHAPTER XII

In June 1899 when Hadley Prep. unlocked its grim doors and spewed forth the fifteen-year-old Neale for his third vacation, he did not as he had always done before, go at once with Mother to West Adams and the saw-mill. The invariable program of his journey there, Mother's two weeks' stay with him to get him settled, her going on to visit vague relatives of her own elsewhere in Massachusetts, and her return to spend the rest of the summer with Father, was upset by the news from the West Adams Crittendens. Jenny, the hired girl, had been to visit friends in Troy, and had fallen ill on her return. The doctor thought it might be typhoid. Certainly they did not want a boy visitor bothering around, until the matter was settled and they knew whether they were in for a long siege.

The Crittendens like all methodical people were quite at a loss when circumstances interfered with their routine. If there was one part of Neale's year the rightness of which they did not doubt, it was the summer spent in the country where his father had grown up. Now they were confronted with a perfectly new aspect of the problem of what to do with him. They solved it by not doing anything for the present. Mrs. Crittenden went off to visit the usual relatives in Massachusetts, delicate old ladies, whose nerves could not hold out against the idea of a great ramping boy; and Neale was left temporarily with his father to wait developments in West Adams.

The first days of liberty were sweet enough, after the strain of examinations. Neale loafed or rode his wheel (he had a new 24-inch frame bicycle now) at random up to Hudson Heights, and beyond on the Palisades. But less than a week of this was enough. He tried to amuse himself with baseball again, but it was not as he remembered it. The three years he had been at Hadley Prep. had separated him from his old friends. They were no longer to be found. Some were at work, some had moved away. The boys playing ball seemed absurdly young. The vacant lots themselves were absurdly small and rough. How could he have played there? He gave the thing up and moped.

What was there to do? He got on his wheel again and went out over the Plank Road as far as Passaic, swung left through Montclair, the Oranges, out to Elizabeth and home through Newark. Home was just as dull as he had left it. Neale was bored to desperation, and on a chance went into the parlor and opened the book-case. He was no great reader. In his own room there was a fair collection of Henty, G. Manville Fenn and Harry Castleman, but none of these seemed worth re-reading. He didn't suppose these grown-up books in the library could be worth anything, but he took down a volume to see.

"Ours was the marsh country, down by the river, within twenty miles of the sea. My first most vivid impression of the identity of things seems to me to have been gained on a memorable raw afternoon towards evening. At such a time I found out for certain that this bleak place over-grown with nettles was the churchyard . . . and that the dark flat wilderness beyond the churchyard intersected with dykes and mounds and gates, with scattered cattle feeding on it, was the marshes; and that the low leaden line beyond was the river; and that the distant savage lair from which the wind was rushing, was the sea; and that the small bundle of shivers growing afraid of it all and beginning to cry, was Pip.

" 'Hold your noise!' cried a terrible voice, as a man started up from among the graves at the side of the church porch. 'Keep still, you little devil, or I'll cut your throat!' "

Half an hour later Neale was still standing by the book-case, the book in his hand, his mouth hanging open, shivering in the clammy mist together with Pip and the man with the iron chain. An hour later he was tucked into the Morris chair, among the cushions of which he hid the book when the dinner bell made him reluctantly lay it aside.

What made him hide it? An invincible sense of moral de-

cency made him hide it. He would have shuddered and
cowered like a modest girl whose bed-room door is opened in-
advertently by a stranger, at the very idea of carrying the
book to the table and pouring out to his father what it made
him feel. With a shy, virginal delicacy he stood guard, half-
frightened, half-enchanted, over the first warm gush from the
unexpected well-springs of emotion in his heart. If his father
had come into the room, had seen what he was reading and
asked him how he liked it, he would have answered briefly,
"Oh, all right."

But for the next three days he did nothing but live with Pip,
and feel intolerable sympathy, far deeper than anything he had
ever felt in his own healthy life, for the convict victim of
society. On the afternoon of the third day, his heart pounding
hard with hope, he was in the row-boat, in the track of the
steamer. The Morris-chair in which he sat, swayed up and
down to the ocean rhythm of the great deeps which bore him
along. He peered forward. There was the steamer at last,
coming head on. He called to Provis to sit still, "she was
nearing us very fast," . . . "her shadow on us," . . . and
then, oh, *gosh!* . . . the police-boat, the betrayal, the summons to surrender!

Neale's soul recoiled upon itself in a shudder of horrified
revolt. He recognized the traitor, a white terror on his face.
Grinding his teeth, Neale leaped at his throat. With a roar
the water closed over their heads . . . he would never let
him go, never, never. . . . Down they went to the depths, to
the black depths, fiercely locked in each other's arms. Neale
smothered and strangled there . . . and came up into another
world, the world of books.

At the table that night, his father looked at him and asked,
"You're not getting a cold, are you, Neale?"

"No, I guess not," said Neale, blinking his reddened eyelids, and eating with a ravenous appetite his large slice of rare
roast beef.

After that, time did not hang heavy on his hands. The days
were not long enough. The volume which stood next to
"Great Expectations" was called "The Tale of Two Cities."

"Which two cities?" Neale wondered. He opened it and began to read. In a moment, wrapped in a caped great-coat, shod with muddy jack-boots, he was plodding up-hill beside the Dover Mail, his hand on his horse-pistol. The panting rider on his blown horse—the message, "Wait at Dover for Mam'selle,"—the answer in capital letters, "RECALLED TO LIFE!" With a long quivering breath Neale slid back a century and a quarter, into a world vibrating with sorrow, hope, indignation, hatred, love.

He dipped his handkerchief in the muddy wine spilled in the street; he looked up, not surprised to see the squalid joker scrawl "BLOOD," on the wall; he climbed the filthy staircase, and averted his eyes in horrified sympathy from the ruin of humanity who sat in the dark, cobbling shoes.

And then, brushed in with great colorful strokes, the causes and authors of the filthy stairway, the squalid joker, the ruined man, the endless misery. With the four serving-men pouring out the chocolate of Monseigneur, Neale began to burn, like a carefully constructed bonfire, alight at last. He had never in his life before, given a conscious thought to social injustice or the poor, but every instinct for fair play, sound and intact in his heart, flared up hotly and honestly, as he gave himself naïvely to the spell of the magnetic exaggeration and over-emphasis of the story. He had "had" the French Revolution in his history at Hadley Prep. and could have recited correctly almost any date in it. But, quite literally, he had no idea until after he had finished the story, that this panting, bleeding, weeping, thundering book had any connection with what he had learned at school.

"David Copperfield" was good, not so terribly exciting as the others, but solid food on which Neale, aware for the first time of his hunger, feasted with a deep content—all except the parts about Dora, who made him tired. After this for a change, he reached up to a shelf above and took down at random one of the set in green and gold binding. This was "Kidnapped." Thereafter he read nothing but green and gold, till his eyes gave out and his father drove him out to spend a whole afternoon on his wheel.

CHAPTER XIII

ALTHOUGH he had gone reluctantly, once he was out it seemed fine to be on his bicycle again. His forgotten body reacted with a rush to exercise and fresh air. Generally he expected to make at least fifty miles in a half-day but to-day was hot. Pedaling easily through Nutley he caught sight of a young man playing tennis against two girls and stopped in the shade of a maple to watch the game, still sitting on his wheel, his right pedal locked over the curb-stone. Tennis was not so universal then as now: Neale knew little about the game.

Presently a chance stroke sent the ball into the street. "Out!" announced the young man, and turning ran back to retrieve it. As any American would do anywhere in the world when a ball is in question, Neale stooped, picked it up and was just going to toss it back when amazement paralyzed his arm. Could this slim youth in immaculate flannels possibly be Don Roberts? Don, the big boy who had played shinny and vacant-lot baseball with him, whom he had never seen but with a dirty shirt and unkempt hair! The elegant youth cried out, "Neale Crittenden! I'll be blessed if it isn't old man Crit! That's luck! Come on and meet my friends and we'll have a set of doubles."

He ushered Neale up to the net, where laying a patronizing hand on his friend's shoulder, he presented him. "Ladies, my old friend, Crittenden. We used to be boys together long ago. Neale, the Misses Underhill, Nutley's peerless blondine duet, Polly and Natalie. Now, how about some doubles? Neale can use my old racket."

"But I don't play," said Neale, alarmed at the idea. "No, I honestly don't. I've never had a racket in my hand. I'll watch."

"Oh, fudge! That's all right. You'll learn. Nat and Neale, that's your team. Polly, my dear, come over to this court and back up your Uncle Don. No fair banging everything at Polly."

The essential rudiments were explained. Neale gripped the racket and the game began. At first his partner politely kept her own court but as the completeness of his ineptness became awfully apparent, she began covering more and more territory, running across and snatching the ball from in front of his hesitating racket. In vain, for Don continually placed his return down her undefended alley. The set was soon over, 6—love.

"Now, Crit," said Don, jumping over the net, "we'll have sex against sex."

The second set went better. Now that he was playing on Don's side, Don gave him a little coaching. Neale learned to run in to the net and found volleying much simpler than playing ground strokes. Natalie's low returns often went through him and he did nothing with her service, but not infrequently he managed to pat back Polly's gentle offerings. When points were needed Don monopolized the court. The boys won,—a love set.

Don lit a cigarette and pretended to fan himself with his racket. "How about lemonade for the victors?" he cried, but the girls demurred. It was five o'clock, they had to go home and dress. They laughed over nothing at all, shook hands with Neale, told a few friendly lies about his progress, and walked off laughing over nothing at all, swinging their rackets; white-shod, yellow-haired, pink-skinned.

"Dear little sweethearts, aren't they?" commented Don. "A little insipid like most nice girls, but you have to take what you can get. Polly's a dub at tennis, of course, uses her racket like a snow-shovel, but she's not such a worse little flirt. Look here, Crit, old boy. I've got to stay in this stinking hole all summer, cramming for deficient exams. The old man won't let me go to the Water Gap till I can answer those damn questions. And there isn't a soul to play with but those girls. It's rotten for my game. Why don't you come out here? Come to-morrow. Of course you can't play, but I'll teach you. I can teach anybody."

Neale blushed and accepted the magnificent offer.

"Well, ta, ta, old man, sorry you can't stay to supper."

Neale mounted his wheel with a very high heart. This was something like. Something was beginning to happen in his life. Wasn't Don great? As he rode home he decided that he would ask his father to let him go to Princeton. Don was at Princeton.

But he didn't. Father read him Mother's latest letter, all about the particular great-aunt she was visiting in Cambridge, and after they had commented on this, Father looked at his evening paper sideways as he ate, and Neale went over in his mind the events of the afternoon, and the wonder of Don Roberts turning out such a splendid fellow, such a good sport, such clothes, such a way with him. Neale thought about him a great deal more than about the girls, and with vastly more admiration. He was sure that David Copperfield's Steerforth was nothing to Don Roberts. Once when he glanced up, he saw Father looking at him instead of his newspaper.

"Well, Neale," he asked, "what are you up to these days?"

This was his opportunity, Neale knew it was, to introduce the subject of Princeton, but he could not think of any way to do it. Instead he said vaguely, "Oh, nothing much. Sort of hanging around." And then with a great effort, he brought out, for once, a vital piece of news, "I'm learning to play tennis."

"That's *good*," said Father. "It's a great game."

This seemed to be final. He looked back at his newspaper. But after a while, as though something had occurred to him he asked, "Who's teaching you? Where do you play?"

"I ran across Don Roberts, over in Nutley. They used to live here, on Central Avenue. He used to go to Number Two School." He wanted to go on and tell about Don's being in Princeton, but could not propel himself past the full-stop, where an inadvertent cadence of his voice had dropped him.

Next morning he found Don with a whitewash brush touching up the marking of the court. For three hours they practised—a most exhausting three hours! He thought he began to make a little progress. He knew he was almost all in, when noon came, worn out far more by the mental strain of struggling his way into a new technique, than by the physical effort, although that had been enough to leave him blown and panting, as they went into the house to have lunch.

The two boys were alone at the table. Don swaggered a little as he served his guest. "No one at home," he explained. "Mother and the girls are down at Asbury. The old man doesn't get back from the office till the 5.45. I can hear his train whistle from here. He finds his loving son deep in his books, you bet."

Through luncheon Don fired Neale's enthusiasm with stories of Big Bill Edwards, Arthur Poe, Lady Jayne and other heroes of his Alma Mater. Afterwards he strolled to the living-room, sat down at the piano, and sang "The Orange and the Black,"—"There's a college we call Princeton." Then lowering his voice, with many nods and knowing winks, he sang a long song with the refrain, "Keep your eye on tricky little Sarah."

Neale's play on the streets and in vacant lots with perfectly heterogeneous and casual little boys had given him quite enough of a vocabulary to understand the words of this song; and odds and ends of the older boys' talk overheard in the locker-room at Hadley made the spirit of it by no means unfamiliar. But this was the first time that either words or spirit had ever been more than one of the casual by-products of boy-life. What put it in the center of his attention now was his admiration of Don as the model of colorful, sophisticated life. Evidently this was a part of such life. Neale applied his mind therefore to the words and the spirit and learned to hum the air.

That evening Father read another uneventful letter from Mother; then they sat in silence till, as father was filling his pipe, he remarked, as if it had just come into his mind, "Oh, I thought you ought to have a racket of your own, Neale. I got one. It's in the hall on the coat-rack."

Neale bounded upstairs and carried his prize to his room.

There was not only a Sears racket, but three Wright and Dit-
son balls, Spalding's "Tennis Guide," and a little pamphlet
on "How to Play Lawn Tennis." Neale dropped into his
Morris chair and devoured both books before going to bed.

The hard protective husk of his little boyhood was so
newly sloughed off, that his adolescence had as yet received
scarcely a mark upon its new freshness to impression. Ready
now, responsive with an inward quiver to a whole range of
experience to which he had been blind and deaf before, he was
catching up from the chance materials about him, the stuff
with which to construct his new world. And here was material ready to his hand. The editor, an enthusiast, an idealist
of sportsmanship had put a great deal in his little treatise
beside his copious advice as to the proper grip on the racket and
the laying out of a court. Without the slightest self-consciousness (because he had the not-to-be-imitated single-heart-
edness of the sincere devotee) he had charged every section
of his treatise with the spirit of the game, the spirit of sport,
not of border warfare. So matter-of-factly was this message
conveyed that even the adolescent soul, half-crusader, half-Hun,
did not guess that it was being preached to. The word
"honor" was never mentioned, yet Neale understood perfectly the significance of what he read, under the caption
"Tournaments:" "The committee should provide adequate
linesmen, for while the contestants themselves can generally
tell whether a ball is good or not, yet close decisions occur
in every match and it is obviously unfair to force a player to
penalize himself (as he naturally would feel bound to do)
by giving his opponent the benefit of the doubt on all uncertain cases." He nodded approvingly over the phrase, "as he
naturally would feel bound to do." It did not strike him as a
new idea, but merely a clearer statement of something he had
always felt was in the air about sports. Yes, that was how a
college man would act, how Don would act.

Again, among the illustrations he was struck by a photograph
of the winner and runner-up shaking hands after the Newport
tournament. Neale looked long at the expression of cordial
congratulation and admiration on the loser's face. He moved

uneasily in his chair at the recollection of a nine of disgruntled urchins muttering after a defeat, "Aw, you bunch of stiffs, wait till we get you on our own diamond." Neale had been one of those who muttered, one of those so stung by defeat that the idea of admiring the better playing which had beaten them would have been inconceivable to him. Neale knew himself well enough to know the fierceness of his lust for victory. He knew it was going to be a job to tame that lust to this civilized code. But he would try. Morally on tip-toe, he resolved to be worthy of Don's friendship.

When he turned the last page, relaxed the intense concentration with which he had been absorbing the essence and spirit of the book, and stood up to stretch and yawn before going to bed, he felt that he had learned a lot. And he had. Silently, with the incalculable silence of natural processes, an ideal had crystallized in his heart around a standard of conduct.

And yet this was all under the surface. As he dropped off to sleep, his mind retained as the chief lesson of the book a mass of stimulating suggestions about rolling strokes, the reverse twist service, and the advice for a solitary beginner to practise against a brick wall.

He knew where such a wall could be found; in a vacant lot on Poplar Street, just off Summit Avenue. He often had played hand-ball there in the old days. Next morning he went there after breakfast, postponing his ride to Nutley till after lunch. The result was so good that thereafter he spent every morning there.

The summer days went by. Neale progressed far in his imitation of Don and Don's manner and standards. He learned after practising with a box of his own, to accept the cigarettes Don constantly offered him. To be like Don, he learned to call the girls by their first names without choking, although he never could bring himself to squeeze their hands or pat their shoulders or stroke their hair as Don did so casually;and he did manage to pick up a fair game of tennis.

When he challenged Natalie to singles and beat her 7-5,

Don looked at him with a new expression, and a few days later announced great news. "It's all arranged. Tournament here next Saturday, lemonade, lawn party, picnic-supper, dance. The old man's agreed not to butt in and spoil things. I've got four fellows from here, Peterson, and a friend of his from Montclair. You and I make eight. Just right for a day's tournament on one court."

"But I don't play well enough," protested Neale.

"You'll be put out in the first round of course," Don admitted, "but I need you to make the even eight, and you can chase balls and make yourself useful. Entry fee's a dollar. That'll buy a Pim racket as a prize. I *need* a new racket."

The great day came and Neale, flustered and tense, was put out in the first round according to schedule. It didn't surprise him, although deep in his heart he had had a fluttering hope—but no matter. What happened to him was of no consequence. Don came through easily, of course. After lunch Neale sat with Natalie and together they gasped and clapped and cried, "played!" as Don captured his match in the semi-finals.

"Isn't he splendid?" said Natalie. Neale nodded, too much moved to speak.

The finals were called. Neale focussed himself on the game, blind to anything else. Don was matched against the Peterson boy, a high-school lad from Montclair. Don got the first set. Good. The second set unexpectedly went to deuce. What had happened! Neale leaned forward, his eyes hot from staring, and tried to make out the meaning of what he saw. Peterson didn't hit the ball as hard as Don did, but his long, bony arm pulled off the most impossible of "gets." Deuce, vantage, deuce, vantage. Don put on more steam, served doubles, lost his service. Peterson won his own service, and the sets were even. Don's face was a blank. He walked to his place, hitched up his trousers, pulled the brim of his white felt sports-hat low over his eyes, set his jaw and faced his opponent. Neale's anxious eyes had not left him for a second.

The last set was astounding, paralyzing to the spectators.

Don had gone to pieces and the high-school boy had pulled himself together. His gawky, graceless body and long arms seemed to cover the whole court. Don served with murderous force, his rising fury burning with a sensible heat all around him as he raced and plunged and stroked the ball. Peterson broke through his service again—four-two. Don struck out dazzling drives, but many of them landed in the net. He got by Peterson with wily stroke after stroke—only so many of them landed in the alleys; four-three; five-three. Peterson kept on steadily, with his stiff, mechanical, chopped returns, his intent eyes gleaming in his impassive face. He had Don forty-love. Neale's heart was bursting. Don rushed to the net. Peterson lobbed to the base-line, and it was all over. Don was beaten.

In a flash Neale found an excuse for his hero, "Every one has his off-days . . . but . . ."

Though half-forewarned by the look on Don's face, he could not turn his eyes away from the dashing figure in white flannels, which stood there frozen in mid-flight as the fatal ball fell inside the back-line. Then with a furious swing of his arm Don flung his racket from him as if he wished to break it into a thousand pieces. By good luck it did not hit one of the girl spectators, but fell with a little crash of broken twigs into the midst of a lilac bush. He took a step or two after this, as if he meant to leave the court at once. With an effort, he turned about, walked up to the net where the Peterson boy stood panting, and gave him in silence, a limp hand-shake.

Then he pushed through the spectators, and went into the house calling over his shoulder that Polly was to award the prize. Neale did not dare to look at Natalie; the moment was too awful.

The Peterson boy did not stay to flaunt his triumph. Pleading an impending thunder-storm as an excuse (the sky was as a matter of fact very black and lowering), he scorched off on his wheel back to Montclair with the spoils of victory bound to his handle-bars. With his departure, the atmosphere of gloom among Don's friends began to lift. When the storm broke, as it did shortly, they all hurried indoors. The girls set about getting supper with a great clatter of chafing-dishes, and much screaming, with each clap of thunder. By the time the cheese was melted, Don reappeared in blue serge and negligee silk shirt. Coming down stairs he passed Neale standing apart with his back against the newel post.

"Oh, drop your grouch, Crit, old man," he said. "Forget it! Of course Nordhoff's a pretty rotten umpire. I suppose he thought he'd give the kid a chance, but he needn't have stung me on *all* the close ones."

On this, he passed lightly to the supper-table, where later, on being loudly called, Neale followed him, starting up from his moody silence as though he had forgotten where he was. It was his first supper out with young people, the first time he had eaten welsh-rabbit; the first time he had seen anything prepared over a chafing-dish; the first time he had encountered the traditional young people's menu of that date—welsh-rabbit, fruit cake, nut-fudge made on the spot, all washed down with ginger-ale. It might have been bread and milk for all Neale knew. What he saw was the photograph in the Tennis Guide of Davis shaking hands with Whitman.

Presently loyalty flared up. If Don fell short of the standard perhaps the standard was wrong. . . . It would not do, even as he thought of this excuse, he knew it would not do. He was aware of a streak of iron in his soul. An idol might sweep away the warmth and color of life by its fall—let them go then! No warping of standards could keep it on its pedestal. But the real sorrow in his heart drove him to try to find excuses for Don. Great Scott! it *was* hard to lose! How could you blame anybody for not coming up to such a terribly high standard? Anybody on earth would naturally feel sore at being beaten in such a . . .

Even as he tried falteringly thus to lower his ideal to fit his affection, he was aware of something stern and relentless within him. The gallant face of the defeated player in the photograph stood out beside Don's startled, angry resentment at a wound to his vanity. Nine generations of Puritan forebears would not let Neale abandon his ideal because it hurt him.

He passed into a condition of acute amazement at the others. How could they take it so light-heartedly? Perhaps they didn't care. Or perhaps they felt themselves obliged to pretend since they were still in Don's house. Yes, of course, he ought to pretend too.

Smarting, he sprang up at a new word of command. "How about a little rag-time?" Don was crying in his role of master of ceremonies. "Polly, you to the piano. Get the old banjo, Dick. Clear the floor, boys. Oh, pitch the rugs out of the window, a little rain won't hurt 'em." For through the open windows came the steady voice of a summer downpour.

The musicians struck up "Whistling Rufus," couples were formed and racketed noisily to and fro from the dining-room to the sitting-room and back, with much bumping and giggling at the congested doorway. Neale danced absent-mindedly with a girl whose name he could not remember, and whom he exchanged for a similarly anonymous girl when the tune changed to the "Georgia Camp-meeting." He went on thus, setting his body to do the decent thing, while his spirit lay prostrate within him.

They were dancing harder than ever now, racing long-leggedly from one end of the room to the other, the boys carrying the girls bodily off their feet at some of the turns, the girls abandoning themselves like romping children to the whirlwind of the insistent rhythm, which they marked by shouting out as they danced, "Oh, la la, la, la-la, la la la! There'll be a *hot* time in the *old* town *to-night!*" Neale danced on with the rest. Under his grimly silent exterior, something fine and high and deeply wounded, cried out silently to the others, and received no answer.

The music ended with a crash, the exhausted couples sank into chairs, gasping and fanning each other. Neale's heart leaped to see, half-way up the stairs, Natalie sitting alone as if she had not been dancing. Why, of course. There was Natalie! He had forgotten her. She had understood. The tragedy of the afternoon must have gone home to her. *She* was a good sport! With a warm glow he hurried up to where she sat, and sank down beside her, his stifling sense of isolation gone.

She lifted the sweet, flower-like mask of her youth to him, her eyes gleaming in the half-light of the stairs. But at the moment, Neale had forgotten whether she was a girl or a boy. She was a good sport. That was what he needed. He started to speak, but a shout of laughter burst out of the room below them. They looked down. In the center of the vociferously amused circle of spectators, Don was making fun of his late adversary's gawky manners and poor eye-sight. He had a racket in his hand, and glaring through it with a burlesque of Peterson's intent short-sighted gaze, he was mimicking the school-boy's strained awkward position at the net.

Neale fell back appalled, and looked to Natalie for sympathy and understanding.

Natalie had also leaned forward, and as they turned towards each other, her face was so close to his that he could see the peach-like bloom on her cheeks.

All the pretty face was quivering with mirth. "Isn't Don the *wittiest* man!"

Neale got up stiffly and walked down the stairs without a word. Nobody in the crowd of laughing boys and girls paid the least attention to his silent passage through them. He went out on the porch, the beating down-pour of the rain suddenly loud in his ears. Oh, all the better! He'd like getting soaked.

He found his wheel on the side-porch, mounted it without troubling to light his lamp or turn up his coat collar, and delighting in the clammy discomfort of the streaming water, pedaled stolidly over the nine miles to his home.

Alone in his room he took off his steaming clothes, rubbed down and got into pajamas and a bath-robe.

"Crittenden," he said sternly, "the world is no place for you. You're a lone wolf. A lone wolf."

CHAPTER XIV

WHEN Neale turned out his Welsbach burner and rolled into bed, he encountered a strange, new sensation, an immense relief just to lay himself down, and to have darkness about him. For the first time in his life he was consciously very tired, for the first time he knew the adult sensation of having lived to the point of weariness, for the first time he felt the passive sweetness of the resigned adult welcome of repose which is perhaps a premonition of our ultimate weariness and our ultimate welcome to death.

For a moment Neale lay there, drowned in astonishment at this new, unguessed-at pleasure. Then, without warning, the thick cloud of a boy's sleep dropped over him like black velvet.

The next morning, his father, passing on the way to his cold bath, looked in and saw the boy, sunk fathoms deep in sleep, the bright new sunlight of the early morning shining full on his face. Heavens! How can children sleep so soundly! His father stepped into the room, walking silently on bare feet, and drew down the shades. The shadowing of the room did not waken the sleeper. He still lay profoundly at rest and yet profoundly alive, one long, big-boned arm thrown over his head on the pillow, as he always had slept when he was a child.

"As he had when he was a child!" His father was struck by the phrase and looked again at the tall, rather gaunt young body flung on the bed. That was no child who lay there, nor was that a child's face, for all the pure, child-like curves of the young lips, firmly held together even in this utter abandon to sleep. The older man stood by the bed for a moment, looking down on his son, his own face grave and observant. He would be a fine-looking fellow, Neale, with those honest eyes, wide apart under his good, square forehead. Yes, Neale's father had always known the extreme satisfaction of being able to respect his son, there was no doubt about that. But there was something else, the something that had always baffled him, that he had never been able to penetrate, the closed look, locked tight over . . . what? Was it locked tight over something, or nothing? Did Neale have a real personal life? Would he ever have? Would there ever be anything, anybody who would have the key to unlock and set free what was there, before it died of its imprisonment?

For an instant the face of Neale's father was unlocked as he stood looking down on his son. Then, with a long breath, he stepped back into the hall-way, silent on his bare feet, and went on to shave, and to take his cold bath.

It was after ten when Neale awakened and the day had sunk from its first fresh hopefulness into the resigned apathy of a hot mid-morning, with the stale smell of dusty, sun-baked pavements, the slow, unimportant jog, jog, jog of the horse hauling the grocer's delivery-cart, and the distant, jingling of the scissors-grinder's bell.

Neale came slowly to himself and rolled over, a very bad taste in his mouth, both physically and mentally. He had not noticed it at the time, but he now thought, scraping his coated tongue against his teeth, that melted cheese and cake and nut-fudge and ginger-ale were a darned bad combination to be swallowing of an evening. And as for the rest . . . oh, gosh! Never again!

He turned his big, strong feet out of bed and sat sunk together for a moment, recalling it all, and steeping his soul in wormwood once more. *Now* what?

The telephone rang; he heard Katie answer, and clump up the stairs to see if he were awake.

"Somebody to talk to you, Neale," she said, seeing him sitting up. Neale's father might note he was no longer a child, Neale's mother might keep her hands from fussing over him, but for Katie he would always be the little boy she had helped to bring up. She laid her hand on his head now, and Neale did not mind.

"*You* answer," he said stolidly.

"It's him that's always telephonin'," she explained. "He's after wantin' you to go and play tennis."

"You tell him I can't go," Neale repeated.

Katie retreated astonished. Neale heard the sound of her voice at the telephone two flights below. Then she shouted up, "Neale!"

He went to the stairs and answered crossly, "What?"

"He wants to know will you be goin' this afternoon?"

"*No!*" shouted Neale, leaning over the banisters.

In a moment she cried again, "He wants to know will you be goin' to-morrow morning?"

"NO!" shouted Neale again, and going into the bathroom locked the door behind him.

When rather damp as to hair, he came out, silence and the smell of frying bacon told him that Katie had left the telephone to get his breakfast ready. Gee Whiz! He didn't want any breakfast, not with a taste like that in his mouth.

To act the part of a lone wolf of sixteen, one must read poetry. He had never read much poetry except some of Milton's Paradise Lost, for a specially loathed English Literature course at Hadley. But there were plenty of poetry books in the library at home. After some false starts, Neale began to know his way among them, concentrating on the slim volumes with paste-board covers and paper backs.

> "Beneath the bludgeonings of chance . . ."

Yes, Neale too would hold up an unbowed, bloody head.

> ". . . without fear, without wish,
> Insensate save of a dull crushed ache in my heart. . . ."

> . . . "Just to reach the dreaming,
>   And the sleep."

Sitting alone in the darkened library how Neale soaked himself in this sort of thing, hunting up one page and down another till he found the voice that spoke to him.

> "The irresponsive silence of the lands
> The irresponsive sounding of the sea
> Breathe but one language and one voice to me
> Aloof, aloof, we stand aloof!"

When Katie's carpet-sweeper and feather-duster and kind, gossiping voice sounded too close, he escaped out of doors, but not on his bicycle. That, like his tennis-racket brought up painful memories. Every evening he walked to the Boulevard, and gazed over the Hackensack meadows till the sun set.

> "No sweet thing left to savor; no sad thing left to fear. . . ."

On the evening of the third day, a letter from West Adams arrived, announcing that Jenny was up and around, and the farm-house was ready for Neale. The evening after that, Neale was undressing in the slant-ceilinged big-beamed, whitewashed bedroom, as familiar to him as his room at Union Hill —but uncontaminated with any of the new, troubling sensations. The air of the hills blew in at the window. Neale felt that it was a different air. He began to feel a difference in himself, but fell asleep in the midst of this perception. The next morning, scorning the mill, the barn-yard, the brook, he climbed to the highest back-pasture where the young white birches and quivering aspens, skirmishers of the unconquered forest, were leading the way in the reconquest of the fields man had taken from them. Here he lay down and prepared to nurse his sorrow. . . .

> "Pain gnaws at my heart like a rat that gnaws in a drain. . . ."

But what was this? What was this? As unexpectedly as the impudent little mick had sprung out of the ground to carry off his shinny ball, so did a cheerful little imp of high spirits spring up in his heart, leaping and skipping to meet the glory of the great sun pouring down its mellow gold upon him through the flickering, tricksy aspen leaves. He lay back on the soft, deep moss, his hands clasped under his head. Huge, jovial-looking clouds floated, piled up in strong, rounded masses against the summer sky.   Miles off in the valley he could see the Hoosick River winding its way among the green, green hills.   He was warmed, cool, alive . . . and, oh, yes, there was no use in pretending otherwise, mighty well pleased to be alive.

The ten-year-old Neale when suddenly the glamor had faded from his lead soldiers, had never wasted time in pretending that it was there.   He had risen at once, left the little heap of clumsily-made mannequins to lie foolish in their flaking paint, and sliding down the banisters, had gone out of doors in a great hurry.   Well, he wasted no time now.   He looked with an ironic eye upon the glamorless lost illusion, with the paint flaking off, and hurriedly turning his back on it all, he went, metaphorically, out of doors.

What had happened after all?   He'd thought the world of Don Roberts, who had turned out a four-flusher.   Well, he'd been stung.   But why holler so about it?   And whose fault was it?   His own, for not knowing better.   Don hadn't ever pretended to be any less of a four-flusher than he was.   It was just that he, Neale, had been taken in by a cheap, flashy guy when any kid ought to have had enough sense to see through him, and those would-be smart college-man airs and manners.

But anyhow if that was a false scent, it had put him on a true one.   There was a lot inside those slim, paste-board covered books beside rats gnawing in drains, and twilight and all-goneness.   You bet your life there was.   Neale had never dreamed what was inside them, poems that stood up to a glorious day like this, and called it brother, poems of foot-free wanderings and high-hearted scorn of prosperity and conventions.

> "I tell you that we,
> While you are smirking
> And lying and shirking
> Life's duty of duties,
> Honest sincerity,
> We are in verity
> Free!
> Free as the word
> Of the sun to the sea;
> Free!"

Neale's voice quavered with another sort of emotion . . .
that was the doctrine! "Off with the fetters!" He pictured
himself in a blue flannel shirt and flowing neckerchief, alone,
or with some perfect comrade, knowing reality, sneering at
railway trains and cities.

It was a gorgeous dream . . . but of course the first Tuesday in September found him back at a desk at Hadley with all
the grinding and polishing wheels of that well-appointed educational mill at work on the corners of his individuality, bent
on turning out the fifty young Seniors smooth and identi-
cal, the perfection of the Hadley type. And since this was
the last year, the faculty speeded up the hunt and all the
pack put their noses to the ground and ran their legs off
in pursuit of mathematics and science. The pace was cruelly
hot, and it was specially hard for Neale because he had yielded
to the captain's entreaties and had come out for the football
team. He made left tackle with little competition and through
October and November practised almost without coaching
(Hadley permitted athletics but was too busy to encourage
anything so childish), and played and was beaten with painful regularity.

Neale found himself dropping far below the rating he had
maintained in the lower classes. He began to pant and strain
as he had the first year. It was a gruelling race; but temper-
amentally he liked races and his wind got better as the months
went by. He cut out all superfluities—no dancing—no reading for amusement except on Sunday mornings, and then only
short poems about Vagabondia and the Open Road. Work,
work, work through every waking hour. By April he had
risen to sixth in his class, and felt grimly sure of holding his
stride to the end.

On the night of Easter Monday, Neale was bent over his
desk with a green eye-shade, trying various combinations to
solve a problem in analytical geometry, when his father knocked
at the door, walked in and sat down on the bed. This was so
remarkable that Neale knew something was up. One of the
things that Neale had always taken for granted in his home-

life was that his room was practically inviolate when he was in it. His father and his mother respected his privacy in this as in other things with scrupulous exactitude. It was a little corner of the world which was his, where he could come out from his tightly-clutched shell, and move about freely with no fear of intruders spying on his nakedness. The security of this privacy had been one of the well-squared stones Neale had found ready to his hand, when slowly, rather later than most boys, he began to build. Hence it was now apparent to him that Father must have something on his chest. He looked up, nodded and greeted him with, "Hello, Dad."

"Hello, Neale," said Father quite as casually. "Don't want to interrupt your studies. How late do you expect to keep at them?"

"Sometime between eleven and twelve, I guess. His Nibs gave us some stinkers, and I haven't touched the German prose yet."

"That would be pretty late for me. We'd better take a few minutes now. The fact is, Neale, we mustn't let you slide along any more without some sort of an idea what you are going to do next."

Neale having no idea beyond that night's work, said nothing.

"The work you're doing this year has given your mother and me a great deal of pleasure," Father went on. "Your marks are getting better and better. I did think of putting you through an engineering school, but I notice you seem to do better at the liberal subjects. Have you set your heart on any college in particular?"

"I'm not sure I want to go to any college."

Oh, now for a break into the Open Road, and a flaming neckerchief and far lands!

Mr. Crittenden looked thoughtful.

"I'll admit it's a waste of time for some, but I don't think it would be for you. I understand your wish to get to work, and begin to make your own way, but it's wiser not to start with too little preparation. And there's no need for it yet.

It's no hardship for me. It's a real pleasure for us to be able to help you to an education. . . ."

Neale chewed his pen hard. How hard it was to have things out with a father! When a man takes it for granted that if you don't want to go to college you must want to be a bank-clerk or sell shoes, how are you to make him understand anything about Freedom and the Open Road and Comradeship and Vagabondia, distant countries and ships that smell of tar and salt like the wharves. How could a man in a three-button, pepper-and-salt cut-away understand? A man who wore a derby hat and went to his office in the city every day? And Father was getting fat, too, the three-button cut-away was heavily rounded. No—all that was in another world. There weren't any words to express any of it to a Father. So he said nothing, jabbing his pen into the blotting paper. Presently Father went on, "Of course, I should like to have you go to my old college, Williams, but Mother feels—we both feel—that it would be a pity to break up the family circle. What would you think of Columbia? They say since it has moved up to Morningside Heights there is more college life—and of course it's one of the leading Universities. . . ."

Another pause, so long that Neale felt bound to say something.

"Oh, I guess I would like Columbia as well as any," he finally brought out.

Father looked at him several minutes. Then he stood up, "We needn't settle it to-night, of course. Think it over; we'll talk it over again."

But of course they never did. They never talked anything over. The subject was not raised again. Nevertheless it was somehow understood in the family that Neale was going to enter Columbia. And Neale made no protest. To tell the truth, as spring advanced and all his classmates began talking over their plans for next year, the uniformity of having a recognized respectable destination was not disagreeable. It saved talk, and useless talk about his affairs was one of the things Neale detested. Till he could be really independent and do as he liked without suffering the ignominy of having people know about it and talk him over, it might be better just to slide along the grooves provided, get the usual labels stuck on you. It couldn't do you any harm. They'd soak off easy enough, later on.

CHAPTER XV

WITH June came examinations at Hadley. Long, long experience and concentration on the subject had taught Hadley administrators exactly how to time their training so that when examinations came, the boys would be in the pink of condition. Two weeks later they would be stale, horribly, sickeningly stale, but nobody at Hadley cared a continental what happened two weeks after examinations. That was no business of theirs. Weary, but still docilely answering the crack of the ring-master's questions, the thoroughly disciplined Troupe of Trained Boys went through subject after subject, with the automatic rear and plunge of circus-riders breaking paper hoops. That was all right. Those were only the Hadley examinations. They expected to be able to pass those.

But now for the College Entrance examinations, the Apollyon which from afar their professors at Hadley had pointed out to them, straddling over all their roads, belching out brimstone-fire on all who tried to pass. With much trepidation hidden under his usual decent impassivity, Neale journeyed up to take his first examinations at Columbia. He was glad that the first chanced to be in history. That was one of his good subjects. He stood a better chance there. With a careful air of carelessness, he went up to the proctor's desk, took one off the pile of the printed examination sheets, and with it in his hand, not entirely steady, he went back to his seat. Safe from observation there, he laid it before him and his eyes leaping to know the worst, took in the first three questions at one glance. Holy Smoke! Was this all? Was it for this he had sweat blood! There was an outline map of the United States, with a request to mark on it the location of such idiotically well-known places as Acadia, Pittsburg, New Orleans. There was *"French and Indian Wars. State causes immediate and remote."* There was, *"What do you consider to be the relation between the Missouri Compromise and the Civil War? Justify your opinion in 500 words."*

Neale leaned back in his chair faint with relief. Why, he could eat it up like candy. And he ate it up like candy; emerging from it, his head in the air and the world at his feet. This aspect caused him to be chastened by a gang of Sophomores who played hare and hounds with him (he was the hare), through Riverside Park from 120th to 81st Street, where his long legs finally distanced them.

The other examinations were of the same sort, exactly the same sort, of a childish facility compared to anything the Hadley professors had described. Why—it came to Neale with a shock—why, the Hadley purpose had not been to enable them to pass the exams.—it had been to use Hadley boys to exalt the name of Hadley throughout the collegiate world! He felt a deep resentment, a burning bitterness as at having been taken in; and by people who had consciously intended to, who had known very well what they were about, and had taken advantage of his defenselessness. He thought of those four years of driving drudgery and causeless dread, and hated Hadley as the quintessence of cheating. The idea that the subjects of his study had any value other than as legal tender for college entrance, that he was the better off for his thorough acquaintance with them did not once cross his mind. In that respect, too, he was a product of Hadley.

He came away from the last examination, as stale and worthless as an overworked colt. The Sophomores let him alone. He looked to them as though he had not been able to pass.

A wide, green pasture with running brooks is the best place for a tired colt, and it was such a one that Neale now entered, his head hanging, his big legs like cotton twine. Oh, shucks! What was the use of anything?

Grandfather and Grandmother kept a Crittenden shut mouth about his drawn face and sallow skin, and at first were careful to keep out of the way and let him even more alone than usual. He fell into bed at eight o'clock, unable to keep his eyes open another moment, and lay as though he were dead for twelve or fourteen hours every night, awaking to see the country sun shining in on the slant, hewed beams over his head, and to hear the country sounds, as clear as crystal coming in through the open window; the mill-brook chanting, the wind in the big maple, the bright, brazen call of the rooster, the sociable grunting of the pigs.

The pigs were a great comfort to Neale at this time. After he had washed in the brown rain-water in his wash-bowl, and had gone down to the clean, sunny kitchen, always empty at this hour, and had eaten heartily of the fried potatoes, hash, and pan-cakes which he found waiting for him in the warming-oven of the kitchen stove, he sauntered out, a doughnut in his hand, to lean over the pig-pen and commune with the pigs. He stood there an hour at a time, occasionally scratching their backs as an excuse for staying so long with them, but for the most part gazing dreamily down, lost in the magnificent sensuality of their joy in life. They had always been fed an hour or so earlier, so there was no excitement in their profound beatitude, none of the homeric scramblings of meal-times. Neale was not ready for that yet. What he needed, what slowly floated him up from the depths, was their rapt ecstasy of repletion, their voluptuous pleasure in sinking thoughtfully into the cool, wet filth and the glow of their peace as they stood sunning themselves, visibly penetrated to every fleshly cell of their vast bodies, by the most perfect accord with the scheme of the universe, as they saw it. Neale gazed at them as they lay sprawled in the mud, or moved about very slowly, grunting very gently, occasionally turning upon the boy a small, wise, philosophic eye; and they did his heart good, like medicine.

When he was ashamed to stand there any longer . . . although no one ever commented on it, and indeed no one was there to see it, except Grandmother and Jenny busy in the house, he loitered along the path which led to the seldom-used foot-bridge across the mill-brook. The sound of the water always threw him into another contemplative pause here. He often lay down on the rusty-colored pine-needles and lay looking up at the distant dark green branches of the forest-roof, the voice of the water rising and falling, so insistent that he could think of nothing else, so unintelligible that it made him think of nothing at all, sliding, breaking, turning, slipping down, leaping up, like an endlessly curving line drawn endlessly before his eyes. He usually shut his eyes after a little, and not infrequently added an hour or two of sleep to the fourteen he had spent in his bed; this time, sleep not black and opaque, but shot through with the gleaming pattern of the brook's song.

One morning when he woke up, while he still lay in bed staring up at the beams over his head, some chance association of ideas made him think of Hadley and he was astonished to find his resentment against Hadley had gone. Hadley seemed very remote and vague to him. He did not hate it any more. He could scarcely remember what Hadley had been like. Nor anything that he had studied there. That day for the first time he went down to the mill, walking, not sauntering, his legs solid under him again.

He found Grandfather and old Si "making out" very badly, with no boy to "take away." The last one had followed all his predecessors into the cotton-spinning mills at North Adams, and as this was haying-time no other help was to be had. The two old men had to stop the saw every few minutes till Si could run around and catch up on taking away. It was fretful work, like trying to lace up your shoes with one hand. Neale stood and watched them for a while. Then although he had not really meant to say it, he was not sorry to hear his voice suggesting, "Why don't you take me on? I haven't got anything else to do."

"What say, Si?" asked Grandfather, laughing so at the idea, that Neale was nettled and had a picture of how unutterably lazy he had looked for the last fortnight!

Si spit tobacco-juice into the mill-race and shifted his quid.

"Wa'll, I know hands is scurse these days, but land! have we got down to taking *any*body?"

Neale was used to the Yankee roughness which they meant

for humor, but this touched him a little closely. Didn't they think he could do any work?

Grandfather puckered his old face into a grin and nodded him into the job.

"If so be so, then so be it. Kin or no kin, I guess we can afford to pay him what we were giving Hubbard."

So Neale bought a suit of overalls at the general store and began to work. For the first three days he wished with all his heart he'd kept his mouth shut. Handling green beech for ten hours a day was very different from helping out a half-hour at a time. Besides, his muscles and above all his hands were pitifully soft after an indoor winter and his fortnight of vegetating. It didn't seem worth while to make an ox of himself for five cents an hour and board—the wage of unskilled labor in that non-unionized Arcadia—but he was ashamed to quit on a job that was always handled by boys of his age. Nobody had asked him to do it. He had offered himself, pushed himself in. It would be too worthless to back out. But, oh gee! he was tired when he got through at six o'clock, and clumped heavily up the hill after Grandfather and Si, walking, it seemed to him, with as stiff and aged a gait as theirs. He shovelled supper up, starved, starved to his toes, and staggered to bed immediately afterward. The first week he lost five pounds. Thereafter he gained steadily, and all solid muscle.

After a time he mastered the mill-hand's basic axiom, "Never lift a plank if you can slide it," his hands stopped blistering and hardened, and he grew muscles in various places up and down his back, where he had never had any before, so that the boards became singularly lighter in his hands.

And then, just when he had mastered his job, the water-god took a hand in the game. Since the spring rains, there had been nothing but the gentlest showers. The mill-pond had shrunk to a pool, and grass began to show far down its dried-up sides. The water no longer ran over the mill-dam. One day about five o'clock the mill stopped, with a log half-sawed.

"No water," said Silas, "got to shut down till the pond fills up." They sat down instantly, hanging their empty hands over their knees, in an ecstasy of idleness. They managed to finish that log by supper time, but the drought held.

Soon they could saw only by pondfuls. A couple of hours in the early morning, a scant hour after lunch, and somewhat less after supper, in the twilight. Between times Si patched belts, or hoed corn, or sat and smoked, Grandfather pottered around the garden, or sat and smoked as he waited for the pond to fill.

This was delightful—just enough work for exercise, and lots of blameless leisure. But with so many hours to read, Neale ran through at an alarming rate the books he had brought with him. Even "Vanity Fair" didn't hold out forever, and with Dobbin and Amelia finally united, Neale was at the end of his literary resources. Boredom settled down heavily. Si's reiterated anecdotes lost all savor; he had read all the books on the sitting-room book-shelves, or had given them up as hopeless. He felt bound by his contract to be on hand whenever the mill could be run, so that long walks were out of the question.

At last as he sat gloomily killing time trying to whittle a wooden chain, and making a botch of it, he seemed to remember one rainy day when he was a little boy, wandering into a room with another book-case in it. Not being a little girl, he had had small interest in exploring the inside of the house, and where that room was he had forgotten; but if there had been any books in it, they were there still; no single decade ever made any change in that house. It was worth having a look.

Anybody but a Crittenden, dealing with Crittendens, would have gone to Grandfather or Grandmother and asked where that book-case was. But it did not occur to Neale to do that, and if he had thought of the possibility, he would never have done it. That would have meant talk about his wanting to read, about what books he liked, and why he liked them . . . all sorts of talk from which Neale shrank away as he did from physical pawing-over. He set off silently, with a casual

air, upon his search, looking first into the darkened best-room,
and going from that to the garret, the attic over the ell, and
the woodshed loft. There were scattered books in all these
places; in the best-room a few big, illustrated, show-off books,
with gold on the bindings, like the Doré Bible he had so
often looked at, and the big Pilgrim's Progress that he had
opened only once. In the garret were dusty old school-books
of past generations, and in the attic over the ell, piles of well-
bound black books, with gold lettering, which turned out to
be, desolatingly, nothing but by-gone Congressional Records
and Census Reports. But he had not found the little brown
book-case which he dimly remembered. Perhaps it wasn't
here at all. Well, he'd try the chambers, mostly vacant now,
which had been so full in the days Grandfather liked to tell
about, when he was a little boy, one of fourteen children all
growing up tumultuously together in this big old house.

Neale went down the attic stairs and began to open doors.
Nothing doing. Everywhere the same sparsely furnished
room, with painted floor, braided mat, dark old bed and
battered dresser, and ladder-back, flag-bottomed chairs. Their
vacancy struck cold even on Neale's not very impressionable
mind. "A room that hadn't been lived in for a long time was
the limit, anyhow," he thought.

But at the other end of the hall from his own low-ceilinged,
little boy's room, he found one like it, rather more cheerful.
The sun came in through a dormer window as it did in his
own room. He remembered now that this was the room
Father had always had, till he went away to college and after
that to New York to live. And there, sure enough was the
little book-case. Of course. He must have seen it lots of
times, going by when the door was open. Now, what was in
it? Maybe, after all, nothing to his purpose; probably this
had been used like the shelves in the attic as a place to put
volumes that nobody wanted to read.

Mather's Invisible Providence—sounded religious. Neale
did not even take it out. A big, old book with the back off
proved, when he opened it, to be Rollin's Ancient History.
With a true Hadley horror for learning anything out of hours,

he slammed it shut, and took down the next one, Butler's Analogy. Seemed as though he had heard of that one. He sat down on the edge of the little four-poster, and opened it at random, skimming the pages. Oh, awful! Fierce! *Worse* than religious! He put it back, discouraged, and ran over the titles on that shelf. A name struck his eye. Emerson. Wasn't there a poem by Emerson at the beginning of "The Children of the Zodiac?" Neale like every one else at that time had read a good deal of Kipling, although he was vague as to Emerson.

He took down Volume I, and opened to the first page.

"But thought is always prior to the fact; all the facts of history pre-exist in the mind as laws."

"Pretty rough sledding!" thought Neale, "bad as Butler."

He turned over a page. His eye was struck by a thick black pencil-mark along the margin; a passage that had interested somebody. Neale read, "I have no expectation that any man will read history aright, who thinks that what was done in a remote age, by men whose names have resounded far, has any deeper sense than what he is doing to-day."

An idea knocked at Neale's head. He looked up from the book to take it in. It echoed and re-echoed in his brain, the first idea about history which had ever penetrated to fertilize the facts piled up by Hadley. Gee! there was something *to* that! Neale began to walk around it speculatively. Wonder if that's true? Sounds good.

Were there perhaps more passages marked? He turned over the pages again and came on another of the black pencil lines in the margin.

"When a thought of Plato becomes a thought to me—when a truth that fired the soul of Pindar fires mine, time is no more."

"Time is no more . . . ." The grandeur of those four words unrolled a great scroll from before Neale's eyes.

Say, who was it who had marked these places, anyhow? Who was it, who, before Neale, had sat in this low-ceilinged room and had caught that glimpse of timeless infinity? Neale turned back to the fly-leaf and found written in a familiar handwriting, "Daniel W. Crittenden, Williams 1876."

Why, that was *Father!*

Neale stared at the name. Could it be Father? Yes, he had gone to Williams and although 1876 was incredibly long ago, that might have been Father's class. And this was Father's room! He looked about him, astonished.

For the first time in his life it occurred to Neale that his father had not always been a father and a successful, conservative business man of forty-something, but that long, long ago he had also been a person.

The idea made Neale feel very shy and queer as though through the pages of this chance-found book he were spying on the privacy of that unsuspecting person. But all the same, it was too strange that *Father* should have . . . what else had he marked? Intensely curious, Neale turned the pages over. What else had struck the fancy of that young man, so many years ago, before he dreamed that he was to be a business man and a father. It was like looking straight into some one's heart; the first time Neale had ever dreamed of such a thing.

There they were, those glimpses of what had fed his father's spirit. Neale read them because they were marked. Some he understood, others he only felt.

"In every work of genius we recognize our own rejected thoughts; they come back to us with a certain alienated majesty."

"There is a time in every man's education when he arrives at the conviction that he must take himself for better, for worse, as his portion; that though the wide universe is full of good, on kernel of nourishing corn can come to him but through his toil bestowed on that plot of ground which is given to him to till."

"Life only avails, not having lived." Good enough!

"For every stoic was a stoic, but in Christendom, where is the Christian?" every word underlined in ink.

"Crime and punishment grow out of one stem. Punishment is a fruit that unsuspected ripens within the flower of pleasure which concealed it." On the margin the note was, "True, think of E. B." "Wonder who E. B. was," thought Neale, "but the old man's right."

Ah, this is bully! "Life itself is a bubble and a skepticism, and a sleep within a sleep. Grant it, and as much more as they will . . . but thou, God's darling, heed thy private dream; thou wilt not be missed in the scorning and skepticism; there are enough of them. . . ."

Why, this was not marked! The old man must have been asleep at the switch.

Neale stopped turning the pages and jumping from one marked passage to another. He began to read for himself, a deep vibration within answering the organ-note which throbbed up at him out of the page.

"This," he said to himself, after a long, absorbed silence, "this is my meat."

There was a good place on top of the plate-beam of the mill, dry and safe. One morning before Grandfather and Si came down to work, Neale climbed up to this, dusted it clean of the litter of a century or more and put the three volumes there. Whenever the water got low, and the mill shut down, and Si went off to oil the harness and Grandfather to have a visit with Grandmother in the kitchen, Neale clambered up and clinging with one hand, reached in and took out a volume . . . any one of the three. From there to the top of the highest lumber-pile outside, in the clean sunlight.

The pungent smell of the newly-sawed wood, the purifying wind, wide space about him, solitude, silence, and this deep, strong voice, purifying, untroubled, speaking to him in a language which was his own, although he had not known it.

*"TO-DAY SHALL BE THE SAME
AS YESTERDAY."*

CHAPTER XVI

March, 1902.

FLORA ALLEN found she was not following the words on the page, and let the book slowly fall shut. As it lay there among her hair-brushes and cold-cream pots, she looked at it with a listless distaste. How sick she was of reading instructive books! She never wanted to see another! She turned sideways in her chair with the gesture of a person about to stand up, but the motive power was not enough, and she continued to sit, one arm hanging over the back of her chair. Why get up? Why do anything more than anything else?

How horribly lonely she was! How horribly empty her room was!

The emptiness echoed in her ears. It was an echo she often heard. She always heard it more or less. She told herself that it was like the emptiness of a long stone corridor along which she seemed to be always hurrying, hoping to come to a door that would let her out into life—the warm, quivering life that other people—women in books for instance—seemed to have.

Now she was tired. She had almost worn herself out in the long flight down the empty passage-way that led from birth to death. She began dreadfully to fear that she would never find a door. Wherever she thought she saw one ajar, it was slammed in her face.

Looking back, how she envied her earlier rebellious unhappy self, bright with the animation of her naïve hatred for Belton and America; quivering with her aspiring cry of "Europe" and "culture!" She had been married almost sixteen years—was it possible! A life-time! A life-time filled with nothing. A life-time spent between Belton and Bayonne! Oh, it wasn't fair! She had never had a chance—never! And soon it would be too late for her chance!

How hideously fate always discriminated against her. She was always thrown in the dreariest places with the dreariest dead-and-alive people, flat and insipid and tiresome.

Other women encountered big and moving things in their lives, knew adventure and excitement, had something to look forward to, something to look back on. But she had nothing but stagnation. And nobody to care *what* she had, because they all assumed that if sawdust and chips were good enough for them, that diet ought to be good enough for any one.

The days, that might be so precious, slid by, one like another, and there were not so very many days left to her, when vivid personal life might be possible. Where was she to find it, where, where? She was so *tired* of stagnation.

She was reduced to envying the exciting life of the women of the demi-monde of whom she was aware here as never before in her life, of whom everybody was conscious. It was indeed precisely to avoid resembling their bright colors and gaiety that all the appallingly respectable women wore such ill-fitting dark clothes and heavy shoes on the street, never broke their solemn silence in a public place, and never laughed freely anywhere except safely behind walls. The women they were so determined not to resemble seemed from a distance to Flora Allen the only people in France who openly enjoyed life as she thought people in Europe did, the only ones who bore the slightest relationship to the vivacious, animated picture of European existence as she had imagined it in Belton. Except, of course, such dusty, vulgar excursion-train crowds of common people as you saw at Lourdes. Flora hated vulgar people.

And yet—ugh!—life couldn't be all gaiety and brightness for the women of the "half-world." That evening last year, when she had tried to lighten the deadly dullness by a little, playful flirtation with M. Fortier, such as any American would have answered by half-sentimental banter—she had never forgotten how frightened she had been by his instant misunderstanding—the horrible spring he had made at her in the dusk of the carriage; his brutal hands on her shoulders, his flabby, old face suddenly inflamed; the terrifying weight of his obese body against her hands as she pushed him furiously away!

For months afterwards she had been afraid to smile at any man, as she said "good-evening"; and she read in their eyes, in all their eyes, what they would think of her if she but looked squarely and frankly at them.

But wasn't there *ever* to be anything for her, between the deadly flat propriety of things like those awful progressive-euchre parties in Belton and *that* sort of thing?

Isabelle came into the room now, floor-brush and cleaning cloths in hand. She was surprised to find her mistress still before her dressing-table at half-past ten in the morning. To herself she made the comment, not by any means for the first time, "Well, the good God certainly never created a lazier good-for-nothing." Aloud she said respectfully, "I beg Madame's pardon for not knocking. I thought the room was empty. Do I disturb Madame by coming to clean?"

Madame got up hastily, murmured a "no, oh no," and disappeared down the hall. Isabelle opened the windows, fell on her knees and set to work with energy, suppressing (lest her mistress still be within ear-shot) the lively dance-air which came to her lips, as she rattled the brush against the furniture and base-boards. She would be nineteen at her next birthday. What a lovely spring day, how sweet the air was, Jeanne had promised to let her walk out beyond the city-walls next Sunday afternoon with Pierre, and she had a new pair of shoes, real leather shoes, to show off there. Perhaps Pierre would take her to a confiserie and buy her some candied chestnuts! Her pulse beat strong and full, the dance-tune jigged merrily inside her head, she reached far under the bed with her brush, and enjoyed so heartily the elastic stretch and recoil of the muscles in her stout shoulders, that she reached again and again, although there was no need for it. "Jig! Jig! Pr-r-rt!" went the dance tune in her head . . . new shoes . . . sunshine . . . candied chestnuts . . . Pierre . . . kisses.

Her mistress, detesting the sight of Isabelle's broad, vacuous face had walked aimlessly away, anywhere to escape the slatternly flap of her heelless sandals, and the knock of her brush as she went through the never-varying routine of the morning cleaning. Around and around, every slow dawn brought exactly the same sequence of tiresome, insignificant events. Only stolid, vegetable natures like Isabelle's could endure it. Flora's small, thin, white hands fluttered piteously out into the air as though trying physically to lay hold on something else. There *must* be something else. The tears stood for a moment in her blue eyes, not so blue now as they had been—oh, she knew how they were fading!

She went through the corridor into the salon, and pulling the curtains aside, stepped into the alcove where her writing desk stood. But she had no intention of writing a letter. To whom? If she wrote what she really felt, there was nobody to understand her. She did not now, as had been her habit in the first days, go to the window and amuse an idle hour by looking down on the crowd below, the ox-drivers, the fish-women, the soldiers, the Spanish peddlers, all the bright-colored, foreign throng that had seemed to her like a page out of a book. Not for nothing had she lived four years in Bayonne! That first simple candor of hers was darkly dyed with new knowledge. She knew now that people talked about a woman still young enough to be desirable, who showed herself at an open window. She knew they talked, and she knew what they said. That hearsay knowledge had been sharpened by her gradual perception of the way certain men among the passers-by had looked up at her; and it had been driven deeply home one day, by one of those men. As she leaned out, her fair hair bright in the sun, a passer-by, a well-dressed man with a walking-stick in his hand, had stared hard at her, caught her eye, hesitated and looked again. Flora had not avoided his eye. Why should she? It was early in her life in the half-Spanish town. She did not fear men's eyes. When he saw this he turned and mounted the stairs to ring at the bell. Isabelle had let him in, not knowing him from any other caller. He stepped quietly to the salon, where the lady of the house, not dreaming that any one had entered, still stood before the window. When she turned in answer to a discreet little cough on his part, she had seen him standing there, hat in hand, waiting, with a singular little smile on his lips, a smile she never forgot.

Oh, he had been perfectly polite, indeed quite desolated at having made a mistake, and had speedily bowed himself out of the place, apologizing gracefully to the moment of door-closing. But that very day, Flora Allen had the swathing lace-curtains put back in their original position, covering every inch of the glass; and when dusk fell, she was always the first to think of drawing the heavy damask curtains over them, so that there seemed to be no windows at all in the room.

That seemed to her to express her life—no windows except these opening on what was physically sickening and coarse; no doors save those leading back and forth between the deadly familiarity of the imprisoning rooms.

What was it she had not done which other women did to let them into the center of life, while she was exiled to the outer fringes? How was it that while other women's arms seemed to close about warm, living substances, hers grasped at shadows. Or did other women only pretend to be satisfied, for fear of facing the emptiness which echoed in her ears more and more loudly?

Did they really and honestly find the absorbing joy in their children, which was the sentimental tradition? And if they did, how did they manage it? She loved Marise, nobody had a nicer little girl, nor a prettier. But the plain facts were that a little girl and a grown woman were very different beings, with very different needs and interests. There was nothing she would not do for Marise, she often told herself, if Marise needed it. But Marise apparently did not need a single thing her mother could do for her, any more than any healthy little girl absorbed in her school and play. There was no sense in doing uninteresting things for people when they were just as well off without them. She often looked at Marise across the dinner-table, fresh and well-groomed by Jeanne's competent hands, and wondered with a sincere bewilderment how any one could expect her to make an occupation out of loving a very busy, self-centered, much-occupied little girl, who left the house before her mother was out of bed, was gone all day, spent most of her few free hours with her music teacher, and in the nature of things went to bed just at the beginning of the evening.

From time to time, when they had first come to Bayonne, she had made various attempts to connect her life with Marise's, annoyed by the affection Marise showed to Jeanne and to that singularly unattractive Mlle. Hasparren. Breaking through the tyrannical regularity of the child's hard-working life, she had carried her off, now for a day on the beach at Guéthary, now for a day in the shops at Biarritz, once for a week-end at Saint Sauveur. But she had come home after such attempts, mortally weary and depressed. What was the use of trying to pretend that the things which delighted and amused a child were not inconceivably tiresome to a grown-up? Those endless hours while she sat in the sun on the sand (which got into her shoes), and watched Marise inanely prance in the surf, or dig for clams which she did not care to keep after she had caught them! How could she see anything but very visible repulsiveness and dirt, and quite probably diseases in the lank stray dogs and cats which always turned up when Marise went along a street, and which Marise always felt an inexplicable and perverse desire to fondle? And those cheap bazaars, where Marise loved to linger, gazing with dazzled eyes at the trumpery, papier-maché gimcracks and playthings . . . ! Of course, as Marise had grown less childish, walks had been free of hoop-rolling with its inevitable encounters with irascible old gentlemen's legs, but she had developed other tastes quite as bothersome. Flora's pretty, slender feet ached with fatigue at the recollection of the long hours she had stood beside Marise, who, sucking hard on a barley-sugar stick, and hooking her elbows over the parapet of the bridge over the Adour, gazed endlessly down on dirty, smelly ships being unloaded by dirty, smelly workmen.

Flora had come to the conviction that the European custom of sending a servant around with children was based on a realistic recognition of facts. It was better for both sides; for she knew that, although she tried to be patient, Marise felt her lack in interest in chatter about whether the stone would hit the tree *this* time, or how long Marise could walk over flagged sidewalks without once stepping on a crack. Good Heavens! What difference did it make! It was inevitable that a servant's vacant mind should be naturally more nearly on the childish level.

And yet, once in a while, when Marise came into the salon to kiss her mother good-night, Flora's arms caught her fast, wistfully, feeling an aggrieved, helpless resentment at somehow being cheated out of what seemed to mean so much more to other mothers. Marise always felt instantly this special mood in her mother and always flashed up in an ardent return, straining her mother to her in a great silent hug. It was a good moment for them both, but so quickly gone.

She looked now at her watch and remembered an engagement at her dress-maker's to try on a new house-dress. It suddenly made her sick to think of bothering with it. What was the use of a new house-dress? Who would see it except Horace, who never saw anything, or perhaps some one like Madame Fortier or Madame Garnier, who would think it unbecoming for a married woman to wear pretty, frilly things, or to think of anything but how to shove their husbands and sons and daughters ruthlessly ahead of other women's. Heavens above! How tiresome they were about their families! They never saw another thing in the world! Except scandalous suppositions about other people's actions.

She discovered that she did not feel at all well, not nearly well enough to go to have the dress tried on. She was always tired. The enervating climate certainly did not agree with her. The doctor paid no real attention to her case, and the sulphur baths at Saint Sauveur had done her no good, for all they cost so much. How she had hated the dreary little village, full of sick women, perched on the narrow ledge, from which the sanitarium and the bathing establishment looked dizzily down into the frightful gorge where the gave of Gavarnie boiled among its rocks. It had given her materials for many a nightmare, that long black cleft in the earth, so full of the wild haste of the waters that the ear was never for an instant, asleep or awake, freed from their plunging roar. It had given her nightmare; and the sulphur baths had not helped her worn feeling of prostrated weakness in the least. And now she feared there was something else—her heart was certainly not quite normal. There were times as now (she put her fingers to her wrist) when sitting perfectly still, she felt her pulse drop almost to nothing. A muffled, listless beat, like a clock that is running down. . . .

"Running down?"—the chance phrase caught her attention. Was she running down to middle-age, without once having . . . ? She started up, stung by the thought, frightened, angry—a way out into life—a way to escape from the stagnant pools where Fate always cast her—a way to find some vibrant stirring aim—if it were only for an hour—something to care about intensely! Other people did—women in books.

Jeanne, passing the door on her way out saw her mistress standing in the alcove, and paused to ask a question. ". . . if Madame wished Mademoiselle Marise to wear a white ribbon in her hair that afternoon? Because if so, a fresh one was needed." Her old voice thrilled as she pronounced the child's name.

Madame brought her thoughts back from their wanderings with an effort. "A white ribbon?" she said vaguely.

Jeanne reminded her, "The annual competition for the prize in music at Mademoiselle's school. The young ladies are to dress in white." Madame remembered, "Oh, yes, yes, yes." A pause, while she seemed to begin to drift away again, and then, with a perception that Jeanne still stood before her, waiting, "Why, yes, of course, buy a white ribbon if she needs it."

Jeanne took her tall, black-clad body off into the hall and thence into the street, her mistress instantly gone from her mind. She had no time or strength that momentous day for anything beyond her passionate absorption in her dear girl's ordeal, Marise's first step into the battle of life. Her little Marise almost a young lady, her fifteenth birthday so near, contending with rival young ladies! Jeanne ground her strong yellow teeth and prayed furiously that the other competitors might all have cramps in their fingers, that a fog might come before their eyes, that they might have blinding headaches or at least that their petticoats might hang below their skirts and disgrace them as they walked across on the platform.

She went to the best shop in town for the ribbon, the only detail lacking in the spotless costume which had been ready for days, pressed by Isabelle and pressed over again by herself. Jeanne had all the possible shades brought down; dead white—ivory white—pearl white—cream, she took them to the door to see how they looked in full daylight, and withdrawing herself by a swoop of her will power, from the clattering confusion of the street, she held up the rolls of ribbon one by one, imagining, as though Marise were there before her, each one against the gleaming dark head. Not the dead white—no, that looked like nun's stuff, and there was nothing of the nun in Marise, thank God! Not the pearl white—that bluish tinge—oh, no! that was only fit for a corpse— The cream? No, the white organdie of the dress would make it look dirty. The ivory—yes, the ivory.

She carried the others back and looked hard at the ivory on both sides, making a deft fold or two with her stiff old fingers, to see how it would tie into a bow. She held it out at arm's length, her tightly-coifed, gargoyle-head on one side. She drew a long breath, having been so absorbed in the ribbon that she had forgotten to breathe for some time. "Well, give me a mètre and a half," she said finally to the clerk, adding scornfully, "if that's the best you have!" Cloth-of-gold embroidered with pearls would not have satisfied her.

As she came out, she turned her head sideways to estimate the height of the sun, having a low opinion of the accuracy of clocks, and was startled to find it so late. If she were to get across to the river, to the Holy Ghost Church, to set a candle burning before Our Lady for Marise's success, she would need to hurry, and of late Jeanne had found hurrying not so easy a process as it had been. If Marise was older, so was she, seventy-six her last birthday. It was harder for her to stretch her long legs to the old stride. Something happened to her breathing, all the blood seemed to go to her head and a blackness came before her eyes, so that once or twice she had been obliged like any weakling Parisian to lean against a wall or table till the roaring in her ears stopped and the dull heavy fullness in her head subsided. But Jeanne despised people who gave way to little notions like that, and had no intention of putting on any such airs. Certainly not now, when Marise's welfare was at stake.

Of course she must make her prayer for her darling's success, and set a candle burning before Our Lady. The easy way to do this was to step up the street to the Cathedral but Jeanne did not care for the Cathedral, where all the heretic tourists from Biarritz went to stare, and which was as big and bare as the waiting-room of a railway station. How could Our Lady notice one little candle or one old woman there! No, Jeanne was set on lighting her candle in her own half-ruined, dark Church of the Holy Ghost, where the Basques go on pilgrimages to pray before the holy "Flight into Egypt." Our Lady of the Saint-Esprit had already performed many miracles for good Basques. . . . Oh, for a miracle now!

She began to pray as swiftly and violently as she walked, "Blessed Mother of God, be with her this afternoon! Holy Infant Jesus! Help her! Blessed little Saint Theresa, help my darling!"

She cast herself so vehemently into her supplications that she felt her heart blazing like a torch. She soared high out of her body. She was swinging along through space among the clouds, wrestling with the Saints, clinging to their knees, dominating them by the fury of her prayers. . . . No, they would not *dare* refuse her. . . . She would not give them an instant's peace . . . !

"Blessed St. Cecilia, stand at her side! Oh, most Holy Mother of God, guide her fingers . . . !"

". . . a way out into life? How could she find it? Other people did . . . women in books. . . ." Flora Allen's eyes moving slowly about the room fell on a photograph of the South Portal of the Bayonne Cathedral. It was framed in dark wood with a little Gothic arch at the top. It made her sick to look at it. How much trouble she had taken to get that photograph and to find the frame that would suit it. How eagerly she had hung it on the wall; and then had turned round to find it had made no difference in her life, or in any one's life. She looked at it now, her pretty lips set bitterly. What an idiot she had been! What difference *could* it have made? What had she ever thought it could do for her, she and the other women of Belton, everlastingly studying something or other, going after culture with such eagerness, bringing it home, hanging it on the wall, and turning round to find it had changed nothing, nothing. How silly they were! Nobody over here cared anything for "culture" or art, or sculptures —except badly-dressed, queer people with socialistic ideas, like Marise's music-teacher.

And they were right not to care. What was there in it for any one? What could she ever have thought there was? What earthly difference did the sculptures on the South Portal make to her, Flora Allen, driven along through life, without getting out of it a single one of the things women really wanted? What good did it do any one to go and gape at the paintings in the Museum, most of them ugly, and all of them as dead as dead? When what you wanted was to be alive! To have gaiety and sparkle and cheerfulness in your life, not to vegetate and mold like the primitive lower forms of life around you, like Isabelle; not to dry and harden and become a mere block of wood like old Jeanne!

There was nothing unreasonable in not wanting to shrivel and stagnate. It was *right* to want to have an ardent life, full and deep, that carried you out of yourself.

But in her life, as by a fatality, there were never any occasions for emotion, for fresh, living sensations. Nothing ever happened to her that *could* stir her to anything but petulance and boredom—nothing! nothing! If anything seemed to promise to—why, Fate always cut it short. Those wonderful afternoons when Sister Ste. Lucie had taken her to the convent to talk to Father Elie! From the first of her Bayonne life she had felt it very romantic to know real Catholics, who used holy-water and believed in saints, and she had loved to go round with Sister Ste. Lucie in her long black gown and frilled white coif, just like a picture out of a book. But this was different. When the dark, gaunt, hollow-eyed, old missionary-priest had given her one somber look and made the sign of the cross over her, she had felt her heart begin to beat faster. And as he talked to her afterwards, in the bare, whitewashed parlor of the convent, with the light filtering in through the closed shutters, he had made her tremble with excitement, as he himself had trembled throughout all his thin powerful old body. His deep-set eyes had burned into her, as he talked, his emaciated fingers, scorched brown by tropical suns, shook as he touched the Crucifix. How he had yearned over her as he told her that, never, never would she know what it really was to live, till she cast out her stubborn unbelief and threw herself into the living arms of her true Mother, the Church of God. Flora had not known that she had any belief in particular to cast out . . . she had never thought anything special about religion at all, one way or the other. She only wanted him to go on making her tremble and feel half-faint, while Sister Ste. Lucie clasped her rosary beads and prayed silently, the tears on her cheeks! And then the very next day the Father Superior of his Order had sent him off to Africa. Would he ever come back?

Perhaps she *could* become a Catholic. Why not? If it moved you like this just to be in contact with the Church—what must it bring you to be intimately of it? She remembered that in a book Sister Ste. Lucie had given her, stories were told of women who lost consciousness from sheer emotion, when they felt the consecrated wafer of Communion on their tongues; others who were caught up among the saints for hours, hearing heavenly music and when they came to themselves, the room was all scented richly with invisible roses. . . .

Also, without a word spoken she thought she had understood that the Marquise de Charmières and all that old aristocratic set would not be so stand-offish if she were converted.

But as this last idea slid into her mind from behind something else, there came with it as frighteningly as if she had seen the walls of her stone corridor closing in on her, a doubt that cast a stale sallow reflection on all her thoughts;—suppose she were really taken up by the Marquise and all the old aristocratic set, *would things be any different then?* Mightn't that, too, be just something else she had gone out after and brought home and hung on the wall, only to find that it changed nothing? She turned away from this idea, cold and frightened at all it implied . . . that life was not deep at all, anywhere, but a shallow mud-hole, and that she had sunk far enough down to touch the bottom.

She heard now the uneven clattering jangle of the bell, heard Isabelle come out of the bed-room and go down the tile-paved corridor. Her sandals dragged at the heel as they always did in the morning before she put on her street shoes. That slatternly flap and drag of Isabelle's sandals made her mistress sick. She had spoken about them a thousand times. She had come to have a nervous hatred of the sound, had actually flown into rages over it, stamping and shrieking at Isabelle as she despised French housekeepers for doing. But how much impression had she made? For one morning, perhaps two, Isabelle laced up her early morning foot-gear, and after that she always forgot, slid back, flop, scuff, flop. That was the sort of sandals all the chambermaids in Bayonne wore for the first cleaning of the morning; that was the kind they always had worn; the American mistress might as well make up her mind to the fact that that was the kind they always would wear. There was about this trivial matter of the sandals, the same nightmare quality of passive, inert resistance to the idea of any change, which sagged smotheringly down on Flora Allen everywhere she turned in her French life. They called it stability. She and her friends in Belton had called it a "back-ground of tradition."

And yet she knew herself now incapable of going back to live in Belton where she would not be able always to depend on an Isabelle, where at times she would have to sweep her own rooms, and scour her own greasy pots herself. It made her sick to think of living that way again—nobody to bring her breakfast in the morning! To get up in a cold house with all the responsibility for everything on her shoulders. She felt weak at the thought of it.

Isabelle scuffed in, the mail in one rough, strong, red hand, and flapped back to her cleaning. This time her mistress made no comment on her laceless sandals.

What might there be in the mail? Nothing interesting, that she knew beforehand. She turned the letters over, recognizing from their very aspect the flatness of their contents. A letter from America? Oh, yes, only from Horace's old Cousin Hetty, for Marise. How she did keep up that correspondence! Did she suppose for a minute that any child could go on remembering some one she hadn't seen for four years, especially a child like Marise, so self-centered and absorbed in her own life, caring really about nothing but her music.

A bill for Marise's school for the last quarter—to be put with Horace's mail; a circular from that something-or-other society Mlle. Hasparren was always fussing over, trying to raise money to keep some quartet running in Bayonne: a bill from the dress-maker; another circular—oh, as bad as Mlle. Hasparren's, that association with the long name, that took care of foundling babies—they were always wanting money too! A notice from the school, another bill? No, the announcement of the music-contest that afternoon. Heavens! Never again for her! Once was enough, to sit silently all a long afternoon on a teetering folding chair in the midst of stodgy, dawdy mothers, whose boring eyes saw right through the fabric of your dress to the safety-pin with which you had replaced a missing petticoat button, and who had no more interest in the music banged out by the school-girls than you had, except to wish ill to every child not their own.

There was one letter, addressed to her in the pointed, fine convent hand-writing of Sœur Ste. Lucie. She opened this with more interest. Ah, Father Elie was coming back. And wished to see her to-morrow afternoon. She felt a little stir of her pulse, the first in so long. What dress would she wear to the convent? Her black voile—and the little close-fitting hat?

Still thinking of this she turned from the letters to the printed matter. There were a couple of battered, out-of-date New York newspapers, weary with their long traveling, and the deadly little Bayonne paper, with its high-flown, pious articles, and its nasty hints at scandals. She stood leaning against the table, looking down scornfully at it, till her eye caught a name, and her face changed.

Mme. Garnier's son back from his two year stay in New York, where he had been studying American business methods. . . .

Flora Allen looked up quickly at her pretty blonde smiling reflection in the mirror, turning her head to get the three-quarter view which was her favorite. So he was back, was he? So he was back. His dear mama must have decided that he was now old enough to protect himself from golden-haired American ladies. So he was coming back to perch on the front edge of his chair and look volumes out of those great soft eyes of his that were so shy and yet could be so expressive. He was coming back to be so nervous and moved that his shaking fingers could not hold his tea-cup, and yet so persistent that he came week after week whenever she was at home to visitors; so timid that he hadn't a word to say for himself but so bold that he often spent the entire evening, romantically sitting on the bench across the way, staring up at her windows.

He was coming back after his exile in America, was he? And two years older. Well, we would see what we would see. And in the meantime Father Elie could wait.

She had a singular little smile on her lips, as she turned from this item to a card from Horace, saying that business would keep him longer in Bordeaux than he had thought and he would not be back till a week from Saturday. She tossed this card with the letters on the table, and began to turn over the canary-colored books scattered on her desk. No, the volume was not there. She must have put it back long ago in the book-case. She ran her finger along the titles on a shelf near her, found it, pulled it out. With it in her hand she sank down on the chaise-longue. But before she began to read, she sat for a moment, her lips curved, remembering what was in it, and remembering how more than two years ago she had looked up from it to see Jean-Pierre Garnier for the first time. Yes. . . .

She opened the book, fluttered the pages, read a little here and there; and then, as if slowly drawn by an undertow, sank into the book, with a long breath.

After a time Jeanne let herself in, stood for an instant in the door, despising her mistress, and passed on to Marise's room. But the novel-reader heard nothing, drowned deep in the book, reading very slowly, her eyes dwelling long on every word. ". . . I wakened, thinking I heard my name called, slipped out of bed and went to the window. The moon poured liquid silver upon the garden, and there in the midst of it stood Urbain, slim and young as a lady's page, his soft eyes glittering like jewels. With a bound he leaped up towards me, and found a foot-hold on the rough stones of the old wall, so that he stood beside me with only the low window-sill between us. He took my hand in his. He was trembling like a leaf. He looked at me imploringly.

" 'Go! Go! Urbain!' I whispered, trying to steel my heart against his youth and ardor, 'Go, I am like an old woman to thee, a mere child.' His answer was to put one trembling arm around my bare shoulders and gently lay his velvet cheek upon my breast. I felt myself melting, melting in a delicious languor. After all, why not? Where would the dear boy find a more devoted and delicate initiation into life. . . . Think into whose hands he might fall if I repulsed him!

"He raised his face adoringly to mine, drew me down to his lips . . . his young, firm lips . . . sweet as the petals of a rose . . . perfumed with youth. I closed my eyes. . . ."

The only break in the intense immobility of the reader was that occasionally she moistened her lips with her tongue, and once in a while she drew a long, sighing breath.

CHAPTER XVII

"There!" said Madame Garnier, scanning the chair-filled assembly-room from the back, "up there in the second row there are three seats. We can take two and hold one and perhaps after Danielle has played, she can come and sit by us."

They were in plenty of time,, long before the contest began, so that she gave herself the pleasure of walking slowly down the aisle, stopping wherever she saw a familiar face to exchange greetings and to say proudly, "Yes, Jean-Pierre is returned from America. Looking very well, isn't he? Yes, that's the style in America, neither beard nor mustache. But I think after a while he'll let his mustache grow again. I tell him he looks like a priest."

But she did not think that he looked in the least like a priest. She thought him the most beautiful young man in the world, and she was so ecstatically happy to have him back again after the rending anguish of the two years' separation, that she forgave him all the anxiety he had caused them by that foolish infatuation of his. That was in the past now, she hoped. Perhaps he had outgrown his foolish idea, as they had hoped he might when they had sent him away. He had certainly said nothing about it in any of his letters. But even if he hadn't forgotten, if he but knew it, she was more than ready to yield the point to him, to yield anything that would end his alienation from her, that would bring him back to live in Bayonne. She had grown old during those two endless years. They had broken her resolution. He was too precious. She could deny him nothing. If he still wanted it, why, let him *have* his little American girl, as soon as she was old enough to marry. She might be made over into a passable wife for Jean-Pierre. There was no doubt she was pretty and fine, with nice hands and feet; and she seemed gentle and quiet. Once get her away from those impossible parents, into a decent home . . . !

Her heart was rippling full with joy to feel Jean-Pierre there beside her. At times it overflowed, and she all but opened her lips to tell him she would sacrifice anything for him, that she would put no obstacle in his way. But for the moment a prudent thought restrained her. She would wait and see whether perhaps Jean-Pierre had not forgotten that curious infatuation with a mere child. There was no use putting the idea back in his head, if his exile and two years' time had blotted it out.

They sat in a decorous silence, waiting for the beginning of the program. Madame Garnier moved nearer to Jean-Pierre, for the pleasure of feeling his arm, a man's arm now, inside a very well-cut masculine coat-sleeve. She remembered what it had been, the rosy translucent flesh of her first baby, then the little thin, white arm of his long ailing boyhood—how she had fought with ill-health to keep him—all those years, never an instant's relaxation of her care, her prayers, her piercing anxiety! Oh, well, it was all over now. There he sat, a splendid young man, still a little delicate, but sound and well. Her reward had come. How goldenly the years stretched out before her! Perhaps it was just as well to have him marry young, to have his wife come to him intact in the first bloom of her early girlhood. He himself was so unworldly, he would never be able to manage an older woman. A fleeting picture came to her of a rosy baby's face—Jean-Pierre's first child. The thought flooded over her, rich with pride and joy.

She continued to gaze at a certain spot in the curtain, her face framed in her heavy velvet hat, composed in decorous vacancy.

Beside her Jean-Pierre also fixed his eyes on a certain spot in the curtain, and composed his face to quiet. But he was afraid of the silence. He wished his mother had gone on chatting, or that they had sat down near acquaintances with whom he would have been forced to talk. Then he would not have been so conscious of the dryness of his mouth, of the roaring of his pulse in his ears. He stared hard at the curtain, trying to interest his eyes in the design of the tapestry. But they could see nothing but what they had seen for two years, liquid dark eyes looking straight into his heart, his poor heart that he could not hide from them; dark eyes that seemed to be looking wistfully for something they did not find, something that he knew he could give, something that he longed to give with such an abandon of desire that he felt now, as so many times before, the sweat start out on his forehead.

He shifted his position, folded his arms, looked away from the curtain and down at the floor. Come, come, this was becoming nothing more than a fixed idea, a mania! It was idiocy to let it master him so! Good God, what had she been but a little girl! What was she now but a little girl! A girl of fifteen was no more than a child. His heart sprang up at him with a tiger's leap—"only three more years to wait—perhaps only two more—." He frowned, cleared his throat, and taking his handkerchief out of his pocket, passed it across his lips.

And then she might be totally changed by this time; girls often did change. Suppose she had grown very stout —or were gawkily thin like his sister Danielle, or bold and forward, or dull. He rolled himself in the hair-shirt of all the possible changes for the worse, and felt his passion burn hotter. Well, he would see. In a few moments he would see. He looked at his watch.

"It must soon begin," said his mother anxiously, leaning towards him, evidently fearing that the delay might bore him.

He smiled at her reassuringly, and put his watch back. Dear Maman! How she did spoil him! How he had missed her, missed his home, those two years in America. He thought of the boarding-house on 59th Street with a qualm. How good it was to get back to a real home.

But there were fine things in America, too, even if they did not know how to create real homes, even if the men did not know how to love their mothers, or cherish their wives. He had learned a great deal there, a great deal even beyond the revelation of new business methods. What he had learned commercially was enormous! He faced his future here in France, sure of success.

But he had taken in other things too—he was thankful that he had been to Marise's native country and had learned something about the attitude towards women there—not that he would ever, ever treat Marise as American wives were treated, with that rough-and-ready, cowboy lack of ceremony, nor would he ever neglect her, leave her out of his life, as American husbands did. He would know how to combine the American honesty and sincerity with what no American ever felt or showed, with what no American woman ever experienced —tenderness, cherishing tenderness. He would be tender for Marise as no other human being could be; he would find the most exquisite ways to surround her with tenderness, to protect that sweet mouth of hers from bitterness or sorrow, or knowledge of the world's evil.

He looked down steadily at the floor, a knot in his throat, his heart aching, and swallowed hard.

Three wooden thumps sounded from the platform, and the curtain drew itself aside, showing the stage decorated with a stand, two potted palms, an armchair, and a sprawling black grand piano with two cane-bottomed chairs before it.

From the wings trudged in a red-cheeked young girl, with a large bust, and brawny rough arms, hanging down over her starched white dress. Behind her trotted a short withered elderly woman, a black silk waist crossed over her flat chest, her scanty gray hair smoothed down in thin bandeaux over her ears. They sat down before the piano, opened the music, carried by the older woman, waited till she had adjusted drooping eye-glasses on her high thin nose, and had peeringly found her place. Then the young girl began to pound out the Raindrop Prelude while the other turned over the pages.

The audience preserved a respectful silence, bestowing a minute attention on the hang of the player's skirt, the fit of her bodice, the crimped waves of her light brown hair, her over-plump hands, and the bulging patent-leather shoes, which she pressed nervously up and down on the pedals.

Something seemed to break and clear away in Jean-Pierre's head, like fumes drifting away from a shattered retort. So this was a school-girl, this solid, unformed lump of human flesh, neither child nor woman, who had lost a child's poetry and had not yet come to woman's seductiveness. He looked coolly at the girl (his mother whispered her name, the younger sister of a lycée friend of his), dissecting her with his eyes, immeasurably relieved. Was it for an amorphous creature like this, too old to kiss on the cheek, too young to kiss on the mouth, that he had suffered? Why, it was nothing; a mere morbid whim of his ignorant boyhood. How right Maman had been in making Papa send him away from it! He had grown to be a man without realizing it, a man of the world, in no danger of losing his head over chits.

The Prelude was finished. The player got to her feet, and bowed self-consciously to the muted thuddings of gloved palms on gloved palms which greeted the cessation of her activities. She got herself off the stage, walking heavily in her too-tight slippers. Jean-Pierre, who sat at one side could see a little behind the scenes and observed that as soon as she thought she was out of sight of the audience, she gave way to childish relief that the ordeal was over, and skipped forward, running. He suppressed a supercilious smile of æsthetic scorn. Her body, as large and heavy as a woman's, no longer expressed the impulses of the child she still was. She skipped clumsily, with an inelastic energy of gesture like a cow capering in a spring-time pasture. Jean-Pierre felt the keenest pleasure in his ruthless perception of her lack of grace. This was emancipation!

"She plays very nicely," murmured his mother, on the general chance that some member of her family might be sitting within earshot.

"Yes, very agreeably," he concurred.

Neither of them had heard a note of the music.

They continued to sit in decorous silence, looking with vacant faces straight before them, till the next performer appeared. This was Elise Fortier, whom they were both prepared to detest because of her father and mother and brother.

They did detest her, everything about her from her thin, dry hair, frizzed out to imitate abundance, to her shifty eyes exactly like her mother's, from her stooping shoulders, to her long bony hands, which clattered out loudly the Schubert Marche Militaire. When she had finished, "Really quite a talent," observed Mme. Garnier taking pains to be audible; and, "Remarkable for her age," agreed Jean-Pierre.

He was relaxing morally, in an inexpressible ease at finding his head clear, his heart at rest. To own yourself, to look at life from behind a stout wall of critical cynicism—it was to be in safety at last! He barely glanced at the next player, a nondescript, precocious child, who murdered a Moment Musical, her short thin legs dangling from the stool. And the next, the one who played the Liebestraum, a tall young lady with the self-admiring graces and manners of an opera singer on the concert platform. He looked at his watch again and wondered how long it would be before the stupid school performance would be over, and he could get away for an aperitif at the Café du Grand Bouleau on the Place d'Armes and an evening with——

He saw that another player was coming forward, a slim tall girl with thick shining dark hair held back by a white ribbon like the others. She stood for an instant to bow to the audience before sitting down at the piano, and he could look up full into her unconscious face, gazing out over his head impersonally with shy, liquid, dark eyes. She was breathing a little rapidly, her young breast rising and falling under the filmy white of her dress. A timid propitiatory smile curved her sensitive mouth and arched her long, finely-drawn eyebrows.

Not a muscle of Jean-Pierre's face changed; every line of his careless, confident attitude froze taut as it was. And underneath this motionless exterior, he felt his heart hotly, joyfully weeping in a passion of thanksgiving, like a frightened lost child who has come into the right way. He lost all sense of connection with his body and yearning, worshipping, clamoring, imperiously calling, humbly beseeching, he gazed out from the bars of his immobile, well-dressed external self at the girl sitting before the piano. Two years, two long years of exile, how could life ever make up to him for those two lost years? How he had starved! His famished eyes fed ravenously on what they saw, the supple, elastic slimness of the young body, the fine, thin ankle and shapely foot, the creamy forearm, the agile, strong, white fingers, so bravely flinging out harmonies beyond the comprehension of the smooth broad brow, inviolate, intact, innocent, ignorant, which bent its full child's curve over the keys.

Jean-Pierre looked and looked, prostrating himself in awe before the revelation of divine, stainless youth. Never till that moment, he told himself, had he understood the meaning of the holy word, virgin.

And he had thought, those two long years, that he had always held her before his eyes! He had remembered nothing, nothing of what she was. Yet, how could he have divined what she was becoming—that mouth, her pure girl's mouth, cleanly drawn in scarlet against the flowerlike flesh perfumed with youth. Would he—would he know the first cool touch of those young lips . . . he found that he could see her no more, for a mist before his eyes, and yet he continued to strain his eyes through the mist towards where she sat.

Some one touched him on the arm. It was Maman— Maman who looked at him in tender sympathy. As their glance met, she smiled at him, and nodded her head once, reassuringly. She looked as she had when he was a little boy, and she had yielded at last to some desperately held whim of his. Dearest Maman! It was a promise she gave him silently, a promise to help him towards his happiness. She too had succumbed to Marise. Who would not? He pressed her hand gently, and smiled in return. A calm peace came upon him.

Madame Garnier knew very well before-hand when the little American girl was to come on the program, and after that illbred, over-dressed Yvonne Bredier had wriggled and grinned her way off the stage, she felt an anxious, nervous expectation. Jean-Pierre had no idea what was coming. She could feel that. Although she dared not change her position to look at him, she was acutely aware of the relaxed careless pose of his body, and of the nonchalant turn of his head as he glanced at the girl who now came forward on the stage.

And then she felt with that sixth sense of her passion for Jean-Pierre that he had been struck, had been pierced, as though a knife had thrust him through and through. Although he had not moved—because he had not moved, had not changed a line of his careless attitude, she divined that he had been stricken into immobility. What was it? Was it the shock of disillusion, of disappointment at prosaic reality after a long, romantic dream? Or did he still find in the girl whatever strange sorcery had so bewitched his boyish fancy?

She herself sat as stiffly motionless as he, suffering so exquisite a torture of suspense that she dared not bring herself to end it by a look at his face.

Some one back of her coughed, and the sound broke the spell. She drew a long breath and resolutely turned her head towards her son.

"Oh, my Jean-Pierre, oh, my little boy! is it so you feel? Oh, my darling, do you want her, do you want anything in the world like that? My little boy, a man! To think that it is my little boy, thus burning with a man's desire! Oh, yes, Jean-Pierre, you shall have her . . . what is your mother for but to help you have what you want? Oh, poor boy, poor boy, to look at any woman so. . . . Oh, Jean-Pierre, if you knew women, how they only live to fool men . . . no woman on earth is worth . . ."

She saw now that his flaming young eyes were veiled with tears. She touched his arm, she smiled at him, closer to him than since his early childhood. And he took her hand, he smiled back, he looked at her as he had not once since his infatuation began—like her son, her only son once more letting her into his heart. She held tightly to his hand, now happy and at peace.

Thus together, hand in hand, they were looking up at the stage when the girl struck the final chord, and rising, turned once more towards the front to make her bow in acknowledgment of the applause. The excitement, the effort, had brought a shell-like color into her subtly modeled cheeks. Once more she looked out into the audience impersonally and then, as she turned to go, unconsciously drawn by the intense gaze of the couple in the second row, her dark eyes dropped to them for an instant's glance of friendly recognition. Madame Garnier felt her son draw a sudden, gasping breath through half-open lips and tighten his hold on her hand.

During the rest of the program her thoughts and plans rose in a busy circling swarm. After all, there were advantages. It might be much worse! Impressionable, sensitive, inexperienced as Jean-Pierre was, it might very well have been some mature married woman in search of a new sensation who had thus caught his first young passion. Or even not his passion at all. Even if he himself had felt nothing, any woman could have victimized him by working on that foolish sensibility of his. If she could make him think—and his mother always had a scared sense of how easy that would be—that she was in love with him, he would never know how to retreat, as more brutal men knew so well how to do. She had always been afraid of some such entanglement as that, in which Jean-Pierre's weakness (in her heart she called it plainly that, and not chivalry or sensibility) would make him a helpless victim of a woman either an old fool herself or a calculating sensualist. Heavens! How many dangers there were in the world for one's son! And sons could not be guarded like daughters, by keeping them under your thumb. There were also, for such a romantic, unworldly boy as Jean-Pierre, all the variations on the Camille theme. How easily some shrewd woman of the demi-monde could have pulled the wool over his eyes! Madame Garnier had no doubts that Jean-Pierre knew such women. Her son was a man like all other men, for all his poetic, high-strung ideas, and had certainly had his part of an ordinary man's life, especially those last two years away from home, irresponsible and alone. Oh, yes, the more she thought shudderingly of the dangers he had escaped, the more harmless appeared this fancy for a school girl. And if his fancy was to

light on a young girl, in some ways it was more convenient to
have her a foreigner with no family, so to speak, rather than
a girl of Bayonne society, whose family would expect to
have much to say about all the arrangements of Jean-Pierre's
life. Heavens! suppose it had been Elise Fortier—think of
Jean-Pierre saddled with Madame Fortier as a mother-in-law!
Not that that worthless idle American mother-in-law was much
better; except that those people *must* go back to America some
time! Everybody did go back to his native country ultimately.
And too, she was a weak, foolish thing who would never have
the force to make trouble. Look at the way she let herself be
run by her servants. Also, until now, she had paid precious
little attention to her daughter; there was no reason to think
she would develop any more interest in her later on. And
the child herself seemed malleable material. There was no
doubt she would be a pretty woman, and marrying very young,
she would certainly assimilate the standards of the Garnier
family.

When the concert was over, she said to Jean-Pierre, "If you
like, we will wait till the girls come out, and walk home with
Danielle and her class-mates." As she spoke she nodded to
old Jeanne Amigorena, the cook in the American family, who
stood there, also waiting, her young mistress' cloak and hat on
her arm. It occurred to her that one of the first things to
do would be to eliminate that servant. She probably knew
altogether too much about Marise's family. It would not be
prudent to have her around a young menage; and anyhow, old
servants were an intolerable nuisance with their airs of belong-
ing to the family.

Behind the scenes where the girls were waiting for the concert
to begin, there had been a deal of giggling and whispering and
rustling. Mademoiselle Vivier, chosen to turn the pages for
the players because she was so severe it was thought she could
keep them in order, was "gend'arming around" as the girls
called it, pouncing on one group for laughing too loud, and on
another for making too much noise as they executed grotesque
caricatures of the way they intended to make their entries on

the stage. The moment her back was turned, they whispered and giggled and pranced more wildly than ever, turning deep bows into pirouettes, shaking out their full skirts and whirling about like dervishes. Everybody took care to lose her music and get it all mixed up with everybody's else, just to see Mlle. Vivier go into the air.

"Here's that missing sheet from your Schubert, Marguerite! Oh, no, it's Gabrielle's Chopin!"

"Oh, all the scherzo pages have gone from my Delibes!"

"Mademoiselle, Mademoiselle, I feel so faint, I don't believe I *can* play."

"Oh, Mademoiselle, I forgot to bring my—oh, yes, here it is, right under Danielle! Get up, Danielle! Get up! *Mademoiselle!* Danielle Garnier won't get off my music! Oh, Mademoiselle, can't I play my Nocturne instead of the Autumn Leaves! I *feel* like a nocturne; just ready to go to sleep."

Poor Mademoiselle Vivier, single-handed as she was, grew more and more frantic, rushing about, a dark red flush on her thin face, crying, "Sh, *sh!*" much more loudly than the girls were whispering, exhorting them angrily to have some manners, not to behave like so many barbarians, and to realize the seriousness of the occasion, the Gambert music prize at stake!

But one of those flint-like school traditions originating God only knows how, and utterly impervious to exhortations from any faculty, decreed in that school that the Gambert music prize was a joke, a scream of a joke. The girls would kill themselves with work and worry to win any other prize, for dramatic recitation, for dancing, even for French composition, much as they hated that, but care who won the music prize they would not; although, of course, it was exciting to have no classes that afternoon, to wear your best white dress and parade out on the stage. They had handed down from one school generation to another the fixed idea that M. Gambert had been short, red-faced and ridiculously fat, and they enraged their teachers by drawing on the margins of their music, impudent sketches of a paunchy, bald little man ceremoniously bestowing a huge wreath on a knock-kneed, scrawny girl. Whereas, as a matter of historic fact, M. Gambert had been a very good-looking bourgeois, who in his youth had been a dashing lieutenant under Napoleon I. Also the Gambert prize was not a wreath at all but an album of piano music, beautifully bound in bright red leather, which, because the Mother Superior feared arousing the vanity of the winner, was privately bestowed behind the scenes. But historic facts have no bearing on a cherished school joke of long standing. For the girls, the Gambert prize continued always to be one gigantic lark, one of those perennial farces, the indestructible quality of which so endears them to fourteen and fifteen year olds.

This year they had a new variation on their usual fooleries. Elise Fortier told them that her grown-up young lady cousin had discovered something as good as the rouge which was so strictly forbidden to them by the Sisters, that its very name was not allowed to be pronounced in school. If you bent over double and hung your head upside down, way over, thus, till it was on the same level with your knees, and held it there till you felt as though you'd burst, you'd have the loveliest color in your cheeks, just like an actress.

Of course they all wanted to look like actresses. What could be more delightful than to look like an actress!

In an instant the horrified Mademoiselle Vivier was treated to an appalling spectacle. All of her charges utterly forgetting their manners or even decency, were stooping double, their full starched skirts sticking out at acute angles behind, and to the tune of muffled shrieks of laughter were dangling and shaking their heads, like so many lunatics, their carefully dressed hair sweeping the floor. She rushed at the nearest one, Marise Allen, and forced her back to an upright position. But this did not improve things. When Marise caught a glimpse of the others, like great white mushrooms, stooping and shaking, she burst out into anything but a muffled shout of laughter, which brought them all up, one after another, to gaze and scream, and lean, convulsed and hysterical, against the walls.

It was a critical moment. The curtain was due to go up, and the girls were really out of hand. Mademoiselle Vivier could do nothing with them. They had lost control of themselves; her experienced eye knew the signs. In a moment more, one of the more high-strung ones would begin to cry and then. . . . Good God! what a mess! What diabolically infernal creatures girls were to handle! How sick she was of their imbecility!

She ran hastily around to the side door and beckoning in the Mother Superior told her what was happening. The nun nodded understandingly, meditated for an instant, casting about in her mind, and then, her aged face taking on an expression of majestic calm, she swept back to the little room behind the stage. The girls were startled to see her and alarmed by the intense gravity of her face.

"My children," she said quietly in the clear, gentle, masterful voice which had kept the Community in whole-hearted subservience to her for thirty years, "my children." She bent her wasted old face on them, raising one thin white hand, peremptorily. Her long flowing black sleeve gave a commanding amplitude to this gesture. "My little children, lift up your hearts. . . ." She waited an instant, till she held every eye, and then she said reverently, "My children, at every important moment of our lives we must turn to Our Very Holy Mother, to bless us. Before you go on the stage to-day, to represent your school in public, and to do honor to music, which God has blessed as an instrument of good, let us pray Our Mother to be with you, and guide you."

She bowed her head. Hypnotically, all the young heads bowed with hers. She began in a low murmur, "Ave Maria, sancta tu in mulieribus. . . ." All the young voices murmured with her, discharging in the reverenced words, the nervous tension of their excitement and frolic. When they finished, they were all quiet, with serious faces. The Mother Superior raised her hand over them, murmuring a short, inaudible prayer of her own. There was an instant's silence.

"Go tell Mathurin to raise the curtain," said the Reverend Mother hurriedly in a low tone to Mademoiselle Vivier; a command which Mademoiselle Vivier lost no time in executing.

CHAPTER XVIII

MARISE had noticed as she left the stage, that Madame Garnier was there with her son,—oh, yes, Danielle *had* said her brother was back from America. Now he'd be tagging around everywhere, tied to his mother's apron-strings, as Papa said all young Frenchmen were. Yes, they were holding hands this minute. How Papa would laugh to see that, as much as he did when Frenchmen with beards kissed each other. And now he'd be everlastingly coming in with his tiresome mother on Maman's days at home, to fidget and stammer and drop his teaspoon. Oh, well, she thought with a superior condescension, he had been hardly more than a boy, just out of the lycée, only twenty-one. He might be better now. Perhaps he had got rid of a little of his shyness in New York; although twenty-three, for a *man,* was of course no age at all.

The fashion at school just then, was to look down on boys and young men as green and insipid. The ideal of all the girls was an *old* man of forty, with white hair, and black eye-brows, a little pointed gray beard, and such sad, sad eyes! Every girl was waiting for such a chance to devote herself to healing the wounds made by other women, faithless, heartless creatures who had ravaged his youth and destroyed his faith. To prove to him what a woman's fidelity and love could be, and then die in his remorseful arms, of slow consumption brought on by his neglect . . . ! Or, as the pious ones had it, to bring him back to the Church, and have him become a monk after your death. Or, perhaps, as some of the more dramatic ones imagined the matter, to find a plot against his life, and to sacrifice yourself to defeat it, throwing back at the last moment the hood of your long dark cloak, and showing a beautiful white satin gown, stained with your heart's blood, as you gasped out, "For you, for you, adored Réné."

The books from which the girls got these ideas, and many others not so harmless, were kept in a hole hidden behind a big loose stone in the end wall of the school garden. Though they were religiously wrapped in oil-cloth, the damp did more or less penetrate. But spots of green mold and limp damp pages which tore unless you held your breath as you turned them, only added to their charm as you read them, two or three heads bent over the page, while a friend kept guard at the turn of the path by the magnolia tree.

Marise had read them with the others, and although neither Father nor Maman paid the slightest attention to what she read, and there were lots of places in Maman's novels ever so much worse than these, she naturally felt an agreeable thrill at the thought of what an explosion there would be if they were ever discovered, reading love-stories at school. It was the fashion with the girls to do it. So she did, and as dramatically as any of the others. But far down, deep under all this, was a hermetically sealed chamber where she kept a secret disgust for the whole subject of falling in love, a secret distaste for men, old or young, and a furiously held determination never to have anything to do with them. It was all very well to carry on against the rules and to play-act with the girls about something in a book, but the faintest approach of the same thing in reality, froze her stiff with indignation and repugnance. When, walking on the street with Jeanne, some well-dressed young man cast a glance of admiration at her, or some half-tipsy workman called out a rough compliment she shrank away from them, hating them and herself; a feeling which old Jeanne zealously fostered.

She did not often think about the gray cat now, but she had never forgotten it, and she had picked up a great deal more information than she had had, about what made people like Isabelle snigger and grin, when there was talk of getting a husband. She intensely loathed all that she had seen and learned, whether it were the shocked, nauseated expression on the face of one of the older nuns at school, when she forbade any talk among the girls over the gossip that one of the kitchen-girls had let a young man into the kitchen at midnight; or a passage in one of Maman's novels, which she had found lying open on the salon table, and read before she could stop herself. Every such experience was like a blow on a bruised spot, deep under the surface of her life, which was so sore now that it ached at the slightest touch, ached and made her sick. She had learned that she must protect it at all costs, and she fought off blindly whatever seemed to threaten it, fought it off with indignation, with brusqueness, with stiffness, with silence, using any weapon she could snatch up. At school, if she found a group of older girls with their heads together, and a certain expression on their faces, the weapon was often simply to run away into another part of the playground. "I can run away faster than they can run after me!" she told herself, fleeing away to where the little girls were playing hop-scotch and "chat-perché."

There were times of course when you couldn't run away literally, but Marise had other methods of running away, the best one being a sudden change of subject—"Oh, Isabelle, your chignon is coming untied!" or "Gabrielle, isn't Sister Ste. Marie coming down the hall?" "Jeanne, you're pulling my hair!"

And she had found, too, that to head people off from beginning on the sort of thing you had to run away from, there was no better device than lively spirits. If you kept joking and laughing and carrying on, the girls didn't have time to lower their voices, look over their shoulders and begin to talk with their faces close to yours.

She was still flushed from laughing and talking and carrying on, when she emerged from the side-stairs into the half empty assembly-room, looking for her wraps, and saw beside Jeanne, Mme. Garnier and her son evidently waiting for Danielle, for Mme. Garnier had Danielle's hat and cloak on her arm. "Oh, zut! What a bore!" She'd have to speak to them; the young man would fidget and make her nervous, and she did think Mme. Garnier the tiresomest of all the frumps who came to call on Maman. She was an old snake-in-the-grass, too,—to use one of Papa's expressions. She pretended to say such sweet things to Maman, and really they were all different ways to slight poor Maman, who didn't understand half the time. But Marise did, and resented it for her. Poor Maman!

"Good morning, Madame Garnier," she said with a little bow, coming up to them, and, "Good morning, Monsieur Jean."

She remembered to drop her eyes, following the precepts of the teacher of deportment, and profited by the gesture to despise Mme. Garnier's shoes, stuffed lumpily full, like badly made sausages.

When Mme. Garnier finished a long speech, she didn't mean a word of, about how nicely Marise had played, "Oh, thank you very much, Madame Garnier," she answered, looking up for a moment.

Jeanne put her hat and coat on now, as Danielle romped in, talking at the top of her voice. Madame Garnier, with the perfunctory air of one attending to a familiar duty, savagely reproached her for boisterousness, and general heathenishness of manners. Danielle took this as it was meant, and paying not the slightest attention to the rebuke, went on talking at the top of her voice, telling her mother and brother all about the foolishness back of the scenes. "It was simply *killing!*" she shouted, laughing so that no one but Marise had any idea what she was talking about, "I thought I'd die, didn't you, Marise? You never saw anything in your life so funny! All of us wrong side up, with our heads . . . oh, ha! ha! ha!"

She and Marise went off into peals of laughter which they immediately suppressed to giggles and then to smothered muffled gasps, as they saw the Reverend Mother's dignified black draperies moving down the side-aisle. They'd hear from it at school if Reverend Mother caught them in such a breach of manners as *laughing in a public place!*

"Who won the prize, my darling?" whispered Jeanne, in Marise's ear, as she smoothed down the collar of her coat.

"Oh, I did," Marise whispered back casually. She had left the big red album of Morceaux de Salon with Mlle. Vivier, because she knew if she tried to carry it home and passed by a school-mate she would be greeted with howls of jeering laughter. She would bring some paper to-morrow, to wrap it up.

"We may as well walk along together," said Mme. Garnier now. "Our road lies your way."

Jeanne dropped respectfully behind, Mme. Garnier walked with Marise, Danielle with her brother. Marise shot one sideways glance at Mme. Garnier as they started along the side-walks. "Sapristi," as Jeanne said, "what an ugly hat! How could anybody not just drop dead to be seen with such a horror on!" "Yes, Madame," she answered politely, at random, not paying any attention to Mme. Garnier's drone. How vulgar it was to let your dress wrinkle across the back where the top of your corset came. And it was worse to let it cave in in front, at the same place. When she was grown up, she would never let *her* dress do that! Marise reflected with the utmost satisfaction on the excellent cut and hang of her own dress. There hadn't been a better one there, and she had silk stockings while most of the girls had clumsy cotton ones, or at best lisle thread. Jeanne certainly did know how to buy clothes, and Papa never said a word against paying the bills. Well, she could wear them too! She had style. She cast a pleased sideways glance at her slim straight silhouette, reflected in the large window of a shop, saw in the same mirror Mme. Garnier's uninteresting middle-aged figure, and then surprisingly she also caught a glimpse of Jeanne, behind the others, her handkerchief at her eyes as if she were crying. Marise stopped short, and turned sharply to look back. For mercy's sake, what could be the matter with Jeanne? Why, yes, she was, she was actually crying, the big tears rolling down her leathery cheeks. With an unceremonious excuse to Mme. Garnier, Marise left her planted there on the sidewalk, and darted back to Jeanne, asking anxiously what had happened.

Jeanne looked at her fondly, her wrinkled old face bright with love, "I am thanking Our Holy Mother and all the Saints for your triumph, my darling!" she said, her voice trembling. "All this day I have been praying for you, all this day."

Marise's first impulse was to inquire stupidly, "What triumph?" and her next was to burst into laughter as she realized that Jeanne had worked herself up so about that old Gambert music prize, of all things! But these gusts had come and gone before the expression of her face had had time to change; and when they had gone, all she could see was the affection shining in the old woman's eyes. Dear, *darling* old Jeanne! *Let* her think it was a triumph! She should never know anything else about it, bless her!

Marise remembered Danielle, the mocking, and glanced uneasily towards where the Garniers stood, waiting for her to go on with them. No, Danielle had not heard. Jeanne was safe.

Marise had grown so that she no longer needed to reach up to put her arms around the neck of the tall old woman, and kiss her hard on both tear-wet cheeks. "I owe my victory to thee, dear Jeanne, to thy prayers," she whispered fervently. "And I shall never, never forget it."

All this was a lie, of course, but lies were easy to tell, and what harm were they, if you made somebody more comfortable by telling them?

She pirouetted about on her toes, and ran back to take her place with Mme. Garnier. "Jeanne had bad news from one of her family," she murmured pensively in answer to Mme. Garnier's look of inquiry. "Oh, bah!" she thought carelessly. "What was one more lie to head off an old cat like that?" Besides, it was amusing to see how easy it was to lie, how with one little phrase, this way or that, you could change facts.

After she had come in, and gone to her room to change to her usual dark woolen school-dress, with the long-sleeved linen apron over it, Marise happened to glance out through the lace curtain over her window and saw that Mme. Garnier's son was sitting on the bench across the street in front of the Château Vieux. "Well, that was queer, why hadn't he gone on with his mother and Danielle?" She looked again, to make sure, herself hidden at one side behind the heavy tapestry curtain, as Jeanne had taught her, lest she be seen by men on the street. "Yes, it was Danielle's brother, sure enough. Well, what could he be doing there?"

She turned back to her greenish mirror to take off the white ribbon from her hair, and found that she had a dim recollection that before he went away to America, he used to sit on that bench in the late afternoon and evening. There was something unpleasant connected with that vague memory, and after a time that came to her also. She had heard Anna Etchergary, the concierge, and Jeanne laughing about it, and had overheard them conjecture that the young man was no such innocent mother's boy as he seemed, and then they had seen that Marise was there, and stopped abruptly, looking at her with the expression that she hated.

Before she went in to dinner, she looked out once more to see if he were still there. Yes, there he was leaning forward, the light from the street-lamp full on his face. Marise could see that he was pale, but there was a smile on his lips as if his thoughts were very pleasant.

When she stepped into the salon, she did not for a moment see that Maman was already there, because she stood at one side of the window, half hidden in the thick tapestry curtain, looking out through the lace over the glass. By the expression of her back, Marise knew that she, too, was looking at Mme. Garnier's son on the bench. For an instant, as though Marise's fingers had dropped on white-hot metal, the wild idea came to her that it was at Maman that Jean-Pierre was smiling, that it was for Maman that he sat there. She jerked herself away angrily and instantaneously from this thought, ashamed of herself. She was getting like Jeanne, like the girls at school.

Maman had heard her move, and now turned sharply around from the window, with the startled look of some one into whose bed-room you've walked without knocking at the door. But Marise never knocked at the salon door before going in. Why should she have thought of it to-day? Maman drew the heavy curtain over the window with a sweep of her bare white arm. For Maman was in grande tenue with her mauve satin low-necked evening dress on, and a camellia in her hair. Marise's first thought was that she was to have another solitary dinner. "Oh, Maman, are you going out?"

"Certainly not, what makes you think I am?" asked Maman quickly. She added because it was perfectly evident what made Marise think it, "The belt on this dress has been changed and I tried it on to see if it was right. And then I saw it was dinner time."

Marise was about to say something about the flower in her hair, but her antennæ-like sensitiveness to what other people were feeling, made her shut her lips. She looked hard at her mother, who made herself opaque, looking back at Marise, her face and eyes and mouth firmly closed over what was in her mind. Being able to see only the surface, Marise took that in with a fresh impression of not having looked at Maman for some time. How pretty she was, with her hair like gold threads, catching the light, and how different from her crinkly hair like a golden mist around her head, were the thick, thick petals of the camellia, with their dense, close, fine-grained surface.

Jeanne came to the door. "Madame is served," she said in a correct tone, standing aside as they came out. She did not look at Marise at all, but Marise knew perfectly well that she too was wondering about the evening dress and the flower. Marise began to try to invent some plausible explanation for it which she could let drop in talk to-morrow as they walked to school.

Marise had lessons to get that evening, lots of them, and hard ones, as usual. After dinner, she went back to her room, opened her history and began. It was very still in the apartment. No sound at all from Maman in the salon. Of course, Jeanne and Isabelle were both across the landing in the other kitchen, doing the work as they always were unless Maman expected callers.

Marise leaned over her table and concentrated with all her might on the rôle played by Colbert in the economic organization of the seventeenth century. She was trying to memorize the outline of his introduction of sounder account-keeping in government administration, when all at once, there in her mind, instead of Louis XIV and his court, was the picture of Maman standing beside the window, looking out. If Marise were now to step quickly into the salon, would she again find Maman . . . ?

Marise tossed her head angrily at the possibility of her doing such a sneaky thing as to go to see. . . . Like some nasty idea of Jeanne's that was! She drew her history closer to her, changed her position and went on studying. "Colbert a souvent répété que c'est par le commerce qu'un pays s'enrichit. . . ."

Although she had not meant to, she started up and went to the window, opening the heavy curtains a tiny crack, to look out.

Yes, he was still there, two hours after they had left him. He had not even gone home for dinner. But old Madeleine, the flower seller must have passed by on her way home, after shutting up her flowerstand, for now he had a white rose bud in his hands, looking down at it fixedly, turning it about between his fingers, once in a while touching a petal delicately, or holding it up to draw in its fragrance.

Marise pulled the curtain shut, and hurried back to the improvement of the French army from 1680 on. She felt very miserable, as though she'd eaten something she ought not to. . . . was it a headache? She had heard ladies talk so much about headaches, and had never had one. Yes, it must be a headache. That was it, her first headache. By thinking about it she felt it very distinctly now in the back of her head—like a great weight there drawing her head back. She tried to think of Colbert; she looked hard at the familiar picture of Colbert rubbing his hands in glee over all the work piled up on his desk, but what she saw was Maman standing at one side of the window looking out. Was that Maman she heard moving about in the salon?

What time was it? Wasn't it time for her to go to bed? The soapy dark green clock on her mantel piece showed only half past eight. Too early. She started at a sudden sound, her hand beginning to tremble. The door-bell rang. Jeanne and Isabelle were both on the other side of the landing and would not hear. She listened, her hands and feet cold, heard Maman go to the door herself and Jean-Pierre Garnier's voice asking if Monsieur and Madame and Mademoiselle Allen were at home. Maman laughed and said that Monsieur was away on business and Mademoiselle was, of course, busy with her lessons, but Madame was there!

Marise heard Mme. Garnier's son also laugh nervously and

say that he would come in for a moment to pay his respects to Madame. They both spoke English, which Jean-Pierre had learned so well in New York. Well, why not? In America anybody might happen to make an evening call at half past eight. And Mme. Garnier's son had just been in America. Heavens! How her head ached! She would go to bed anyway, whether it was time or not. She undressed rapidly and getting into bed pulled the covers over her head. It seemed to her that she lay thus for ages, her eyes pinched shut in the smothering air under the blankets. Then she pulled them down to breathe and found that she had forgotten to put out her candle, which was guttering low and showing by the clock that her "ages" had been less than an hour. It was twenty minutes past nine.

She blew out her candle, and decided that Jeanne or no Jeanne, she must have more air. She was suffocating. She drew the curtains aside and secure in the darkness of the room, opened both sides of the window wide. The fresh air came in like waking up from a night-mare.

But she had not waked up, for there on the bench across the street was Mme. Garnier's son again. Had she dreamed that he had come to the door? How strangely he sat now, flung down sideways, his face hidden on his arm. As Marise stared, understanding nothing of what she saw, he started up spasmodically as though some one had struck him from behind. Then he collapsed again, his face buried on his outflung arm. After this he was perfectly motionless, like everything around him, the somber wall of the Château Vieux, the sickly light of the street-lamp, the bench, the rough paving-stones, the vacant, gray shutters of the department store further along the street.

As Marise stood there, shivering in her night-gown, staring, she heard Maman's quick light step at the other end of the corridor, and the sound of Maman's voice, humming a little trilling song. She turned her head, and saw the cheerful yellow flicker of a candle coming nearer her open door. Maman was going down to her dressing-room to get ready for bed. She thought of course that Marise was in bed and asleep by this

time and when she came by, looking down at the lighted candle
in the pretty little gilt candle-stick she did not even glance
into the dark room where the child stood bewildered. For
the instant she was framed in the square of the open door,
she was brilliantly painted on the darkness, all the bright
colors of her fair hair, her shining eyes, her red lips, softly
gleaming in the warm, golden light of the little flame. The
picture was printed indelibly on the child's wide eyes sensitized
by the darkness; and long after the sound of the gay little song
had died away, long years after the sound of the light foot-
step was silent, Marise could see, hung on the blackness
around her bed at night, the shining picture, golden-bright in
the quivering, living flame of the candle, the dense waxy
petals of the camellia against the vaporous blonde hair, the
smiling curved lips, the velvet white of the slender bare neck
and arms, the rich sheen of the mauve satin flowing about the
quick, light feet.

She got into bed warmed, comforted. Nothing could be
the matter if Maman was smiling so cheerfully. She fell
asleep at once, desperately tired, giving up as an unanswerable
and no longer very interesting riddle, the question of what
was the trouble with Mme. Garnier's son.

But in the night, without knowing how, she found herself
once more by the open window—she had been dreaming,
she had got up to see about something in her dream—something about . . . why, there he was still on the bench, all
huddled and stooped together now, his face hidden in both
arms crossed on his knees. Perhaps he had dropped asleep
there. Br-r-r-r! he would be cold when he woke up. How
chilly it still was at night! Well, yes, it was evident that she
had dreamed it about his ringing at the door. She plunged
back under the covers, she heard the long sonorous hoot of
a steamer going out to sea, and was asleep before it died
away.

She overslept in the morning, so that Jeanne, when she
came with the tray, ran to shake her and said she must hurry
to dress or she would be late to school. Marise sprang up,
thinking of nothing but the reprimand she risked, and flung

on her clothes, stopping to bite off big mouthfuls of the buttered croissants and drink big swallows of the café-au-lait.
Jeanne buttoned her behind while she brushed furiously at
her hair. "Where are my books? Oh, never mind that
last hook, it'll never show. Oh, just *once* without my gloves!
No I don't *need* my coat, the sun is so warm." She ran out
to the corridor, snatched her hat, and, her teeth set in the last
morsel of her bread, darted down the hall, Jeanne galloping
stiffly behind her, as anxious as she over the possibility of
being late.

But at the outer door, she paused, one hand on the knob,
something imperatively urging her to return. What had she
seen as she passed the open door of the salon? Just the
every morning scene, Isabelle with her head tied up in a cloth,
a brush-broom in her hand, all the windows wide open, the
rugs hanging over the sills, the sun streaming in with the
particular clean fresh brilliance it always seemed to have
early in the morning, while the room was still empty of life.
How could there have been anything threatening about that
familiar sight? It was Isabelle's face. She had been standing
perfectly still, the long handle of her brush-broom held under
one arm, looking down with a puzzled expression at something
she held in her hand.

Marise had wheeled so instantly in answer to the vague
warning of danger, that she was back at the door of the salon,
before Isabelle's position had changed. She still stood there,
looking down at a wilted, white rose-bud. And now her face
was suspicious as well as puzzled. Glancing up she said
meaningly to Jeanne, over Marise's shoulder, "Now, *where*
do you suppose *this* came from? I found it on the floor by
the sofa! There were no roses brought into the house by
any one *we* saw yesterday!"

Jeanne thrust her long stringy neck forward, and passed her
head over Marise's shoulder to verify the fact. Marise could
see the glitter in her eye. Marise cried out instantly, "Oh, my
poor rose! *That's* where it was! I looked for it everywhere
last night to put it in water."

Jeanne and Isabelle turned their eyes on her penetratingly.

She held them energetically at bay, hardening her gaze, defying them.

"I didn't see you have any rose yesterday," said Jeanne. But Marise knew by the tone of her voice that she was not sure.

"Well, I did," she repeated, "Gabrielle Meunier gave it to me out of her bouquet. Oh, I'm so sorry it's spoiled."

"I believe you, that it's spoiled," said Isabelle carelessly, dropping it into the dustpan. "Somebody must have stepped on it to crush it like that."

Her interest in it was gone. She began to hum her favorite dance-tune, "jig-jig, pr-r-rt!" and to shake out a rug.

Marise fled down the slippery waxed stairway, three steps at a time, and dashed out on the street, Jeanne, purple-faced and panting, close at her heels. How she hurried, how breathlessly she hurried that morning; but a thought inside her head doggedly kept pace with her hurry.

CHAPTER XIX

I

Now that she was in an advanced class, she stayed all day in the school and convent, taking her lunch with the "internats" in the refectory. So that it was always six o'clock before Jeanne came for her, with the first, thin twilight beginning to fall bluely in the narrow, dark streets, and sunset colors glimmering from the oily surface of the Adour. That evening when Jeanne came for her, she said that Maman had decided to go back for a day or two to Saint Sauveur for the sake of the change of air and to try the baths again. Jeanne never permitted herself the slightest overt criticism of her mistress in talking to Marise, but she had a whole gamut of intonations and inflections which Marise understood perfectly and hated—hated especially because there was nothing there to quarrel with Jeanne about. Jeanne had told her the news in the most correct and colorless words, but what she had really said was, "Just another of her idle notions, gadding off for more sulphur baths. Nothing in the world the matter with her. And it's much too early for the Saint Sauveur season."

Marise could resent such intimations, although Jeanne was too adroit to give her grounds for open reproach. She had her own gamut of expression and attitudes, with which to punish the old woman. She immediately stopped chattering, looked coldly offended, and walked beside Jeanne, her face averted from her, out towards the street, now crowded with two-wheeled ox-wagons, and donkeys, and men with push-carts starting back into the country after market day. She could feel that she was making Jeanne suffer and she was glad of it.

As she kept her eyes steadily turned through the tangle of traffic across to the side-walk on the other side, not more than ten feet away, so narrow was the street, she caught sight of Mme. Garnier's son. He had a small valise in his hand, and was idling along as though he were waiting for something. As she looked, their eyes met. He looked at her hard, and crossed the street towards her. He came swiftly now, as if, all of a sudden, he were in a great hurry. How oddly he was staring at her! Not as though he recognized her, as though he took her for somebody else. Oh, perhaps he wasn't looking at her at all! Perhaps there was somebody behind them, at whom he was staring so hard. The tall school-girl jerked her head around for a quick glance over her shoulder. But there was nobody else on the side-walk!

The young man had come up to them now, had taken off his hat and stood there, bowing. How white that bluish light made people look! Marise and Jeanne slackened their pace for an instant, thinking that he wished to speak to them, but all that he brought out was, "Good evening, Mademoiselle," in a low voice.

They stood for an instant, Marise feeling very awkward, as though she had misunderstood something. Then he put his hat back on, and stooping forward as though he were tired and his valise heavy, hurried on. Marise looked over her shoulder again and saw that he was almost running. But he had plenty of time to catch that train to Lourdes, which was the only one due to leave Bayonne that evening.

Jeanne's turn had come, in the little guerilla skirmish between Marise and herself. "*Don't* turn around in the street that way!" she cried in a shocked tone. "Haven't you any sense of what is proper? Don't you know if you turn around like that, just after a young man has passed you, he is likely to think that you are *looking after him!*" She had no idea that Marise was really guilty of such a heinous misdemeanor, and had only snatched the phrase up as a weapon.

II

That night Jeanne rolled the little fold-up cot-bed in across the landing and setting it up in Marise's room, slept there beside her. This was what they had done before, when Maman was at Saint Sauveur, on the nights when Father had to be away too. Isabelle hadn't the slightest intention of sleeping over on the other side by herself, and she always came too, bringing her own sheets to put on Maman's bed. She remarked that she couldn't afford to have it said of her that she had spent the night in the apartment without another woman with her. Marise did not see in the least why any one should object to having this said of her, but the tone of Isabelle's voice as she spoke, and the fact that it had something to do with passing the night warned her off from asking any explanation. She had already gleaned from many sources, in and out of books, that there was something about accounting for where you were at night, about which she didn't want to have Jeanne and Isabelle talk. So she began to sing a new satirical verse to the air of "Maman, les petits bateaux" which one of the girls had made up that day.

Everything went exactly as usual the next morning, the absence of the mistress of the house not making the faintest difference. Jeanne and Isabelle went through their usual domestic ritual in exactly the same order, whether Madame told them or not. Indeed, whatever she might tell them, they changed no slightest tittle of what they did, as she had long ago found out. Jeanne brought in the breakfast tray, and did Marise's hair as usual, and although not a soul had stepped into the salon since the day before, Isabelle was skating back and forth on the waxed floor, woolen cloths on her feet, when Marise passed the door. Outside it was a breathless still day, with a hazy sun, very hot for so early in the spring.

As they crossed the Adour, Marise caught the first whiff of its summer smell, compounded of decaying sea-weed, tar and stale fish. She and Jeanne said little, although they had wordlessly made up their tiff the evening before, and had gone to sleep after exchanging their usual hearty good-night kisses. Their quarrels although frequent never lasted long.

Everybody at school was dull, too, from the first heat. The hours seemed very long, with little in them. Marise felt listless and rather cross, and dreaded the exertion of taking her music lesson, although she usually looked forward eagerly to those hours with Mlle. Hasparren, the best and happiest of her days.

At four o'clock the music-teacher called to take her home. She also was hot and tired and fearfully nervous, she said, after a terribly trying day in her class-room, with her forty-five squirming little Basques. As a rule she and Marise had a good deal to say to each other, because Mlle. Hasparren was the only person Marise knew who had any interest in America. The rest never spoke of it, or if by chance they did, they only asked about buffaloes and Indians, and evidently didn't believe her when she said she'd never seen either. But Mlle. Hasparren knew better, and loved to talk about it, and actually knew the difference between the Civil War and the Revolution, and had heard of Abraham Lincoln and thought he was a greater man than *Napoleon!* Marise, who was reading a great deal of Victor Hugo, hardly knew whether to agree with this startling idea or not, but she felt when she was with Mlle. Hasparren, that it was safe to open many doors which she usually kept locked, and to talk with her about things she never dreamed of mentioning to anybody else. Which did not, of course, at all prevent her from wishing to goodness Mlle. Hasparren didn't wear such fearful hats, and that her skirts would hang better.

But this hot day of early spring, she thought neither of America or of hats, as she plodded silently beside the equally weary school-teacher, through the dusty stone streets. The depression which had hung over her all day deepened till she felt ready to cry. Wherever she looked she saw Maman standing in that stealthy attitude, looking out of the window. Mlle. Hasparren's worn, swarthy face, under her home-made hat, was plainer than usual.

Isabelle let them in to the empty salon, with her usual air of being cheered up to have something happen, and bustlingly arranged two seats before the piano. Mlle. Hasparren took off her hat and pushed her fingers through her graying hair. Marise fumbled among the music on the piano and pulled out what they were working on, the Toccata in D minor. She flattened it out with both hands on the music-rack above the keys, and sat down. She raised her fingers, made sure of the notes of the first twiddle, and began to play.

She had not wished to take this music-lesson. She had been hot and listless and tired; with a secret heartache and a dread like a black shadow on her heart. She had sat down before a great black varnished wooden box and,—detached, indifferent, preoccupied, had set her fingers to pushing first one and then another bit of wood covered with white bone.

And what happened?

Out of the black, varnished box, like the mighty genii of the Arabian Nights, soared something beautiful and strong, something that filled the dreary, empty salon and her heavy heart with sonorous life, something which like the genii put its greatness at the service of the being who knew the charm to free it from imprisonment.

"Stronger there, as you come up from the bass," said Mlle. Hasparren, and Marise knew from her voice that she too was soaring up. And yet, although she sounded no longer dull and weary, but strong and joyful, she abated nothing of her exacting rigor. "No, don't blur it because you make it louder. Don't lean on the pedal. Clean power of stroke, that's the thing for Bach. Now try again. Roll it up from that lowest note, like a mid-ocean wave."

She listened, all her personality concentrated on her hearing, her head turned sideways, her eyes fixed on a point in the very far distance. With all her intelligence she listened, and when the immature intelligence of the pupil faltered or failed, she came swiftly to the rescue. "No, take care! you're losing yourself in that passage. You're playing each note correctly but you haven't the sense of the whole thing. There's a rhythmic progression there that starts four measures back, and doesn't end till you swing into those chords. Don't lose your way in what is only a little ornamentation of the line. See, to here—all that is half of the rhythmic figure, and here it is repeated in the bass. Now again! Read it so the meaning comes out."

The nimble flexible young fingers went flying at the passage again, guided and informed by the ripe soundness of the older mind, and from a passage which Marise had physically mastered as mechanically as she would an exercise, she heard the master-voice speak out again.

Her teacher leaned forward beside her, working as hard as Marise, although she did not touch the keys. Four years of incessant work together had made them almost like one mind. From time to time, they wiped the perspiration away from their foreheads with a hasty pass of their handkerchiefs, Mlle. Hasparren's gesture as hurried as Marise's.

"Pearly in the treble—clear, clear—try that bar of triplets again. Again! Again! Once more! There, now start at the double bar—like running water. No, not so much shading, ugh! *no*, that's not classic, let it speak for itself! You don't need to use those theatrical swells and die-aways here. You're not playing Gounod. Start that movement over again. Every note's a pearl, remember, string them together in a necklace. Don't jumble them in a heap."

They were still at it, laboring like slaves, putting their backs into it like ditch-diggers, exalted as young-eyed cherubim, when Jeanne came discreetly to the door to look in on them. This was her decorous method of intimating that she was about to put Marise's dinner on the table.

"Oh, là! là!" cried Mlle. Hasparren, "is it as late as that? And my sister told me to be sure to start early enough to buy some salad for our supper." She slammed on her hat, took her bag, and darted away.

Marise got up, feeling numb, flung her arms high over her head, and stretched herself like a cat, although she knew that like any other vigorous and forthright bodily gesture this would call down a reproof from Jeanne as not being "convenable." But she did not care what Jeanne said to her. She did not care about anything in the world but the deep-rolling waves of rhythm, and the clear tinkling rain of pearls which went on and on in her head as she ate her solitary dinner, and studied her lessons in her solitary room afterwards.

When Jeanne came to set up her bed for the night, she remarked "What a horrid sticky hot day it has been!"

"Has it?" asked Marise, in genuine forgetfulness of the weather. Also, caught up into another world as she was, she forgot for an hour or two all about the white rose-bud.

III

But she was reminded of it as she opened her eyes the next morning. It was her fifteenth birthday and to celebrate it, Jeanne had already been out to the market and brought home a great bouquet of white rose-buds. She was loitering around, pretending to pick up the room, but really waiting to hear what Marise would say, so of course Marise must conquer the nausea that white rose-buds gave her and exclaim that they were lovely, and kiss Jeanne and thank her and lean over them and smell them rapturously. What a lot of this sort of thing there was to do, Marise thought, if you didn't want to hurt people's feelings, or let them suspect things you didn't want them to know.

Jeanne tried to restrain herself to decorum, but her overwhelming jealousy of any one else who touched Marise's life was too much for her, "They're nicer than that one wilted old thing Gabrielle Meunier gave you, hein?" Marise understood then why Jeanne had chosen white rose-buds. Down below the surface where she kept her real feelings she heard a sick sort of laugh. What she said was, with fervor, "Oh, yes, Jeanne, a thousand times better!" (You might as well make it a thousand times while you were about it.)

"Well, I should hope so!" said Jeanne, satisfied at last.

That morning when Marise stepped into the courtyard at school a group of older girls had their heads together over a newspaper, and when they saw her, they all started. Elise Fortier rolled the paper up rapidly and put it in her leather portfolio with her school-books. They looked at her very oddly. Four years ago, Marise would have run up to them, demanding, "What's the matter? What makes you look so funny? What is it in the paper?" That was before she became aware of any mire in the world, invisible, wide-spreading, into which almost any casual inquiry seemed likely to plunge you. Marise knew what it was to have some of that indelibly staining mire splashed upon her, from a look, an intonation or a phrase that meaningly expressed much more than it said. She walked with a desperate wariness now, trying to pick her way dry-shod, in the dark. So that morning she was only afraid that the girls *would* tell her what it was they had found in the paper that made them look so. She pretended that she had seen nothing, ran up to them with a funny story to tell, and went at once to hang up her wraps in the hall outside the class-room door. Sister Ste. Julie passed her and said, "Good-morning, my child." It seemed to Marise that she too looked queerly at her. She reached her hand over her shoulder to make sure her dress was hooked, and felt of the ribbon in her hair. No mirrors were allowed inside the school and convent walls, or she would have stepped to look in one to see what was wrong.

At eleven o'clock while the class in advanced geography was reciting, the street bell rang. Sister Ste. Marie went to answer, and came back to say that Mlle. Allen was wanted. Her maman was ill, and the bonne had come for her. All the girls turned instantly and looked at her without surprise, as though they had been expecting this. Marise started up, suddenly very pale, put on her wraps in a great hurry and ran to where Jeanne was waiting for her. Jeanne looked just as usual, although everything else seemed to have changed in an instant and to look threateningly upon Marise.

"Your maman is home from the baths," said Jeanne, as though she were saying something she had made up to say beforehand, "and she doesn't feel very well. Since Monsieur is not here, I thought we would better come and get you."

Marise seized Jeanne's arm and dug her fingers deep into it, "Jeanne . . . Jeanne . . . nothing's happened . . . Maman's not . . ."

Jeanne said with the very accent of truth, "No, no, no. Madame is not dead—never fear, my darling. She is only very . . . nervous." She said it with the very accent of truth, but Marise knew perfectly well that Jeanne could say

anything she pleased with that accent. She never believed
a thing Jeanne said unless she knew it already.

But in spite of herself she was relieved from her first wild
panic. Nothing so very bad could have happened, with Jeanne
standing there, carved out of brown wood, just as usual. They
began to hurry up the narrow short-cut by the market, and
Jeanne told her a little more. Maman had come back by
the first train. She must have taken the afternoon train
down from Saint Sauveur to Lourdes, and have waited hours
in the station at Lourdes, till the west-bound train from
Toulouse came along. And she had come in, perfectly worn
out, staggering, and pushed right by Isabelle to go to her
room. And she had locked the door, and wouldn't answer
when they knocked, and wouldn't open when they brought a
tray with some food, only called out to them in a queer hoarse
voice to go get Sœur Ste. Lucie. And they could hear her
crying and sobbing, so they had sent Anna Etchergary to get
the nun, and she, Jeanne, had come of her own idea to get
Marise.

Marise read into this Jeanne's dislike of the nun and
her usual suspicious idea about poor Maman that it was all
just some new notion of hers. But she also felt that the old
woman had had a real fright and she walked faster and faster.

The door on the landing was ajar, and inside the hall they
saw a tall old monk, his bare feet in sandals, his bald head
bowed over his clasped hands his lips moving in prayer.
When he saw the girl and the old servant, he made way for
them to pass, and without interrupting his prayers, motioned
them to enter. His gesture was so imperious that without a
word they tip-toed in past him. Isabelle, her eyes wide, and
not as red-faced as usual, was standing uncertainly in the door
of the salon, her apron up to her lips, looking scared, "Sœur Ste.
Lucie has gone in to Madame," she said to Jeanne in a whisper. "She said you and Mademoiselle were to go to Mademoiselle's room and wait until she came."

Jeanne inquired wildly with a silent jerk of the head who
in the world was the monk who stood praying before Madame's closed door; and Isabelle answered with a desperate

rolling of her eyes that she had no more idea of that than Jeanne.

They all went down the corridor on tip-toes, to Marise's room, where automatically Marise took off her hat and coat. She saw to her amazement that Jeanne had dropped down on the crimson quilt on the bed. Nothing that had happened had startled Marise so much as to see this.

Almost at once Sœur Ste. Lucie entered, and coming up to Marise put her arms around her and kissed her very tenderly. Then she turned and motioned the two servants out of the room, "I must speak to Mlle. Marise alone," she said. Isabelle was only too glad to go, but Jeanne looked furious and stood for a moment with darkened face, lowering down on the nun, as if she were on the point of defying her. But she finally thought better of it, and followed Isabelle out.

Sœur Ste. Lucie stood in the open door till they were both well down the corridor. Then she shut it carefully and came back to Marise whose heart was beating wildly and whose knees were shaking under her. Sœur Ste. Lucie sat down, and made Marise sit down, holding both the child's cold hands in her soft, kind, old fingers. "Dear child, there are times in every life when we must ask God for courage. Your mother is not sick or hurt, but she needs all your prayers. She has had a terrible shock, a dreadful tragedy that took place before her eyes, and she will need all the help our Holy Mother can give her, to recover her calm. It seems that——" Sœur Ste. Lucie stopped an instant, as if to consider how to put what she had to say, and changed the form, "Your dear mother was in Saint Sauveur, and by chance a person from Bayonne passed through, whom your dear mother knew. And it seems they went out to walk together, as any one might, and descended the paths and steps, that lead visitors down the face of the Gavarnie Gorge, towards the place arranged so that tourists can look up at the arch of the great bridge. And then—nobody knows just what happened—the water was very high and violent, the other person must have slipped and fallen in, and was instantly killed by being flung by the current against a great rock. Your dear mother saw it, and sensitive and high-strung as she is, it . . . it slightly unhinged her. She said a great many wild things. . . ." Sœur Ste. Lucie stopped, drew a long breath and began again. Nothing that she had said had made the slightest impression on Marise. It sounded far off, as though Sœur Ste. Lucie were reading something out of a book. Marise could not seem to put her mind on it, and when she did, she could not understand it.

Sœur Ste. Lucie went on, "But by the mercy of God, I had just written her that the holy Father Elie was once more here; and after they had got the body out of the water and carried it to the hotel they—your mother remembered about Father Elie and turning in her trouble to the only source of strength, she—your mother wishes to make a retreat for a few days at our convent, and I am sure that it is much the best thing for her to do. It is a shelter for her—Father Elie is with her now, I have sent for a carriage. . . ."

"Oh, but can't I see her? Can't I kiss her good-by? How long will she be away?" cried Marise wildly, starting from the fascinated immobility in which she had gazed at the nun's face.

Sœur Ste. Lucie laid a quieting hand on her shoulder, her kind old face yearning over the child. "Dear little Marise, I think it will be better for your mother not to see you, or any one just now. She needs quiet, perfect quiet."

Marise looked at her hard. She had no idea whether she was being told the truth, or only some kind invention which they thought suitable for her to hear. "Can't I go to see her at the Convent?" she asked in a whisper, giving up the first point.

"Oh, yes, yes, my darling, *any* time . . . only a little later, when your mother is calmer." Sœur Ste. Lucie's face shone suddenly, radiantly, "God uses all means to His great ends," she said fervently. "This may be the means of giving your dear mother in the end, the holy peace of faith."

She looked so serenely trusting and hopeful that Marise felt comforted, "I'll do just as you say, dear Sœur," she said in a trembling voice.

Sœur Ste. Lucie drew a long breath, as though she had been steering a difficult course. She kissed Marise again, told her to stay in her room for the time being, to say her prayers, not to worry, her Maman would soon be all right, and probably happier than she had ever been in her life. All this might open the door to salvation for her.

She left Marise standing in the middle of the floor, and closed the door carefully behind her. But not so carefully that Marise could not, a moment later, hear Maman crying and crying and crying as she went down the hall and out of the door. Marise began to tremble and cry at the sound. She ran to her window, and saw down below, Maman, her hands over her face, with Sœur Ste. Lucie's arm around her, the tall old monk on the other side, cross the sidewalk and get into the carriage.

As the carriage rolled away the weeping child at the window remembered that Sœur Ste. Lucie had not mentioned who the person from Bayonne was who had been killed. Well, what did Marise care who it was!

CHAPTER XX

IT occurred to Marise, and the idea of a responsibility dried her tears with a start, that she ought to get word somehow to Papa. Her heart sprang up to think that perhaps if he knew Maman was so upset he would come back at once. She did *want* somebody so much, beside Jeanne and Isabelle.

But she never knew Papa's address when he was away on business. Perhaps there was something on Maman's writing-desk. She went quickly into the salon, drew aside the curtains which shut off the writing-desk's alcove from the salon, and began rather helplessly to fumble among Maman's papers and novels. There were very few letters of any sort. Maman didn't keep up her correspondence with America very much. Jeanne had heard Marise moving and through the alcove curtains Marise saw her now come into the salon with a basin of water in her hand, pretending that she needed to water a plant. Marise remembered that she must as usual arrange something to present to Jeanne that would not reflect on Maman's fancifulness. But perhaps Sœur Ste. Lucie had told her something. She inquired cautiously but Jeanne said stiffly, still outraged at having been shut out of the room, that she knew nothing. Everything about her except her words, said forcibly that she cared less, and that all this foolishness was a part of the usual nonsense.

"Oh, Jeanne, a terrible thing has happened to poor Maman —she saw somebody swept away in the Gavarnie and killed right before her eyes, and it's upset her fearfully."

Jeanne's sulkiness vanished in the delight of her kind at having any inside information about a violent death or a scandal. Marise remembered how absorbed and excited Jeanne had been when somebody in the apartment overhead had taken an over-dose of morphine and how proud she had been to have everybody in the market stop to ask her details.

"Killed?" said Jeanne with a greedy eagerness, her eyes shining, "how killed? Drowned? or knocked against the rocks? Man? or woman? Have they got the body out?"

Marise did not, as a rule, enjoy Jeanne's interest in murders and deaths and kidnappings, but this time she welcomed it and passed on to the old woman all she could remember of what Sœur Ste. Lucie had told her. Jeanne was much disappointed that Marise had not heard the name of the dead person, but Marise promised to tell her as soon as the paper was out, the next morning, since it would probably be printed. And with the mention, there came back to her, with one of those sickening lurches, the recollection of the girls putting their heads together over the newspaper at school, and then looking at her so oddly and hiding it away. "It was probably in this morning's paper," she said to Jeanne. "If you'll get it, I'll read it to you."

But Jeanne came back in a moment with an astonished face, saying that Isabelle reported that, of all queer things, Mlle. Hasparren, the music-teacher had stopped in that morning and asked to borrow the paper. Jeanne's astonishment never on any occasion remained more than an instant untinged with suspicion, and Marise, who knew the old face so well, saw the suspicious expression begin slowly to color the surprise. "What in the name of God did the Hasparren want with our newspaper?" she asked herself aloud, obviously snuffing around a new scent. Marise hated Jeanne's face when it looked like that,—crafty and zestful, as though she were licking her chops over a nasty smell.

They were still standing in the alcove, beside the writing-desk when the door-bell rang. Jeanne turned to go, heard Isabelle open, and standing between the half-open curtains turned her head to listen. Marise heard nothing but a man's voice, and Isabelle answering, "Oui Monsieur, oui Monsieur, oui Monsieur." But Jeanne started, stiffened, and darting on tip-toe to the door, looked around the corner. The door shut, steps were heard at the other end of the long hallway. Isabelle was evidently bringing the visitor to the salon. Jeanne looked around wildly at Marise, her face suddenly the color of lead, her eyes panic-struck. The steps were nearer, there seemed to be more than one man. Jeanne ran back, pushed Marise into the chair in the corner of the alcove, motioning her violently but without a sound, to keep perfect silence, and noiselessly drew the curtains together before the alcove. Marise heard her step quickly back to the stand where the plant stood and the click of her tin basin against the earthenware of the pot. And then she heard her say in exactly her usual voice, only with a little surprise, "Good-day, Messieurs, what can I do for you?"

"We have been sent," said a man's deep voice and not a "monsieur" but a common sort of man, Marise could tell by his accent and intonation, "to see and question Madame Allen." Jeanne evidently went through some pantomime of astonishment for he explained, "a part of the inquest over the death of M. Jean-Pierre Garnier, but the maid tells me she is already not here."

Jeanne answered, and if she caught her breath or flinched, there was not the smallest external sign of it, "No, M. l'Inspecteur, our poor lady was so terribly upset over seeing such an awful thing, that the doctor has just sent her for a few quiet days' retreat at the Holy Ghost Convent. What a terrible thing, to be sure, M. l'Inspecteur."

The man answered wearily, "Eh bien, we shall have to see her, retreat or no retreat. We have the blanks to fill out by all witnesses, and she is the only witness. This is the inspecteur from St. Sauveur."

"Oh, the poor lady is in no state to be questioned," said Jeanne with an affectionate warmth in her voice. "She is as tender-hearted as a child, and besides had been a great invalid. She took the whole course of baths at Saint Sauveur last season, and was starting in again."

"Oh," said the man as if surprised, "she had been at Saint Sauveur before? For the baths?" and then as if speaking to some one else, "it would be harder then, to establish that she was there to meet the young Garnier."

Jeanne seemed so astounded at this idea, that she could scarcely get her breath to protest. "Oh, M. l'Inspecteur, oh!

Who ever heard of anything so wild! Is *that* what people are saying? Oh, why!" she laughed out in her amazement, "she hardly knew him by sight."

"Why," said the man evidently not speaking to Jeanne, "didn't you say that she ran down along the bank of the river, screaming that he had killed himself for her sake?"

"Yes, I said that," answered another man's voice, astonished and on the defense, "and she *did* too! and when the body was pulled out she flung herself down on it, and shrieked that she wanted to die with him."

Jeanne broke in now, at the top of her voice, calling Heaven and earth and all the saints to witness that she never heard of anything so preposterous in her life, and that anybody in Bayonne could tell them so, and what crazy stories would people be making up next out of whole cloth? "Some one is trying to play a joke on M. l'Inspecteur from Saint Sauveur. Nobody *could* have heard our Madame say such things, because she couldn't possibly have said them, any more than she could about a clerk who sold her a yard of cloth over the counter. For she didn't know any more about the young man than that! Why, she *never* knew him except as the son of one of her friends. He never came to the house, and more than that she hadn't even laid eyes on him for more than two years. He had been in America and is only just returned, day before yesterday. *Any*body you ask here can tell you that."

"Nom de Dieu!" said the first man's voice in extreme surprise. "Hadn't seen him for two years!"

"No, he hasn't even been in France since he was a little young boy!" The first man laughed as though the joke were on his comrade.

The second man's voice said, still defending himself, but now uncertainly, "Very queer his following her right up there, if he scarcely knew her—what was *he* doing in Saint Sauveur at this season, I'd like to know, if not . . ."

"Oh, as to that," said Jeanne carelessly, "I happen to know why he was there. I saw the young monsieur day before yesterday, just as he was about to take the seven o'clock train, valise in hand, and I had a talk with him, our young mademoiselle and I."

"Why, I thought you hardly knew him by sight in this house and he never came here," broke in the second policeman suspiciously.

"I didn't say it was here we saw him," said Jeanne, "and I said it was Madame who hardly knew him. But he is the brother of a little girl class-mate of our mademoiselle. They are all children together. Well, every evening at six, except the days when Mademoiselle takes her music lesson, I go to the school to fetch her home, and that afternoon, as we were coming up the rue Port Neuf, we met the young man going towards the station, and when he saw our mademoiselle, he stopped for a moment for a chat, as young folks will. He was in high good spirits and said he was off for a fine business trip to the mountains and expected to have a good time as well as do business, and would be in Cauterets the next morning. Well, you know Cauterets is just over a ridge of the Pyrenees from Saint Sauveur and Mlle. Marise said, 'Why, is not that queer, my maman is at Saint Sauveur just now! Why don't you take the other train at Pierrefitte-Nestalos and run up to Saint Sauveur for half a day and take Maman a message from me, something I forgot to ask her before she left,' and the young man said he had been half planning to go to Saint Sauveur on business anyhow, and to tell him the message and if he saw her maman, he'd repeat it. Only he said, 'I don't believe your maman knows me,' and Mlle. Marise said, 'Well, you tell her you are Danielle's big brother, and she'll know. She knows all about my schoolmates,' and the young man asked which sanitarium it was in Luz and Mlle. Marise reminded him, 'No, it's at Saint Sauveur where Maman is,' and told him the name of the sanitarium, and then he said he hoped he'd get a little fishing in the Gavarnie, and I said the water would be too high, and he said he'd go and have a look at it anyway. And then he went along with his valise. Mlle. Marise is at school or you could ask her all about this too."

"Eh *bien*, my friend from Saint Sauveur!" said the first

man's voice, in a rallying tone of jocularity. "This sounds as though some of you country-people must have lost your heads a bit. Come now. Did you yourself *hear* her, saying all that?"

"No, of course I didn't," said the other man stiffly, "I was in the office at Luz. How could I know anything was happening? But the men who got the body out said she was awful to hear."

"Oh, I don't doubt," agreed Jeanne, "that she was. Any woman would have been driven half crazy by such an awful thing, the only son of a friend, killed before your eyes. And she is terribly nervous into the bargain, the least little thing sends her off into hysteria. Some nights I have to rub her back until eleven o'clock to quiet her. And the doctor has warned her against the least excitement. Why, two days ago there was an important prize-contest at our mademoiselle's school and the poor woman, although she would have given anything to go, was forbidden by the doctor. He said the excitement would be too much for her, and she would feel it so if her daughter were defeated. You can ask any one whether she was there! And that evening, although Mlle. Marise had won the prize, she was so worked up, I had to give her a sleeping draught to get her a little rest, poor thing. . . ."

"Were they *sure* of what she said?" asked the first man of the other. "Would they swear to it?"

"I don't see how anybody could hear anything!" put in Jeanne. "In ordinary weather the gave of Gavarnie makes such a noise down there in that gorge, you can't hear your own voice even if you yell. I remember last summer when Madame was taking the cure, when we went to see her . . . and now in flood . . ."

"They'd certainly swear to her being in a terrible state of agitation," said the other in a rather nettled tone. He went on, "You saw for yourself what was put in the paper about it this morning, how they had met there by design and spent the night together at the hotel and all."

"You won't get far in an inquest, my young friend, if you

take what a newspaper says. Newspapers are always wrong,"
said the first man pityingly, in a tone of experienced scepticism.
"If this happened at ten in the morning, they can't have been
together more than an hour. If he was seen here in Bayonne
at six o'clock the evening before, he couldn't possibly have
reached Saint Sauveur before nine the next morning. You
know you wait three or four hours for the connection at Lourdes. To my mind there's nothing in it. I will take you to
the convent to see her, if you insist, but I have no liking for
scenes with hysteric women."

"Oh, messieurs!" said Jeanne shocked at the idea, "you
couldn't possibly expect to see her *now!* Not for a week, at
least, the doctor said."

"A *week!*" cried the second voice, dismayed, "sacrebleu, I
can't kick my heels for a week, waiting."

"Well, suppose we go through the usual routine?" suggested
the other. "Go to see the family of the young man, and if
they confirm all this . . . there's no use going further. There
is plenty of time for you to get all the facts you need for
your report, and catch the one o'clock train back to Saint
Sauveur."

Jeanne said now jocularly, with a change of manner to the
intimate knowing tone of a servant-girl speaking to a policeman, "If you're not in a hurry, you must stay to have a glass
in honor of the house. We have an excellent white wine, and
the patron never counts the bottles."

Marise heard her lead them down the hall and across the
landing to the dining-room, and then in an instant heard her
come back and run on tip-toe up the hall. She thrust her head
through the curtains, showing a haggard gray face, glistening with sweat, and whispered, "Don't move, don't speak
to a soul till I get back. I must see the Garniers before they
do."

Even without this, Marise would have been incapable of
moving hand or foot. Half an hour later, she was sitting
in exactly the same position frozen and deathly sick, when
Jeanne let herself in cautiously. From the gust of sounds
that came in from across the landing, as the door was opened,

the two policemen seemed to be greatly enjoying both Isabelle and the white wine.

Then Jeanne shut the door on the loud voices and laughter; and in their place Marise heard the sound of dreadful hoarse gasps as Jeanne tried to get her breath after running. It did not sound like the breathing of a human being, but like that of some large animal, like a horse or cow, exhausted and panting.

Jeanne came up the hall, fighting thus for her breath, and dragging her feet. She shuffled heavily into the salon, and across to the closed curtains, where locked in her nightmare, the child waited for some one to come to the rescue.

The old woman drew the curtain a little aside. Marise caught one glimpse of her face, now swollen and darkly congested. She saw that Jeanne was nodding reassuringly at her; she heard Jeanne say in a whisper, "They understood, it's all right, they . . ." Then, without the slightest warning, she turned to one side and fell headlong inside the curtains.

For an instant she lay as if dead, her ghastly face at Marise's feet. But almost at once she opened her eyes and tried to smile and to speak. Only a guttural sound came from her lips. A look of terrible anxiety came into her face. She motioned with one hand passionately, that the curtain should be drawn shut to conceal her.

Marise, frightened out of her palsy, was kneeling by her sobbing, "Jeanne, Jeanne."

She thought of what Jeanne had done for her mother, and flinging her arms around her as she lay, she kissed her furiously, the tears coming in a flood and pouring down on the dreadful face, now strangely twisted to one side. Jeanne put one arm around her, and tried again to say something. But her tongue moved senselessly in her distorted mouth; the sweat stood out on her forehead as she struggled to speak.

Finally she gave up her desperate attempt, and put her finger to her lips, exhorting Marise to silence. Such a wildness of apprehension was in her eyes, that the girl muffled her sobs, hiding her face on the inert breast, clinging with all her might to the half-dead body.

She thought that Jeanne was dying. She thought that she herself was dying. She longed to die, there, that instant, and escape the shame and sorrow and misery that buried her so deep, so much deeper even than Jeanne knew.

The sound of laughter and voices chimed out merrily again. Isabelle had opened the other door. Marise held her breath, her face buried on Jeanne's breast. The old woman tightened the clasp of her arm. They strained their ears.

Then they heard the men's feet clatter down the stairs.

the way Jeanne saw things. With all her immature personality, with the pitiably insufficient weapons of a little girl, Marise had fought not to accept Jeanne's way of seeing things. That had been the real cause of their quarrels. But now the weapons were struck from her hands. Jeanne had been right all the time it seemed. That was the way things really were. Now she knew. With a long breath she admitted her defeat.

"No, *specially* not Papa," she whispered.

II

It was four o'clock that afternoon. They had had something to eat, talking quietly about indifferent things, and they had found Papa's address in Bordeaux and sent a telegram to him, before Marise thought to ask, "But, Mademoiselle, how is it you can be out of your class-room to-day?" She had often known the teacher to drag herself to work when she was scarcely able to stand, and knew how the stern discipline of her profession frowned on an absence from duty.

"Oh, I arranged this morning to have a substitute come. I heard—I heard your maman was not well, and I knew your papa was not here, and I wasn't sure that any of your maman's friends might be able to come to look out for you."

As a matter of fact, Marise never saw one of her mother's callers again.

That evening, Anna brought up a blue telegram from Papa, which since it had been sent in English, as Papa always insisted on doing, was perfectly unintelligible, reading:

"Com inga nmorninjtrain ta kigo adca rof Maman."

Papa.

Marise who had with Maman puzzled over many other similar telegrams from Papa, made out "morning-train" and that was enough.

The doctor had sent in a nursing sister to take care of Jeanne during the night, and Isabelle had gone off to a tenement near the Porte d'Espagne where some relations of hers lived and had brought back an old cousin to help her with the work and marketing and to sleep with her in the other apartment.

Mlle. Hasparren slept in the folding-bed beside Marise's so that every time Marise, with a great scared start, realized anew that what had happened was not a bad dream, she felt the other's hand reaching for hers in the dark, and holding firm. She said very little and Marise was glad of that, but the clasp of her muscular musician's hand pulled Marise out of the black pit many times that night.

Later on Marise fell into a real sleep, deep and unbroken, and when she woke up, much later than usual, to find Mlle. Hasparren all dressed, the folding-bed put away, the window open and the sunshine coming in, she found that she seemed to have grown stronger since yesterday, that the black pit was not so fathomless. She felt infinitely older and as though she would never laugh again. She lay in bed, looking up at the ceiling, thinking fixedly about what had happened, and found that she could endure it now without crying out or bursting into tears as she had done yesterday. She could stand up under her burden, because there was no other way. But she felt her shoulders bowed and aching with the weight.

Mlle. Hasparren heard her stir in bed, and sensed the awakened quality of the movement. She came to look anxiously down at her. Marise looked back and remembering that, so far as she knew, Mlle. Hasparren knew nothing beyond the surface of the happenings of yesterday and so might expect her to be able to smile, she produced a faint smile.

"I overslept," she said, in order to say something. "Has somebody brought your breakfast?"

"No, I waited for you," answered Mlle. Hasparren. "I'll ring for Isabelle now."

When Isabelle came, very self-important at taking Jeanne's place, she reported that the Sister said Jeanne had passed a very good night and was perfectly comfortable, with no complications. "She says Jeanne may get all over it and be as good as ever. All old people have these seizures, she says," chattered Isabelle, setting down the tray and pouring out Marise's café-au-lait. She was full of her new dignity, and bustled off to give orders to her assistant, leaving Marise and Mlle. Hasparren to eat their breakfast. Mlle. Hasparren did not seem to feel like talking much, and neither did Marise. She was trying to think what it was she was to tell Papa. She must remember now just what it was that everybody was to be told

An hour later, as they went down the hall, on their way to the station to meet the morning train, they saw the salon as usual at that hour, the chairs pushed about, the rugs hanging over the window-sills, the fresh, clean, new morning sun streaming in through the wide-open windows on the familiar spectacle of Isabelle on her knees, a brush-broom in her hand reaching under the piano for dust. The alcove curtains were drawn back, the cheerful sunshine poured in, glittering on the dark polished wood of the desk, on the yellow-covered books, on the pretty little inlaid chair which stood beside the desk.

Was it only yesterday that Jeanne had flung her into that chair? She stood in the door, as she put on her hat, looking steadily at the alcove. No, that had been somebody else . . . a little girl, a lucky, lucky little girl, who had no idea what things were like.

"Come, dear," said Mlle. Hasparren, looking at her watch.

It had been agreed since there were so few trains in and out of Bayonne and since as yet no news had been sent to Jeanne's family, that if Marise's father did come on the train from the north, Mlle. Hasparren would board it as he left it, and go on down to Midassoa to tell the Amigorenas about their mother's illness. "But do tell them, Mademoiselle," Marise said over and over, anxiously, "that we will take care of Jeanne, that we will do everything for her that anybody could, that they needn't worry. I know Papa will see that she's taken care of. I *know* he will, if I ask him." But really she was not as sure as she said. She did not know Papa so very well, after all. She had very little idea what he would feel or say about anything. And then everything depended on the way things turned out . . . !

They stood there in the smoky dusk of the station, a long ray of sunshine thick with golden motes striking the ground

at their feet. They still said very little, Marise not daring
to talk for fear of making a mistake, for fear that she would
not remember just what and how much Mlle. Hasparren knew.
The music-teacher held the girl's slim fingers close. Marise
answered their pressure with a nervous fervor, inexpressibly
grateful to the other, loving everything about her from her
steady face and kind, shadowed eyes, to her heavy, badly-cut
shoes, dusty now, which would be dustier later after they had
trudged along the hot white road at Midassoa. Never, so
long as she lived, was she able to forget how Mlle. Hasparren
had looked to her, when she came quietly into the salon and
lifted her up from Jeanne and said in a plain matter-of-fact way
as though nothing were the matter but Jeanne's sickness, that
they must get a doctor and probably Jeanne wasn't as sick
as she looked. She had just taken Marise by the hand and
showed her how to go on living . . . when it seemed to Marise that she had come to the end.

They heard the train whistle shriekingly in the distance,
and the somnolent porters roused themselves. Marise tightened her hold on the strong fingers which held hers. Her
heart ached with longing, with confusion. Suppose Papa did
not come . . . what *would* she do? But suppose he did . . .
wouldn't it be impossible not to make mistakes, not to forget
what you were to say and what you weren't?

But when the train came in, and Marise saw at the other
end of the long platform her father's massive bulk heavily de-
scending from a compartment, and saw his eyes begin to
search the crowd for her face, all her confusion melted away
in a great burst of relief. . . . Papa was there, something of
her very own in the midst of all those strangers! Her heart
almost broke with its release from tension.

And yet before she ran to meet him, she put her arms around
the music-teacher and kissed her hard on both swarthy cheeks.

III

Then she ran with all the speed of her long legs, and flung
herself upon Papa's broad chest and tried to put her arms

around him, as she had around Mlle. Hasparren, and began
to cry on Papa's great shoulder. How good it was to feel
him, to feel him so entirely as Papa always felt! It would
not have seemed like Papa if there were not more of him than
she could get her arms around.

Her tears, her agitation gave Papa such a turn that he
set his satchels down hastily and looking alarmed, shook her
a little, and asked what had happened to Maman.

In the hurry and noise and bustle of the crowd it was easier
than Marise had feared to get over that first moment when
Papa must be told. It all came out straight, just what she
had planned to tell him, that nothing had really happened to
Maman, she wasn't sick or anything only she had had a
terrible nervous shock, had seen somebody killed right before
her eyes, and it had pretty nearly driven her wild.

"Oh!" said Papa, evidently relieved, and caring as little as
Marise had about the person who had been killed. He picked
up his satchels again (by this time the porters at the Bayonne
station were resigned to his strange mania for carrying his own
hand-baggage), and said, "Well, yes, that's too bad! I remember I saw a brakeman killed once, and it made me pretty
sick, too."

They walked out of the station together. Not two minutes
had passed since his arrival, and already Marise's joy that he
had come, had faded to a frightened sense that he had not
come at all, that he was still very far away, that he would
never really come, as he used to.

And yet Jeanne had been right of course; whatever else
she did, she must not tell Papa.

"When did it happen?" asked Papa now, as they turned the
corner and were finally escaped from the last of the clam-
orous cab-drivers, who had not yet accepted, as the porters
had, the eccentricities of the American gentleman.

As they crossed the bridge, Marise told him the version she
had prepared, the version Jeanne had presented. She had
had a good deal of practice in saying something different
from what she thought, and she got through this without
any hesitation or mistake. But every word of it set her

further away from Papa, raised a wall between them, the wall of things she knew and Papa must never know.

"Well, to be sure," said Papa, when she finished, "you certainly have had goings-on, for sure."

"Oh, Papa," went on Marise earnestly, "you *will* have Jeanne taken care of! It was when she was working for us, she got her paralysis. *Don't* you feel we ought to—for always, for always? It was for us. . . ."

"Oh, as to that," said Papa, "anybody of Jeanne's age, who rustles around as Jeanne does, is apt to get a stroke, whether she was working for us or not. It might have happened just as easily in her own home."

Marise's heart went down.

Papa added, with a change of tone, "I don't like her lying very well, but the old woman has been awfully good to you, Molly, awfully good, more like your grandmother than the cook, and I guess we'll see that she's taken care of, all right."

Marise squeezed his arm hard, and said nothing. After all, wall or no wall, Papa was there, good old Papa, so broad and solid, her very own Papa; somebody who, even if he didn't understand much of what went on, would look out for them all, Maman, Jeanne, herself.

IV

Papa went in at once to see Jeanne and told her through Marise—for Jeanne had never learned to understand his brand of French—that he would see that she was well taken care of till she recovered. Jeanne contrived with her one living hand and her eyes, to convey her respectful thanks, and to conceal everything else which Marise knew she must be thinking.

Then Papa wanted to go at once to the convent, and bring Maman home. What had he come back for, if not for that? As a matter of fact, Marise was not very sure why he had come back, or why she had felt it so necessary to get word to him at once. Now that she had had time to think about it, she realized that she dreaded very much having Maman see

Papa just now, right after . . . after all that. It would have been better for her to have had a little time to get over it, and like Marise, to think what to say.

But, of course, this was one of the things she could not speak to Papa about. All she could do was to find out that lunch was nearly ready and they would better eat that before they went to the convent.

Isabelle, her head turned with the sudden removal of Jeanne's heavy-handed authority, had prepared a gala luncheon with the best silver and linen, and "What a pretty bunch of flowers," remarked Papa.

Marise looked silently at the white rose-buds, now opening into roses. Was it only yesterday morning that Jeanne had given her those? Was it only two days before, that she had been walking along with the Garniers, with nothing in her head but mockery of Madame Garnier's shoes and hat? No, that must have been somebody else, some one she had distantly known, that girl who had laughed with the others so, over their foolishness behind the scenes.

"Let me see," remarked Papa, "you must be almost fifteen, aren't you, Molly?"

"Yesterday was my birthday."

"Funny kind of celebration."

Marise looked at him across an immense chasm, and said nothing. She couldn't ever remember having a meal at a table alone with Papa before.

"Don't you want to go with me?" he asked later, as the dessert was served. "I don't know how to find my way around a convent—of all places! Whatever possessed your Mama to go there anyhow?"

"She and Sœur Ste. Lucie are such good friends," explained Marise. She decided not to say anything about the old monk, because she didn't know whether Papa knew about Maman's going to see him before; but after thinking for an instant she decided that it would do no harm to add, "Sœur Ste. Lucie wants Mama to be a Catholic, you know."

Papa said quickly, "What's that?"

Marise was surprised at his tone. Perhaps that *was* one

of the things she oughtn't to tell about. "Why, would you mind if she did?" she asked.

Papa thought for a moment, and dropped back into his usual slow casual comment, "Oh, no, I guess not, if she wants to." There was a silence broken by Papa's saying something else, in an earnest tone as though this time he really wanted Marise to listen to him. "All I *ever* want, Molly, is for Mama to have things the way she wants them."

Marise's heart was nervously sensitive that day, in a sick responsiveness to the faintest indication of what was in other people's hearts.

She could not put another morsel of food to her lips. She sat looking down at her plate, trying to master or at least understand the surge of feeling within her. *"All I ever want is for Mama to have things the way she wants them."* There was so much to think of in that, that she was still lost in thinking, when Papa pushed back his chair and got up, pulling down his vest, with his usual after-dinner gesture.

"I'll have a look at the mail while you get your things on," he suggested. Evidently he was still set on going at once to see Maman. Perhaps more than he admitted, he really didn't like her being in a convent.

Marise went to get her hat, and with it in her hand, went to join her father, standing by her mother's writing-desk in the alcove. He had an American newspaper in his hand, his forefinger inserted in the wrapper.

He tore it open and stood looking at the head-lines, while Marise put on her broad-brimmed sailor-hat and, tilting her head forward, slipped the rubber under her hair behind.

"All ready?" said Papa, and they set out.

How much less *exciting* everything was, now that Papa was home. But would it be—if he—but he never would! Who would tell him? Not Maman certainly, although Marise wished that poor Maman could have had a few days more without seeing Papa, to get over being excited so she could be surer of what she was saying. Not Jeanne. Not herself. Nobody else knew him well enough to tell him anything. If Maman could only get through to-day all right. . . .

V

At the convent they waited in the usual bare, white-washed
convent parlor with the shutters drawn, with the usual little
rush-bottomed chairs, so light that the one Papa sat down on,
groaned and creaked under his great weight. The usual black-
walnut book-case displayed the usual Lives of the Saints.
Through an open door they could look down a long, long,
gray stone corridor, very empty, till they saw Sœur Ste. Lucie
hurrying noiselessly down it towards them.

As she came near, Marise saw that her sweet face looked
anxious and worried. She told them at once that Madame
Allen had been taken very ill, that they had been up all night
with her and had sent for the doctor early that morning.

Papa was startled by this unexpected news, and apparently
never dreamed of what occurred to Marise at once, that this
was just something they had made up to prevent anybody's
talking to her. Marise thought it a good idea. She had hoped
something like that could be arranged . . . in case those
horrible sergents de ville came back again. She was not alarmed
by Sœur Ste. Lucie's worried face, because this was by no
means the first time that she had observed how easy it was
for people's faces to look anything they wished to have them.

Papa was asking rather sharply, "What is the matter?
What did the doctor say? Is it the effect of nervous shock?"

All the same, it was too bad, thought Marise to have Papa
worried for nothing.

Sœur Ste. Lucie shook her head hurriedly, "Oh, no, something much more acute than that, a terrible, terrible chill
which has gone to her lungs. The poor lady must have been
in soaking wet clothes, for nobody knows how long. Monsieur
has been told of the . . ." She hesitated and paused.

"Yes, yes, I know she was with some one who fell into a
river somewhere and was drowned. But did she fall in, too?
How did she get wet? Why *weren't* her clothes changed?"
His voice rose as he asked the questions.

Sœur Ste. Lucie explained in a low, hurried, agitated voice.

"Nobody knows of course just what happened. Perhaps she tried to save the poor fellow. Perhaps she slipped as he did. In any case she was too distraught to think of herself or to realize the danger of going so long in wet clothes. And every one there was so absorbed in the tragedy. . . ! She was all alone among strangers, the poor lady. She must have sat in her dripping garments in the cold train all the way to Lourdes, and then half the night in the unheated station there, waiting for the train. It was terrible. The doctor said it was terrible to think of—weakened with the shock, as she was, and no food!"

Papa now said ungently and impatiently, yet as though he were restraining himself, "Well, we must get her home at once, where we can take care of her!" Marise could see that he believed every word that Sœur Ste. Lucie said.

But of course Sœur Ste. Lucie hadn't the least intention of letting Papa take Maman away. "I'm afraid that is impossible," she said, "the doctor came back this afternoon, is here now in fact, and says"—her voice broke—"he says she is much too ill to be moved."

At this Papa burst out angrily, his face very red, "Why under the heavens didn't you send word of this to her own home? Here I have been there, ever since the morning train, eating my lunch . . . with no *idea* that . . ."

The nun defended herself reasonably, sadly, showing no resentment at his anger, "No one knew you were come back, Monsieur, and I was just starting to fetch our dear little Marie."

Marise saw over the nun's shoulder a gentleman with a bald head, a great brown beard and very white hands coming down the corridor, "Here is the doctor, now," said Sœur Ste. Lucie, drawing in her breath quickly. Taking Papa and motioning Marise to stay where she was, she stepped down the corridor. Marise watched them, her eyes on the doctor's serious, spectacled eyes. Something about the way he looked at Papa made Marise for the first time wonder if Maman really were a little sick after all.

They all came back to where Marise stood. Papa's face was no longer red. He said to Marise in a queer voice, "The doctor says that Maman must not be disturbed, but we may go in to see her for a moment if we will be quiet and not talk."

They turned, all of them, and started down the long, gray stone corridor. Marise tip-toed along beside her father. She was a little frightened in spite of herself, at a loss to know what to think or feel or believe. The emptiness of the corridor echoed around them. Marise's ears rang with the emptiness of it! And how long it was. It took them forever to walk through it. Marise looked up at the small windows set high in the wall, and wondered when they would ever come to a door that opened out.

But the only door was at the very end, and that opened into the white-washed room where Maman lay in a narrow bed.

As soon as she saw her mother, Marise was sure again that she was not really sick because she looked even better than usual, with a deep shell-pink in her cheeks. She did seem a little tired and sleepy, however, for her eyelids looked heavy and kept dropping down over her eyes. They stood there for a moment, looking at her, till she should open them again.

When she did, and saw Papa there, she flung out her arms towards him. As he stooped over her she clung to him with all her might just as Marise had at the station.

She did not look at Marise at all, only at Papa. He patted her shoulder, and smiled at her, and Marise saw the tears run out of Maman's eyes in a gush.

Papa sat down on the little chair by the bed which creaked under his weight, and leaned forward, his arms around Maman, his cheek against hers. She said to him in a hurried, frightened whisper, "Horace, I want to go home. I want to go home."

He answered steadily, "It's all right, Flora . . . we'll have you home in a few days."

She closed her eyes again, all the expression dropping out of her face. The doctor stepped to the other side of the bed, and his fingers on her wrist, his eyes on his watch, motioned them silently to leave, with a sideways jerk of his head.

They tip-toed out and down the long, gray, empty corridor.

Marise's mother died that night, without seeing them again.

AN EDUCATION IN THE
HUMANITIES AND THE
LIBERAL ARTS

CHAPTER XXII

September, 1900.

THE first weeks of Freshman year were like a return to the formless impersonality of little boyhood. Just as Neale had felt himself an amœba-like cell among the finished, many-membered adults of his parents' circle, so he was now again only one more wriggle in the mass of Freshmen. Nobody could tell him apart from any other Freshman. He could scarcely tell himself apart from the other Freshmen.

This did not afflict him as it might a more sensitive, self-conscious boy. Indeed he rather enjoyed the anonymity of his condition, the space and vacuum about him which it created, where he floated free from any threat of the handling or pawing-over which was his especial fear when he entered into relations with other people. There was so much that was new to him in college life that it was occupation enough to look on without taking any part. He enjoyed the variety of his experiences, from the Greek-and-Roman feeling that came with walking up the Library steps, to the fairy-cave enchantment of floating on the shimmering water of the electric-lighted, marble-lined swimming pool. And he enjoyed most of all his aloof spectator's scorn of footless classes like Rhetoric A, or class-meetings where a few loud-mouthed blow-hards ran the show, while the real scouts like himself preserved a cautious, sardonic silence. He discovered the perilous secret, always a temptation to natures like his, that if you attempt nothing, share in no effort, you are automatically freed from any blame for the inevitable foolishness and blunders; you can stand on your safe little hillock and scorn the poor fools who try to do things and fail. The lone-wolf motive sang seductively in his seventeen-year-old ears. Nothing in any of his classes, nothing in the Library or in any of the books in it gave the seventeen-year-old a hint of any valid, compelling reason for his assuming the heavy, distasteful burden of responsibility.

Then one day, word was passed around that the Flag Rush would be held that afternoon; the Flag Rush unanimously deplored by the directing forces of the University; the Flag-Rush, that out-burst of meaningless brutality so shocking to all the European members of the Faculty, secretly contemptuous of the prosperous, illiterate, childish country where they taught.

Neale never dreamed of staying out of the Flag Rush. There was a row on, and his class needed his muscles and his head. He went to the Gym. at the appointed hour, where all the Freshmen were assembled. Gathering confidence at being all together for once, they marched in a body over to South Field. There they found the Sophs. gathered about a tree, from a branch of which fluttered a 1903 flag. Juniors took charge of the affair, coaching and urging on the Freshmen. Still buoyed up by their mass, by being together, they advanced to the charge. They were uncertain, and for the most part, amiable big little boys, who really cared nothing about that flag, who really cared only about doing what was expected of them. As they advanced, they began to hurry, to rush forward nervously. Several detached Sophs. dived in at the leaders' feet and broke up the formation, but there was mass impetus enough to carry the rush forward. The Freshmen crashed into the defenders of the flag, pushed them back, circled them round . . . at the first physical contact with the enemy they were no longer big little boys doing what was expected of them, they were young Berserk fighters, blind and furious with the delight of battle. A roar went up, a roar from their very hearts, like the yell which had burst up from their little-boy game-centers. Except for a few rare and artistic natures, who were suffering horribly from shock, every one of them was twice what he had been two minutes before. A Freshman somehow shot up through the crowd, hoisted on his classmates' shoulders, and laid his hands on the sacred branch; but defenders spouted up around him, grabbed his legs and

pulled him down. With this, all semblance of organized purpose left the rush. It broke up into a disorganized mêlée,
rolling and tumbling, panting and struggling in a hundred separate encounters.

Neale rolled and tumbled, panted and struggled with the
rest, far, far from any cool Olympian detachment. He was
one of the biggest and strongest of the Freshmen and felt his
responsibility. He did what he could. But that was not
much. The Freshmen did not know one another, and had
no plan. Sometimes Neale collared his own class-mates by
mistake; sometimes a couple of Sophs. tackled him together,
ran him back and dropped him on the grass.

A half-hour later the flag was still in the tree, and the furious
boiling over of insensate young life had cooled to a simmer.
The Juniors called the rush off, the Freshmen began to stream
back to the Gym. Neale was surprised to find one sleeve to his
jersey missing and innumerable rips and tears all over his
other garments. He was bruised from head to foot and spat
blood from a cut lip. Calmed, appeased, exhausted, he made
limping for the gate.

As he passed through it, he passed through another and
invisible gate, opening into quite a different path from the
solitary, self-satisfied way of aloofness which he had been
following. He did not, as a matter of fact, pass through the
invisible gate. He was shoved through by a vigorous hand
that slapped him on the shoulder. Turning, Neale looked into
the masterful face of the Varsity Coach. "Report for football
practice to-morrow!" was the order. "I'm Andrews!"

The information was unnecessary. Neale would not at
this date have recognized President Low or Dean Van Am-
ringe, but he knew the football coach. The next twenty
hours were beatific. His mind refused to grasp facts. It
wandered off into gorgeous day-dreams. He was on the Varsity . . . no, he was a sub, called in at the last minute . . .
a long run! . . . better, a recovered fumble . . . then down
the field, shaking off one tackler after another.

He would wake up to real life, blushing, swearing at himself for a condemned fool. And yet a few minutes later, in

fancy he was the last defender between the goal line and a rushing Yale back. . . !

Not the faintest hint of any of this appeared on the surface. At home he preserved his normal appetite which was his mother's gauge for his health and spirits, and although he told them, not unwillingly, about the Flag Rush, he preserved the sacred secret of his summons from Andrews, as though it had been his first sentimental rendezvous. The next day dragged endlessly, filled with the paper-like silhouettes of talking professors. But three o'clock was finally there, and he was at the Gym., silent, his face composed, his heart given to sudden swelling bulges, which made it hard for him to hear what was being said.

They gave him a suit. He trotted with the squad, *with the Squad* over to South Field!

"Ever played?" asked the scrub quarter.

"Yes," said Neale. He did not feel obliged to tell how little.

"What position?"

"Half-back," he lied brazenly, having made up his mind that he hadn't the weight to aspire to the Varsity line.

They ran through signals. Then a scrimmage started but Neale was not in the line-up. A scrub back had his wind knocked out and didn't get up quickly enough for the coach. "Put in that Freshman bean-pole. Jump in, what's your name?"

Neale jumped and floundered for five minutes, then the peppery scrub quarter consigned him profanely to the side-lines. For two days after that he moped without a job, although still in a suit, out in the field. Then he had another trial.

Gradually he made sure of his place as right-half on the scrub—not that he was any good, as they told him plainly: but because in those days the whole squad, including hopeless dubs, seldom numbered over thirty men, and thanks to the work in the mill at West Adams, Neale was physically fit.

With this place, minor though it was, came the great privilege of dinner, after practice, at the foot-ball house. There he picked up a little of the theory of the game from the blackboard talks; there after the Pennsylvania's guards-back had battered through for thirty points, he heard the coach, white and shaking with emotion, pour out his biting post-mortem. "You, Jackson," shaking his fore-finger at the left-guard, "did you shoot your body in low and spill them in their own territory? No, you STOOD UP!"

Neale's flesh crept, he was almost glad that he had escaped the fearful responsibility of being on the Varsity. It was terrible, such a weight on your shoulders. He shrank from it, and with all his being, aspired to it.

He made no impression on the football world, but his own interior world was transformed. He was no longer an isolated, formless Freshman, dumped down into the midst of the most callously laissez-faire of Universities, he was no more a forgotten molecule with no share in, or responsibility for the ultimate reaction. He had a shelter for his personality against the vast, daunting indifference of the universe. He was on the football squad.

He had feared he might have some trouble in explaining his absence from the supper-table at home, but that proved unexpectedly easy. The second evening after he began to play on the scrub, he found Father in the library at home, reading the sporting sheet of the Evening Telegram.

"Any other Crittendens in college, Neale?" he asked.

"Not that I know about."

"That's you on the foot-ball team, then?"

"Only on the scrub, yes, I'm trying. We have dinner together after practice. You don't mind, do you?"

"Me? Of course not," said Father.

Mother heard all this, apparently had known it before, and did not ask him to take care of himself and not get hurt. Neale looked over at her gratefully. Mother was all right.

The foot-ball season slid along, the Varsity improving every week. Neale glowed with caste-loyalty as Saturday after Saturday he watched the prowess of his big brothers. Every day he felt himself stretching up, broadening out, nearer to their stature, though nobody else gave him a thought. Life was full of big and generous and absorbing matter.

Then came Thanksgiving Day, the climax . . . and oh, after that, what a vacuum! Nothing in life but classes! Holy smoke! It was fierce! What did the fellows do who hadn't had anything but classes! How could they stand it? But of course, it wasn't such a come-down for them.

Going home as Neale did every afternoon, he had none of the scanty, ill-organized college social life. Sliding into college as he had, with no introduction from the right kind of Prep. school, and with a noticeably colorless personality, he was not thought of as a possibility for any fraternity. Time hung heavy on his hands. Lectures took up but three hours a day, on the busiest days. To fill in the rest of the time there was the swimming pool, the Gymnasium and the Library. He swam, practised the overhand racing stroke, dived; in the Gym. he fooled awkwardly on the parallel bars and side-horse; he tossed medicine balls with any pick-up acquaintance; what he really enjoyed was the line of traveling rings which hung in front of the visitors' gallery—but one day he heard an upper classman refer to these as "Freshmen's Delight," and thereafter he avoided them.

The Library, the first one to which he had had access, wasn't so bad. Neale went there first to look up a reference for Comp. Lit. A. Of course you ran the risk of being thought a grind if you spent too much time there, but you could kill the hours very pleasantly with the bound volumes of the magazines in the shelves about the general reading-room. Neale and most of his friends wasted an unconscionable number of hours on those magazines: but little by little the library habit began to form itself, by slow, infinitesimal accretions. He found it a good place to study, wrote English A. themes there, finally even got into the way of running through the card catalogue, and drawing books with titles that sounded good.

Christmas came. Father, recognizing manhood achieved, gave him a box of a hundred Milo cigarettes. Mother—poor, dear, ignorant Mother!—gave him a white sweater decorated with a light blue C! Even more than by smoking Father's cigarettes, Neale proved that he had begun to outgrow the cruel egotism of adolescence, by kissing Mother and thanking her, without telling her that almost any fool finally gets his diploma, but only the chosen few—and these as Juniors or Seniors—win the right to adorn themselves with the proud insignia of their Varsity letter.

After Christmas came the mid-year exams. Neale went into them confidently enough—and to his astonishment emerged with passing marks, but with no great credit. D in German was the worst, and he'd studied German since he was a little boy! Greek, English and Latin marked him as mediocre with a C. Comparative Literature alone rated him B—and every one knew that Comp. Lit. was a snap course. Neale had never thought of himself as a grind, but he had been used to high marks at school, and the low grades nettled him. He began to see that there was more to this college work than he had understood. The studies themselves were not unlike those of high school; indeed they were easier than the science and mathematics that had been hammered into him at Hadley. But the point of view was different, and that had fooled him. There was a "take it or leave it" attitude about everything at college; the professors did not, as at Hadley, hold their jobs only because they were able to drive the bright, the dull, the scatter-brained, the sluggish, all through passing grades for the next year's work. No, these college professors and instructors gave themselves no such trouble. They set out their wares. If the students helped themselves, so much the better: if they didn't, so much the worse—for the students. Neale mis-called the professors for lazy time-servers: but he wasn't going to let them put it over on him that way another time. He would read everything they suggested and more! They would be astonished by the brilliance of his finals. But just then baseball practice started in the cage and Neale forgot all about his vendetta against the professors.

At baseball he expected to shine. This he had really played before coming to college. April saw the Freshman baseball squad practising on South Field. It was a terrible jolt to Neale to find himself in the discard. His vacant-lot, light-of-nature game had not compared favorably with the play of graduates of well-coached Prep. schools. He was thrown back on the Library. Perhaps it was just as well, he told himself with sour-grape philosophy. After all he was there, among other things, to get an education.

CHAPTER XXIII

THE event of that summer, the only one that counted for him, was a long, timber-cruising trip which he took, as chain-boy and camp-helper, up into the mountains of southern Vermont. Grandfather's whole life had been spent in handling timber in one way and another and all his old friends and associates were in that world. Every one had the greatest respect for old Mr. Crittenden's "timber-sense" even now when he was so old that he could do no more cruising, engage in no more active speculation. Sitting around on the lumber-piles at the mill, or on the porch of the Crittenden house, Grandfather somehow had a finger in many a timber deal. People came to consult him, and to get him to go halves on buys bigger than they had capital for. From the time he had been a little boy, Neale had been the unconsidered witness of innumerable such interviews, and had laughed inwardly with considerable family pride to see how completely Grandfather in his baggy old country clothes held his own and better against the smartly-dressed younger men who came to talk business with him.

The summer after Neale's Freshman year, the proposition was a big buy of wild land from which Grandfather himself had skimmed the cream thirty years ago and sold for nothing afterwards, but which old Mr. Crittenden opined, cocking a shrewd old eye in reflection, must have again come to some exploitable value. Three men were to go up unobtrusively, and timber-cruise through it, back and forth, zig-zag, till they could make a fair report on what was there. The plans were being made, one evening, out on the porch where they all sat in the long, clear summer twilight. Grandfather had not seemed to notice Neale's half-wistful interest in the talk of camp outfits and compasses and packs, but suddenly, looking down to where the boy stretched his long, gaunt body on the porch-floor, he said, "What say, Neale? How'd you like to go along? You could carry chain when they had to run a line, and I guess you're smart enough to keep a fire going and help make camp, ain't you?"

That had been a great month; full of discomfort and hardship and fatigue and deep, deep satisfaction. Neale was the only boy with three men, hardened, wiry woodsmen, who had spent their lives in forests, not at all in the loafing irregular manner of sportsmen, with occasional spurts of nervous effort, and with long periods, in unfavorable weather, of idling around a camp-fire. Neale's three companions had always worked in the woods as regularly as his father worked in his office. Rain and heat and cold and insect-plagues were nothing to them. The main business of every day was work: and camp-life was organized sketchily (without much regard for comfort), not to interfere with work. Neale found that his gymnasium-practice, athletic-sports, college-life had left him as soft as dough beside these lean, iron-like men. He doggedly sweated himself into a hardness that made it possible for him to keep pace with them. At first when they turned in under their blankets at night as soon as dark came, Neale had been too exhausted to sleep and had lain awake aching, every one of his big bones bruised by the roughness of the hastily-made balsam-bough bed. But inside a week, he was able, as his companions did, to stretch out with one long, deep breath, and to know nothing more till morning came, and the light woke him to roll over and open his eyes to the unimaginable freshness of dawn, filtering through the thick-leaved branches over his head. He drew in a chest-full of the sweet, new air, a heart-full of immaculate beauty, and fell heavily asleep again, till half-an-hour later one of his companions kicked him awake to take his share of getting breakfast and packing up for the day's tramp.

The three timber-cruisers talked very little of anything, most of their prodigious capacity for effort going into their work, and they never talked at all of the beauty which was the background of their lives; but they occasionally paid a silent, offish tribute to that beauty by going a little out of their way to some "look-out" evidently, from their talk, familiar to them since boyhood. This was generally the top of a cliff or rocky slide, where there were no trees to obscure the view. Arrived there, they never did anything but sit and swing their feet over emptiness, pitch stones into the void below them, and quarrel with each other about the identification of different peaks and hollows in the vast wooded expanse of mountains before them. But they were always more than usually silent after such a glimpse of the spaciousness of the world and, for one, Neale found a greatness in his heart to match the greatness which had filled his eyes.

Once as they sat thus on a crag, throwing stones and smoking, the head timber-cruiser, old Martin Hoardman, remarked to Neale, of whom they usually took little notice, "See that high range . . . and then that other beyond it, the one with the three-peaked mountain in the middle?"

Neale nodded.

"Wa'l, you'd never guess it, but there's a valley down in between them two, with a sight of folks in it, and farms and everything."

Another man said, "Why, old man Crittenden's got a brother lives there. Ain't that the Ashley valley? He runs an old-fashioned water-power mill there."

Martin observed, "Yep, I've drawed many a load of logs to the old man's mill."

Neale remembered the sharp-spoken old man who had visited Grandfather's mill one day when he was a little boy. He had said then, he would go up to Ashley some day and make Uncle Burton a visit. Well, if he were a crow or a hawk, he could do it now, in about half an hour. He sat dreaming, his eyes fixed on the two hazy blue lines of mountains which stood up so high and so close to each other that they entirely hid the valley between. It must be a quiet, sheltered spot, that valley.

"Time to be movin' on," said old Martin, getting to his feet, and striding off into the woods, with his strong, unelastic, never-tiring gait.

At the end of five weeks they were plodding back up the road to the Crittenden house, Neale not to be distinguished from the other men. The road seemed hard and narrow and foolish to them, the house and barn like toys, the world about them on so small a scale that their widened eyes could scarcely distinguish one thing from another. Neale had the distinct impression, when he stepped into the kitchen that if he stood up straight, he would put his head through the ceiling. And what a comical, trifling thing a chair was! He felt afraid to let his whole weight come down on it and expected it to go to pieces in his hand, it felt so flimsy.

But his bed was good—oh, very good. He slept till noon the next day and was wakened by Grandfather coming up to see what the matter was. He scrambled up, half-awake, rubbing his eyes and staring, his pyjamas open upon his broad chest, his long arms bare. Grandfather stood looking at him for a moment before he went back down-stairs. He did not say a word except, "You're going to eat breakfast and dinner together, I guess," but Neale knew that Grandfather was very well pleased with what he saw. Grandfather was a pretty good old scout, anyhow, he thought, as he washed gingerly in the white earthen-ware basin, which seemed appallingly breakable to him.

CHAPTER XXIV

AND then it was time to go back to college. Sophomore year was *entirely different*. What a change from his cat-in-a-strange-garret sensation of a year ago! Now he was blatantly sure of every step in the elaborate and illogical ritual that makes up undergraduate life. He stood between College Hall and the Library all one happy afternoon, wringing the hands of Sophomores, as uplifted with their status as he. There Griswold the Assistant Manager hailed him and carried him off to the football house on 117th Street. He found the office on the first floor crowded with all the leaders and hangers-on of the football organization.

Andrews shook hands with him and actually remembered his name instead of calling him "Freshman Bean-pole"—it was great to be a Soph.! "Report in the Gym. at three," said Andrews, "you'd better live at the house this season; fix him up with a room, Charley." He turned and went on talking with McClurg, something about officials for the Fordham game.

Bixby reached over and picked up a paper from the welter on his desk, "Top-floor, Crittenden, you'll find a lot of cots in the front room; take any one that's loose."

"I haven't any clothes with me," explained Neale. It had never occurred to him that he would be accepted into the very center of things this way.

"Never mind, bring 'em to-morrow; but you'd better beat it up and stake out your claim to a cot now. . . ." The telephone rang and Bixby snatched it up, "Columbia football house, yes, this is Bixby speaking. No, that *won't* do! Those shoes were promised for this afternoon. Yes, yes, you can make it if you send them right away. See here, there are lots of sporting-goods firms who want our trade. . . ."

Neale went upstairs and found a room, with six cots made

up. Four of them had suit-cases or books on them to show
occupancy. Over by the window he saw Billings, last year's
full-back, sitting at a table with a thin, slight upper classman.
Neale thought he recognized him,—Grant his name was—
one of the college leaders, debating team, Spec. Managing
Board, Phi Beta Kappa; that sort of chap. Billings' big
body was hunched miserably forward over a book, his forehead wrinkled. As Neale looked at them, Grant reached forward, shut up the book and pulled it towards him.

"No use, Billings. It'd only ball you up to keep on with
that math. Not a chance! Don't try the exam. Anyway
they can't keep you off the team with only one condition.
But, God, how *did* you manage to flunk Comp. Lit.? Any
child of three ought to pass Comp. Lit. But don't you worry!
We'll get you through. Have you learned those pieces I gave
you?"

Billings straightened up and recited in a stumbling sing-
song, "As Shelley beautifully says, 'I could lie down like a sick
child and weep . . . and weep . . . and weep! . . .'"

"'Away this life of woe,'" prompted Grant. "And it's like
a 'tired child.' . . . No, don't change it! It'll look less as if
you were copying a crib if you don't get it quite right. All
right for that. Now, let's have the other ones."

At this point, Billings said violently in very forcible language, that poems were all such damn silly rot he couldn't
learn them. And Grant, unsurprised and peremptory, answered
that it didn't make a damned bit of difference how silly and
rotten they were, they could be learned. "You've got brains
enough to get a racing-dope sheet by heart, you can memorize
poetry too. Now, your time's up. Beat it over to the Library
where you can't talk and learn all *three* pieces! Remember
you're to work 'em in, no matter what he asks. And if you
have a chance, praise Shelley and knock Matthew Arnold.
That's his line."

He turned to Neale, "You're Greenway, aren't you, with
two years' conditions in French B?"

"No," said Neale, "I'm Crittenden."

"Oh, are you? Not on my list. You ought to have reported before. I can't do everything at the last minute. No matter, I'll give you till Greenway shows up. He's only a sub-end anyway, and we're lousy with ends. What did *you* flunk?"

"I didn't flunk anything," Neale admitted, half-ashamed that he might be considered a grind.

Grant jumped up. "What, *nothing!* And on the football squad, too." He stared hard at Neale as at a strange animal, and conjectured aloud, "Well, you must be a dub, of course. Never knew a Varsity man whose brain-cavity wasn't stuffed with cabbage-leaves."

Neale apparently showed some of the alarm this caused him, for the upper-classman added, "Oh, you'll get your chance just the same. Judging by the number of boobs Alpine and I are coaching, any dub who is eligible will have a smell at the Varsity, at least for the early games, till we can shove the regular Varsity men through their conditions."

"Everybody over to the gym.," roared a voice from the lower hallway.

Neale tossed his derby on one of the unpreëmpted cots and ran downstairs. As he bounded down flight after flight he could hear Grant leaning over the top banister yelling to the Manager to have Greenway found and delivered to him at once.

It was great to breathe the sweaty air of the dressing-room again, to strip and pull on your rough jersey and feel it rubbing the skin of your shoulders, great to hail the men you knew and have them slap you on the back.

"All over. . . . On the jump!" The squad clattered out, their cleats scraping and slipping on the marble steps.

Practice that afternoon was what the coaches called light —that is, no bones were broken: they fell on the ball, and it gladdened Neale's heart to see the new men hop into the air and bang down on one hip, just as he used to last season. They tackled the dummy, they went down under punts that sultry September afternoon—all of them, even the line men, time after time, till the sweat soaked even through their elbow-pads. Neale was dog-tired as he hobbled back to the dressing-room and pulled off his dripping jersey. What luxury to slip under the shower, hot first till the dirt was all off, then turn the handle, cool, cool, cooler, cold—to lean forward and feel it patter on your back, lean backward and feel the cold hard drops sting your face and chest. As he lay in Pompeian ease on the rubbing table, Josh went so far as to tell him that his muscles were in pretty fair shape compared to some of them. That was the timber-cruising trip. And how he tore into the roast-beef that night! It was good to be alive—to be a Soph.—to be on the football squad!

Grant's prophecy turned out correct. Four of the regular Varsity men were debarred by the faculty committee and the eligible subs made the most of their opportunity. One of the vacant places was left half-back and Neale, who that summer had grown some flesh and muscle on his lanky limbs and now weighed a hundred and sixty-three stripped, put his whole soul into the quest and nosed out Biffy McFadden for the job. McFadden knew more than Neale (the coach made no secret of Neale's lack of sophistication) but he weighed less and was only a little faster.

So Neale was given, although grudgingly, his chance and took it as though it had been his one chance to save his soul alive. He played against Rutgers, proud, half-scared, yet reassured at lining up by the side of big Tod McAlpine, and was fairly translated when he went over the line (just as easily as if it had been in practice) for one of Columbia's five touchdowns. Against Williams a week later, he played again and did nothing either very good or very bad. Just before the Harvard game, Garland was squeezed through a special examination in Latin and after that Neale had no chance for the Varsity. But he *was* considered about neck and neck with Biffy as first sub for the back-field, and he and Biffy grew together in a loyal comradeship, as brothers-in-arms.

Like a young tree which suddenly puts out a long new shoot in a new direction, Neale learned a lot of things that autumn, different from anything he had learned before. In the first place, living in the constant unrepressed society of thirty other young men, he acquired a good deal of social ease of a rough-

and tumble sort, learned much profanity, many foul and a few funny stories by the aid of which he was able to piece together the isolated facts he had already picked up about sex, and appear to his brothers a great deal more sophisticated than he was.

He also learned much technical football: to pick openings in a broken field, to jump from a crouching start the instant the ball began to move, to find his stride and be going at top speed in three paces, instinctively to hurdle when the defense was on the ground, to bull over it with churning knees when it was waist high, to lower his head and ram through when it was standing up, and always to kick, crawl, squirm the ball forward even if it was only a half an inch.

He learned a great deal more than that. All that autumn he played football, thought football, dreamed football, lived football. The savage Spartan football code was his code: to do anything, everything for a team-mate, for the team; to fight as hard in midfield with the score hopelessly against him as half a yard from the enemy's goal-line; to endure the agony of being tackled on muscle-bruised thighs, to get up and drive back as hard as ever into the line to the same certain torment; to go to any length to put an opponent out of the game—any length except being caught and having his team penalized by the officials; and no matter to what outbreaks of emotion his exhausted body and over-strained nerves might give way in the dressing-room, to walk out of it with his jaw set, his face impassive and never let an enemy rooter see a tear in his eye. It was by no means the education in the humanities and liberal arts with which the University was supposed to be providing him, but an education of a kind, it certainly was. Above all, at a period when his raw new personality was all one huge void, clamoring for something to fill it, football filled his life full to the brim. There was no vacuum left to be filled either by culture or deviltry.

All through the rest of that in-and-out season he played regularly at left half-back on the scrub, relishing to the full those afternoons when the scrub, with all the best of the decisions, scored on a crippled Varsity; rejoicing even more (for it meant power to the team) when the Varsity struck its gait and pounded rough-shod over the bleeding and prostrate scrub.

After the season Neale found himself entitled to wear the "Varsity stripe" and monogram. This gave him a certain position in his class. He was somebody. Two fraternities made discreet overtures to him. Neale considered, encouraged Lamma Kappa Pi, which seemed to have more athletic men than the other, was duly pledged and initiated.

And now came a change in his manner of living. The chapter needed roomers to help pay the rent for the Frat. house. Couldn't Brother Crittenden move into a top-floor bed-room? Neale broached the subject to his father and mother, pointing out how much more time he would have for study if he lived near the University. They surprised him by treating the matter with unexpected solemnity and delaying decision for several days; but in the end they gave their consent.

It did not occur to Neale as he slung his clothes into a trunk that he was saying good-by to his home-life; and if it occurred to his mother, silently helping him pack, she kept her thoughts to herself. An event that seemed of much more importance to Neale was a move that Father made on his own initiative. After a long homily on responsibility and learning the value of money, he proposed to grant Neale an allowance of fifty dollars a month to be paid on the first of the month in advance. Out of this Neale was to buy food, shelter and incidentals. Father was to go on paying college fees.

So Brother Crittenden installed himself in the top-floor hall bedroom, and according to fraternity practice, decorated it with pennants, foils and masks (although he did not fence), and sword bayonets, because they looked impressive and were cheap at Bannerman's. To make a real college room, he knew by comparing it with others, it should have a dozen girls' photographs, but Neale knew no girl well enough to beg photographs from her. He excused this lack by telling himself that he had no use for women, he was at college for the stern man's business of making the football team. Nothing that might interfere with the pink of physical condition or the singleness of mental resolution should have a place in his life.

And indeed for the six weeks which separated the end of the season from mid-year examinations, he stuck to a monastic schedule. The mandate had gone forth that football men must somehow manage to pass a majority of their subjects, and Neale's fraternity brothers never tried to coax him away from the table where he sat wrestling with Cicero's Letters or the Carolingian Empire, not even to play poker, or go night-hawking around little Coney Island.

But after mid-years it was different. Nobody could possibly start worrying about the finals for three months yet. The basket-ball season began and with it the informal Gym. dances after each game. "Nunc est bibendum, nunc pede libero" was in the air, not only in Latin classes. Neale went to the first games in the cap and sweater he wore about the campus, and when the dance began, sneaked out, dodging behind pillars to avoid compromising those of his chapter, resplendent in evening clothes with girl partners more resplendent still. But such seclusion was not to last. Other fellows, the "fussers" of his chapter were caught with extra girls on their hands, sisters or cousins, or ex-girls, and Neale in spite of his avowed principle of dancing only when he couldn't run away fast enough to escape, was hauled in to be the necessary extra man for the more or less anonymous out-of-town girl to be provided for.

Logically enough, other advances followed. Finding that they had landed not only a promising athlete in Brother Crittenden, but a passable social member, the rest of the chapter hastened to count him in. He learned to play poker; to drink more beer than he wanted; to keep a pipe going without burning his mouth; he learned where to go for chop suey; to sniff at a cigar, and look wise before he bought it; to pretend to like his cocktails dry, although as a matter of fact, he did not like them at all; he learned to rattle off a line of bright, slangy compliments at college dances or Frat. teas, and to take a flashier line with chippies at the dance halls; he added to his store of oaths and smutty stories . . . the chapter thought well of him and he thought even better of himself.

By the time spring came Neale felt happily sure that he was seeing life without making a fool of himself, which was, according to his latest philosophy (borrowed from Horace) the right thing to do. He would be nineteen in a few months now, time to attain a calm, mature, unsurprised acceptance of the world. No half-baked enthusiasms about anything. Except football, of course. That was far above all philosophies of life. In the spring of his Sophomore year Neale was consuming pipefuls of tobacco and meditating on what he called his "past life," censuring or approving his actions by the newly acquired yard-stick of the "golden mean." What a youthful idiot he had been about Don Roberts! That was so long ago that he could smile cynically at both his enthusiasm and his disillusion, each equally far from balance. Balance. Poise. That was the right dope for a man of the world.

And yet, spring was in the air, and it was hard, even for the ripe maturity of nineteen to be perfectly balanced. Neale had no girl at hand, and was betrayed into working off the excitement of spring days by writing an English theme on the tulips in Union Square. So much early May, both of style and personality seeped into this, that the jaded, discouraged young professor of English felt his heart leap up with incredulous hope and pleasure. To encourage the writer he read parts of it aloud to the class, while Neale's very soul scorched with shame. One of his non-athletic classmates, a brilliant, precocious, foreign-born fellow, with literary aspirations, came up to him afterwards and congratulated him enviously on his success. It was a terrible experience all around. Neale vowed furiously to himself that never again would he let any real feeling slip into a college theme.

CHAPTER XXV

WEST ADAMS and Grandfather's house looked queer and countrified and old-fashioned. It was a long, long way from a Frat. house on 113th Street to that plain bedroom so full of his little-boy and prep-school personality that Neale felt ill at ease and restless there. How could you live up to your ideal of Horatian calm and sophisticated tolerance towards human life in the presence of people who had known you when you were in short trousers, who only a few years before had been giving you hot lemonade for a cold and tucking you up in bed? No, West Adams was impossible! He looked inside the Emerson one day, remembering what an impression it had made on him, and found it like West Adams, very dull. "The man is so terribly in earnest!" he told himself and was enchanted at the superior, Oscar Wilde tone of his dictum.

The next day he thought of Billy Peters and knew that he was saved. Billy was the most amusing of his Frat. brothers, the one now nearest to him, for he remembered that Billy spent the summers in the Berkshires. He wrote to Billy asking him to come up for a couple of weeks and go camping with him, somewhere up the Deerfield. Neale would meet him at whatever station Billy could make and they would start at once. He didn't invite Billy to Grandfather's, not because he was ashamed of Grandfather's—not at all—he just didn't think it would interest Billy there. In due time Billy's answer came, asking Neale to cut out the wilderness project and come down to make him a visit in the Berkshires. Neale considered, he liked Billy; and West Adams was deadly dull. Why not? There was no good reason why not; he packed his suit-case and went.

Billy met him and drove him to the Peters' cottage, a re-modeled farm-house several miles from town. Mrs. Peters was cordially polite, Billy's little high-school kid sister turned blue, admiring eyes on her big brother's friend, who was presented as a most prodigious athlete. After supper, at Billy's suggestion they walked over to the hotel, two remodeled farm-houses with shingled sides joined by mission-furnitured piazzas. Billy introduced him to the "finest little girl ever" and Neale was only half-surprised (knowing Billy fairly well) to find she wasn't the same as the "finest little girl" of the winter before. But that was nothing to Neale; there were plenty of other girls, all delighted to buzz around him, to have him dance or play ping-pong, to make fudge, or walk in the moonlight. Some were pretty and some were not, some were bright and some just boisterous. And it was all the same to Neale. The Horatian pose was a great success. He was delighted with himself.

At the end of a week he prepared to leave. But Billy couldn't see it that way. It was true that Polly was going to have a couple of girl friends at the house next week, and would want Neale's room, but then they'd want Bill's room too. If Billy was to be exiled to a tent, why couldn't Crit keep him company? They'd move the tent up into the Glen, and really camp out, cook their own grub and everything. Crit had said he wanted to camp out! Why not? After all there wasn't any real reason why he should go . . . ! Next week there was the coaching parade, and all sorts of fun, decorating the hotel three-seater, with ferns and daisies. Then there was a boating excursion to Long Pond where Sarah Davis fell overboard and Neale pulled her out.

Then there was a fateful straw-ride in the August full moon, very near to Neale's nineteenth birthday, and there he met Miss Austin, a new arrival at the hotel. She was almost as tall as Neale, which was very tall indeed for a girl, and she looked to Neale as though she might have stepped right out of a Gibson illustration. This utterly superlative impression of beauty and good form was not lessened even in broad daylight the next morning, when he saw her again on the tennis-court, where she said good-morning with a special look for him in her very fine gray eyes. She did not play tennis, she sat on a bench at the side, under a purple silk parasol, her long, full, white skirts frilling out in a plaited cone, her pretty, fluffy, brown hair arranged in a high pompadour, which stayed impeccable as the tennis-playing girls grew hot and red, their hair straggling in straight wisps across their shining wet foreheads.

Had Neale ever thought he scorned girls who sat cool and dressed-up on a bench while others played tennis? As soon as the set was over, he went to sit beside her. She glanced at him out of her gray eyes and looked away again. Neale's pulse beat more quickly and he looked hard at the curve of her cheek. Then they began to talk. Before she went in to lunch, she had told him with a wistful note in her voice, that she was glad she'd met him, because most of the people at the hotel bored her so. Neale answered (the truth striking him for the first time), that *most* of the people bored him too.

If other people were what bored them, they certainly must have been free from ennui for the next few days, for they saw little of any one but each other. Neale's days and evenings were good or bad, according to the extent of his success in monopolizing Miss Austin. On the whole the evenings were the best, the evenings when they sat in a far corner of the hotel piazza and compared notes about their views on life and literature. Miss Austin paid Neale the compliment he most appreciated. She affected to consider him as well-read as she was—what did he think of Meredith, and Ibsen? She discussed Bernard Shaw and "The Second Mrs. Tanqueray." Neale had to trust to copious bluffing: to confide heavily in his taciturnity, letting her run on, till she expressed opinions tangible enough for him to agree with her.

The climax of the season was the fancy dress dance at the Prospect House. Everybody went; Billy in a blanket, woodchuck skins and turkey feathers considered himself a passable Uncas. Neale who had caught the early morning train up to West Adams and the milk train back, wore his football suit, with his white sweater like a cloak, the arms tied under his chin—hot but very becoming.

With Billy he started conscientiously to dance in rotation with all the girls from their hotel. His second dance was with Miss Austin. She was in black with a black lace mantilla, and pinned in her hair was one of the roses Neale had ransacked Pittsfield to buy—he forgot the others—forgot everything but the rhythm of their steps together—they danced, sat out on the verandah—danced again.

It was pointed, shameless—the chaperon, whose daughter was sitting a disconsolate wall-flower, glared at them—and they danced on. Had this red-blooded young blade, giving himself up wholly to the glamor of the moment, had he ever taken the cold, dry, heartless doctrine of Horace as a guide to life? He danced on—had he said he only danced when he was caught and had to?—he danced on, thrilling to the rhythm, like the swinging beat of hearts in young bodies. At last, the piano, violin and cornet (the "orchestra" imported from the city of North Adams), broke into "Home, Sweet Home," and the last waltz began; slow, languorous, the climax of the wonderful evening for Neale.

Then Miss Austin staged her dramatic effect. As the party broke up, she said, putting out one hand to Neale and resting the other on her mother's arm, "Good-night, Mr. Crittenden, and . . ." she looked down at the roses he had given her, "and good-by. Mother and I are leaving on the morning train. I only waited to have that last dance." She waited an instant to let this have its effect, and added in a lower tone, "Thank you—thank you for—for making my stay here so pleasant."

Now there was, under Neale's skin, neither a calm Horatian philosopher nor a dashing red-blooded young blade. There was only a shy, awkward boy of nineteen, taken entirely unawares, struck dumb by the surge of emotion within him. Helpless and inarticulate, except for a muttered "good-by" he shook Miss Austin's hand and walked away with apparent steadiness.

But afterwards. . . ! When Billy was snoring inside the tent, Neale sat on the platform outside, and wrestled with Destiny. What a stiff, frozen lump he had been, not to have

been able to speak out what was in his heart. She was *going!*
And he had no photograph of her. . . ! What an idiot never
to have thought to ask for one! Not a keepsake! Not even
a kiss! It was too hideous. No man with any virility would
let Destiny ride rough-shod over him like that. He would
be masterful. He would take the same train with her in
the morning, he would be reckless, follow her up . . . Great
Cæsar's ghost! But it was cold out there! The night damp-
ness pierced through even his thick sweater. He staggered to
his cot, rolled up in the blankets and fell instantly asleep.

He half-wakened once at dawn with the first rays of sunlight,
rolled over, looked out into the breathless, pure beauty of the
new day dropping slowly in a rain of golden light through
the great trees, thought hazily that he was timber-cruising
in the Green Mountains again, and fell asleep more profoundly
than ever. He was really very tired and his old faculty for
prodigious sleeping reasserted itself.

When he finally awoke, the day was ripe, and the light had
a late look. Sure enough, his watch said a quarter past eleven.
He sat up and stretched, and rubbed his hands back and
forth through his frowsy hair. Billy had eaten his breakfast
and gone. But he must have brought up the mail and left it
for Neale to find; for a letter now fell off Neale's cot to the
floor.

The letter was typed, brief and direct like the writer.

"Dear Crittenden:

"We have a hard schedule ahead of us this season. I want
all last year's squad to report at the football house for practice
on September 1st. I can count on you not to be late.

"R. McAlpine, Capt."

Neale read it over and over, stupidly at first and then with
growing excitement. Alone in the tent, he allowed a broad,
childish, unrestrained smile of pure pleasure and pride to
shine all over his face.

Then the date struck his eye. He was to report on September first and this was August twenty-fourth. Gosh! Less than a week to get into condition! Not a single minute to lose. His chance might depend on his being in condition.

His chance. . . ! He tossed the blankets off and sprang up, making plans rapidly. The coffee-pot left by Billy was still warm in the banked ashes, but Neale put it aside. No coffee! After his breakfast of oat-meal and toast, he looked longingly at his pipe, but did not light it. No tobacco! He remembered that this was about the time for Miss Austin's train, but he did not change his clothes to go down to see her off. No girls!

Still in his football togs, just as he had danced the last waltz, he set off for the first of his training, a two-mile jog-trot over the hills.

CHAPTER XXVI

September, 1902.

AFTER the first day's practice Neale and Biffy McFadden were jogging back to the dressing-room together.

"Great, isn't it?" grunted Biffy, rubbing his jersey sleeve over his sweaty forehead. "Looks like a job for either you or me."

"I'll have to step lively, if I get the job. Just you wait till I get some of the fat off me. I'm soft yet." He thought bitterly of time wasted on the hotel piazza.

"Soft? Hell!" cried Biffy. "All I'll say is I hope you never tackle me when you're hard—thought you'd slapped me with a piece of lead pipe just after I caught that punt."

McAlpine and Andrews were standing outside the Gym. door. Neale stopped to shake hands with his Captain whom he had not seen before practice. McAlpine punched him appraisingly in the abdomen.

"Not so bad. Some fat but there's muscle behind it."

Neale made way for Atkins of the '99 team, an alumnus always hanging around the squad every season. He was supposed to be devoting his heart's blood to bond-brokerage, down on Wall Street, but, a wistful exile from the world to which he had given the passion of his youth, he always came uptown in the fall to watch football practice. Also, which was of much more importance, he spent his summer vacation looking up available football material, "out in the bushes" as he expressed it. He now stopped in front of the Captain with a grin of pride, and jerking his head towards an approaching player, he inquired, "Well, how about him?"

McAlpine replied with enthusiasm, "Built like a piano, isn't he? Where'd you raise him?"

Neale followed their eyes and saw a squat, swarthy, two-hun-

237

dred-and-fifty-pound linesman rolling past them towards the Gym. door.

"Where'd I raise him? Stole him from the U. of P. Father's something or other up in the coal-fields—oodles of money. Son was all set up to go to Pennsy, but we got him down here and led him up and down the Great White Way a couple of nights. Nobody could coax him away now —unless there's a University at Paris."

McAlpine stared after the powerful back and shoulders filling the doorway. "God, what a brute! Baby hippo walking on his hind legs. What's his breed anyway?"

"Some sort of hunky. I'm not up on their stud book, but I'd say off-hand he's a cross between a Slovak cart-horse and a Ruthenian wild boar—lots of space in his garret, but you can't hurt him with a pick-ax."

"But, how in merry hell, are we going to keep him eligible? What courses did you get him entered for?"

"Oh, assorted snap courses—English Lit. mostly. And he has a tame tutor that lives with him and does the studying. How'd you suppose he ever got through High School?"

Neale left them talking and stepped into the Gym., admiring enviously the massive bone-structure of the new student of English Literature.

There were horribly emotional ups and downs in the Junior football season for Neale, ups and downs that ploughed and harrowed his young soul, planted many seeds in his heart, and left him at the end of the season with so much new knowledge of himself and others to digest, with experiences so rich and varied, dark and brilliant, to look back on, that he needed the entire rest of the year to grow up to them. The other students, those who did not play football, seemed to him like little boys, fooling around with marbles and kites, so little did they know of the black depths of depression and despair, and the hard-won heights of exultation which crammed his own personal life full, and gave him a premature maturity of experience, like that of a boy who has been through a war.

The day after his third game on the Varsity, Father called him on the telephone and asked if he couldn't come home and have dinner with them to celebrate his success—would that be breaking training? Oh, no, Neale answered, not if he got back to the house at nine. So he went home to a specially good dinner, just the kind he remembered as a little boy, when there was company. They talked football mostly: that meant he and Father talked and Mother saw to it that the plates of her two men were filled. After dinner they went into the library, the library where he had first plunged into the world of books, and there he and Mother sat on the sofa, while Father sat in his own chair, and they visited some more. Neale found it surprisingly easy to talk to his parents now, almost as easy as if they were strangers. During the last year he had lived away from them except for week-ends and short visits. In that time he had acquired a little perspective; and the new shell to his personality had set hard enough so that he no longer felt an irritable, shame-faced distaste of being looked at by people who had known him as a little boy. Great Scott! Had he *ever* been a little boy? The college Junior looked around on the walls, books and furniture that had not changed a hair and remembered with difficulty that he had once been a care-free child in these surroundings.

When he went away, he shook hands with his father, as he always did, and stooped from his great height to kiss his mother as he always did. Why not? It did not occur to him that he might not kiss his mother.

But apparently it had occurred to her, for when she felt on her lips the cool, fresh, boyish, matter-of-fact pressure of his lips, she gave a sob and flung her arms around him, holding him close and crying a little on his shoulder.

Why, dear old Mother! What was the matter with her? Neale put both arms around her and gave her a great hug, as he used to when he came home from West Adams.

It had done him good to see his folks, he thought, as he strode off down the familiar, but not much-loved city street.

He thought affectionately about his father and mother for
quite a time thereafter, as far as the ferry-house indeed, when
the build of a deck-hand reminded him of the new Swede on the
team. After that he thought football intensively, a strong
color of Junior cock-sureness tinging all his thoughts. He was
making the team! He wasn't so worse! How green, how incredibly green the thumb-fingered Freshies were who came out
to try for the squad. And he had beaten Biffy to it, although
Biffy had almost killed himself with trying.

The weak opponents of the preliminary season were easily
swamped. McAlpine, Rogers, Neale, with one of the tackles
back, the big Swede, Gus Larsen, or Atkins' coal miner (whose
name, Vaclav Blahoslav, stumped the squad till it was short-
ened to "Mike") tore over Rutgers, Fordham, Hamilton
and the other small fry. True, the battering-ram machine
broke tragically down before Princeton's even stronger attack,
but none of the blame for that attached to Neale. He was
kept out of that game by a wrenched ankle, and Biffy's rotten
luck let him into the line-up for the first defeat of the season.
Neale really had luck on his side, he thought with some com-
placency. By next Saturday his ankle was all right again and
he trotted out on Franklin Field supremely confident, trotted
out to fall straight into the black depths of the bottom-
less pit.

For after that swelling supreme self-confidence came a
queer slowness of mind. He found it hard to keep his thoughts
on his work as they ran through signals. His eyes kept stray-
ing to the rioting, flag-waving grand-stands. The whistle blew,
the kick-off came straight to Neale. For the first time since
Freshman year he felt a sinking dread that he might fumble.
The ball hit him on the chest and bounded off. Tod Mc-
Alpine fell on it and the rushing game began.

For the first half it was anybody's game. Either team when
it got the ball could gain but could not score. Something was
the matter with Neale. He wasn't all there. He knew he was
playing mechanically, but couldn't seem to summon the energy
to do better.

He sat listless, almost sullen while Andrews harangued the

team between the halves. He was hardened by this time to the Neapolitan frenzy of emphasis which marked exhortations to play your best football or die. He'd do his best, he told himself, looking down at his feet. Nobody could do any more.

The second half began with an exchange of punts. Playing behind the cyclopean Mike, Neale hadn't much work to do on the defensive, but once Mike was boxed out on a straight buck, Neale shot his body in to plug the hole and turning, caught a bony knee in the back, right over the kidneys. As he lay on the ground gasping for breath, he could see that he hadn't even stopped the play. It had gone over him for two yards. Oh, Hell! What was the use? How his back ached! The Penn. quarter seemed to know he was feeling wobbly. All the plays were coming at him and Mike, and most of them got by. Where *was* the ball? Sometimes it came straight through and the next minute on the same formation swung outside—and Neale uselessly buried under the interference. He'd have to stop it somehow—soon. He glanced back out of the corner of his eye, and saw the goal posts less than five yards behind. The Penn. formation was on his side again. Mike charged like a buffalo. Neale rushed in behind him, but blindly. Then all at once he picked out the man with the ball—too late. His sideways drive for a tackle missed and as he fell, his arms empty, he saw the red-and-blue jersey go over the line.

He got up shaken, feeling very sick of himself, not meeting anybody's eye. While Penn. was kicking the goal, Neale saw Biffy come bounding out from the side-lines, "I'm to take Crittenden's place," he reported.

It was like a blow in the face. And he had earned it. Neale walked to the bench, took a blanket, looking carefully away from the sub who held it out to him, wrapped himself up, forced his face into its usual expression of impassivity and watched the game. It was not much to watch: Columbia badly up in the air, Pennsy getting stronger every minute.

He dreaded the post-mortem at the football house, and took as deserved Andrews' verdict. "Crittenden, you were a total loss. I knew you weren't much of a defensive back, but

I didn't suppose a whale like you would let a skinny little runt of a Penn. sub ride you back five yards and dump you on your tail."

Day after day went by, with Neale in exile, playing once more on the scrub. The night before the Brown game, when the line-up was announced, he got together a show of good-will as he shook hands with Biffy and wished him luck. But he lay awake in the dark that night, heartbroken, sternly motionless and rigid on his cot, his great hands clenched hard. It was his virgin sorrow, the first real suffering he had ever known. The first real sorrow of most lives is usually tempered to the softness of immature hearts by the self-preserving instinct to lay the blame on something or somebody else, by merciful self-pity. But for Neale there was no Fate, nor chance, nor enemy, nor fickleness of woman on whom to lay the blame. There was no one to blame but himself, and before his time, he felt the pure rigor of this knowledge cut deep like a clean steel blade. It cut out a part of his boyishness forever. It was the first scar of the initiation into manhood. Neale stood up to it like a man, although so young a man. "No squealing!" he commanded himself savagely.

The next day he sat all through the game on the edge of the subs' bench, his big muscles quivering with readiness to respond to an order to jump into the game, his heart sick, sick within him because the order did not come. Nobody so much as looked his way. There he sat, a big, useless lump.

"What's the matter with me?" he cried out behind his Iroquois mask of insensibility, "I've got the strength. I've got the speed. *Am I a quitter?*"

The sweat stood out on him at the idea, and at first, helpless before the dramatic quality of young imagination, he felt that must be the answer. Yes, he was a quitter. As well die, and be done with it.

Then the nucleus of what was to become Neale hardened itself against this easy, inverted sentimentalism, and small as the nucleus was, it set itself to consider the matter in judicial, objective judgment. Neale went over his football for the last week as though it had been that of another player. "I did quit in the Penn. game. But other fellows have had a slump and pulled out of it. And since then, by God, I've played myself out in every practice. I've given all there was to give and then some!"

He held up his head at this. And yet, if he wasn't a quitter, what *was* the matter with him? "Biffy isn't any world-beater. Yet he must be better than I am, or Andrews wouldn't give him my place. *Andrews is square.*"

He said that with the accent of the mystic who affirms that God is good; and it was very much the same sort of corner-stone in the house he was building to live in.

Along in the second half, Atkins (the grad. who had discovered Mike), stopped his caged-tiger prowl up and down the side lines and dropped into an empty space beside Neale. "Look at that!" he cried suddenly, "Did you see that?"

Neale had noticed nothing in particular—just a general tangle of brown and blue jerseys. "I don't think they gained," he said.

"Great Scott, no! Haven't you any eyes? They lost about half-a-yard. The Brown left-half tripped over Mike's legs, but if he'd been a foot further out, he'd be going yet. McFadden was suckered."

Neale took his eyes for a moment from the field to look around wonderingly at Atkins. He had never thought of him before except with pity as an old exile, who couldn't play any more. Could he really see all that in a play, see just what every man had done? Atkins went on now, stiffening with his concentration like a pointer dog. "There it goes again—see, he's charging right on top of Mike. Just luck if he gets the man—missed him! It was Tod who stopped the play. Next time they hit the left side of our line, watch the way Rogers handles it." Atkins bit savagely on a mouthful of gum, "There!" He dug his finger nails into Neale's wrist. Neale could see Rogers rock a second, undecided, on tip-toe; side-step an interferer; and then shoot his body like a projectile into the play. "Spilled 'em-for a yard-and-a-half loss: that's the stuff!"

He looked around sharply at Neale. "If *you* could use your head like that, you'd be worth something to the team."

Neale stared at him, his young face candid with the astonishment of feeling a brand-new idea inserting itself into his mind. Maybe *that* was what was the matter with his game.

He reached up, as he would have said, to the upper story, and turned back to watch the game with new eyes, eyes sharpened by intelligence. He concentrated on the back-field defense and began for the first time to understand the inwardness of it. He couldn't attain Atkins' hawk-like vision of the play and what every man in the back field had done; but he made out a great deal more than he ever had before.

Next Monday at practice Atkins came and stood behind Neale (the bond-selling business never seemed to exist for Atkins during football season). To Neale, as he played on the scrub, Atkins poured out his accumulated tactical lore, the wisdom that choked and strangled him because he was no longer allowed to put it into action. Seizing on Neale, whom he did not know personally at all, he forced his way into Neale's attention and held it fiercely on the business of playing football intelligently.

"Have a look! Have a look! Secondary defense finds the play before it stirs out of its tracks! No, you shouldn't have tried a tackle that time," he yanked Neale to his feet, "they were too bunched. I made just that break in the Princeton game in '99 and I've never forgiven myself. If you'd spilled the interference, your end would have got the runner. Watch the ball! don't run in till you *know* where it is—and then *go to it!* Sometimes you can tell by the back's eyes, give themselves away by looking where they're going to go, but, an old hand will cross you on purpose. The knees are safer, mostly they lean a little just before the ball goes back. Got, to use old head! Bill Morley himself couldn't stop a play if he didn't know where it was. Ah! *that's* the stuff! That was just right—not too soon or too late—and see how easy it was!"

Day after day the Wall Street bond-broker wrestled with

Neale's latent acuteness and forced it into action. With shame, with praise, with reproach and enthusiasm, he drew out of Neale more than Neale had dreamed could be there. If one—even one—of the teachers of English or Greek or chemistry or economics had taught Neale as this semi-illiterate, wealthy young barbarian taught him . . . ! If Neale had given even a tenth as much attention to any of his courses . . . !

Neale clambered up over himself, raging with hope; up over his first realization that there was infinitely more to this problem than he had ever supposed; over his next, that he did not know even the rudiments of the game he had thought he knew so well; over his occasional glimmers of understanding, why he failed sometimes and succeeded at other times; over an increasing percentage of successes, and finally stood, a little giddy with the new height, on the peak towards which Atkins had urged him, where he waited clear-headed, strong, confident, behind the tackle, hoping the next play would come his way.

The play did come his way. The Varsity tried out against the scrub its new delayed pass from close formation. To the left it worked very well. But when they tried it to the right, Neale dropped Rogers for a loss, three times in succession. The look on Atkins' face was glory.

The next afternoon Neale was back on the Varsity and Biffy on the scrub.

There was a pang in his beatitude, a painful moment of generous distress when Biffy came up to congratulate him. The two hard-faced, frowsy-headed, gum-chewing young savages gripped each other's hands in an inexpressive silence; and each saw deep into the other's big heart as he was rarely, in all his life thereafter, to look into any other human being's inner chamber.

Biffy carried it off splendidly, Neale thought, but he couldn't fool a man who had just been there himself. He felt sorry for Biffy. He remembered to be sorry for Biffy till the whistle blew for the Annapolis game.

CHAPTER XXVII

AFTER the Thanksgiving game, a great peace, a lying-fallow time, a period of unconscious adjustment and assimilation of all that mass of experience.

Neale moved back to the Frat. house, rooming with Harry Gregg, a classmate of his and a fine fellow, thought Neale, even though not athletic. He and Gregg had chanced to take much the same courses and were in the same class-rooms in several subjects. After a preliminary stagger or two, like a man coming indoors after living in the open, who cannot walk across the room without tripping over the furniture, Neale's mind settled down to his studies. He found them rather more interesting than he had expected. A course in general European history especially held him, and he gave much more time to the outside reading prescribed than he would have confessed to any member of his Frat. except Gregg, who took it as a matter of course. He encountered some personalities there who held him and about whom he often thought, big figures who dwarfed the life around him when they stood up beside his study table. Cromwell was one and Garibaldi another. But they were not all soldiers. Wise old scouts like Sully, Oxenstierna and Plombal who did the real work and let the cloth-of-gold opera-tenor kings and potentates prance around in the lime-light, they took Neale's fancy too. They were the boys for him! He used to sit back and laugh to himself to think how much more they must have enjoyed the real exercise of their own strength than the silly sovereigns could have enjoyed their silly lime-light. As for Henry IV and his lady-loves, he reminded Neale so forcibly of Mike and *his* lady-loves that he could never take that white-plumed monarch seriously. Henry of Navarre made him laugh at Mike and Mike made him laugh at Henry of Navarre, and over both those hilarities Neale drew the decent veil of his calm, pipe-smoking stolidity.

One day browsing around in the Library, he saw the title of one of the books Miss Austin had spoken of the summer before, one of the books Neale had pretended to know and had never heard of. He drew it out (it was "Richard Feveral"), and read it, entranced, until early the next morning. After that he looked up, one by one, all the books she had mentioned, and read them, some with delight, some with blank incomprehensiveness, some with scorn.

He killed a lot of time discussing things in general with Gregg, reading Gregg's books. He fell especially hard for a worn volume of Poems and Ballads. For six weeks he was convinced that Swinburne had said the last word, a blighting word, on ethical values. Then one day he noticed that his favorite credo, "From too much love of living, from hope and fear set free" could be sung to the tune of the well-known, extremely coarse and very unpoetical song called, "Some die of drinking whiskey, some die of drinking beer," and it occurred to him suddenly that when you thought about it, both expressed the same philosophy. It was disgusting! It wasn't argument—but just the same it somehow put a crimp in Swinburne! He went back to his history and economics. But you couldn't stew over your books all day long; he drifted more or less with Billy Peters' innocuous, evening-dress, dancing-fussing set.

Outwardly he passed as a good fellow, a passable mixer though rather silent. Inwardly he had given up his pose of Horatian calm. It didn't work—not for him. He found himself very much alone and friendless. The other men on the football squad—well, they had been his blood-brothers during the season, but after the season they were mostly illiterate young rakes without a single mental spark even when they were drunk. As for Pete Hilliard's crowd and their small-town, back-alley ways of amusing themselves—hell! Neale felt for them the amused scorn of the native-born great-city dweller for the uneasy provincial who thinks he can hide his provincialism best by assuming a boisterous nastiness.

For the first time Neale began to wonder about himself, to wonder what sort of a human being he was anyway, that he didn't seem to fit in really, with any crowd. There was always so much of himself left over, shut out from companionship, left in the dark, alone and silent, while with a little corner of himself he danced and talked to girls, and drank and played poker, and talked to Gregg; for there was an immense lot of which he never spoke even to Gregg. For instance they never talked about girls, and Neale was thinking a good deal about girls. When he read love-poems his breath came and went fast, he felt tingling all over. He longed to put out his hand and open the door into the wonders and marvels that lay beyond it. He drew back from the fear of failure, of making a fool of himself at an unfamiliar game. But he never feared that there was nothing beyond the door.

At dances, sometimes he stood aloof, trying to look Byronic to save himself from looking wistful, sometimes he danced steadily, always with a calm exterior, beneath which weltered a confused mass of bewildered uncertainties and longings that rose choking to his very throat: and yet not a word of it could he ever get out.

What was it he was missing? Moody, out of humor with the bright, warm May sunshine, he put the question to himself as he sauntered aimlessly down the Library steps. Why, he was missing everything that made life worth while! Was he always to live alone with most of him hidden and silent? Would he never find his crowd, or at least one other person, to meet whom he could go forth, all of him, light and free, without the ball and chain of his endless reticences? Other fellows seemed to find something satisfying in life. Why not he? Was it his fault, or life's, that he walked in inner blackness? He was framing a sweeping indictment of life as he passed the gate to South Field.

Somebody ran out and grabbed him by the neck, a tall Senior. "King's Crown playing the Deutscher Verein," he explained. "Speed up and get in, Crit. Get your coat off. Never mind your togs. You've got to catch next inning. Purdy can't hold the ball if I put a hop on it, and the Dutchies are swatting my slow curve. There you go, that's the third out. Get busy. Give me one finger for a fast one; two for an out; and the closed fist for the drop."

The pessimistic philosopher, exiled to eternal solitude, shed coat and collar, put on mask and mit. A ball, a strike, a high foul. As he sprinted behind the back-stop to get under it, Neale sloughed off the parched skin of introspection. From that time on, he forgot everything but the game. He rattled off encouragement to the pitcher, "Keep workin', old man *that*-a-boy, make him hit it! Got him swinging wild!" He improvised wild flights of kidding to get the goat of one batter after another.

After the game when he and his pitcher were shaking hands and grinning at each other, he became aware of Berkley and Berkley's girl. What was her name? He'd met her at the Junior Ball—oh, yes, Miss Wentworth. They stopped to congratulate him. Neale was conscious, wretchedly, unphilo-sophically conscious of a very dirty face, a more than dirty shirt—and torn trousers. But Miss Wentworth didn't seem to notice. Perhaps she was a good sport. It was conceivable that a girl might be. She made a sensible comment on the double play which had saved the game in the eighth. Why, she was intelligent as well as good-looking. Neale fell into step, forgetting his disheveled looks, and walked along to the drug-store at 120th Street, where they all had sodas.

He met her again that spring, in the waiting-room of the 125th Street station, of all prosaic places! He had stopped in for a time-table to see about getting up to West Adams and she was evidently waiting for a train. He touched his cap. She smiled. He stopped to pass the time of day, "Vacation's almost here," he said.

"What are you going to do with it?" she inquired.

He hesitated. She wouldn't understand. But he was never very good on quick bluffs, and so said briefly, "I've got to learn to kick this summer—to kick a football, I mean. I—I play football a little."

She threw back her head and laughed, "Oh, you needn't explain. I know you play. I'm a regular fan. I haven't missed a home game in three years, and I read the athletic news. McAlpine graduates, so does Johnstone. There's nobody left at Columbia who can punt. So you're to learn! More power to you. I'll come and root for you next autumn."

He took with him. to West Adams• a mental picture of a strong, capable body in a shirt-waist and golf-skirt, fluffy yellow hair, smiling lips, laughing, honest, blue eyes.

He carried also what was more· tangible and important· in his summer plans, a worn brown football, the center of many an afternoon's battle between scrub and Varsity. As soon as he was installed at West Adams he went to work. The spare, thin grass on the upper meadow had been cut. There, a good mile Neale jogged every day, and there, all the morning, he practised punting: booting the ball high and far, racing down, trying to get to it while it was still bounding; then kicking it back again, experimenting with different ways of holding it. He always kicked at some target. "I'll drop that on the stone pile," he would say to himself, and before he kicked. again, he would try to analyze success and failures. He no longer needed an Atkins to spur him to use his brains. By eleven o'clock, pretty well fagged-out, he would jog down again, take a plunge in the inlet above the mill pond, where no one could see him for the thick growth of alders, and come in to luncheon at noon, cool and ravenous.

In the afternoon he worked at the mill, or lay round and read. He had brought a lot of books up from college in his trunk, but nothing seemed to fit his present serious régime as well as Emerson. After much running after false prophets the clear, brutal sanity of the Essays was as refreshing and tonic as the plunge into the icy, clear water of the inlet. He found in them too, what had escaped him at the first reading, an austere sonority in the best passages. "Let those fear who will. The soul is in her native realm, and it is wider than space, older than time, wide as hope, rich as love. Pusillanimity and fear she refuses with a beautiful scorn. They are not for her who putteth on her coronation robe and goeth out through universal love to universal power." He rolled it under his tongue. It beat about his ears like the low, dignified threat of distant thunder.

One Saturday in August, a little before his twentieth birthday, something happened which cast a long ray of light back on Neale's life. It began by the great surprise of seeing Father and Mother drive up to the house, in a buggy from the village livery-stable.

It was perfectly evident from the moment they set foot in the house that there was something in the air, but being a Crittenden, Neale's father was in no haste to say what it was, and waited to explode his bomb-shell till dessert time, as they were eating the peaches and fruit-cake which Grandmother served to honor their arrival. Then it came out.

"We've been doing a pretty big business in cabinet woods lately," Father began, looking at no one in particular. "Coco-bolo, rosewood, lignum vitæ, mahogany. The selling end is all right but it's a job to get the stuff delivered. The firm has made up its mind that it will pay to send a man through the West Indies and Central America to look the production end over, get options, sign contracts for regular yearly delivery. There's a big territory to cover, the field goes as far south as Brazil—it'll take a couple of years at least, maybe three or four. I'm telling you all this because they've offered the job to me, and Mother and I have about decided to accept."

Mother looked hard at Neale as Father announced this, and they both waited to see what he would say. Neale was so astonished at the idea of his stationary father and mother being anywhere but in the house on Union Hill, that he found nothing to say for a moment, staring at them. Then he said (it was the first thing that came into his head), "But what will you do with the house? All those things?"

Mother said eagerly, "Oh, we could rent it furnished. We already have a good offer for it."

"Well, what do you think about that!" exclaimed Neale in a stupid astonishment at the idea that somebody else could live in their house.

He went on eating his peaches and thinking about it in silence since he saw no reason why his opinion on the subject was of any interest to anybody. It did not dawn on him till afterwards, when he and Father took a stroll along the mill-brook that Father and Mother wanted to *know* how he felt about it, and would not do it if he very much disliked the idea of having no home nearby. This astonishing fact became apparent to him along with another matter even more astonishing, that apparently the Union Hill house had been arranged largely for his benefit, so that he could have the stability of a home atmosphere.

"We always wanted to roam, rather," explained his father casually, "we were pretty young when we married. Your mother was only twenty and I was twenty-four. We had talked a good deal of cutting loose and seeing the world. But— well, you were born the first year afterwards, and we thought probably there would be other children. It seemed better to put it off, settle down till we had raised our family—though you turned out to be the only one."

In the twilight of the maples, Neale was doing some think-ing. Mother had been *married* when she was his age; with all her life before her, and she'd never had a bit of it till now; only Union Hill and more Union Hill. And Father, too. . . . He murmured something muffled and inarticulate, which made no particular sense to the ear, but which Father understood, and answered with some vehemence, "No, Great Scott, *no*, Neale! Don't think that! Heavens, no! I didn't mean we'd sacrificed anything for you—we just got into a rut, the way people do, and stayed there so long we began to think we couldn't get out and now when this opportunity comes, your mother wanted to make *sure* it's all right with you, that's all! Your mother and I, you've been a great com-fort to us. We don't want . . ."

He was almost as muffled and inarticulate as Neale, but Neale understood him, and reaching for his hand, gave it a hard grip. He did not try to say anything now. The two men, silent under the old maples that had sheltered their childhood, exchanged a quick glance of understanding and affection, nearer to each other now, at the moment of parting than ever before.

Then they went back to the house, silent as Iroquois, and Neale went in to where his mother was playing dreamily on the old piano, to tell her bluntly that he would not in the least mind their leaving Union Hill, since he could be at home very little in any case during his Senior year.

She turned around on the piano stool to listen to his sober statement, and to look at the great fellow, towering up over her.

"Yes, you're grown up now, Neale, aren't you?" she said faintly, putting a hand out towards him and he knew he had hurt her by his bluntness. And yet it was the truth he told her, and also what she wanted to hear. He could not take it back. But he did stoop to her and take her in his big arms for a little-boy hug.

Father came in then and they lighted the lamp and tried to talk a little about what Neale was going to do to earn his living when he graduated. They had often tried to talk of that. But they never got very far, and no farther this time than any other. Neale had no ideas on the subject, and being Neale, he would not imaginatively play up to what was expected of him, and say he had. No, he did not feel that he would like to be a doctor. No, certainly not a lawyer! He wouldn't mind engineering, but the old grads in his Frat. who were engineers seemed to have a way of turning up, out of a job every once in so often. He didn't think much of a profession where you were so entirely at the mercy of people with money. It was too much like being a turtle that had to wait for somebody to turn it over before it could go on its way. Father looked at him rather queerly and remarked that he'd find it difficult to get any work in the modern world, where he wouldn't be at the mercy of people with money.

Neale said, he thought very pertinently, "Grandfather never has been."

Father looked as though he considered this mere arguing for the sake of arguing, and said something drily, looking around at the plain, old countrified room, about Neale's not being willing to live as his grandfather had, two generations ago.

The upshot of the talk was, as it always was, that they

agreed once more to let things run on and perhaps something would turn up.

The next morning Father and Mother went back to New York, to finish the preparations for their adventure. Mother cried a little when she kissed Neale good-by, but Grandmother kissed her son without a quiver, though she clung to Grandfather's arm. She and Grandfather and Neale and old Si and Jennie stood in the front yard looking after the carriage. It was almost like seeing a newly married pair go off after the wedding. Neale's mother kept turning to look back at them, her April face like a bride's, colored through tears by excitement and anticipation. Neale stood up, taller than his tall old grandfather now, broad, massive, his tanned face like a man's. But, to his amazement, there awoke in his heart for the last time, a little boy, a little boy who was frightened and grieved at being left alone.

Half-way down the hill, the carriage stopped and they saw Neale's mother spring out and run back up the hill, beckoning to Neale.

"Forgot something," conjectured Grandfather.

Neale bounded down towards her. They met half-way between the carriage and the house. Mother's face was still wet with her tears but she was not crying now. A glory was on her tremulous face. Neale never forgot how she looked at that moment.

There was something she was trying to tell him and although all she could bring out, as she took his big hands in hers was, "Neale, dear, dear Neale," she knew by the look on his face that she had told him.

The little boy in Neale's heart, appeased, consoled, comforted, melted away forever, without bitterness, without regrets. The over-grown young man looked down at his mother, with an absolute trust in her love, and a robust confidence in himself. "I'll be all right, Mother dear," he told her heartily, meaning a great deal more than he said.

Then she went back to her husband, and Neale went back to his punting.

As he ran furiously after the ball, reeking with sweat under the brazen August sun, it came to him suddenly, so that he stopped short for an instant to think of it, wonderingly, that he had never seen his father and mother look at each other, except with affection. And besides this old, old knowledge which had hung there so long he had never seen it before, there was a new picture . . . the animation and excitement on their faces, as they talked of their setting off together for distant travels, the gaiety of Mother's laugh, as they told of the fun they were having to make ready for the unknown, to get the right clothes, to learn Spanish. . . . "I've been on the point of buying a mantilla," she had said. "Don't you think I would look well in a mantilla, Neale?"

Mother had never seemed half as young to Neale as now. She must have been an awfully nice girl, he thought, going soberly to recover his ball.

CHAPTER XXVIII

ALTHOUGH he had of late seen very little of home, and had occasionally felt irked to know that his parents expected him to make a semi-regular appearance there, Neale found New York rather queer and empty at first with no back-ground whatever but the football house.

He encountered something of the same queer, gone feeling as he lined up in the first game of the season, with all of the trusted Old Guard disappeared, with no Tod McAlpine beside him, on whom to leave the responsibility for the outcome of events. Of all the old supermen in whom he had put his trust, only Marshall the Captain was still there, at right guard. Things looked black to Neale. Such raw beginners could never hold together against any seasoned team.

And yet they did. Week after week of the early season, they registered victory after victory; never with sensational scores, but with steady defense that kept their goal line un-crossed, with drive enough to punch out a touch-down of their own. It came to Neale slowly that this was no kid team after all. It had about the usual proportion of seasoned players and recruits; only now he was one of the old timers. It came to him also that Bunny Edwards the Soph quarter was obviously trusting in him as he used to trust in Tod McAlpine. At first it was horrifying to Neale to have some one depending on *him!* He had all he could do to stand up under his own responsibility, heavy on his own shoulders for the first time. Presently he realized that possibly Tod McAlpine had had his own secret misgivings too, in the days when Neale depended on him. It was by no means wholly physical and muscular, the hardening and maturing that went on in Neale, those first weeks of his last football season.

This deepening of his sense of responsibility deepened his capacity for emotion along with the rest of his personality.

The other Seniors, even good old Gregg theorizing and spinning talk about things he'd read in books, seemed off in another world to Neale, a light, bright, boyish, somewhat foolishly unreal, although very care-free world. But although he sometimes groaned at the fierce, stark suffering which was the inevitable penalty of caring so fiercely and starkly about anything as he cared about football, he did not envy Gregg and the other outsiders. Envy them? Heavens, no! They were playing at life; he was living!

Yes, he was living and at a higher emotional pitch than he had ever known. He did not think of himself as an individual. He was flesh of one flesh, bone of one bone with his teammates. Once in the Amherst game a smash into the line had piled up without gain. The heaped mass of legs and bodies squirmed itself apart, friends and enemies crawled to their position. All but one, and that was the big Slav tackle, who lay limp and white as if dead.

"Time out!"

Neale flung himself against Fate. He fell on his knees beside the prostrate man, and took the bullet head into his arms. "Mike," he pleaded. "Not now! *We need you, Mike!*" Like a mother with a baby lying between life and death, he hung over that coarse, bruised face. All the love he had ever felt for any one seemed shallow compared to his yearning over this debauched, foul-mouthed, hairy boozer.

He could have kissed the ugly blue mug as the eyelids flickered, the color came back, and the giant rolled to his feet and lumbered back into the line.

The season rolled along. The luck seemed finally to have changed. They were almost through, with the best record in years. Then two days before the final game, Marshall the Captain broke a bone in his foot. The faces of the team were grave (all but that of Dodd, the sub thus let into the Varsity) as they gathered in the dressing-room before the game. The coach looked them over, casting about for the right note, and had the inspiration to lay by his usual impassioned, florid appeal.

"Nicholson will play center," he began, his plain, heavy words like iron; "Burke and Dodd guards; Mike and Larsen tackles; Greenway and Huggins, ends; Edwards quarter. Crittenden and Wallace halves; Bascomb full-back. Crittenden will act as Captain." He looked full at Crittenden, "It's the last time you'll wear the blue and white, Neale Crittenden!"

Neale throbbed like a great brazen bell, struck by the hammer.

Andrews turned his eyes on the team and made the rest of his speech short and hard.

"Boys, it's easy to lose and it's hard to win. Don't be fooled by the rooters saying you made a game fight. What *would* you do? Run away? Take it from me, there's a time in every game when either team can win. It's the team that has the sand, that's got the guts to put in an extra pound *right then*, that wins! I'm not telling you this Cornell team is easy. They're damned hard. But you've got weight enough, you've got speed enough, you know football enough. Now you go out there on the field, and show me you've got guts enough to win!"

With set jaws and grim, resolute hearts, the team, Neale at their head, trotted out on the gridiron. "It's the last time you'll wear the blue and white, Neale Crittenden!" He was clanging to that note.

They were lucky to get through the first half with a clean slate. Cornell came fast and hard, but time after time they held them and punted out of danger. The ten minutes' intermission seemed to last barely ten seconds and they were at it again, dead-locked, swaying from one forty-yard line to another. "Looks like a tie-game, barring a fluke," thought Neale, and then with an angry throb of alarm, "By God, I believe we're letting up! Here's where we put in that extra pound!"

"Six, n-int-e-e-n-f-o-r-t-y-f-i-v-e!" the quarter was droning. "No!" cried Neale, "Change that! Four-seven-two-eight!" It was his own straight buck, and he went into the line with a headlong hurdle. "I'll give the signals for a play or two, Bunny," he called to the quarter as they lined up again, "Seven-fourteen-thirty-three," he barked and took the ball on a cross buck, rolling and plunging for four yards, "Three-seven-nine-four." Again he started on the cross buck, bluffed at receiving the ball, hit the defense head down, yelling, "Help me!" and just as he fell saw Wallace skirting outside of tackle with the delayed pass, stiff-arming the end, shaking off the defensive quarter and on for a good ten yards. As he got up, Neale grabbed Edwards round the neck and whispered, with lips close to his ear, "We've got 'em started, Bunny! You run the plays now. Get the idea? Shoot 'em outside, till they open up, then plug Billy and Mike through the guards. Keep mixing 'em up, and speed, *speed!*"

Bunny got the idea. He snapped out his signals, and shot his offense like a boxer hammering a groggy opponent. With Mike back, he ran Neale and Wallace outside, inside, across, on the weak side: then suddenly dropped back to straight battering-ram football, and sent Mike at the apex of a straining, stamping tandem, straight through and over the defense to the fifteen yard line. The team was crazy with success—prancing like stallions. "Come on, boys!" Neale went a yard on a straight buck, dug his toe-cleats in as he fell, plunged and squirmed for another yard and a half. Wallace shot through a quick opening for three. With Larsen back and first down, Billy sheered off inside for a couple of yards, the Swede got another two straight ahead, Mike running from position made only a bare yard, but enough!

"First down, to the line to go!" said the referee. Neale heard his signal. "Damn the torpedoes, go ahead!" he thought. He flew at the line, bone and muscle transfigured by flaming will—a hard body dove against his knees—he staggered, leaned forward, churned his knees up and down a tenth of a second that seemed to drag for an hour, forward he staggered, strained forward, then fell. When the mass got off him he found he had got to the two-yard line. "Give it to me again!" he whispered, passing Bunny.

Larsen stuck his blonde head close up to theirs, "For Christ's sake, let *me* take it! It's my last game. I won't play no more after to-day!"

"Neither will I," thought Neale, but he nodded and they lined up with Larsen back.

"Look out for a funny one," cried the Cornell quarter, as the signals began. "Cap and quarter had a consultation—"

As the center's fingers contracted for the snap-back, Neale shot out of his tracks, and crashed into the defensive half. "Got him flat-footed," he thought, remembering as they both went down to swing his feet wide in the hope of getting the defensive quarter as well. He rolled clear at once, and looked back to see if he could be of any help. It wasn't necessary. Practically all the two teams were heaped in a human haystack, from the base of which emerged a grinning blonde face. Under the face were two huge hands some six inches over the line, clutching the ball, on which emotional Swedish eyes were weeping beatific tears.

Neale kicked a fairly easy goal. The trainer let him suck a little water from a sponge, whispering out of the corner of his motionless mouth, "Andy says minute and a half to play. Hold the ball and line up slow!"

But the team had tasted too much blood to stall. They went down on the kick-off like a pack of wolf-hounds. They smashed two plays for a loss, and after a punt, they punched the ball to mid-field before the whistle blew and the game was over.

Nicholson tossed the ball to Neale. "Here's your ball, Cap!"

Neale saw Mike Blahoslav kissing Bunny Edwards. He himself was hugging Gus Larsen, when the pandemonium from the grand-stand struck them. He was lifted on a platform of shoulders and carried to the gate surrounded by a cheering singing, crazy mob of rooters.

"That's so," he thought, "there *was* a crowd looking on!" He had not thought of the bleachers, or heard a cheer since the second half began.

They packed into the 'bus, Varsity inside, scrub on top.

The 'bus went off at a gallop. For a few blocks the rooters ran along, throwing cigarettes and cigars through the windows. Neale leaned back and luxuriously lit a cigar. He had been thinking about that first cigar for the last month. Oh, faugh! It tasted hot and dry and burned his mouth. No matter! He threw it away and leaned back in a golden reverie.

Would he ever again know such blessed unalloyed content? Probably not.

CHAPTER XXIX

The end of the football season was a door slammed in Neale's face forever. He had given four years of his life to football, flung them joyfully and proudly to feed the sacred flame. Now for the rest of his life, he was to be shut out from the temple of the only religion which had as yet been offered him. For the rest of his life—he was no post-mortem Atkins to hang enviously and piteously about watching other men doing the real thing.

Neale did not find this realization tragic, because it seemed to him that it was the common lot, and he had a poor opinion of those who cry out melodramatically against the common lot. The thing to do was to accept the common lot without undignified comment. So he did not give a Latin groan, nor cry out a Russian curse on Destiny, when he woke to the knowledge that the aim of his life had been taken away, that he had lived the last of his Homer. He set his jaw and began to try to adjust himself to the life without any goal which he was henceforth to share with the rest of the under-graduates.

But the days seemed very long and empty, none the less, in spite of his grim refusal to complain.

Into the middle of one of these empty days dropped a note from Miss Wentworth: "Dear Mr. Crittenden: Now that you can stoop to earthly affairs, won't you go Palisading with a party of us next Saturday? *Please say yes*. We take the 9 o'clock boat from 125th St."

The first thing he noted next Saturday was that Berkley was not of the party. He still thought of Miss Wentworth as "Berkley's girl," and he was annoyed at the pleasure he felt in finding her unpre-empted. The second thing was that she never did anything to block his manœuvering to break up group formation and string out the party two by two—

Neale and Miss Wentworth being the important two. But that might very well be only because she wanted to talk football. She had seen all the home games, knew the players' names, and for a girl, remembered an astonishing number of the more spectacular plays. The morning passed quickly. At noon they huddled around their camp-fire on the edge of the cliffs, ate broiled bacon sandwiches and drank coffee. Then they started back. On the last stretch of the road when the other girls began to tire, Miss Wentworth still swung along unflagging, and Neale saw to it that he was by her side. They ran out of athletic reminiscences. She ventured hesitatingly on books and her uncertain face cleared when Neale chimed in enthusiastically.

"She's surprised to find a football man who's got beyond Munsey's," thought Neale. No, he hadn't read "The Egoist," but "Richard Feverel" was *great!* And wasn't "Harry Richmond" a racy, crazy sort of tale? Did she know "The Second Mrs. Tanqueray?" He grinned internally with an amused cynicism, remembering for whom he had crammed up on this line. But he felt a difference. When she spoke about Henry James, he admitted frankly that he'd never heard of him. There was an honest quality about Miss Wentworth that made it seem underhanded and unnecessary to bluff.

Silent they stopped where the road pitches steeply down to the river. Speech seemed impertinent when the Hudson lay below, vast and mystic in the early-falling December dusk.

Then the rest of the party came up, shrieking out, "Oh, didn't he *r-a-m-ble!*" Neale saw Miss Wentworth home to the door of her apartment house, 114th Street, just off the Drive. He noted the number of the apartment. And found it again a good many times in the months to come.

There were other things which helped fill the void left by football. One of these, quaintly enough, was class-work! Many electives were open to Seniors. Neale had chosen rather at random; Philosophy, Ethics, Anthropology, English Lit. and Modern History. There was really nothing whatever to do now with his time except study, and to his surprise, those courses which had been but names printed in the catalogue, turned out very much alive once Neale began to put his mind on them.

Another interest was what he called with pretended scorn, "Gregg's gab-fests." It amused Neale to poke fun at Gregg's pretensions to being an intellectual, but he liked and admired his room-mate none the less. Their room came to be the favorite loafing-place of all the speculatively minded of their acquaintance, and Neale was surprised to find how many there were of them, who liked, as much as he and Gregg to discuss "things in general."

Every Friday evening, unless there was a dance or an athletic contest, from ten to two A.M. some of the Gang would haunt the Den, lolling in the shabby, easy chairs and on the beds, smoking pipes, drinking beer and spouting out all they knew of modern thought. In theory the meeting was open to all shades of opinion, but the boys were without exception filled with the painless misanthropy of youth, afraid of nothing except appearing priggish (by which they, like many other people, meant reasonably clean-mouthed), carelessly ready to agree to any sweeping indictment of mankind; this, although their youth and gloriously perfect digestions made them serenely confident that their own little rafts would eventually drift to a smiling harbor in the country of easy money and orange blossoms.

They took their pessimism, as they did their beer, in great undiscriminating gulps, which affected their healthy organisms no more than the blowing of the wind. With it they drugged their bodies, swigging away heartily at both narcotics till at last they dropped to insensibility, only to crawl out from under the table the next morning, their young eyes invincibly bright, their breaths sweet, their stomachs indomitably craving good food, finding the honest winter sunshine flooding in at the windows, in no way incompatible with the flat, stale beer and stinking cigar-butts left from the night before. An adult might have drunk of the bitter waters of disillusion with more caution, have carried his load of pessimism with less outward unsteadiness, but later on, what dead pussy-cat fur upon his tongue, what a sick loathing for wholesome fare! But these gilded youth swilled down each his kegful of Nietzsche and turned with equal zest to handfuls of gum-drops like "The Cardinal's Snuff-box."

As for Neale, he joined in the discussions as briskly as any, but with reservations. He never quoted or mentioned Emerson, although he thought of him a great deal. He never discussed anything or any one he really cared a snap about. In occasional moments of insight (which came to him because he talked less babblingly than the others and listened more) he suspected that all the other slashing young radicals and iconoclasts might also be holding back secret articles of faith from defilement.

One element in his life that he never mentioned to the Gang, was the amount of time he was spending with Miss Wentworth. He had called on her one evening shortly after the Palisading trip, alleging as an excuse that he owed her a dinner call for the picnic lunch she had provided. He had called several times since then, with no excuse at all. He had been one of her box-party at "Candida" and somewhat over-paid his debt by taking her to "Out of the Wilderness," and Barnum and Bailey's circus. He had dined several times at the Wentworth apartment, discussed the Republican Party with her quiet, widowed, impressive father, and had learned to leave him in peace with his Evening Post after dinner. Miss Wentworth kept up on her college athletics, and Neale took her to the Basket-ball games, the Dual Gym. Meet with Yale, the Hockey games, the Indoor Track Meet at the 69th Regiment Armory. She had a great passion for walking, so they walked in the afternoons along Riverside Drive, in Central Park, along the driveway by Fort Washington Point. By the time the ice had broken up in the spring, Neale had discovered two things: first that Miss Wentworth was not like any other girl he knew, she didn't flirt, wasn't piqued if he was silent, he felt no impulse to bluff or play-act before her, she was more like another fellow than a girl—only a very much more attractive fellow than he had ever met. The secondary discovery, which alarmed as well as thrilled him, was that if three days passed without his seeing her, he found himself missing her very much indeed.

Meanwhiles the mid-years were long past, spring almost at hand, the tongues of the Gang, after all the winter's practice, wagged more freely than ever. The first Friday in April, Elliott came in, pulling from the deep pocket of his rain-coat, a bag of limes and a bottle of gin, and announcing something better than beer for that evening.

"It's up to you, kid," Neale ordered Robertson, the Soph., whom they tolerated because his self-important airs amused them, "you're the youngest. Beat it to the drug-store and bring back as many siphons as you can carry."

After the rickeys were mixed, the cheese cut, the cracker-tin set out, the tongues began to clack, and the resounding generalities to unroll themselves before the fresh gaze of those young eyes, dazzled by the brilliance of their explorations into the nature of things. Elliott was saying wisely, "Laws? Everybody knows that laws are a conspiracy among mediocrities to keep the strong from taking too much property." He let this soak in and went on, "And moral systems are similar conspiracies to prevent monopolies of less tangible things." Elliott delighted in polysyllables, which he did not as yet always handle with entire accuracy. Gregg, who did not like either polysyllables or Elliott, commented on this, "What book did you get that out of? And what's the moral?"

"The moral is, that morals are a sham. Man obeys the law only because he is afraid of the herd-majority. But a free spirit doesn't mind the criticism of mediocrities, he glories in it."

"So he feels all right, does he?" asked Gregg, "when he clears out to Canada with the contents of the safe, or his best friend's wife. As a matter of fact, he feels like a dirty dog."

"Oh, but that is just force of habit, race-superstition, cowardice before convention."

"Shucks! You fellows are on the wrong track," broke in Brown, "all man really cares about is his three meals a day. That's what makes the world go round! When the caveman's wife was stolen, he went on the warpath for the same reason a cow-boy lynches a horse-thief, because he can't afford to lose valuable property. Now the modern woman is no longer an asset, but a liability. . . ." He paused, so filled with admiration for his own metaphor struck out in the heat of discussion, that he could not go on. Great Cæsar's ghost! That wasn't so bad! He'd have to remember that in the next theme he wrote.

Gregg was disposing of him sardonically, "Oh, yes, we know Brown's soaking up the economic interpretation of history like a sponge. Have a mind of your own, Brown. You don't have to believe all your Prof. tells you. What do *you* think, Crit?"

Neale sailed cautiously a little nearer his real thought than he usually ventured, with the casual comment, "Well, there do seem to be some things a man can't bring himself to do, no matter how much he wants to. I wonder if maybe it isn't just inherited race-experience warning us off from what's bad for man in the long run."

Brown came back for revenge, "Oh, yes, we know the rest, what's that but the anthropology course? Have a mind of your own!"

"As a matter of fact, pleasure's the only motive," Elliott laid down the final dictum. "Every time you do something you do it because you'd rather. If you didn't, you'd do something else."

Some one brought out another profundity deep enough to match this, affirming, "Oh, of course, everything's relative!"

And this was still so new an aphorism to them, that they let it alone, the party breaking up over a last round of weak rickeys squeezed from the bottle.

Neale waited till he saw Gregg deep in "Venice Preserved"; then he opened a small volume, and shielding it from any random glances of his room-mate, began reading, "The Last Ride Together."

CHAPTER XXX

THE two had passed a long evening together. Miss Wentworth's father was attending the annual banquet of the American Philological Association and the young people, left to themselves, had dined downtown at the Lafayette. It was their first meal alone together, all the more intimately alone because of the shifting crowd of strangers about them. How natural it had seemed to look across the table and see Miss Wentworth there! As natural as though he could look forward to an endless succession of days together; yet so tinged with romance that even the banalities of their small-talk had vibrated with emotional significance.

When dessert and coffee and Neale's cigar could be dragged out no longer, they had strolled side by side up deserted lower Fifth Avenue.

Now they were standing silent, watching the periodical rise and fall of the gushing fountain in Madison Square. At first the pool lay quiet; then the surface was troubled; then swelling, mounting, the jet of water burst through and shot upward, to sink again, leaving only waning ripples behind it. It made the young man think of a great many things, which were none the less moving and poignant to him because they have moved every thoughtful human being since the beginning of time. As he looked gravely down on the pulsations of the gleaming water, it symbolized to him the rhythm of the universe; the recurrent rhythm of the generations—human life with its one little spurt of youth and glory sinking so soon, so fatally soon to the sterile, routine movements of age. But when he spoke, his voice was as casually off-hand as ever.

"There's a fountain in Rome," he said, "where, if you throw a coin in, you're sure to come back to it. I wonder if it would work with this one!"

"I didn't know you'd ever been in Rome."

"I haven't. I got that out of Crawford's 'Ave Roma.'"

"What makes you so anxious to come back to Madison Square?"

"I'm not. I'd rather find a fountain that would send me round the world. But there isn't much chance of that, and I thought if you'd throw one in too—both at the same time, you know—it might fix things so that we'd come back together."

She gave him a steady, thoughtful look, took a penny out of her purse. "All ready, go!"

The two coins splashed into the pool. "I hope there will be as lovely a moon then as there is to-night," she said.

"I wonder," thought Neale, "just how much she meant by that."

When Neale got back to his room, the Gang was not there in full force, only Robertson, the knowing little Soph. and Gregg, drinking beer and smoking their pipes. Neale kept back a grimace of distaste at seeing Robertson, his broad boy's face set in its usual expression of solemn, self-conscious wiseness in the ways of the world. The rest of the Gang found Robertson comic and enjoyed having him around to laugh at, as many people enjoy a visit to the monkey-house in a zoo, and see nothing but the comic in the humanness of simian antics. But he disquieted Neale to his very soul, as another set of people are disquieted and troubled by a visit to the monkey-house and see nothing to laugh at in simian antics.

One evening of little Robertson and his loud-proclaimed disillusion with the world and the human race moved the rest of the Gang to delighted howls of laughter for days afterwards; but though Neale laughed with the rest (nobody could help laughing at Robertson, he was such an owl!), it rather took the shine off Schopenhauer and pessimism, and that was a real privation for a Senior.

As he came in, Gregg was quoting,

> "But sweet as the rind was, the core is;
>   We are fain of thee still, we are fain,
> O sanguine and subtle Dolores,
>   Our Lady of Pain."

Neale lifted a stein from its hook, poured it full from the pitcher and took a long drink.

"Go ahead, Johnny," he said, "sounds lovely—like any other fairy tale."

"Fairy tale!" cried little Robertson. "Fairy tale, you blue-nosed Puritan! That's all *you* know. You've been neglecting your opportunities."

Neale answered sharply, "Puritan be damned! I'm no Earl Hall Christer! I know Swinburne enough sight better than you do."

At the sight of Robertson's round eyes goggling at him under his bulging forehead, he was amused at his own annoyance, and taking another drink went on indifferently, "All I'm saying is, maybe prostitution was a dainty art in Ancient Greece, or maybe Swinburne knew some high class practitioners, but here in New York, on the Heights—maybe the thought of Becky Blumenthal without her shimmy gives you an æsthetic thrill, but if it does, you've got a stronger stomach than I have. Take it from me, kid, if you want any poetry out of all that, you'd better stick to Swinburne."

"Yep," agreed Gregg, "I'm with you, Crit. I don't like the professionals. They're a mercenary crew. They're 'out for the stuff, and if you ain't got enough, biff, kerslap, out you go!' Why doesn't some gay little lady just looking for a good time give us the high sign, the way they do in books. Does she? She does not!"

The subject of the discussion pleased Robertson immensely, of course, but he was outraged at the middle-class narrowness of his elders' views. He got up languidly, put on his cap, and standing by the door, pronounced judgment.

"All women," said little Robertson the Soph., "belong to the Trade, more or less, in one way or the other. I won't go so far as to say that every woman has her price, only *I* have never met one who hadn't!"

Neale and Gregg gazed at him spell-bound. He turned away, calling airily over his shoulder, "Well, ta! ta! A May night's no time for debates. I'm going out for a stroll on Morningside to prove my theory."

After they had had their laugh out, Gregg said, "Doesn't he think he's a heller?"

"Wants *us* to think so," grunted Neale. "Where's all the Gang?"

"Oh, some of them are boning for the exams. and some are chasing chippies, and Billy Peters is off on some of his usual footless fussing. Been calling on a girl all winter and I don't believe he's even had his arm around her yet, except at dances. The kid!"

Neale filled his pipe, held the match over it and puffed gently until the tobacco glowed an even red all over the top. What would Gregg say, he wondered, to his attitude towards Miss Wentworth? And Gregg himself! Neale knew perfectly well Gregg wrote long, weekly letters to that innocent-faced up-state girl whose picture stood on the dresser over there. He also knew perfectly well that Gregg was a regular Sir Galahad when it came to her. Oh, Lord! How like that blatant idiot Robertson, they were! It made him feel like a fool kid himself, the bluff they always kept up. Weren't they getting grown-up enough to drop this inside-out hypocrisy?

He kept all this to himself, smoking in thoughtful silence. When the pipe was finished, he yawned and stretched, "Guess I'll turn in. Going to read all night?"

Gregg looked up from his book, "I'll put the shade over the light so you can get to sleep. I want to finish this Philosophy A stuff, Plato's Republic. Have you read the last book yet? It's great dope!"

The next day Neale and Miss Wentworth were sitting by their little gipsy fire in a nook among the Palisades, over-looking the river. Luncheon had long been finished, the dishes packed away, and they continued to sit still, Miss Wentworth looking at the view, Neale looking at her and turning over in his mind the problem, "How can a man with no money, and no prospects of ever earning any, ask a girl to marry him? He can't. But suppose there's a chance that the girl . . . well, no matter what she may be thinking, wouldn't it be the decent thing to let her know how he feels? Of course he ought to! What's the answer, then? There isn't any answer."

"A penny for your thoughts, Mr. Crittenden."

"I was wondering," Neale lied glibly, "whether you didn't know me well enough to stop calling me Mr. Crittenden."

She met his eyes squarely, "All right, I'll call you Neale, if you'll call me Martha. I hate formality between friends."

He weighed her intonation carefully. Had she accented the word, "friends"? Did she mean it as a warning? Well, whether or not she meant it, that was the only line he could decently take.

As they started on the five-mile walk back to the ferry, their talk dodged personalities. They talked about the trees and rocks and wild-flowers and books and music—the music to which Martha had been introducing Neale that winter, the music which, little by little, was beginning to speak to his heart more powerfully, more directly even than poetry. Then, gradually, with a deep sense of tranquil comradeship, they stopped dodging personalities, no longer felt any need to talk, strode forward side by side, silent, each sure of the other. Neale felt quiet and happy and at the same time miserable and uncertain. Could he find words to tell her? Must he in honor wait till he had a place in the world to offer?

At the end of their long march, they came to the edge of the cliff and stood for a long time staring down at the great river, shimmering and iridescent far below them in the spring haze. Only a few miles further south along these cliffs and only a few years ago, the little Neale had sat alone and swung his feet and dreamed. How simple life had been for him then!

Still without a word, they went down the zig-zag path to the ferry landing, and stood waiting for the boat. It was very still, except for the water splashing on the stony beach. Without thought, without planning it, the fullness of Neale's heart unsealed his lips. He began to speak in a low tone, his voice rough and uneven with emotion.

> "Listen! you hear the grating roar
> Of pebbles which the waves draw back, and fling,
> At their return, up the high strand."

He was aware that the girl was very still, listening with bent head.

> "Sophocles long ago
> Heard it on the Ægean, and it brought
> Into his mind the turbid ebb and flow
> Of human misery; we . . ."

his breath failed him and he was silent. Over there beyond that wide expanse of lapping water lay the world with its houses and railways, its business, its spider-web of human relations. Here in the shadow they were alone together.

> "But now I only hear
> Its melancholy, long withdrawing roar,
> Retreating to the breath
> Of the night-wind, down the vast edges drear
> And naked shingles of the world."

He stopped. Now that he had come to what he wished to say, he dared not.

"Don't you know the rest?" asked the girl softly.

"Yes," said Neale huskily, "I know it."

She waited for him to go on, and when he did not, she said, "Well, no matter. I know it too."

She stood beside him in the blue twilight, her fair head raised, her eyes looking far over the water. Neale was certain that she too was silently repeating,

> "Ah, love, let us be true
> To one another! for the world, which seems
> To lie before us like a land of dreams,
> So various, so beautiful, so new,
> Hath really neither joy, nor love, nor light,
> Nor certitude, nor peace, nor help for pain;
> And we are here as on a darkling plain
> Swept with confused alarms of struggle and flight,
> Where ignorant armies clash by night."

The great day was over. The Yew Tree had been planted and orated over. The scared Valedictorian had stumbled through as much of his speech as he could remember. Neale, with a hundred other Seniors had stood up and received the degree of Bachelor of Arts, which the President, "By-the-authority-in-him-vested" scattered broadcast over them. Neale was through with college. College was through with Neale.

Father and Mother were there, come up specially from the other side of the Equator, though Father tried to pretend that business had brought him north. They strolled about the campus, went down-town and had luncheon together, all three outwardly calm in the traditional Crittenden manner, in spite of the emotion boiling under the surface of their little family party.

What boiled hardest under Neale's surface was a great haste to find his place in the business-world, to begin to make money, to have something to offer Martha. Before he had met Martha he had had dreams of asking to go back to college for a Master's Degree—in anything, just to go on with the studies he had found so interesting, to play football again, to sit, care-free, smoking his pipe and talking philosophy with Gregg. But even in his dreams he had felt that all that was only a little boy's scheme to dodge real life. And now he felt no sympathy with dreams. He wanted to get out and tackle real life with all his strength. He smarted under the feeling that he had no right to speak to Martha.

So when Mother went up to her room to rest from the strain of throttling her feelings down to her men-folks' standard of outward calm, and he and Father went into the lobby to light cigars, he said at once, "Father, I want to start in to-morrow to hustle for a job."

Father looked pleased. It even occurred to Neale that Father looked relieved. "Anything special in sight?" he asked.

"No, I'm just going to knock at all the office doors till I find one where they don't throw me out."

Father puffed awhile. "Naturally I'd like to have you with me, but I couldn't offer you anything but a clerkship. And I'm convinced that the opportunities to rise are greater here at the center of things. Now I've worked a good many years for the firm and I believe Gates would give you a job on my recommendation. Want to try it?"

"I'll try anything that'll give me a start."

"To-morrow too soon, if I can make an appointment for you?"

"I'll be there."

"Of course you won't draw much of a salary at first; I think I'd better keep your allowance going for a few months at least."

"Nothing doing, Dad!   It's white of you to suggest it, but I'm on my own now.   If you get me a job, that's more than plenty.   If I can't live on my wages, I'll black boots after office hours."

CHAPTER XXXI

May, 1905.

NEALE had never, so to speak, received any letters in his
life until his parents had gone off to Rio; but since then
letters had filled what personal life he had found time for.
It was surprising how much more freely people spoke out in
the written word than in talk. The weekly bulletins from
Mother, and Father's occasional letters gave him more of a
feeling of intercourse with his parents than he had ever known
when they lived under the same roof. And he was sure that
in no other way could he ever have come to look into the
clear integrity of Martha's heart as he had in the letters which
had come to him from all over Europe, where she had been
wandering with her father during his sabbatical year of freedom.

In the April after his graduation, Martha had written from
England that she was hurrying the end of her travel-year so
that she could be home to take a Palisading walk with him
on May sixteenth. May sixteenth was the date of their last
walk together on the Palisades, the walk which had ended
in the sweet, wordless understanding between them. Her frank
recognition of it as an anniversary to be remembered showed
how far along the year of separation and frequent letter-
writing had brought them.

He was thinking of Martha, the wonderful Martha her
letters had revealed, as he waited for her on May sixteenth
in the parlor of her father's apartment. He found it almost
impossible to listen to what Professor Wentworth was saying,
and tried in vain to answer the traveler's questions about
Columbia news. The Wentworths had been in Norway and
Spain and England and Greece, while Neale had not been out
of New York; but he knew no more of Columbia than they.

With the bestowal of the impersonally broadcasted degree, Columbia had dropped him as unceremoniously as it had failed to welcome him when he arrived—"and quite right, too," thought Neale. He detested the florid sentimentality of some other universities, the maudlin old grads singing of bright college years!

So he knew nothing whatever about Columbia to report. Besides, Professor Wentworth naturally enough was inquiring about what had been happening to the faculty during his absence, and Neale had never had the faintest guess that any of his professors led a three-dimensional life. But most of all, his year in business, in an office surrounded by men who had never been near a university had set him immeasurably far from the academic world. In an attempt to satisfy Martha's father he now made a great effort to look back at college life, but he was looking back at it from the wrong end of a telescope. It was inconceivably small and far away. He had not realized till now how much the year in business had changed him, how rapidly he had left behind him the horizon of his college years. Well, that was as it should be—to live hard in the present without brooding over the past or dreaming of the future. . . .

Then Martha came in, and he forgot college altogether, forgot Professor Wentworth, he even forgot the business world as he looked half-shyly, half-confidently into her blue eyes— the same, but, oh, how startlingly more real and alive than the dream-like memory picture he had been treasuring all those months.

They crossed the ferry, they stepped off briskly up the zig-zag path, then when the last house was hidden behind the rocks, they stopped. Martha lifted her smiling face to his. As their lips touched, Neale was thrilled by a wave of emotion,—exaltation rather than passion. "How dear, how sweet, how incredibly pure and good she was!"

The moment passed; as they walked on from time to time their eyes met frankly. "Oh, but I'm glad to be walking with you again, Neale," said Martha at last. "It's as if we hadn't been separated at all—yes, you do look older—ever so much older—and yet about the same."

"Oh, I'm just the same, Martha," he told her briefly with a weighty, significant accent.

It was the only reference made by either of them to what was in their hearts. But it was enough for both of them. What a *fine* girl, Neale thought, not to want, any more than he did, a lot of goings-on to express feelings! As they tramped along energetically, Martha was talking of what the year had been to her. She spoke of picture-galleries and Gothic cathedrals, and palaces and ruins; but what she said, and what Neale heard was that nowhere had she met any one whom she liked better than Neale. Neale felt himself relax in an ineffable content, and knew by contrast how anxious he had been.

Then they made their fire and cooked their bacon, ate their lunch, and Neale lighted his pipe peaceably and happily. They sat in a sunny, sheltered corner of the rocks, overlooking the river, their hearts sheltered and sunny, and in the intervals of their talk they looked at each other in quiet satisfaction. How good it was to be together again!

Neale's report of his year took longer than Martha's because they both felt that hers had the irrelevant passing interest of a vacation-time, while his was to have enduring importance for them both. It was, he told her, the same phase in the business world as a freshman year in college, and although he had not made a brilliant outer success as yet, he felt, on the whole, satisfied with the way he had got his feet under him and had begun to know his way about. He gave a droll little color to the account of his job in the office, the one they had evidently given him as an experiment, to be tried out in cheap materials first—he representing the cheap materials! The business had grown and grown; at first, a generation ago, the product of Mr. Gates' business ability; later on, too large even for what the "old man" could keep under his remarkably capacious hat. Then twenty years ago, other people—Mr. Gates' son, Neale's father, the clever and forceful manager of the Chicago office, a branch-manager in Ottawa,—had begun to keep it under their respective hats. Important matters were decided orally in a personal talk between the different department heads, who, having the required information at their finger-tips, needed no figuring or statistics to help their decisions. This had lasted all the while Neale was growing up, but by the time he graduated, some of the younger members of the organization had begun to feel that perhaps the stock of information vital to the conduct of the business ought to be copied off from the several brains which possessed it, and set down in some more accessible form. Mr. Belden, the Ottawa manager, knew all about the lumber market in eastern Canada, the average quality of mill-run spruce in each section and what the chances were of getting it on time for a given order; Mr. Gilman, at the Chicago office, could snap back over the long-distance wire any question you cared to put about Wisconsin or Northern Michigan lumber regions. But they were neither of them so young as they had been nor was Mr. Crittenden, whose specialty was the selling-end of Eastern and foreign lumber markets. Even the "young Mr. Gates" was now over fifty. They were all mortal, the health of the "young Mr. Gates" was far from good; and furthermore the business kept steadily growing so that it was very inconvenient to have to wait to consult men widely separated.

"Do you get it?" asked Neale, lying in the sun on the Palisades, smoking, looking up at a sweet, well-beloved face and delighting in her eager, intelligent interest in his story. "Do you get it? Half the bunch thought a card-catalogue the foolishest, new-fangled waste of time; half of them didn't know whether it was or not; all of them wanted some sort of tabulation of inside information, and none of them knew how to go about it any more than if they'd been asked to bake a batch of bread or write a theme on the Crusades. The half that wanted to stick to the old ways and keep it all safe under different people's hats were dead set against spending any money on any fool system of collecting and classifying information. And the other half weren't by any means so sure of their ground that they wanted to spend a lot of cash to get an expert. And, anyhow, where could you find an expert? If you let one of those 'business-system' people inside the office he'd be trying to run the whole works. Maybe the idea was all right, but you couldn't get it executed. Well, while the whole proposition was up in the air, and everybody chewing the rag about it, somebody knocks at the door, and who is it? Why, Crittenden's son, just out of college, wanting a job. All nonsense, college, and yet what *would* it have taught a boy if not how to straighten out and classify information? Anyhow you could get him for next to nothing: boys out of college never expect to be paid anything to speak of, and a good reason why; because they aren't worth anything. Give him a year's try at it! Crittenden's son ought to have a *little* natural sense. It won't cost much; he can't do any harm; maybe he might work out a system that would be useful.

"So they offered the job at slightly more than office-boy wages to the college graduate. And what did *he* think about it? How had he been trained for such work? *You* know, Martha, how he'd been trained. What he knew about orderly arrangement of information was about what would go on the head of a pin! He'd been learning a *few* scattered items about English Literature and Greek Philosophy, and the latest inaccuracy about atoms; and a whole lot about how to get a football over a given line under given conditions. But incidentally and on the side, he'd had a pretty thorough course in poker, and a poker-face was the necessary equipment for *that* situation!"

He and Martha laughed, a light-hearted young laugh, that did them good and made them feel closer than ever to each other in the conspiracy of two against the world.

The rest of the year had been, Neale told her, a slow, dogged struggle to find out what after all it was nobody's business to tell him; to invent a system of recording what he found out that would not only be fool-proof but stenographer-proof; to collect exact statistics as to the cost of production and transportation; and to bring together items of account-keeping that had never before had even a speaking acquaintance with each other.

"I've traced a plank from the tree to tide-water, inch by inch, my note-book in my hand, setting down every sixteenth of a cent per board foot that it cost till we sold it to the retail dealer, watching it as if it were the prince-royal of a reigning house and I the secret-service man set to keep track of him! I've covered reams of paper figuring out the cost of the office-work of getting that plank sold—extra office-work, you know, not ordinary overhead;—and, by heck, I don't see how they've ever managed to run their old business a minute, the haphazard way they've been going at it! Nobody knew anything, not *all* of anything! I seem to have been marking time, but just you wait till I get out of the office and into the real game. I know more about some things than any of the buyers, even the old-timers."

"Well, there must be a big profit in business or they wouldn't be able to conduct it that loose way," said Martha.

"Oh, the profits are big, all right," Neale concurred. "Old man Gates has more cash than he knows what to do with. And not one of his grandchildren amounts to a whoop. When his son, the one who's our General Manager now, retires, there won't be a Gates left in the Gates Lumber Company."

"They won't mind," said Martha.

"You bet your life they won't *mind*," said Neale. "Far from it! Most likely they've hardly heard the name of it. They're all living in Europe now, buying villas and things out of the money the Company makes. Our Mr. Gates never sees any of his family except when he takes a vacation and goes to Florence or England. All *they* want out of the lumber business is a fat wad of easy money."

"That's not right," said Martha suddenly. "That's not right."

"It's not right if getting something for nothing is wrong," Neale agreed casually. "But what are you going to do about it? There you are. That's the way things go."

Martha made no answer. There was a little silence. Then she said: "All that account-keeping, that detail work—it doesn't seem so terribly interesting to me, Neale. Haven't you found it awfully dull sometimes?"

Neale rolled over and sat up with an effect of entering again into active and energetic life. "Well, I might have," he said finally. "But you know, Martha, that I have a special reason for wanting to get on quick in business, and I've been mighty glad enough to grab hold of any end that was handy." He smiled at her confidently. "All a fellow needs in the business world is a crack in the wall to get his toes into for a start. I've got my crack. Now you just watch me climb!"

It was perfectly understood between them what he was climbing to reach.

CHAPTER XXXII

FATHER had written from Caracas that Mother was taking the next boat back to New York because she needed a lot of dental work done and hadn't any confidence in Venezuelan dentists, but when Neale met Mother at the dock she told him at once, laughingly, that the dental work was only an excuse, and that she had come to have a visit with her son. She had added with a whimsical defiance that, such being the fact, she had no intention of putting up the usual Crittenden bluff of something different.

"I'm not a Crittenden," she told Neale gaily in the cab on the way to the hotel, "though I married into the family so young! And now that I've worn a mantilla, with a rose in my hair, I'm not going to try any longer to pretend that I am."

Neale looked at her, admiring her now quite distinguished appearance, but feeling a little alarm at her tone. She sounded almost disturbingly electric.

"I've come up to have a real New York spree with my big son and his nice girl, now that he has condescended to let us know he has a nice girl," she told him, her smiling eyes at once tender and a little mocking. "You can afford it, can't you, since your last raise?"

"Oh, I can afford anything in reason."

"Your father says they tell him you're getting on splendidly."

"They never let on as much to me," said Neale drily, "though they are treating me very white as to pay."

They were at the hotel door now, where Mother made arrangements for a stay of a month.

"Dental work takes so long," she told Neale gravely in the elevator, making him laugh outright. She looked very well pleased at this, and after they were inside her room, stood up on tiptoes and gave him another kiss.

He had never entirely recovered from his father's chance remark that Mother had been only twenty when she married. She must have been about as old as he was now when he first began to remember her. Just a girl,—and she had seemed older to him then than now.

He told her this as he unstrapped her valise. "You seem younger to me everytime I see you—lots younger now than when I was six or seven years old."

She laughed out. "I was a child myself when you were six or seven." She turned grave for a moment. "If I had you to bring up, now that I am a really grown person with a personality of my own and some experience of the world, I'd do it very differently. I'd make a better job of it."

"You made a good enough job," he protested mildly. "How can you look at me and think you could have done any better?"

She stopped her unpacking to laugh. "It just spoils a person for other forms of joking to live with one of you dry Crittendens. Other people's humor seems so flamboyant. I *like* the Crittendens," she pronounced judicially, "though I did waste about twenty years of my young life trying to make myself into one. I'm glad you're one. But if you try to make Martha into one—"

"Martha's one already," he told her triumphantly. "We're exactly alike—the way we think and do things. That's why we get on so well together." At this Neale's mother looked at him so hard that he felt a little annoyed, and turned the talk back to its earlier channel.

"How else would you have brought me up, I'd like to know?"

"I'd have taken dynamite to you," she informed him briskly.

"Dynamite?"

"Oh, you don't understand. And I daresay it would have been too early anyhow. You'll probably get your share of dynamite when your turn comes." She changed the subject: "How's business? Seriously!"

Seriously he told her of the results of his promotion six months before from the "intelligence bureau," as he called it, to the real business of life, to buying and selling. "The only real money is in that," he told her, warming as he spoke. "All those other jobs, office jobs, don't lead you anywhere. Buying and selling, especially selling, that's where you get ahead. I'm earning twice what I did, and by this time next year I'll be doing twice what I'm doing now. I may soon be able to do a little on the side, on my own hook, pick up something good and dispose of it well. Grandfather is sure I can. He may have some tips for me later on. Grandfather is a wise old scout."

Mother laid some underwear away in a drawer. As she shut it, she asked casually: "Do you read any Emerson nowadays, Neale?"

How in the world did Mother know he had ever read Emerson? "No, I don't," he said.

She noted the shortness of his tone with raised eyebrows, and began to hang up her dresses in the closet.

Neale looked at her back with some uneasiness. He felt his privacy threatened, and, stiffening, put up the bars. And apparently Mother sensed the change, for she at once dropped her intimate tone and began making gay plans for "having some fun" during her stay, plans in which dental engagements played a conspicuously small part. It turned out to be a very light-hearted month, Mother's month in the dentist's chair. Neale and Martha were quite shaken up out of the quiet, jog-trot routine of their peaceful days and long evenings of serious reading together. Mother took them to the theater and to dinner at out-of-the-way restaurants of which, like most sober resident New Yorkers, they had never heard the names. In the daytime, she and Martha, of whom she had grown very fond, went around a good deal together, looking at the innumerable expensive and occasionally beautiful objects on view in the shops of a big city; or visiting museums, or going to matinées. They heard a good deal of music, all three of them. Mother had chosen a hotel near Carnegie Hall, so that frequently, when they had nothing else to do, they strolled up on foot and listened to whatever was being played. They had an occasional dinner with Professor Wentworth and Martha in their apartment on 122d Street, and Mother went off by herself to look up the old friends of Union Hill days, the few who were not scattered.

Once in a while Neale talked over his business prospects with Mother when she asked him about them and he couldn't get out of it, and they agreed that he would be able to marry in another year. And having agreed in this opinion, Mother was apt to fall very silent for a time. But this suited Neale, who found intimate personal talk disconcerting. It always made him uneasy when another human being rattled the handle of the door to his inner secret garden. One of the things he most loved in Martha was that she took so much for granted without talking about it. They understood each other instinctively, he felt, without need of explanation. He suspected that Martha had her own inner garden, and prided himself on respecting her right to it. *He* was no one to go rattling handles of doors that were none of his. He found Martha especially restful and satisfying after one of these talks with Mother, lightly and passingly as Mother glanced over those sensitive places. He constantly felt that Mother was trying to open a door he wished to keep shut, that she was trying to say something that he had no desire to hear. He and Martha were all right. What business had Mother to look at them that way?

She did nothing after all, beyond looking, and went away at the end of her month, having committed no greater crime than to whisper brokenly to Neale as she kissed him good-by, "Neale, it's not enough to— Neale, you must *love* Martha. You must *love* her—not just—"

At this Neale had quickly assumed the cold look of distaste which she knew so well, and she had ventured no further.

After her departure, Neale fell with relief back into his old routine of quiet, comfortable life-in-common with Martha, with none of the prickling electric uncertainties he had felt in Mother. Odd how much better he knew Martha than he did Mother; how sure he was beforehand of what Martha would think and say, whereas he had been uncomfortably unsure of Mother. He felt he knew Martha as he knew himself, through and through.

This conviction was a great satisfaction to him. He often thought of it with pride, and with a secret pity and scorn for people who found life and human relationships so complicated and mysterious. That sort of thing was just a novel-writer's rubber-stamp convention. What was there so darned mysterious about your own nature, about a sensible woman's nature? Nothing. If you were a sane, normal man, you found your mate in the world just as normally as you found your place in the business world. With a healthy, honest, fine girl like Martha, there would be none of those double-and-twisted emotional complications you read about in books.

He was away from New York a good deal at this time, taking, as one of the younger salesmen, the more difficult and less remunerative territories, and when he came back to the city it was like coming home, to ring the bell of the Went-worths' apartment and have Martha herself come to open the door for him, her eyes as clear and honest as sunlit water.

They always had a good deal to tell each other after these separations. Martha about her work at the Speyer School, where she had begun to help a little in visiting the families of the poorer children, Neale about his business, which he was finding more and more absorbingly interesting, for which he was feeling much of the zestful passion he had felt for foot-ball. He talked a great deal to Martha about the resemblance of football to business. One of the many things he loved about Martha was her knowledge of football. Of course, strictly speaking, like all other outsiders, she knew nothing whatever about football; but she knew as much as any spectator could, and, brought up from birth as she had been in one or another college community, she had a second-nature familiarity with the psychology of the game, with the fierce, driving concentration, the eager, devout willingness to devote every throb of your pulse, every thought in your brain to

winning the game; and it seemed perfectly natural to her,
as it did to Neale, to step into another world where all the
mature energies were focussed in the same way.

"It's just like football," Neale often told her, his eyes gleaming. "Having played football gives you as great an advantage
as though you were in training and the other fellows soft.
I often feel as if I ought to go and look up old
Atkins and thank him. He was teaching me enough
sight more than how to play backfield defense! That
everlasting pounding of his on the idea of knowing where
the ball is before you go for it— Gee whiz, you'd never
guess how many fool mistakes that's kept me from. I see
the other fellows wasting money on buying drinks and tickets
to shows and champagne suppers for hard-shelled old buyers
who haven't an interest left in life beyond screwing the price
down an eighth of a cent—wallowing in any-old-how just to
get going,—the way I used to; and I think of old Atkins,
lie low, keep my mouth shut, and size up the enemy's formation till I see their weak place, *and then!*" The brilliance
of his eye, the grimness of his set jaw, the impact of one
great fist in the palm of the other hand showed what happened
then. He went on. "One game's just like the other,
and the thing that wins in both is *wanting to win* more than
the other fellow does." He turned serious, almost exalted,
and said: "Sometimes I used almost to think it was the
way religion must be for people who believe in it—it puts
you in touch with some big force—I've felt it in football—I
guess everybody always feels it who really gets going enough
to *care* about anything with all that is in him—if you give
every bit of yourself—don't keep anything back—want to
win more than anything else in the world—why, all of a sudden
some outside source of power that's hundreds of volts higher
than normal begins to flow through you—and you *move* things.
It's wonderful, but you can't have it cheap. It costs you all
you've got."

One evening as they sat thus, Martha perched on the arm
of Neale's chair, the quiet air about them crackling and
tingling with the high-tension current, Martha caught and

grasped a comparison which had long been floating elusive in the back of her mind. She jumped up and ran to the piano. "Listen, it's like this," she told him, and played with one hand, clear and defiant and compelling, the call of the young Siegfried. "That was how it was in football. And now—" She sat down before the piano, and, stretching out both hands over the keys, she filled the room with the rich clamor of the same theme reinforced by all the sumptuous strength of harmony.

Neale sprang to his feet. "You know what Siegfried went through fire to find," he cried, stooping to put his lips on Martha's cheek. "All he wanted was to get to Brunhilda. And that's all I want, my Brunhilda! All I want in the world!"

CHAPTER XXXIII

He had called her "his Brunhilda" with honest sincerity; with all his heart he thought he meant it. Of *course* he was fighting for success to put in Martha's hands. His honor was pledged to win for Martha's sake. His deep affection for Martha underlay his delight in learning to play the game. All this went without saying, and he said it even to himself with less and less frequency during the next year.

He had, as a matter of fact, less and less time and strength to give to anything outside his business. This focussing of energies began to have its usual result. He felt the eyes of the older men in the organization turned on him with curiosity, with approval, and with a little jealous alarm which gave him the utmost pleasure. He saw in the younger men's eyes the appraising, combative, watchful look with which one tackle surveys his opponent. All his life-long mystic intensity of conviction of the worthwhileness of winning games, flared and blazed hot and lusty in his heart as he recognized that he was now head over ears in the turmoil of the biggest game he had yet encountered.

Of course the real purpose of the game was to take care of Martha—that was axiomatic!

The middle of his third year in business was marked by a considerable raise in salary and an enlargement of territory with corresponding increase from sales commissions, which proved conclusively that he was now accepted as one of the live-wires of the organization. And when barely a week later, Professor Wentworth was notified of his appointment as exchange professor for the next academic year to one of the German universities, the moral of the two events was clear. It was time for a rather long engagement to end; time for

Martha to set a definite date for the wedding before her father's departure for Berlin.

With the setting of the date the relations of the three took on another aspect—like a change of lighting at the theater. Everything was as it had been, and yet everything was different. Professor Wentworth considered himself already eliminated by the younger generation, and although they invited him to share the new home on his return from the year in Germany, he assured them that he would under no conditions cumber up the background in any such fashion, and began to make plans for joining forces with another widowed professor whose children were now all married. His resigned, philosophic acceptance of his soon-to-be exit from their stage set them further from him and closer to each other, as if he had already stepped out from their lives and closed the door behind him. They occasionally felt a little self-conscious awareness of being alone with each other which was new to them. As Martha quaintly phrased it, she now began to feel not only that she was engaged but that she was going to be married. The feeling was a new one, gave a new color to her thoughts and sometimes made her feel a little queer.

Neale told her that he understood this and felt with her that he was stepping forward into a new phase of their relation; and he did feel this at intervals. But while this was the only change that had occurred in Martha's life, it was overshadowed in Neale's by his intuition that he had now come to a crucial moment in his business career. He recognized perfectly the feel of the moment in the game when one side or the other wins, although half the time may yet remain to be played through. In football it lasted but an instant, that well-remembered poise on the very crest of the will-to-win. In business it would last—he had no idea how long—but he felt that he had been well coached by life, that his training had left him with the endurance to stick it out—years if necessary. His pride as a fighter hardened and set. He felt again the single-hearted passion to win out at any cost to himself or others which had been the meat and marrow of his football days. In short he began to be considered by all the experienced eyes about him as a remarkably promising young American business-man.

But now for the first time he did not pass on to Martha the excited exuberant sense of triumphant force, the salty tang of pushing a weaker man where he had not wished to go. Nowadays when he stepped into Professor Wentworth's apartment he found Martha with excitements and interests of her own—of her own and his too. After the first slightly startled recognition that he had opened the door upon a quite unexpected scene, he always focussed his eyes to the other distances, and discussed as animatedly as Martha the relative advantages of suburban and upper-west-side locations, and looked over with her the list of apartments to let. But when he left her, he had scarcely reached the bottom of the stairs before he was again in his own world, crouching warily with tense muscles, alert to catch his opponents off their balance. He occasionally cast a mental glance back at the scene he had left, but it was already out of focus. As a matter of plain fact he did not care a picayune whether they lived in a suburb or on 145th Street, or in what kind of book-case they kept their books, nor whether they had twin beds of mahogany or white enamel. He told himself that what he did care about was that Martha should be suited in those details about which she seemed to care so much.

One evening he found even as he was with her, his attention wavered, dimmed, and fixed itself on a deal he was planning with his grandfather, a small affair which he hoped to put through on the side, but from which, as he was to handle it by himself, he expected quite a brilliant percentage of profit. He answered Martha at random, came back to her world with a guilty start, excusing his lapse by explaining to himself that he was eager for that profit only because it would considerably add to the sum he was laying by for the equipment of the new home. As he sat listening to Martha and agreeing with her, and at the same time speculating about the age and condition of the oak on the tract he hoped to buy, and how much of it was big enough to make quarter-sawing profitable, he thought whimsically that he was as good as married already, that he was doing just what was done by all the husbands he knew.

Martha stopped suddenly, as if he had spoken aloud, or as if she had been struck by a new thought, "Neale, do you realize it! We're really going to be married—just like anybody else. I don't believe I ever thought we really would!"

"Didn't you?" he said. "I always had a sort of notion we would." But although this was not the first time she had expressed this feeling, something about her accent, or aspect, crystallized into tangible form anticipations which had been as vague in his case as in hers.

About this time he began to notice that instead of misty, in-the-distant-future glances at what marriage was to mean, came concrete, definite, recurring pictures of one scene after another in the life before them. His imagination, never very quickly aroused or very flexible by nature, began to be prodded by circumstances into an unwonted activity on the subject of Martha and this marriage. He saw her in his mind's eye across the breakfast table, on the other side of the hearth, or even sitting on the arm of his chair with his arm around her, as she often sat now while they talked over their plans. But (it was one of the first intimations he had of the storm before him) he encountered some curious dumb resistance deep in his heart when he tried to think of her more intimately with the veils of girlhood gone, as his wife. Something within flashed up with chivalric swiftness to shut out such thoughts. He amazed himself once or twice by feeling his face hot, as though with shame at the idea of making Martha, Martha whom he loved so much, his wife. What sort of morbid prudery was this? As soon as it was passed he found it incredible; and felt it again. "Perhaps it wasn't so incredible after all. Maybe that was the price you paid for knowing something about life." It was inevitable—what must be felt by every man who had not been brought up in a vacuum. And it was really all right and nothing to be squeamish over. Human nature is what it is, and there's no use dressing it up in high-sounding names!

If that had been all he had to worry him! But there were other things. More than once he had felt a new exasperation rise in him when Martha would go on discussing the color of wall-paper and window-curtains. Hang it all, he was ready to agree with her whatever way she wanted it—wasn't that enough without dragging him into a discussion of details he didn't understand or care about? Nothing of any great importance, such passing moments of impatience, and yet he had gloried in his certainty that Martha and he agreed on everything! More troubling still—he remembered so distinctly the first time—bending together over a book, a strand of Martha's hair had touched his cheek. He could still feel the shiver with which he had drawn away—true, he had not realized what was taking place—had felt subconsciously as if a spider were walking across his face—but just the same, three years ago though he might have recoiled, his next impulse would have been to snatch that tress of hair and kiss it. Why didn't he kiss it now? Why, here it was again, just as if they were married already: that was the way so many husbands he knew acted with their wives! Of course all this was to be expected, too: you get used to things; you can't go on being thrilled by familiar sensations. In the nature of things marriage could not be as transcendent as people pretended, when men and women are so far from being transcendent!

And yet little by little whenever in the pauses of his business he gave a thought to his personal future he felt it all there again, heavier and heavier, weighing down leadenly every thought which he tried to send ahead into the life he meant to make so happy for Martha.

At this, for a short time, he fell into an inner panic, lost his head, thought himself abnormal, incapable of ordinary human life. He was afraid to see Martha, and was in his heart immeasurably relieved when she was called off by a wedding in her Aunt's family to a somewhat lengthy visit in Ohio. He wanted to have it all out with himself while she was gone —make an end of all this nonsense. But what he did was to think of it as little as possible.

With Martha gone he was able to occupy his mind entirely

with business problems, and the release from tormenting personal worries was grateful to him. He had been intensely ill-at-ease. He was relieved that his discomfort was passed, quite passed.

He opened Martha's first letter with pleasure. Letters were all right: they didn't harry you with emotional overtones. He read her entertaining account of the prostrate condition of both families over the elaborate wedding ceremony impending. Everybody it seemed was frantic with nerves—except the bride-to-be and her young man, of course, who paid no attention to anybody or anything but themselves. Neale thought he felt a note of good-natured satire in this, and smiled appreciatively. That was exactly what *he* felt about fussy weddings. Martha always felt as he did.

With the thought an inner door clanged open, and sickeningly there was the whole thing to begin again! What if Martha *had* been feeling as he had? What did a decent girl feel before her marriage anyhow? Did she dread it perhaps—or on the other hand, had she too lost the thrill—were they already like some of the married couples he knew who kissed with listless lips, looked at one another with stolid glassy eyes? No, Martha was all right! Martha wouldn't change! But didn't that make it worse? What did she expect to find in marriage? Could he give Martha what she expected to find in marriage? He had never once before thought of that, absorbed as he had been by his own disquiet. He was overwhelmed by this new complication, and for many days would not allow himself even to glance at it. He hated the idea of thinking about it. He hated the whole idiotic tangle he kept getting into. Why, damn it, getting married was no such complicated affair! Look at all the imbeciles who sailed into it, a vacuous smile on their lips and nothing whatever in their heads, and made a success of it! A man wasn't a woman, thank God! and couldn't be expected to divine what a woman wanted out of marriage. People who did not expect too much of it, or of anything, were the only ones with intelligence.

Just at this time he got his first chance at a big order. An industrial suburb was projected to house the operatives of a

new machine-tool manufacturing plant in the Connecticut valley. The contractors had never been Gates customers and no
one in the office thought that young Crittenden had the ghost
of a show of landing the order—no one, that is, but young
Crittenden himself. The contract would run up into the millions of board feet: forgetting Martha, marriage, every personal element in life, Neale started after it.

He studied the buyer, the situation, the sort of lumber
needed. He sat up nights going over the architect's specifications; made up alternative schedules for spruce, oak, yellow
pine interior trim; clear or "grade A" shingles. Then, delving
deep in the information he himself had collected, he rechecked
his figures, shaving the margin of safety down till he was sure
his bid would be lower than any other firm's, and yet safe—no
danger of leaving the firm in the hole. The Gates Lumber Co.
could count on its usual percentage of profit and Neale Crittenden on his biggest commission yet, to add to the sum he
was laying aside for the new home.

When his bid was finally in the contractor's hands, and
routine office and road work threatened to leave him with time
to think, Neale turned hastily back to his private deal with
Grandfather. Grandfather's intimate knowledge of all the
possible timber-tracts in his region was a gold mine. There
were always wood-lots in the back valleys being sold for taxes,
or for very little because, all the older generation dying off, the
western heirs did not care enough about the little old family
land-holdings to come east and investigate them. And even
if they had, knowing nothing of the eastern or indeed of any
lumber market, they had no notion of the potential value of
their inheritance. Neale resolved to take part of his little
savings for the use of the new household, to buy up a few such
wood-lots, and turn them over at a big profit. He felt sure of
himself now, sure he could swing such an operation, and taking
advantage of the Labor Day vacation, he went up to West
Adams to spend the week-end and talk it over with Grandfather.

Nothing ever changed in Grandfather's home. Grandfather
and Grandmother did not look so very much older to Neale

at twenty-four than they had to the eight-year-old, having always looked as old as possible. Jennie, the hired girl, had aged more than the old folks, he noted, as she went with him up the steep stairs to the little slant-ceilinged room now incredibly low and tiny.

He sat down on his little-boy bed, a thousand forgotten memories standing thick about him. He saw his mother leading in the sleepy little Neale, and now he saw that she was young, young as Martha, so young herself . . . as young as Martha! He was the strong, purposeful, determined young man, sitting on the bed and looking at that long-past scene, and yet he was also the sleepy little boy, feeling on his lips his young mother's kiss. "Good-night, Neale." "Good-night, Mother."

"Oh, damn it!" he cried impatiently, dismayed to feel that with the memory of his mother, he was aware as though of a palpable presence in the room there, of women . . . of women as different from men, emotionally exacting, wanting something different from men, with some fine-spun impossible ideal of what could be had out of human nature, troubling, hampering the real business of life . . . and yet all the time an inevitable part of things! For an instant he felt brutally angry with them, with their superfine weakening notions, and had for the first time the exasperated feeling that they were an element in life which you could neither do anything with, nor do without. The ewig-weibliche,—good heavens! All it did was to snarl things up! Neale got up from the bed and went over to the wash-stand, amazed at himself, his fit of fury passed, unable to conceive what had started him off on such an explosion. What under the sun possessed him, veering around like a crazy weather-cock from one high-strung mood to another, more shifts of feeling in a day than he had ever used to know in a year! He would put it all out of his mind, all! He simply would not allow himself to think of it again, to think of all that, he would not!

He went hastily down the stairs and fell to talking business with Grandfather, talking to very good purpose, too. To-day their projects went far beyond the little tract of second-growth oak they had first thought of. Grandfather, wily old spider,

at the center of a wide-flung web, knew many tips which he
was more than willing to pass on to his favorite, Neale,—
Neale who had the other half of the combination and could
sell at top prices what Grandfather could buy at rock-bottom.
He was in fact delighted with Neale's ideas and the energy
with which Neale laid his plans. "Why, you're worth two of
your father!" he cried exultantly, as they sat again, the next
morning on the porch and went into details. "I never could
see why Dan'l didn't get on better! He never seemed to care
enough about it, and by thunder, you got to care if you're
going to get anywhere." The old man paused, took breath,
and brought out, with an attempt to sound casual, "I've
thought sometimes 'twas your mother made him that way.
She's a nice girl, your mother is, Neale, but I never thought
she *pushed* your father the way she ought to."

He glanced at Neale a little apprehensively, but the young
man said nothing. He was following out a thought, not entirely new, a guess which he had subconsciously made before,
that there was a long hostility between his mother and his
grandfather. The idea stirred a great deal in his own head,
which he felt no desire to examine.

"I tell you what, Neale," said the old man, observing the
other's silence and emboldened by it. "I tell you what, Neale,"
the old man took his pipe out of his mouth and spoke more
loudly, "don't you get to thinking women are too darned *important*. That's what your father did. He was going good
. . . but that softened him right up."

Neale still said nothing, a succession of well-remembered
scenes from his early home-life evoked by his grandfather's
words.

The old man cried out now, in a burst of long-contained resentment, "Your father ought to have gone enough sight further
than he did! Yes, he had ought to!" He looked keenly into
the hard, strong face of his grandson and said proudly, "But
you will!"

Neale felt so queer a disquiet at all this, that he got up
abruptly and clapped on his hat. All kinds of different pieces
were fitting together before his eyes into some sort of a pat-

tern. He wanted to get away by himself and look at it to see what pattern it was.

"I'm going up to the far wood-lot," he said. "I can remember when the pines were just coming in there. I want to see how much they grow in fifteen or twenty years." But he had no interest in the young pines, and he was not at all thinking of them as he strode hurriedly up the stony sunken wood-road. He was thinking of Martha. Out of nowhere there had come to him the recollection of saying good-by to her at the station. He had kissed her good-by, and as clearly as though he had just now stooped to her, he could remember that the very instant their lips met he had been wondering if he would have time to get down to the office before Mr. Gilman came in from Chicago. He wanted Gilman's support for his scheme to follow the shifting center of supply with a branch office in the Gulf States. Were the figures he wanted filed under L for Louisiana or Y for Yellow pine?

He laughed rather grimly to himself, marching rapidly up through the second-growth birch on which with one corner of his eye he was automatically setting a possible value. If Grandfather only knew, he wouldn't think he needed any exhortation to avoid uxoriousness. He was not very proud of that remembered moment at the station. It was all very well not to be uxorious but . . .

When a clear tiny brook crossed the road, he stopped to draw breath, for, without knowing it, he had been hurrying as if not to miss an appointment up on the mountain. He saw his father stooping to say good-by to his mother at the train as the yearly summer vacation began. He had seen that good-by every June of his little boyhood, but he had never looked at it, till, a man grown, he now stood stock-still on the mountain and stared back through the years into his father's face. What he saw there was startling and troubling to him. He stood frowning sternly down at the brook. He was very, very unhappy and he resented his unhappiness. But his unhappiness was nothing to the remorse which now shook him. If that was what marriage could mean to a man and a woman, what right had he to ask Martha to accept what he had to give? Martha was so fine, so true—dear, dear Martha! To his amazement, almost to his fright, he saw the brook waver and flicker and knew that the tears were in his eyes. For God's sake, what was the matter with him?

He sat down on a fallen log, looking back down towards the valley and found that far beneath him lay the sunburned, flat, upper pasture where in his junior year he had practised so fiercely to learn how to punt. He cast a glance of heart-sick envy back at the sweating, anxious boy who could conceive of nothing worse in life than to have a kick blocked. How lucky kids were, only they didn't know it, never for a moment to dream of such a heavy burden of obscure misery as that which now sickened his heart.

What was the trouble? What *was* the trouble? He had everything in the world a man could work for. Why then, did he stand there leaden-hearted, as wretched as a man who cannot pay his debts?

The feeling of oppression, of weight was intolerable, like a physical constriction. He stretched his great arms and shook himself and drew a long breath, trying to throw it off physically. In the back of his mind stood his father, looking down at his mother, but now he would not look him in the face, for if he did he would see that he was not in love with Martha, deep and tender as was his affection for her.

With this sudden involuntary formulation of what he had been fighting not to formulate, the trouble and restlessness and disquiet dropped away, and left Neale, sitting, his face gray and grim, looking steadily at what he ought to have seen long ago, at what he had known for a long time.

That was what the trouble was: he *was* a man who could not pay his debt, and he owed it to the person he loved best.

Well, it was better, infinitely better now that he knew what there was to face. He could face anything, anything, if he could see it. His native energy rose up, that energy which had been so carefully and steadily trained to aggressive strength. He wouldn't take anything lying down! He would stand up to this!

The young man with the hard strong face sat as silent and

motionless as though he did not breathe. The bright sun wheeled slowly across the sky. The shadows stretched longer.

When he finally rose to his feet, stiff and lame with his long immobility, he had constructed a new little world in which to live, different from what he had foreseen but tolerable, probably all that could be expected by any one who had an honest mind. At least it was constructed on things exactly as they were.

These were the foundations and boundaries of his new world: a profound doubt as to whether any one outside of books is ever in love as men and women are traditionally supposed to be; a certainty that with his deep affection for Martha, his respect for her, his liking for all her ways, he could make her happy . . . happy enough . . . ; and be happy with her . . . as happy as any one in this world was likely to be; the probability that a normal healthy man married to a young and comely woman would fall in love with her sufficiently at least to satisfy any conception she would be likely to have of love, sufficiently to satisfy what any honest open-eyed man had a right to expect from love; a guess that in the long run such a marriage would be more to his taste (possibly also to Martha's) than a more absorbing, exciting union. It would certainly be all right for Martha if they had children. The point was that he could do infinitely more for her, advance and succeed and triumph, unclogged by too much personal life. He did not, he decided, looking back over his life, seem to be the sort of man who really cared much for personal life. He never had. His few tentative steps towards it had always made him miserable, a fish out of water. What he really did care for, what he had always liked when he got it, was a chance to use his strength and wits in competition with other men. Wasn't that after all the real business of life? Wasn't that after all what women wanted of men? That was at the bottom of the marriages he saw about him, in the homes of the older men where he occasionally was asked to dinner. He could give Martha all they gave to their apparently quite-satisfied wives . . . and more, much more! . . . because Martha was such a dear, dear girl.

And that was enough! Enough for any one! He did not feel very light-hearted, it is true. But life evidently was not a very light-hearted business. And he was no grimacing, God's-in-His-Heaven, professional optimist. You took what was coming to you. And what was coming to him was plenty good enough for anybody!

The thought of Father and Mother knocked at the door, but he turned the key in the lock, and started down the mountain to his grandfather, the most promising young business man who had ever entered the employ of the Gates Lumber Company.

CHAPTER XXXIV

Martha came into the room with a little rush as though she had been waiting impatiently to see Neale, and yet when she saw him she gave a little quavering "oh!" as of fright, and stood stock-still near the door.

Neale, conscious of nothing but his own heavy heart, was so startled that he had for an instant the fantastic notion that his mountain colloquy with himself was perhaps written on his face, and that Martha had read it at a glance. But before he could move, she had moved herself and come towards him as swiftly as she had first entered the room. She spoke swiftly too, as though she were afraid of losing her breath before she could say what she had to say; and yet she had already lost her breath, and was panting.

"Neale, dear, dear Neale . . ." her voice was quavering and very low, "I must tell you quickly. Neale, I'm afraid I've done you a great wrong. Neale, I love you better than any one I ever saw, but," her voice sank so low Neale could scarcely hear her, "I don't want to marry you."

Her lips began to tremble. She hung her head, and Neale could see the dark red flooding up to the roots of her hair.

He was for a moment literally incapable of speech. She went on falteringly, "Out in Cleveland, at Margaret's wedding you know, everybody talking about getting married, and Margaret . . . she's like my sister . . . we're so near each other . . . and we talked. She was just going to be married, and she thought I was, too. And I thought so. Truly, Neale, I'd never dreamed of anything else. And she talked to me as one woman about to be married talks to another—not girls' talk."

She began to cry a little now, though she made a great effort to control herself, drawing long, long breaths, and halting between her words, trying to bring them out quietly, "Neale,

I'm afraid you won't understand. I don't know how to tell
you, I don't know how to tell you! You see I never knew my
mother and I never liked to talk intimately with other girls
about . . . about . . . but Margaret is so fine and——"
She cried out what she had to say in one burst, in a loud
voice of pain, "Oh, Neale, when I saw Margaret with her lover
I knew, I knew, I'd never loved you at all. I knew I'd hate
you if we were married."

She turned away and leaned against the wall, sobbing, her
face hidden in the crook of her arm. "What's the matter with
me!" she cried desperately, brokenly. "Why don't I? Am I
different from other women? I can't bear to hurt you so! I
want to love you! What can I do with myself if I don't?"

The two stood there, the broken pieces of their life lying in
a heap between them.

Over the heap, Neale took one long step and put his arms
around Martha, so tenderly, so quietly, that she did not start
or shrink away. She stopped sobbing, she stood still in his
arms, breathlessly still as though she were listening intently,
as though she were taking in some knowledge from a source
not articulate.

She turned her face to his, and said abruptly, "Neale, it's
just come to me. . . . I hadn't thought of that . . . perhaps
you don't really love me either, not in *that* way . . . perhaps
you never did. Perhaps I've just found all of it out in time."

Neale was startled, frightened, unutterably desolate but he
made no pretense of being taken by surprise. "I can't bear
to give you up, Martha," he said looking down at her. "Perhaps what we have is all we could ever have. We may lose
this and have nothing. Perhaps there really is nothing else.
What we have is . . . is . . . very good to have." His face
contracted in a pain that really did surprise him by its keen-
ness. He was horrified at the idea of losing Martha altogether.

Martha gazed steadily into his face as if trying to understand
what he said, their old habit of sharing things, of talking
things over, strong on her. He noted how pale and drawn
her face was, with dark rings under her eyes. She had been
suffering, she too had had broken nights. And as he looked

he saw from her eyes that she was no longer seeing him, but some inner vision.

She shivered and drew away from him. "Yes, there is something else . . . something we haven't . . . and it's what makes it all right," she said. "I'd rather have nothing at all . . . nothing . . . *ever!* than something that would make part of me shrink away from you. I couldn't stand that! I couldn't stand that!"

She had said the last words wildly, and she was back by the door now, as if ready for flight.

Neale sat down heavily in a chair, and hid his face in his hands. "All that this means," he said to himself as much as to Martha, "all that this means, any of it, is that I have not been man enough to make you love me."

At this she came flying back to him, incarnate tenderness, "No, no, Neale, I *do* love you. I know in my heart that even if I should ever marry any one else, I'll never feel for anybody the affection, the trust . . . I couldn't . . . it's not that. Loving you as I do only makes it more impossible, more utterly impossible. You mustn't think this is just the nervous reaction from any sudden shock of knowledge. I knew . . . I *knew* well enough what marriage is! But I hadn't felt it."

She moaned aloud in her bewilderment, "How can I tell you? How can I make you understand? I don't understand, myself. Why can't I give you what Margaret has to give?"

She was bending over him and now snatched his hand and caught it up to her breast, "Neale, I'd give anything to want to marry you! Anything! I've tried and tried. It's like a mountain between us . . . I can't reach you through it. Neale, perhaps we're too much alike. Perhaps that is what brought us together, but that is what keeps us apart! We can't unite! I thought of so many things! We're like two chemicals that can't combine. They can't! That's the way they're made!"

Neale found himself resisting her certainty, although it had been his own. He sat up, suddenly astounded at all that was being said, and cried roughly, "Martha, do you know what this means? You are sending me away. What can I do without you?" He caught at her hand. "Martha, why hunt for rainbows when we have the pot of gold in our hands?"

She shook her head. "It wouldn't be the pot of gold," she said sadly. "It would be a mess of pottage, and you mustn't sell your heritage for it, any more than I."

He looked at her hard, and saw that he had no hold on her.

"Oh, it's finished for me!" he cried bitterly, out of all patience. "If you send me away for some romantic notion, you need have no idea that I will marry any one else. I shall never have anything to do with a woman again."

She said steadfastly though her lips were trembling, "I think when it's a question of what's the finest in us, that nothing at all is better than a halting compromise."

"I don't know what you're talking about," he said angrily and for the moment truthfully. "You're ruining our two lives for some hair-spun fancy."

She grew paler, and said in a deep voice, "Neale, I have told you that I would hate you if you were my husband."

He turned away to the door. "Good-by," he said coldly.

She did not answer.

He went out of the door, and down the stairs. At the bottom he turned and came up again. He found her standing where he had left her. He said gently, "You're right, Martha."

She held out her arms to him. They kissed, sadly, wistfully, like brother and sister parting for a long separation.

Neale went away silently in a confusion so great that from time to time he stopped on the sidewalk till the street straightened itself out before him, and he could see where to take the next step.

CHAPTER XXXV

Neale had set the wheels of his business life whirring at such speed and there were so many of them that they continued to turn clatteringly around and around after Martha had gone away, not only from him but from America; for she had sailed at once with her father for Berlin. Neale watched them whirring for weeks before he perceived that they were running down, and for weeks after that before he perceived that he felt no impulse to keep them moving. There didn't seem to be much point to things, any more. Martha had done what in his heart he wanted done. And yet he was far from satisfied. He missed her outrageously, missed having her there, didn't know what to do with himself. And yet he had not been overjoyed at what he had been on the point of doing with himself. He must be hard to suit, he thought, fretting to feel himself still confused and uncertain, with no zest in things. Damn it, what *did* he want?

A week after Martha's departure he had a letter from Grandfather, written on blue-lined paper, reading, "Dear Neale: Wharton just came in to say he wants the Melwin spruce and heard you had bought them. He wanted 'em for twelve hundred (couldn't find out what you'd paid for them I guess). I said fifteen hundred and stuck to it. He squirmed some. But I knew through Ed that he wanted them for a New York order he's got for big stuff. And there aren't any others around here that'll come up to his specifications. So I made him toe the mark. He left a check for $300 (which I enclose) and will pay spot cash for the rest before beginning to cut."

Neale sat at his desk, looking hard at the piece of cheap paper which brought him the news that in a short time he would have eight hundred dollars more in the bank than he had had before. And without turning his hand over. All he had done was to know that the Melwin spruce were worth a lot more than was thought by the Iowa cousin who had inherited that distant woodlot. Easy money! Somebody had paid him high for that piece of knowledge,—who? Wharton, of course, would certainly get it out of somebody's else hide, or he would never have gone in for the deal.

He sat dreaming, remembering his timber-cruising trip, remembering the choppers and woodmen he had known around Grandfather's. Men like that would work all a year around in all weathers, all their days, to get as much as he would have for doing nothing.

He drew a long breath and turned to enter the check in his check-book. A queer sort of a world. And after all, he stood in much the same relation to the Gates family as the lumbermen did to him, working enough sight harder for enough sight less money. That seemed to be the way things were. But it didn't seem quite square.

A hasty mental calculation showed him that with this money he would have over two thousand dollars. Clear. Not so bad! He considered the matter, wondering why he felt no more elation, and decided that it was because he could not for a moment think of anything he specially wanted to do with two thousand dollars. Always before this he had thought he was making money to give to Martha. Was it possible that he had been using Martha as an excuse? No, no, he explained hastily to himself, the point was that Martha had, all women had, some definite use to make of money. It bought things they wanted and thought important, suburban houses and mahogany twin beds and what not. Martha could easily have spent that sum to buy things that pleased her. The only use he could think of for it was to use it over again to make more money. And then what? It didn't seem much of a life to do that over and over.

He looked around him at the busy outer office, filled with haste and a sense of the importance of its processes. There was more to it than making money. That was the foolish, reforming-professor's idea of "sordid business." You were in it, not because you wanted the money but because it was the biggest game in the world, and it was fun to win out. All right then. He *would* win out.

But no matter how much time he put into his efforts to win out, there was a lot of time left over. Neale did not succeed in filling that leisure to his satisfaction. He went out more than he had ever before, accepted invitations to dinner from all the married men in the office and lunched with all the unmarried, and had them out for meals with him. But still there was time left over. He went to the theater, to loud hearty farces that made him laugh, at first; but they very soon seemed all cut by the same pattern and he found himself sitting them out as grimly and smilelessly as Americans read their comic supplements.

It was not that he was lonely because he was alone. Never in his life had he found the slightest alleviation to loneliness in merely having some one, any one, with him. The truth was that when he was alone he fell to thinking. And he did not know what to make of his thoughts. They mostly consisted of an answerless question, so answerless in the nature of things, that it was foolish to formulate it—the same old question you always ran into when you stopped to think, "what are you doing all this *for*, anyhow?"

In football days that question had been silenced by the instant fierce, all-sufficient answer, "For the team!" What was the present equivalent of the team now? It looked remarkably like Neale Crittenden, all by himself—not such a very big inspiring goal when you stopped to think of it. The best thing evidently was not to do much stopping to think.

One evening unwarily he allowed something alarming to happen to him, something worse than stopping to think. After a solitary dinner at Reisenweber's he strolled along 59th Street, and, as it seemed too early to go back to his room and he had nothing else to do that evening, stepped into a concert at Carnegie Hall. He stepped in to get rid of a few hours of his restless uneasiness and he came out so devoured by restless uneasiness that he could not think of going to bed, but walked up and down the streets for hours trying to forget the

shouts of the brass, the long sweet cries of the violins. They
seemed to call his name over and over . . . to summon him
out, up, to some glory . . . little by little they died away, leaving him in the same flat, inner silence as before, hearing nothing
but the banging clatter of the elevated and the clang of the
surface-car bells. A little before dawn he went back to bed,
exhausted. What sort of a life was this, anyhow?

He was less away from the city than usual, now, spent more
time at his desk, which was usually in those days heaped with
work that had formerly been done by other men. The office
was shifting its routine, rearranging the work to meet the
strain of the Manager's failing health. It was whispered that
Mr. Gates—the "young Mr. Gates"—though only fifty-three,
might have to pull out altogether. That would mean promotion all around. Neale knew by the character of the work on
his desk that when promotion was served out, he would get
his share.

Flittingly once or twice, it occurred to him that all the
managers of departments were but mortal, and that in time all
their private offices would be filled by the men now working at
desks in the outer rooms. How would he like in the end to
move into Mr. Gates' office, he wondered? This thought,
casual and fantastic though it was, moved him to inquire whatever was the matter with Mr. Gates' health anyhow? He was
told that the older man was "threatened with a complete nervous breakdown due to overwork." Neale like all other American business-men had heard that phrase all his life. The
very wording of it was as familiar to him as the name of a
standard make of soap or collar. But he found he did not
after all really know what it meant. What happened to anybody who had a complete nervous breakdown? Mr. Gates
came and went about as usual although not so regularly, looking about the same—spare, dry, hard, well dressed, well shaved,
attentive, silent. Neale looked at him with some curiosity,
wondering how a threatened nervous breakdown showed itself,
and deciding skeptically that there was probably the same
amount of nervousness about it as about everything—less in
it than people made out—money for specialists mostly.

One day he was consulting a letter-file near the door to the manager's office, which stood ajar. Over the file, Neale could see the familiar scene: Mr. Gates' private secretary standing to the right of his employer in a respectful attitude, a bunch of letters in his hand. Mr. Gates adjusted his eye-glasses, their fine gold chain gleaming yellow against the hard gray of his thin cheeks. He took a letter off the pile and held it up before him. To Neale's astonishment the paper shook as though a high wind were blowing through the room. A look of anxious effort came into the older man's face. He leaned his elbows on the table and tried to take the letter in both hands, but it fell out of his trembling fingers upon the desk and slid to the floor. Mr. Gates stooped, secured it with difficulty and lifted his head to recover his position. As he did this, with rather a jerk to get his balance, the drooping loop of his eye-glass chain caught on the key of the drawer and tore his glasses off. They fell on the desk with a little tinkling clatter, broken; and instantly Mr. Gates flung the letter from him, put both hands over his face and burst into tears. Neale heard the sound of his sobbing. His secretary, looking concerned, but not surprised, sprang to the heavy door and slammed it shut.

Neale stood frozen with one hand on a letter in the file, frightened for the first time in his life, so frightened that it made him sick. When he recovered presence of mind enough to move, he tiptoed away to his own desk and sat down before it, shaken. So that was a nervous break-down! Good God!

He wasn't so sure he wanted to move up ultimately into that office.

For a long time after this he was haunted by the recollection of that scene, and especially by the sound of those strange, shocking sobs. Sometimes they woke him up at night, as though it were a sound in the room. They recurred to him at the most inopportune moments, in a train, at table, as he undressed for the night in a bedroom of a country hotel.

He would have given anything not to have heard them. He tried everything to drown them out.

He turned again at this time to books, and took down from

the shelves, volumes he had not looked at since college, books of speculation, abstract thought, history. He found Gregg's marks in one or two and wondered how Gregg was liking it being a professor out in California. That was far away, and so was Gregg. And so were the books. They looked different in his hand; remembered pages had not the same message. He could not seem to put his mind on them as he had. It wandered to other things. A long time since he had tried to use his mind in that way. He had had mighty little time for reading abstract stuff.

Once, starting off on a trip sure to be tiresome, with a long wait in the late evening at Hoosick Junction, he chanced to put into his valise a volume of Emerson. He read the newspaper on the train up, the news, the financial page, and what was going on in the world of sports. But he left the paper in the train, and as he settled himself for the dreary wait in the dreary, dusty, empty station he opened the Emerson. What were some of those places he used to think so fine? . . . "Society is a joint-stock company in which the members agree, for the better securing of the bread to each shareholder, to surrender the liberty and culture of the eater. The virtue in most request is conformity. Self-reliance is its aversion. It loves not realities and creators, but names and customs. Whoso would be a man must be a nonconformist. . . .

"The other terror that scares us from self-trust is our consistency; a reverence for our past act or word. . . . But why should you keep your head over your shoulder? Why drag about this corpse of your memory, lest you contradict somewhat you have stated in this or that public place? Suppose you should contradict yourself; what then? It seems to be a rule of wisdom . . . to bring the past for judgment into the thousand-eyed present, and live ever in a new day. Leave your theory as Joseph his coat in the hand of the harlot, and flee!"

He slammed the book shut again. It made him feel as that confounded music had, stirred up, restless, unhappy, ashamed. It was a voice from another sort of world, a voice that he would rather not hear, because there was nothing to be made of what it said. What could you *do* about it? Neale detested stirring up ideas about which there was nothing to be done. And he knew a great deal more now than he once had about the many, many things that could not be done.

But shutting the book, even slamming it shut, did not silence the voice. He sat alone under the one smoky kerosene lamp, staring into the dusty, dreary, empty waiting-room and heard it clear and calm and summoning, "Leave your theory as Joseph his coat in the hand of the harlot, and flee!" He looked about him desperately, but there was not a soul in the station save himself, nor a house near the tracks. There was not a sound to drown out the deep humanity of that summoning, challenging voice.

He made an impatient rebellious gesture. Summoning? That was all very well. But to what? To something better than he had, more worth while than he was? Well, what was there? Where could it be found? Those vague high-sounding phrases were easy enough to write, but what could you *do* about it in real life? What was the matter with what he had?

The matter with it was that it was bare and dingy and empty, like the room in which he sat. But what was not? Everything was like that, if you didn't believe the nonsense written about it, if you looked at it and saw it. It wasn't to be supposed that he, Neale Crittenden, would go and be a missionary, was it, or any of those pious priggish make-shift devices to pretend that you were doing something worth while? Or join the Salvation Army and beat a drum? He was an American business-man. What in hell did Emerson think you *could* do?

He got up and walked restlessly around the dreadful little room, helpless before its bareness. Nothing to read in the place, not even a time-table. Nothing but the Emerson. He went over to where it lay on the bench, opened his valise, put the book back in, down among his shirts, and snapped the valise shut on it. A whistle sounded down the track. He looked at his watch. No, his train was not due for half an hour yet. He went to the door and watched a through freight roll past, noting the names on the cars as they flashed into the light from the station-agent's window,—N. Y. Central, Père Marquette, Wabash, Erie, Boston and Maine,—shoes and groceries and hardware, structural-steel, cement—all the thousand things needed every day to keep the wheels of daily material life moving, all made, bought and sold, shipped and handled by men like him. All necessary honest goods, all necessary honest work . . . but that couldn't be *all* of life! The train pounded off, the silence of the night closed in on him, and in that silence he heard the echo of those appalling sobs, and the slam of the door. Queer thing, human life was, wasn't it? Think of poor Mr. Gates paying that price, and very likely for something he didn't care so much about when he got it. It wasn't the price you paid, that bothered Neale. If it were something worth your while, you were willing to pay all you had. But to pay so much, just to make money for Neale Crittenden . . . he couldn't see it that way. He'd have a smoke on it anyhow.

As he filled his pipe it came to him that once before he had felt the same aching restlessness, so intense that it was pain. That was the time when he had gone stale. He'd been put out of the game, and had sat on the side-lines eating his heart out. He was there again, gone stale, out of the game. He had the strength, he had the speed, now as then. Why was it he stood outside the game? Other men were giving their souls to it. Maybe he *was* a quitter, after all. There had certainly been quitting or *something* the matter in his relations with Martha . . . how empty life was without Martha. . . . But he was mighty glad he wasn't going to marry her.

He was a fine specimen anyhow!

"Well now, well now," he shook himself together, "let's consider all this. What's the best thing to do when you go stale and have a slump?" Atkins had showed him what to do that other time. He had actually profited by it in the end, profited immensely by being temporarily out of the game, so that he could consider and understand the real inwardness of what it was all about.

Why, perhaps that was what he needed to do now, pull out

for a while, get away from the whole thing, look at it from a distance, get a line on what it was all about.

He sucked on his pipe, cocking his head sidewise to look at the ceiling, his hands deep in his pockets. There was nothing to hinder his taking a year off. He had money enough. And not a tie on earth to prevent his doing as he pleased. He'd lose his job, of course. But he didn't seem to be just madly in love with his job anyhow. And there were other jobs.

"Well, by George, why not?"

Where should he go? Anywhere that wasn't the lumber business. There was the whole world, the round globe hurtling through the infinite. What in God's name was he doing in Hoosick Junction?

There was England; and France; and Italy; and after that, why, anywhere again! Wherever he pleased . . . the East, China, and where there were Malays and jungles. When his money gave out, if he still wanted to stay on he could earn his living as well there as here. "There!" That meant anywhere else. Anywhere else must be less dusty and frowsy and empty than here.

Why under the sun had he not thought of this before? Their damned old labels do stick after all. But he would soak them off!

His heart unfolded from its painful tight compression. The way out? Why had he been so long in seeing it? The way out was to put on your hat and go.

BIRTHDAYS IN
SEVERAL LANGUAGES

CHAPTER XXXVI

I

Ashley, Vermont, May, 1904.

HORACE ALLEN'S cousin was astonished to the limit of astonishment by the news, and cried out accusingly, "Why, I thought the other time it was only because Flora wanted to go. I thought you thought it would put you on the shelf altogether. I thought you hated it."

Horace considered this, sitting heavily on a bench while cousin Hetty pruned a near-by rose-bush, rigorously. Although she did not break in on his silence with a, "Well?" or, "Did you hear what I said?" she made him quite aware that she was relentlessly waiting for his answer.

"Well, I did," he admitted finally, "and I do yet. And it did put me on the shelf. That's all I'm good for now. It's because of my experience in Bayonne they want me to take charge of the Paris office."

"You don't have to go if they do," she pointed out; and this as she expected, brought out the real reason.

"Those four years in France have spoiled me for living here," he said and awaited doggedly her inevitable cry of amazement.

"*You!*" She stood up from her shorn rose-bush, her huge shears in one clumsily-gloved hand, a large thorned spray in the other, "Well for goodness' sake, *how?*"

He was in no haste to answer this either, meditating silently, the spring sun pouring an incongruous flood of golden young light on the sagging heaviness of his middle-aged face. Cousin Hetty let him alone again, and went on with the ruthless snip! clash! of her great shears.

When he rose again to the surface, it was with a two-fold explanation.

"Everybody that's worth anything over there has learned

319

how to do his job. No slap-dash business. And there's plenty of cheap slave-labor. You're waited on! You're made comfortable. You've heard people talk of the charm of European life. What they mean is cheap labor. There's nothing more charming for the employer."

"Well!" commented Cousin Hetty. After a time she remarked, resolutely gathering up the villainously prickly shoots she had been cutting off, "I should think you'd be sort of ashamed of the slave-labor part of it. An American!"

She was not one to hesitate, either to handle thorns herself, or to thrust them upon others.

"Oh, I am," admitted Marise's father casually, and then as though it gave him a faint amusement to shock her, "I forgot to mention their cooking and good wines."

She scorned to take any notice of this, going on, "And I *should* think," she stayed her steps for a moment, as she turned away to carry the pruned-off trash to the spot where the spring bon-fire with its exquisite coils of blue smoke faintly dimmed the exquisite clarity of the mountain air, "I should think that if you found good workmanship such a fine thing, you might try to do something towards getting more of it in your own country, instead of just going off where it grows already."

"Oh, heavens! you don't see me trying to 'make the world a better place to live in,' do you? What sort of Harold-the-Uplifter do you take me for?" he protested, with a yawn.

Cousin Hetty stepped off to the smoldering bon-fire, threw her armful of rejected life on the flames, and came back, her wasted elderly face looking stern.

"How about Marise? Will it be the best thing for her?"

"Oh, the best thing. . . ." her father disavowed any pretentious claims to ideas on that subject.

"Horace, don't pretend you don't know what I mean. Right in the middle of her college course!"

"Shucks for her college course!" he said. "How much good does anybody's college course amount to? Her music is worth forty times that to her. Besides she can keep on going to school in Paris, can't she? What's to hinder?"

The reference to music seemed to give her a new idea as to his plans, an idea which she challenged with suspicion, "What do you expect she's going to do with her music, anyhow? What do you *want* her to do?"

"What do I expect her to do with her music? Oh, what does anybody do with music? Use it to get what she wants. I expect her to succeed on the concert platform. And get a lot of applause. And marry one foreign monkey after another. And hate every other musically gifted woman, like poison. And get so dependent on flattery that she can't live twenty-four hours without a big swig of it from no matter whose flask. And die of wounded vanity because a younger woman is beginning to be applauded. That's what I expect, of course. What else is there to expect?"

At the end of this prophecy which he had brought out slowly and coldly, with long pauses between the sentences, he closed his eyes and relapsed into silence as though it were all a matter of no consequence.

His cousin made no comment but waited patiently for what he had not said. He turned his bulky body sideways on the bench, his shoulder to her, like a sulky boy, to indicate that he had no intention of adding anything.

But presently her persistent, silent demand for what was really in his mind brought out, "Marise's music-teacher in Bayonne was pretty near the only human being in the whole damn town that didn't make me tired. She was pretty nearly the only human being I ever saw anywhere who had enough sense to come in out of the rain. She was an old-maid school-teacher, ugly enough to stop a clock. But she was all right. She didn't want anything for herself. She was safe. Her music had put her where nothing could touch her."

Cousin Hetty was struck by the quality of this statement. She looked at him softly.

"That is what you want for Marise," she said, and continued to stand before him, looking down at him.

He was as much annoyed as though she had cried out emotionally, "Oh, you *do* love her! You *do* think of how to be a good father to her!" and he cut short her sickly, sentimental display of feeling by affirming stolidly, "Well, I won't get it."

"But you don't see any other chance for her."

He felt that she was taking an unfair advantage of a chance lapse on his part and, dismayed and disgusted by the pious color of their talk, was pointedly silent, conveying the impression that he was trying to command his patience till she should consent to stop talking foolishly.

"Marise isn't a bit old," she pointed out, half to herself, half to him. "She's just seventeen to-day. And she's not plain, either."

"You bet your life she's not. That's why I know what her music is going to do to *her*."

"Well, for goodness' sakes, why take her out of college to go on with it?"

He evidently felt that he had more than explained this, for he made no answer. She said then, a very plain, human anxiety wrinkling her old face, "Do you honestly think, Horace, that you are the right person to bring up a pretty, seventeen-year-old girl?"

"As good as anybody else," he said drily, averring the complete incompetence of all the world for that task.

"But she is getting on so well at college—she stands so high—and the youngest in her class. She is so bright."

"Oh, that hasn't anything to do with her being bright. That comes from the schooling she's had in France. She learned to keep at whatever she was doing till she got it right. —Lord—the sloshy work in an American college—as easy as sliding down hill for her. She may or she may not have a good mind. She's learned to work, that's all."

"That's what you're going back for, because of good work," stated Cousin Hetty.

"Oh, I'm not expecting to do any of it myself," he enjoyed his usual satisfaction in making no pretense to virtue, "but I like being able to hire other folks for a nickel or two, to work like that. And I like being able to hire other folks to make it their business to keep me comfortable. And don't forget the cooking. And the wine. And the beds. There's not a decent bed in America."

She made him feel by a lift of the eye-brows that she considered this a rather self-conscious, sophomoric continuance of the pose of knowing sophistication. At this he looked nettled and cross.

A little later, as she stopped in front of him, with an armful of pruned-off shoots, on her way to the bon-fire, she asked, "But will Marise have a good time over there? Young folks here do have such good times."

In his turn he showed her by a lift of the eye-brows that he considered this too unimportant to answer. She stood looking down at her shears, cruel, steel-bright and keen, "Oh, well . . . I don't suppose I let my roses have such a good time," she said to herself.

II

After supper they went out on the bench while he smoked his cigar. Cousin Hetty did not mind tobacco smoke inside the house, but her elderly hired girl did. They were both still under the impression of the tepid warmth of the afternoon sunshine, and were surprised to find the evening air so cold.

"Feels as though there were still snow on the mountains," he remarked, recognizing the peculiar, raw, penetrating chill.

"There is," she told him, drawing her shawl about her.

By his tone he had intimated that he had passed out of the prickly irritation of his afternoon mood. By hers, she had told him that she would, as usual, meet him half-way, in any mood he chose to feel.

They sat down together on the wooden bench; he began silently to smoke, and she to think.

"My visit's over. I must take the noon train to-morrow," he said, "and I've half a notion to ask your advice about something."

She refrained from any expression of the astonishment and skepticism she felt and said briefly with a friendly accent, "All right."

"About Marise," he said.

"Oh, yes, of course. What is it?" she asked in an altered tone of quickened interest.

But for a time he said nothing more. He waited, drawing on his cigar. He drew so hard that it began to gleam redly through the dusk. At this, he took it from his lips and held it down, his fingers out-curved at his side, where he did not see the raging coal at its tip. He had never thought consciously about this gesture, but it was an invariable one with him. There was something distasteful to him about the naked, raw hotness of a newly-lighted cigar-tip. He preferred it later on when all you could see was the ghost-form of the burned-out tobacco, the long, fine ash held together by nothing at all, ready to be shattered at a breath into floating particles of nothingness.

"About Flora, Flora's death," he added presently, knowing although she had given no sign, that she was listening intently, "I never told you. It wasn't just pneumonia. . . ."

He was silent as if he did not know just how to get on with what he wanted to say, and finally said, irritably, "There's nothing to it—nothing! But I can't ask you what I want to, unless you know something about it."

She divined that he would not have told her if they had not come out where it was dark, where he could not see her.

She made herself small, cowering under her shawl, and listened forebodingly, as he went on, his intense distaste for every word coloring his rough, abrupt statements.

"I was up in Bordeaux on business and one morning didn't I see Flora's name in the headlines of the nasty little local paper from Bayonne! An accident at Saint Sauveur—that's a kind of Hot Springs where Flora went sometimes for sulphur-baths. A young man had fallen into the river, or had jumped in. It was in flood, with melting snow. And he was drowned. And because Flora happened to know him and be there, the reporter who'd written up the accident jumped to the conclusion that he and Flora . . . to the conclusion they always jump to about everybody."

Cousin Hetty did not stir, allowed herself no inward comment lest she color the impersonal attention she was giving, which, she understood well enough was, with the darkness, the only condition on which he could go on speaking.

"Hell, wasn't it?" he said briefly before continuing. "I didn't know anything about French inquests, but I could make a guess they would take care to make this one as uncomfortable for Flora as they could. Sounded like a good chance for blackmail too. So I telegraphed back to the house that I'd be back on the next train. I found out afterwards that Marise had wired me, but I never got her telegram. Then before the train started, I beat it to the office of a French lawyer in Bordeaux, and found out all I wanted to about French inquests. I found out then, that there wasn't any real danger, that they couldn't do a thing except talk about it. But, Heavens! their talk was apt to be a-plenty. It was up to me to get back and look out for Flora. Poor Flora! You know she had no more harm in her than a kitten."

Cousin Hetty felt a long, rigorous tremor run through her, partly the cold of the mountain evening, partly an inner chill.

"Poor *Flora!*" she said now in a trembling voice. It was the only word she spoke, the only comment she made on what he had told her, on what he was to tell her.

"Well, when my train pulled into Bayonne the next morning, there was Marise to meet me, and great Scott! she almost scared the life out of me, crying and hanging on to me. I didn't know what *had* happened, besides what was in the paper, what she had heard! But in a minute, she got over that enough to tell me what *she* thought the matter was . . . her mother all shaken up from the nervous shock of seeing somebody killed, all upset, gone to a convent for a rest-cure. Lots of folks do that in France, instead of going to a hospital or sanitarium, as they do here. I didn't think from the way she spoke she even knew who it was who had been killed. You'd better believe *I* didn't say anything about who it was, either! I wanted to go easy and find out how things were. I kept my ears and eyes open: but I didn't get anything that would give me a lead from Marise, except that I found that her music-teacher had piled right in and stayed by her till I got there. And I was pretty sure she wouldn't have told Marise anything, and would have kept anybody's else mouth shut. It came out casually, for one thing, that she had sequestered that newspaper I saw, before Marise had a chance to look at it. Well, it looked as though the first thing was to get Flora home where I could stand guard over her, till the thing blew over." He burst out savagely, "Good God! How was I to dream that she was so sick!" He made some violent gesture which his old kinswoman felt, but could not see in the darkness.

"But she was. When we went to see her that afternoon, the doctor was there with her, and told me there wasn't a chance in a thousand for her. Double pneumonia. We saw her for a moment that afternoon, and the minute Marise went to bed that evening, I went back. But I was too late. Hetty, you never saw anything like how young she looked . . . like a little girl, as if she'd died without having lived. The nice old Sister who had taken care of her had put flowers around her, white roses. And she was crying. She was about the only friend Flora had, the only one of them who didn't want something out of her."

Cousin Hetty's face was wet with tears, but she let them fall silently, not stirring a hand to wipe them away.

Her cousin stirred a great deal, moving restlessly on the bench, folding and refolding his arms impatiently.

"The next three days—I never went through such a crazy performance—enough to drive a man out of his mind. The music-teacher I told you about took Marise off with her, up to the mountains somewhere where her old home was, until the day of the funeral. I don't know how I could have managed without that. I *couldn't* have had Marise around, while I was trying to hush up the coroner's men, or whoever they were.

"As soon as I got in touch with the dead boy's family, I found out where a lot of the trouble came from. The police had come down from Saint Sauveur, just as a matter of routine, to go through the motions of an investigation and had gone to where we lived, because they thought Flora was there. But she'd gone to the convent, so they saw our old cook and

asked her a lot of questions. And Jeanne, instead of telling the truth, which was that she didn't know a thing about
it, saw a chance for some tall and fancy lying such as she
made a specialty of. She got off a long story about how
she'd met the boy on his way to the train, and he'd told her
he was going on business, and Marise had asked him to take
a message to her mother, and he'd said her mother didn't
know him by sight—oh, God knows what! I take it she
thought she was safe-guarding the family honor, by making out that Flora didn't know the young man, but she certainly got everything tied up into knots. She'd beat it off
to tell the dead boy's family what she'd told the police, so
their lies would be of the same color as hers. Oh, it was
the damnedest mix-up! Of course they were all set to do
their share of lying. They wanted as much as I did to keep
the police out of it. Jeanne had beat them to it, and so they
repeated her version rather than start something new. But
naturally, rattled as they were with the suddenness of it, they
didn't get it exactly straight, and that started the police off
on an idea they hadn't had before, that maybe there was
something more in it than met the eye. They asked some
other questions around in Bayonne, and then it was all up.

"Of course Jeanne's story couldn't hold water for a minute.
They found out first that he hadn't any business that could
possibly have taken him up to the mountains. And the old
hag that kept a flower-stand on our street said he had sat all
the evening before Flora went away, on the bench across the
street from our house, that she'd sold him some flowers at
eight when she shut her stall, and when she came back at
six the next morning he was there again. And our concierge
said—oh, hell, you don't need to know all the details. Everybody was lying and everybody sure that everybody else was,
and those fool police inspectors were sure they'd unearth
something if they only kept on. Inside twenty-four hours, I
saw there was no sort of chance of getting anything straightened out by getting down to the facts, which didn't amount
to a whoop anyhow. So we did what you always do in
France when you want to get anything done. We used a

pull. Garnier, this boy's father, was a business acquaintance of mine, and quite a level-headed man. We got together, away from his wife. She was just crazy over her son's death. From one day to the next she looked twenty years older. And the way she cursed us all for ever coming to Bayonne —not that I cared. She was out of her mind, anyhow. All the same, the things she said . . . and poor Flora in her coffin. . . ."

He drew a long breath, and cast his dead cigar from him with a vivid gesture of disgust.

"The up-shot was, that Garnier got busy the right way. He furnished the political pull, and I furnished the money. We stopped fooling with the police and went straight to the Préfet, and they passed the order down quick from one office to another, to have that inquest settled at once, with no more noise. When that hit the police who'd been bothering us, they curled up and dropped off. I bribed a reporter and the editor of the local newspaper, and when the music-teacher brought Marise back to the funeral, the whole mess was buried."

In the momentary silence which followed, as he drew breath again, Cousin Hetty's self-control gave way. He could feel that she was shaking uncontrollably and hear that her teeth were chattering.

He was startled, having forgotten that she was there, forgotten that this was anything but one of the sick, silent evocations which blackened so many hours for him. ·

"Great Scott! Hetty, you're freezing to death," he cried, helping her roughly to her feet. "Why under the sun didn't you *say* you were getting cold?"

She did not intimate that she was shaken by anything but a physical chill. Stiff and bent, clinging to his great arm, unable to stop the nervous chattering of her teeth, she hobbled back to the house beside him.

The light from the fire on the hearth set them miles apart, as she had known it would. His face closed shut. He would never mention all this to her again. He was irritated that he had spoken. He blamed her because he had spoken. But she cared less than nothing whether she were blamed or not. As soon as she was able to control the nervous trembling of her hands and lips and head, she asked, "How much does Marise know?"

He said impatiently, "I don't know. I haven't any idea. I thought perhaps *you* might have. Why *else* do you suppose I told you about it?"

"What do you think?" she persisted.

"Well, I don't see how she could. That music-teacher had gone directly to be with her, and stayed with her practically every minute I wasn't, and I know she'd never tell her anything, nor let anybody else. But you never know. You never know. There are a million underground ways—in France especially. You find out everything you ever know through the back of your head somehow, or by putting two and two together that nobody meant you to. Servants— gossip—though, thank God, Jeanne had a stroke of paralysis just then, that kept her from saying a word till after we had left Bayonne. If Jeanne had been able to talk, I'd have been *sure* that Marise had heard forty times more than there was to know. Damn Jeanne! and yet she'd have died to get Marise a new dress or something good to eat, any day! I don't see how Marise *could* have heard anything. And of course, if she didn't—least said, soonest mended. But if she did, it's a dead sure thing she got it all twisted, and I suppose she ought to have it straightened out."

His old cousin broke in with a rush, "Well, I think you'd better tell her," and felt instantly that this was not at all the answer he had wished for. "You don't want to do it," she said.

"Oh, I never want to do anything," he admitted. "It's always the easiest way."

"The easiest way lands you in some pretty hard places," she observed.

He made no comment on this, but his silence did not save him from her further going on, "Look where it landed you with Flora."

He was stirred to a moment of heat, "What are you talking about, Hetty? By God, I never refused Flora anything she wanted. If you call *that* the easiest way!"

She flared up in a momentary impatience at his denseness, but wasted no words on an issue no longer vital.

"Well, I think you'd better tell Marise," she repeated stubbornly.

He set this on one side for a moment as irrelevant, and said, "All I want to know from you is whether you've ever seen a sign in her to make you think she had heard anything. Did you ever notice when she speaks of her mother . . . or whether she doesn't speak?"

She scorned, as he knew she would, coloring the truth to win a point, "No, I never did," she stated honestly.

"Well then, that's all I wanted to know. I know you'd have seen it, if it were there, she's been so much with you."

"But I think you ought to tell her," she persisted.

"Why, under the Heavens, *why?*" he asked. "Why put ideas in her head, if she's perfectly all right?"

"I think everybody ought to know about everything," she answered sweepingly, "and they're not perfectly all right unless they do. At least, if she *has* heard anything, she ought to know that you don't blame Flora, that you don't think there was anything but talk. You could talk it over with her, get it out into the light."

"It would be poisoning her mind against her mother to mention it."

"I don't believe," Cousin Hetty held to her point steadily, pale, very much in earnest, "I don't believe that the truth can poison anybody's mind."

"Well, I believe in using ordinary horse-sense about everything," he said conclusively, with a peremptory accent.

Cousin Hetty fell back from this brute assertion of his authority.

"You'd made up your mind what to do before you ever spoke to me," she told him, not without bitterness.

"That isn't fair, I didn't know enough to make up my mind. You told me what I needed to know," he answered.

"I wish I *could* tell you what you need to know," she flamed out at him.

But she evidently found it useless to try any longer, and sank again huddled in her low chair. He got up carelessly and shook himself to start the blood through his great frame, numbed by immobility. His eye was caught by the expression of the old woman's face as she looked up at him. He stood still, considering her, "You're going to miss Marise," he said.

She turned back hastily towards the fire, to hide the sudden trembling of her lips, and presently said in a dry voice, "All I want is for her to have what is best for her."

He agreed to this with relief, "Sure! So do I. Poor kid. *She* never asked to be born."

Later, as he started up the stairs, his glass kerosene lamp in his hand, he said, "You know, Hetty, as well as I do that it doesn't make any difference what we do, or don't do for her. She's got to take what's coming to her just like everybody else."

His cousin looked down at the steady, commonplace little flame of her own lamp, "I don't suppose I'll ever see her again," she said in a low tone of profound sadness. But she added stoically, as she began to climb the stairs after him, "Not that that makes any difference to anybody but me."

CHAPTER XXXVII

"Holá . . . p-s-st! Allen!" called Marthe Tollet, as Marise passed through the glass-covered verandah, on her way to the street door. In her haste to stop Marise, she used the abrupt surname hail which the girls thought so very chic and truly English, which the older teachers forbade as rude and barbarous, a typical manifestation of the crumbling down of civilized French ways under the onslaught of modern Anglo-Saxon roughness.

"Eh bien, the little Tollet, what is it?" asked Marise in the same vernacular, pausing in front of the concierge's door. Marthe left the Swedish ladder, where she was twisting her flexible young body in and out of the rungs, and coming up to Marise remarked casually, "Oh, I just thought maybe you'd like to go to the dormitory and see that little compatriot of yours. She's crying like everything, la pauvre, and nobody can do a thing with her."

"The pretty little girl with blonde hair?" asked Marise, somewhat vague as to the younger girls in the lower classes. "What's the matter with her?"

"A perfectly horrible attack of homesickness, they say. The English teacher is up there—she's the only one who can talk to her; but you know how likely the MacMurray will be to put balm on a sore heart, eh? And you could make a wooden man split his sides laughing, once you get started. *You* could cheer her up."

Marise hesitated, looked in at the clock in the concierge's loge, and nodded. She started towards the door of the dormitory building, stopped and called back, "O là, the little Tollet, what's her name?

"Eugénie," said the other, "Eugénie Mille."

As she climbed the dark, winding, well-waxed stairs, Marise

reflected that that didn't sound like an American name, and made a guess that, as had happened to her before, she would find that the "American girl" was from Martinque, or Peru or Saō Paulo.

But it was English, sure enough, that Miss MacMurray was talking, as she bent over the sobbing blue-serge heap, on the narrow iron bed. She was saying helplessly, "There now, it's verra har-rd, I know, I'm far from home, mysel'," patting the heaving shoulders with one hand, and anxiously looking at her watch. She was due at a private lesson in ten minutes, and a private lesson meant five irreplaceable francs.

She welcomed the tall American girl with relief, "Ah, that's right, that's right, you'll know how to get her quieted down," and fled before Marise could protest that she did not even know the homesick child.

Rather at a loss, and very unenthusiastically, Marise stood looking down on the crumpled, untidy bed, and the mass of disordered golden hair, noting the fineness of the tailored blue serge, and the excellently made small shoes. They were unmistakably North American in their shapeliness. Nothing Peruvian or Brazilian about them!

What could you do for somebody who was homesick? She certainly did not know from experience. Nobody had ever done anything for her. She sat down on the edge of the bed, laid her arm over the narrow shoulders, and said cheerfully, "Hallo there, what's the matter? You'll run out of tears, if you aren't careful!"

At the sound of her voice the sobbing stopped abruptly. The girl on the bed started, dashed the floating brilliant hair from her face, and turned on Marise, blue eyes dimmed with tears. She looked exhausted by her passion of sobbing.

"Why, you poor kid!" said Marise compassionately. She hadn't thought it was as serious as all *that!*

The other with a rough, scrambling sprawl, got herself to her knees and sat up, rubbing the tears away from her eyes with the backs of her hands, and drawing long, quivering breaths. Her lips were swollen, her cheeks fiery and glazed.

Marise was touched, and putting out her arms drew the

other into them. "Here, you must let me help you get used to things. *I've* been homesick, too."

The girl tried to speak, was on the point of bursting into tears again, struggled wildly to get the better of her excitement and emotion, and finally brought out in a strangled voice, "I'm not *homesick!* I *hate* my home! I wouldn't go back theah for *any*thing!"

The words in themselves were sufficiently astonishing to Marise, and the raging accent with which they were cast out made them even more disconcerting. She felt that the little quivering body in her arms was clinging desperately to her, and sat silent, holding the unhappy child close, because she did not know what else to do with her.

Presently, however, she ventured to ask, "Where is your home?"

"It *was* in Arkansas," said the other, in a muffled, defiant tone. "It isn't anywheah now. It's heah."

Marise not being very intimately acquainted with the shades and phases of certain American prejudices, saw nothing peculiar in having one's home in Arkansas. Why not?

Apparently some hint of this reached the other, for after a moment of silent, expectant tension, she lifted her face from Marise's shoulder and looked up searchingly into her face. How pretty she must be, thought Marise, when she hadn't been crying. She must look like a pink lily in the midst of the dark-skinned, dark-haired, city-sallow little girls of her class.

"Have you any of your family here in Paris with you?" she asked now.

"I haven't any family left, only some lawyers and guardians and things," said the other. She spoke as though she were glad of it, Marise thought, so that she suppressed the *"oh!"* of sympathy which she was on the point of uttering. What a strange little thing!

The strange little thing now looked up at her. "Do you know what I was crying for just now?" she said. Marise could not understand why she asked this in an accusing tone of blame.

"No!" said Marise, as utterly at a loss as ever in her life. "How could I?"

"Because I hate myself so, because I hate my looks and my clothes and *every*thing!" the other burst out passionately, "I feel like po' white trash. They had plenty of money! Why didn't they send me here befoah?"

"*Before!*" cried Marise. "Why, you're only a child now."

"I'm almost as old as you are," said the other. "I'm seventeen and you're eighteen."

She flung it out like a grievance.

"Eh *bien!*" cried Marise in great astonishment. She had not thought the other girl over fourteen.

She said now, sitting up straight and looking wistfully at Marise, "*Will* you be friends? You came of your own accord to be nice to me. Tell me about things. *Everything!* I want so like sin to know! I'll do anything to learn."

"Know what?" asked Marise, bewildered, looking about her, as if she might catch a glimpse of the things the other wanted to know.

"What they all know oveh heah . . . everything *you* know."

Marise drew back with an abrupt gesture, "No, *indeed!*" she cried, her face darkening, the words leaping out before she could stop them.

"Oh, I don't mean your secrets. I don't care about that. And I don't mean the way you play the piano, although I know some of the girls are envious of that. And I'd despise to have to study as hard as you-all in the upper classes do. I mean the right way to sit down and hold your hands and speak and weah clothes."

Marise began to laugh, "*I* don't know how to wear clothes. What do you want anyhow? You're prettier than any girl in the school, and you are wearing a dress that cost more than anybody's else, and finer shoes than you could buy in all Paris."

"But they're not right," the girl said petulantly, "or else I don't *weah* them right, or something! I hate them! I have lots of money, but I don't know how to buy what I want."

She flung herself again on Marise, holding her closely, "Help me!" she begged, "help me buy what I want."

Marise was touched by the loneliness which underlay the other girl's appeal. She knew what it was to be lonely! It was the first time that any one had broken through into her loneliness as this quivering, passionate, unhappy little thing had done; the first time anybody had asked her for help. From the very first word of their talk, the light chaffing manner which was her usual shield had been torn into shreds by the other girl's driving directness. She looked deep into the other's eyes, fixed breathlessly on her, and said seriously, "Yes, Eugénie, I'll help you . . . all I can."

"There!" said the other, "that's a specimen. My name's not Eugénie. It's Eugenia. Isn't that turrible?"

Marise did not follow this at all. "It's just the same thing, only in English, isn't it?"

"Yes, but it's horrid and common in English, and it's lovely in French. Why can't I *have* it Eugénie?" She looked up keenly and searchingly into Marise's face, and at what she caught there, she contradicted herself hastily, before Marise could open her lips.

"No, no, I see. It would be silly to change it—to pretend. I'd better make the best of it. There! There's one fool mistake you kept me from making, you see!"

Marise felt that the talk was on a plane different from hers, so that she did not get its meaning, although the words were clear enough. What was all that about Eugenia and Eugénie? She hadn't caught the point of that, at all.

Being only eighteen, she found her bewilderment rather comic, and began to laugh. "I still don't see that Eugenia isn't just as good as Eugénie!" she said, "I honestly don't know what you're talking about, Eugenia, but if *you* do, it's all right."

"Oh, *I* do," said the other with conviction.

Marise was relieved to see that her small, pretty face, although still flushed from her fit of tears no longer looked distraught.

"How strange!" thought Marise. They had never spoken

a word to each other ten minutes before, and now they were sitting side by side, hand in hand, like sisters.

"I'm awfully glad I came in," she said.

"So am I," said Eugenia, "I'd been just crazy to talk to you, but you're so many classes higher than me. Oh, how I *hate* my class—to be put back with all those young ones! And study such *turribly* stupid things! And the teacher! Such an old frump. And I'm not having *any*thing of what I want. I'm not getting on a bit. What do I care what France did in India before the English got there? I didn't come to France to learn those sort of things! Marise—please can I call you Marise? Do you suppose I'll *ever, ever* speak French as you do?"

"Why, of course," Marise answered her reasonably, "every-body does, who lives here. Why shouldn't. you?" The echo of the famished, burning accent of the other struck now oddly on her ear. She repeated, "Of course you will, if you care to," and went on, "but why should you bother to care so much? What difference does it make? They don't bother themselves to learn English."

Eugenia flashed a look of quick astonishment at her. Apparently this was an entirely new idea to her. After an instant's silent consideration of it, she flung it away with the aggrieved cry, "Oh, but you *do!* You *do!*" as though, thought Marise, that incapacitated her from having a valid opinion about it. But this too, like the Eugénie-Eugenia discussion had somehow taken place in another dimension than the one she knew. She was not allowed to ponder the question, however, receiving at this point another impassioned embrace from Eugenia, who cried, "You don't *know* how glad I am you came! Now it'll be all right. And I've been so miserable. Let's talk! Let's talk!"

"I must soon be going to a music-lesson," said Marise, glancing at the little jewel-crusted watch, which hung on a black ribbon around the other girl's neck.

Eugenia caught at her despairingly. "Oh, don't go away. I haven't *begun* yet! I haven't said a *word!*" Then struck by another possibility, "Can't I go with you? We could talk in

the cab, and I wouldn't say a word at your lesson. Yes, *do*
let me."

"I wasn't going to take a cab," protested Marise, "I don't go
round in cabs except when I'm dressed up in the evenings. It
would be pretty expensive, ma foi! to take a cab everywhere
I went in the daytime. Mostly I walk."

"Oh, I hate to walk, let *me* take the cab," the other girl
begged, beginning hastily to arrange her hair. "I've got plenty
of money. It's the only thing I have got." She paused, the
brush in her hand. "Haven't you?" she asked, addressing herself to Marise's reflection in the glass.

Marise was passably astonished at the unceremonious question, but answered it simply, "I haven't any of my own. I
live with my father. And he hasn't any either, but he makes a
good deal, gets a good salary, I mean. He lets me have all I
need."

Eugenia's comment on this was to say bitterly, "Think of not
knowing more than to ask such a question! I told you I don't
know anything. But I can learn. I can learn in a minute if
only I get the chance. I learned then . . . from the way you
looked. I'll never make *that* fool mistake again."

She pinned on a very pretty, costly hat, and Marise saw
that she really did not look like a child, after all. She ran her
arm under Marise's now, and gave it an ecstatic squeeze. "Oh,
I'm so happy!" she cried, "I wish I could buy you a diamond
necklace!"

The talk in the cab as they clattered over the big paving-
stones of the quiet, half-deserted left-bank streets turned on
the school, and very soon Marise was led to say, "But, see
here, I don't believe, Eugenia, you've got into the right school
at *all*. It's not a bit chic, you know, to go to a girl's lycée, and
ours is one of the plainest of them all. The teachers are terrible grinds, the girls are fearfully serious-minded. They don't
care a thing about their looks. All they want is to pass the
competitive exams. for the Ecole Normale at Sèvres, and get
in there for four more years of grind, lots and lots worse than
at the lycée. You'd better believe there's nothing *but*

what France did in India before the English got there, et ainsi de suite."

Eugenia made a gesture of despair. *"There!"* she lamented, "that's it! Not even to know enough to pick out the right school!"

And then a curious expression of suspicion coming into her eyes, she said skeptically, "but *you* go to that school! If it's good enough for.you . . . !"

Here again was something in that baffling other dimension, and this time though she understood it as little as ever, Marise did not like it at all. She said stiffly, "I'm going because you can get serious instruction in some things I need to enter the classes at the Sorbonne next year."

Eugenia sprang at her, remorsefully crying, "I won't again. I don't know what made me." She kissed her once more, rubbing her cheek against the other's shoulder.

Her bewildering alternations of mood, the reckless way in which she threw herself on Marise to embrace her; and the way, very startling to a girl brought up in France, in which Eugenia kissed her on the mouth like a lover, were very exciting to Marise. Not since Jeanne's big double kisses had she been so fondled and caressed, and never had she been kissed on the lips before. That was something closely associated in her mind with secrecy and passion. It made her feel very queer; partly stand-offish and startled, partly moved and responsive—altogether shaken up, more alive, but apprehensively uncertain of what was coming next.

"And what *is* the Sorbonne?"

"It's the University," Marise explained, "I was half-way through a woman's college in America, when we came abroad again. So I wanted to go on and study some more here although I have to work so many hours a day on my music that I can't ever hope to have a degree."

"College? University?" Eugenia was horrified. "Mercy! What makes you want to do that? And music lessons, too. I should think you'd be working every minute."

"I do," said Marise.

"Just study, study, study, and practise, practise, practise?" asked the other, astonished.

"Mostly," said Marise.

"Why, that's *turrible!*" cried Eugenia, beginning to look alarmed.

"That's the way everybody does over here," said Marise.

"They *do!*" cried Eugenia, aghast and astounded. "Why, I thought they . . ."

Marise corrected herself, "Oh, of course not. What am I talking about? I mean the kind of folks I know. There are millions of others, I suppose, yes, of course, all the rue de la Paix clientèle, who don't work at all."

Eugenia was relieved at this, and relapsed for a moment into silence, which she finally broke by asking, "Well, wheah *would* you go to school, if you were me?"

Marise had been thinking of this, and was ready, "There's a very grand private school, I've heard about out at Auteuil, in what was somebody's country estate, when Auteuil was the country, with a château and a park. It's fearfully expensive and so it must be very chic. The girls never go out by themselves, always have a maid, or a teacher with them; the old ideas, aristocratic, you know, that ordinary French people don't hold to any more. Mrs. Marbury could tell you all about it."

"Who? . . . Mrs. Mahbury?"

"Oh, she's an American, who's always lived over here, in the American colony. Her husband and my father are in the same sort of business. We know her. She'd be *sure* to know what was chic."

"Well, I'll go to that school," announced Eugenia. "I just *knew* there'd be a place like that, if I could only find out wheah. I bet you I won't have to study French history *theah.*"

Marise laughed, "You'll probably have to work like a dog, for the teacher who teaches *la tenue.*"

"What's that?"

"Oh, all I know about it is what the dancing teacher used to make us do in the convent-school I went to in Bayonne;

walk into a room, pretend to greet somebody, step into a make-believe carriage and out of it, sit down with him for a talk; and first he'd pretend to be a girl like you, and then he'd pretend to be an older woman, and then he'd pretend to be a man (only of course he really was that), and you'd have to have the right manner for each one. . . . All that kind of foolishness, you know."

"No, I don't know!" cried Eugenia angrily.

The cab drew up and stopped. "I suppose we're theah," said Eugenia, "you tell him to wait till we come out."

She was cautiously silent during the introduction to Mme. de la Cueva, and during the hour of the lesson. But if she gave her tongue little employment, she kept her eyes busy, absorbing every detail of the long, bare room, with its four long windows opening on a balcony overlooking the little, dank, unkempt Jardin de Cluny. After the lesson, Mme. de la Cueva stepped into another room to get some music, and Marise, rather pale with fatigue, walked wearily out on the balcony for a breath of fresh air. Eugenia sprang to follow her, as if she had been wishing to do this, and had not known if it were allowable. But before she looked down on the medieval building below them she said in a whisper to Marise, "You're dog-tired. Why, I wouldn't work that hard for *any*body! And for that fat old dowd!"

Marise looked down at her astonished. "I'm not working for *her!*" she exclaimed. But this was, evidently, from the look of Eugenia's face a fourth dimensional remark for her, for she made no answer, turning instead to look at the gray-black old mass of Cluny.

"What is it?" Eugenia asked.

Marise had not yet wholly emerged from a struggle with an exercise which she had not been able to execute with the inhuman, neat-fingered velocity demanded by Mme. de la Cueva. The hour in that other world to which music always transported her had broken the continuity of her impressions of her new friend. She stared rather blankly at Eugenia's question, and looked from her to the well-known medieval pile below them. It did not for the instant occur to her, that the other

girl did not recognize what the building was. The turn of her
phrase suggested an inquiry about the architecture, and though
she had never thought about Cluny before, the look of it stirred
recollections of a certain fierce history teacher, whose specialty
had been the transitions of the reign of Louis XII. She looked
down on the stone lacework opposite, and said doubtfully,
"What is it? Domestic Gothic, shouldn't you think? But
some of it pretty late. Those square dormer-windows are Louis
Douze, aren't they?"

She looked away from the Cluny and down at Eugenia as
she finished, and had once more a shock of astonishment. The
other's eyes were flaming. "Theah, that's it," she said fiercely,
showing her white teeth as she spoke, but not in a smile.
"That's it. That's *just* it! *Wheah did you learn that?*"

She dashed the question in Marise's face as though it had
been her fist.

Marise positively drew back from her. Too startled to be
anything but literal, she answered, "Why, why, I don't know
where I did. Oh, yes, in my French history class, I suppose.
They make you learn everything so hard, you know. You
yourself were saying what a grind it is."

Eugenia breathed hard and said, "History again, darn it!
But I didn't dream you'd learn *that* sort of thing in it." She
added defiantly, and for Marise quite cryptically, "Well, *I'm*
going to learn it without!"

Mme. de la Cueva came back with the music in her hand.
"Voilà, mon enfant," she said, shaking Marise's hand heartily.
She reached for Eugenia's hand too, which was hanging at her
side, till Eugenia, seeing the meaning of the other's gesture,
brought it up with an awkward haste, a painful red burning
in her cheeks.

Some one came in as they went out, another student evidently, for he had a roll of music in his hand. He stopped and
stood aside with a deep bow to let the two girls pass.

"Good-day, Mlle. Allen," he said, looking at her intently.

"Good-day, M. Boudoin," she answered. Neither girl spoke
as they went down the endless, winding stairs and passed out
to the street.

As they turned into the Boulevard, and jogged past the Jardin de Cluny, Eugenia asked tensely, "What are those queer looking broken-down walls?"

Marise answered circumspectly, fearing another out-burst, "I think they're Roman ruins . . . what's left of the baths the Romans had here."

Eugenia made no answer, but looked at them hard.

Marise went on, "Awfully interesting, isn't it, to see Roman ruins right in Paris, across the street from a café. But I suppose they'd look like small potatoes to anybody who's seen Rome. Mme. Vallery says they look comically small, after Rome."

Eugenia put her arm around her neck, and kissed her once more, fervently, disturbingly, on the lips, "Would you like to go to Rome? I'll *take* you to Rome. I'll hire a private car for the two of us."

And before Marise could answer, before she could even bring out the laugh which rose to her lips, Eugenia said with another of her abrupt leaps, "That young man is in love with you. The one who came in afterwards. He's awfully good-looking, too." She looked into Marise's face with her avid, penetrating gaze, and said, "But you don't like him!"

"I never thought about him in my life," cried Marise, exasperated. She was beginning to feel desperately tired of the mental gymnastics of such talk.

"But there was something you didn't like as I spoke about him. Don't you *like* men? Don't you like men to be in love with you? I do, I love it." She made another flying leap, and asked, "Are many French women like your music-teacher —so fat—no style?"

"She's not French, Madame de la Cueva."

"What, then?"

"A Levantine."

"A what? What's a Levantine?"

Marise considered, "What *is* a Levantine, anyhow? A little of everything, I should say, and all more or less oriental and southern. She's part Spanish, part Jewish from Asia Minor, brought up in Cairo and Paris."

Eugenia sheered off on another tack, "And who is Madame Va . . . Va . . . something?"

"Madame Vallery? She's a . . . she's a sort of friend of mine. Yes, she's a friend. My old music-teacher, when I was a little girl, got us together. She's the wife of a Deputy, you know, like our Congressmen."

"Is she chic, too," asked Eugenia, "like Mrs. Marbury? Is she young? Is she pretty?"

Marise laughed, "No, she's not pretty or young. She must be fifty years old."

Eugenia was shocked. "And a friend of *youah's!*"

Marise explained, "She has more brains than you and I and forty other girls rolled into one. And I've met more interesting people at her house than . . ."

"Will you take me sometime—will you take me?" asked Eugenia.

"Yes, if you like," said Marise.

Eugenia looked around her wildly, as if to find some way of saying her thanks. Something in the street caught her eye. They were passing a florist's shop. She slammed the door open, curved her flexible little body around the frame, and caught at the driver's coat-tails. "Stop a minute!" she cried to him and dashed into the shop. When she came out she had a huge bunch of mauve-colored orchids in her arms.

"For you, for you," she cried, elated at her idea, thrusting them into Marise's hands, and kissing her again. And then, suddenly downcast, "Oh, it oughtn't to have been orchids! What? Roses? Lilies? Violets? . . . Yes, violets."

This time Marise protested energetically against this assumption of meanings in her face.

"I don't know what makes you *say* such things," she cried out helplessly, half-angrily. "Orchids are lovely—*beautiful.* How could anything be better? I never had any before in my life."

But the other was not to be comforted. "Yes, it ought to have been violets," she murmured, and then squaring her jaw, "And it *will* be violets, the next time. You just see!"

CHAPTER XXXVIII

As Marise started up the front stair-way she saw Biron emerging on the run from the foot of the servants' stairway, his apron half-off, a net marketing-bag in his hand. His broad, red face looked cross and anxious. Something must have gone wrong. She turned back, meeting him in front of the concierge's door.

"Oh, Mademoiselle, God be praised you're back in time. Desolation and ruin! The sole has turned—it has been so hot to-day. I swear on my soul as a Christian it was fresh when I got it—unless that blackguard Gagnan changed. . . ."

When Biron turned his torrent of objurgation on the trades-people who sold him eatables there was no stopping him. Marise cut in now.

"Were you going out for another? Do you want me to go?"

"Yes, yes—only not for a sole—there wouldn't be one left—and the dinner was *planned* for sole!"

He ground his teeth, white and sound as a wolf's, "I could send Mélanie if she had the intelligence of an angle-worm —and yet to leave her with my sauce till I get back—I was right in the midst of a *sauce piquante* for the . . ."

He turned as if to rush back upstairs, distractedly, and turned again as if to rush distractedly out into the street.

Marise put out her hand for the market-bag and spoke with the peremptory decision that was always necessary to un-loosen Biron from his temperamental tangles.

"Go right back to your sauce, Biron. I'll have the fish here in five minutes. And have plenty of onion in that sauce. My father thought the last not well-balanced, too much vine-gar. He likes his sauces suave."

"But not a sole, Mademoiselle, not a sole! Any sole that is left on the market at six of the evening is left because nobody would buy it. But the dinner was *planned* for sole!" He stamped his huge, felt-slippered feet in exasperation.

"A mackerel," suggested Marise, "they're good at this time of the year."

He flung his arms over his head. "A *mackerel!* A gross, fat, dark monster like a mackerel to replace a *sole!*"

"Oh, no, of course not." Marise saw his point. "I didn't think. Nor salmon, of course."

He shuddered away from the idea of salmon.

They stood staring at each other, thinking hard, the cook's big, parboiled fist clenched on his mouth, his brows knit together, like those of the *Penseur*.

"Some merlans?" suggested Marise. "You can cook them *au gratin* just *like* a sole."

"But will I have time!" he groaned. "Who knows whether the oven is hot enough?"

"Well, hurry back and brighten the fire, while I rush out and get the fish."

He fled back up the stairs, his slippers flapping. She left her roll of music in the concierge's care and darted out into the street, market-bag in hand. Twenty minutes later the fish were being disposed with a religious care on a bed of chopped parsley, shallots, mushrooms and butter. Biron shoved the baking-pan tenderly into the oven, wiped the sweat from his face, and stopped storming at his wife.

"You were not to blame, after all, Mélanie," he told her magnanimously, and with a long breath, "But it was a close call, by God, a close call."

In the salon Marise was pouring an apéritif for her father, brightly dishing up the news of the day with the sauce of lively comment, and saying nothing about culinary close calls. Her father listened to her, sipping his Dubonnet with an air of intense satisfaction. He took plenty of time for it, allowing each mouthful to deliver all its complicated burden of tang and bitterness and heat before he took another one into his mouth.

"Excellent stuff, Dubonnet," he said appreciatively.

"I'm glad you like it," said Marise. She envied her father his enjoyments. They were, comparatively speaking, so easy to get.

Looking at her seemed to remind him of something. He reached into a vest pocket (with some difficulty, for his vests were more and more tightly packed with each year of good living), and took out a little jeweller's box.

"It's your birthday to-day," he remarked, taking another careful sip of his apéritif.

Marise looked at the present, a little wrist-watch, from a very good house.

"Oh, that's awfully good of you, Father," she said, trying it on.

"You can have one if that funny little friend of yours can," he advanced.

"Oh, if you start giving me everything Eugenia has. . . !" protested Marise.

"Somebody ought to make *her* a present of a little ordinary sense," he commented, with no great interest in the subject. "I've seen her kind before. They tear things loose till they get what they want, and then they don't like it."

"Eugenia just loves it, every bit of it," Marise objected.

"Well, let her," he dismissed her from consideration with his usual nonchalance, and taking the last of the Dubonnet, he rose to go into his room.

In a moment Marise heard an indignant roar, *"Mélanie has forgotten my hot water again!"* Her father came to the door of his room, vast and bulging in his shirt and trousers, outraged by the oversight.

"Oh, yes," said Marise, in annoyance. "You might have known she would. Biron has been in another tantrum and taking her head off. It gets her so rattled she forgets her own work."

"I don't see what that has to do with *my hot water*," cried the master of the house aggrieved.

"It hasn't! It hasn't!" cried Marise hastily, running to tell Mélanie of her crime.

Not till the hot water was safely delivered, and her father's comments on bad service diminished to a distant solitary mutter, did Marise go into her own room to dress. She had no hot water, either, but she washed in cold, scorning with all her heart the childishness of men, and laughing childishly at the picture her father had made, shouting and indignant, billowing in his shirt and trousers. He and Biron! One had always to be smoothing them down and wrapping them up in the little things they wanted. It must be truly lovely to be married to one, as poor Mélanie was! But, after all, Father did his best to be good to her, when everything about the house was all right and he could think of it. She hoped the dinner would be all right. It was too bad about that sole. Sole was so expensive too. Not that Father ever objected to anything the table cost. Oh, *flûte!* she had forgotten to see if Biron had exchanged that Bénédictine for Chartreuse. Father would raise the roof if they served him Bénédictine again. She put on her dress hurriedly, and hooking it up as she went, she stepped hastily down the hall to the kitchen. She never had any help from Mélanie in dressing, not even costumes that hooked up on the shoulders and under the arms, because it was important not to disturb the small quantity of gray matter Mélanie had, at the hour of serving a meal. It was all needed for the matter in hand.

Dinner was over, and had been acceptable. Her father had partaken of everything with his careful appraising attention, and had found no adverse comment to make. Coffee had been served, and the Chartreuse—Biron had not forgotten.

Out in the kitchen Biron (first, taught by much experience, loosening the sash which bound his mighty paunch), was sitting with his wife at table, eating and drinking like a page out of Rabelais. The dinner had pleased his exacting and irritable master (Biron immensely respected him for being exacting and irritable), and it also had pleased Biron. There was plenty of it left and this was a house where the cook was never subjected to the indignity of having inquiries made about *les restes*. He leaned back in his chair, undid the button at his throat, and smiled at his wife, over his glass of excellent Burgundy.

"Life is good, hein, old lady?" he said.

She nodded in agreement, keeping her thoughts to herself in the usual stealthy, secretive, feminine fashion.

Over the coffee and Chartreuse, facing another well-satisfied man sat another secretive woman, talking in one key, feeling in another, and finding the process far from enlivening. Down below the surface of the sparkling, chatting Marise, drooped a listless, dispirited Marise for whom a birthday was a most depressing occasion.

"You're nineteen, aren't you, Marise?" asked her father over his cigar.

Marise nodded.

"Well, that's another one gone! Congratulations on every one you get over with," he commented, sipping the stinging green fire of his liqueur with satisfaction.

Marise thought of nothing amusing to say and was silent.

Her father stirred his big body, with the air of some one arousing himself to an effort. The effort seemed to be to say, "Is there anything you want I can get for you?"

His daughter was at a loss before the comprehensiveness of this blanket question. "What kind of a thing?" she inquired.

He professed himself more at a loss than she. "If I had any idea what, I wouldn't need to ask you, would I?"

But he managed, all the same, at least to eliminate some of the things he didn't mean, "Oh, not dresses or hats," and in a moment, after another sip at the liqueur, to give a little more definite idea of what he did, "Something going on, social life; what girls of nineteen are supposed to want."

"Oh, you needn't bother. I get enough of that," she answered, "between Mrs. Marbury and Eugenia and Madame Vallery." She was surprised at her father's interest. They seldom talked together, except of what they were to eat, had eaten, or were eating, or of the interminable games of chess which occupied any leisure moments of his and hers which chanced to coincide. He seemed to have something on his mind now. And he always hated the effort of bringing out what was in his mind. He stopped beating about the bush now and said heavily, "You're no fool, Marise. I don't know any of the roundabout ways to say it to you, that a woman would have, but you won't mind that. What I mean is, I suppose—I imagine that's what's at the bottom of all of it—is this. Are you getting a chance to meet the right sort of young man, the kind you'd want to marry? For you will be marrying before long, I suppose."

Marise waited a long time before she spoke, so that she would not flame out as she felt. That would not be speaking in her father's vernacular, and if there was one thing which every instinct of Marise's taught her, it was to speak to every one in his own language. Nothing in the world would have induced her to expose her own to other people's casual comments, her own, in which she spoke to herself, bitterly, caustically, skeptically, tragically, as no one had ever heard her speak aloud. When she could command herself to select the right phrase out of her father's vocabulary, she remarked, pushing her tiny coffee-cup away with a gesture of finality, "I don't believe I'm very much of a marrying sort."

Her father's comment on this was to say stolidly, "Oh, every girl thinks that." But if he thought he could get a rise out of Marise with this provocation, he was mistaken. She now turned away from the little table and began with an indifferent air to arrange the coal-fire in the grate. They were sitting in the salon.

"Don't you like men?" he asked presently.

She laughed a little, "To dance with."

He looked at her more keenly than he had and asked, "Don't you trust men?"

She turned this off by riposting lightly, "How much is it safe to trust anybody?"

It was as though a chance stroke had cut through the dyke and let out in a rush, waters that had lain sleeping.

"Never trust anybody but yourself," he told her urgently, the words heavy with the intensity of his conviction.

A moment later he added, more deliberately, his manner tinged with his habitual saturnine humor, "And it's not safe to trust yourself very far."

It wasn't at all what he had meant to say to her. But it was such an undertaking to say anything. And what was there to say anyhow? He decided to let it go at that, drank the last of his liqueur, fell back in his arm-chair and reached for the chess-board.

"I hope you got a good supply of that Chartreuse," he said, beginning to set up the men. "It's very much better than what we've been having. Not so syrupy. I do loathe syrupy things."

After the game was over, he took up his Paris Herald and Marise, freed from the necessity to make talk, went to the piano. She began to play, not Chopin as she would have liked, but a dance from the Arlésienne Suite. Father detested melancholy music.

After she had finished, she sat still, sunk together on the piano stool, staring at the music but not seeing it. She heard her father rustle his newspaper as if he had lowered it to look at her. But for once she made no attempt to arouse herself. She continued to present to him a silent, dejected back.

He must have considered this for some minutes when he finally remarked, "I suppose there are people who *like* birthdays!" Then with a yawn, "But for me, they always make me think of all the ones I have still to get through with, year after year, one by one."

Marise's shoulders bowed under the weight of his words and his accent. She still said nothing.

He took up the newspaper again, but before he began to read he exhorted her, "Oh, well, stick it out! Stick it out, Molly, as best you can. It doesn't last so very long."

CHAPTER XXXIX

Paris, May, 1907.

"Wouldn't you *think*," asked Eugenia, looking about her, "that anybody who could get up such a room as this, such a perfect room, would know how to get herself up better?"

"You don't suppose for a minute that she doesn't know how to!" Marise rejoined. She added after a moment, to tease Eugenia, "Perhaps she thinks it ordinary to be chic. Perhaps she thinks it is more distinguished to have her very own genre."

Eugenia said with a nettled accent, "Well, wouldn't you think if she were going in for a genre of her own, she'd pick out one that was a little more ornamental than her flat-chested, old-maid, provincial school-teacher variety?"

Marise laughed. It always gave her a little malicious amusement to make Eugenia uneasy. To make her still more so, she added, "Yet you know well enough, Eugenia, in any room full of people, let Mme. Vallery come in with that mild, oh-I'm-nobody, don't-mind-me sort of air of hers, and everybody else looks like a dressmaker's mannequin."

Eugenia, alarmed for her standards, annoyed and aroused, disputed the point with warmth, "That's only because you know who she is. If you didn't, you'd take her for the concierge's country cousin."

Marise shook her head exasperatingly, "No you wouldn't. She has *cachet*. You can see it a mile away."

Eugenia suddenly conceded the point with grudging wonder, "How does she *do* it?" she marveled, unreconciled.

"Personality," diagnosed Marise, and then seeing that Eugenia's face looked really clouded, she stopped her teasing abruptly, ashamed of the unkind impulse which drove her to it, and of the malicious pleasure she took in it. What was the inner irritation with everything that kept her so aware of other people's weak points and so easily led into playing ill-naturedly on them. Now, here and now, let her resolve she would never tease Eugenia again.

But she knew she would.

She did, however, resist an easy opening, given her by the next remark of Eugenia's, as she looked across the beautiful room, "What *makes* it all so just right? I'm going to start in at that corner, and look at every single thing, and find out *what* makes it right."

Marise restrained the mocking words on the tip of her tongue, and turned away to the half-open window, near which she stood. Across the empty street in the pale gold of the spring sunshine, the vaporous young green of the Luxembourg showed like a mist through the tall iron palings. The light blue sky above was veiled with hazy white clouds, stirred by a young little spring breeze, which blew languorously on the girl's cheek.

It came over her, all of it, with a soft rush, the invitation to life, the lovely, treacherous, ever-renewed invitation to live. And she drew back from it, with her ever-renewed determination not to be taken in by it. It was always too horribly lovely in May. It made her ache, it made her want to cry, it made her horribly unhappy. How detestable to have it so lovely, looking so seductive as though this were only the promise of something lovelier . . . when there wasn't anything to redeem the promise, when it was all just a part of the general scheme to fool you.

Behind her Eugenia's voice said enviously, "Where did she get all these terribly quaint Louis XVI things?"

How thoroughly Eugenia's English diction teacher had rooted out that "turribly" of Eugenia's, thought Marise.

Aloud she answered, "She began collecting years ago, before anybody else thought of it."

"I shouldn't think a teacher would have much money to collect."

"Oh, she picked them up for nothing, in corners of whatever province she happened to be in, out of barns and chicken-houses and attics."

Eugenia said complainingly, "It seems to me she always has been able to pick up something for nothing. Look at her husband."

Marise said over her shoulder, "Oh, she didn't get much, when she got him. He never would have been anything except his good looks, if she hadn't taken him up. And she didn't get him for nothing—not much! Mlle. Hasparren says—every one who knows them says—that she made him. She writes his speeches now. I've seen her. And never bothers him by being jealous."

"I should hope *not*," commented Eugenia. "She's ages older than he. And he's such a ripping good-looker."

Marise found Eugenia's fervent accent rather distasteful. Not that she minded her latest fad of finding married men so much more interesting subjects than the others. Eugenia's affairs never lasted more than a minute anyhow. But she wished Eugenia would pick out somebody with more brains than Mme. Vallery's husband, somebody not so well satisfied with himself.

"He's an awful imbecile," she said.

"What did Mme. Vallery marry him for, if she's so terribly intelligent?" challenged Eugenia. She delighted in using the words she had formerly mis-pronounced, and giving them the purest, most colorless intonation. There was not a trace now, in her speech, of the sweet, thick, unstrained honey of her original southern accent.

"She has brains for two," said Marise shortly, displeased by the direction of the talk. As a matter of fact, Mme. Vallery had once informed her why she had married her handsome, unintelligent husband. She had said warningly one day, when Marise had drawn back from a match Mme. Vallery had proposed for her, "Don't carry that too far, dear child. You will have to give in to the flesh sooner or later. You might as well do it young, before the growth of your intelligence spoils your enjoyment of it, as wait till you're driven to it, as I was. It's not amusing in the least, to have to take it all mixed with the contempt of your brains. You'll find you have to take your share, one way or another."

Marise looked out frowningly at a great beech tree bursting into life in the garden across the street. It held its huge, flowering crest proudly into the spring air. To look at it was like hearing a flourish of trumpets, triumphal, exulting.

That was all very well for trees, thought Marise, that stupid, yearly emergence into a life that promised so much and brought futility.

Along the gravel-walk, inside the Luxembourg, under the hedge of lilacs, under the new splendor of the great beech, a young man and a girl in a pale gray dress were strolling. They looked at each other, and smiled.

"That's the way my father and mother probably walked together," thought Marise, wincing. "That" was one of the clumsiest, most obvious parts of the general conspiracy to fool you. But when you had the key to the code, as Marise had, there was little danger that you would be taken in.

"I think I hear them coming," said Eugenia, "I do hope Monsieur is with her! Not that he ever condescends to pay the slightest attention to me!" She assumed carefully a pose of unconscious ease on her small, spindle-legged chair. Marise turned around from the window and looked at her with appreciation. Was it only two years ago, that Eugenia had scrambled up from the crumpled bed on which she had lain a-sprawl?

"Nobody can say *your* genre is not decorative, Eugenia," she remarked with the sincere intention of pleasing the other girl, "that's a perfectly glorious toilette, just right. And oh, how divinely that broadcloth is tailored."

Eugenia looked at her resentfully, with a flash of her old suspicion that she was not being treated as an equal.

"I haven't any *cachet*, and you know it," she said, "if Mme. Vallery can have *cachet* do you suppose I'm going to be satisfied with just chic?"

Marise felt one of her claps of laughter rising within her, but kept it back, as the beautifully proportioned paneled door opened to admit their hostess. A tall, spare, stooped, gray-haired woman, dressed plainly in fine black, with a shrewd, wrinkled, fresh-colored face, well-washed and guiltless of the smallest trace of powder. She looked like an elderly Jesuit, one who wields a great deal more power than he likes to show.

"Good-day, my children," she greeted the girls in a clear voice, with the utmost simplicity and directness of intonation. "Have we kept you waiting long? I told Auguste that we were a little late."

Auguste, magnificently tall and magnificently bearded, having now followed her in, the four sacramental hand-shakes were accomplished, Eugenia's this time the promptest of all.

After the equally sacramental exchange of salutations and questions and answers had been achieved, questions as to health and general news, which did not in the least denote any interest in these matters, answers which were pronounced with perfunctory indifference and received in the same way, the necessary civilized preliminaries were considered disposed of, and the first moves of the game could be taken. M. Vallery's gambit was to say, looking admiringly at Eugenia, "Such a piece of the month of May oughtn't to be within four walls. Come over to the balcony a moment, and let me show you your sister, the Luxembourg, in flower."

Mme. Vallery's move was to sit in the winged, brocaded, deep-cushioned *bergère,* and motion Marise to sit beside her.

"Let's get our business done and off our hands first of all," she said, smiling up at the tall girl in an admiration as frank as her husband's for Eugenia, and for Marise, vastly more valuable.

The others, in a little chiming burst of chatter and high spirits, moved off towards the balcony. Mme. Vallery glanced after them with an inscrutable expression and then at Marise with a brisk, business-like manner.

The matter at issue just then, the occasion of the girls' call, was a fête de charité at the lycée, over which Mme. Vallery's sister was Directrice, shoved up to that position, so the lycée teachers said, by the political pull of Madame Vallery herself. But even they could not deny that the connection was highly advantageous for the lycée. There was not another one in

Paris, which felt itself more "protégé" in high places, more sure of its standing with the Ministry of Education. And its annual charity fête, from being the usual small-bourgeois bazar with home-made aprons and pin-cushions on sale, and perhaps an inexpensive conjuror pulling rabbits out of silk hats in the assembly-room to amuse the children, had become one of the most elaborate and unique annual events of the city. A good part of Tout-Paris lent its highly ornamental presence to these affairs, and helpless before Mme. Vallery's energy and acumen, always left much more of the contents of its purse than it had the slightest intention of leaving in the amusingly decorated stalls where pretty, well-trained amateur salesgirls sold the goods furnished at cost (under pressure from Mme. Vallery), by the most fashionable shops in Paris.

This year Marise had been asked to play, along with two other de la Cueva pupils, in the afternoon concert which was the *clou* of the three days' fête. Mme. Vallery had written her to ask her to come to talk over the choice of music, and to Eugenia's surprise and extreme pleasure had mentioned casually that she would be glad to see her pretty friend, Miss Mills, also. Marise had instantly wondered what she wanted to get out of Eugenia, and now behind her fresh, open, unlined young face she was hiding a determination to find out what, and to keep Eugenia from being unduly exploited. She might tease Eugenia herself, but she had an elder-sister feeling of protective care towards her. Eugenia was so awfully defenseless, in spite of her money, and so naïve still in spite of the sophisticated lore and manners which she had so energetically acquired. She had not learned that thorough-going suspicion of everything, which is the only valid protection against life.

But Mme. Vallery said nothing whatever about Eugenia, other than to comment in passing on how excessively pretty she was, a real late-Régence type, such as one seldom sees now-a-days. Marise found herself, as usual, quite helpless before the Vatican antechamber suavity of the older woman, and reflected, not without some resentment, that she probably seemed as naïve to Mme. Vallery, as Eugenia did to her.

After some desultory talk about other features of the fête, they got out a pile of music, went together to the piano, where Marise tried the effects of various combinations, and finally decided on a desirable one.

All this time M. Vallery and Eugenia spent on the balcony, leaning over the railing, the sound of their voices and occasional laughter coming in pleasantly through the open windows. They came in together, when Mme. Vallery summoned them to share the Muscat and hard sweet biscuits which it was part of her genre to serve at four o'clock instead of the newly introduced tea.

"Business is over," she announced, settling herself in the chair back of the little stand, where the tray stood. "Now for some talk." She put her hand to the crystal carafe and held it there for a moment. Another of the ecclesiastical details of her appearance was the beauty of her hands, white and shapely.

M. Vallery seated the girls and then himself, smiling into his beautiful, glistening brown beard. Eugenia too was smiling, with a dazzled look of pleasure. Mme. Vallery looked down at the wine she was pouring. Marise suppressed a qualm of distaste for M. Vallery, and started the talk by laughing outright as at a sudden recollection of something comic. She explained that she had just had a letter from America, from an old cousin of her father, who always kept her au courant of the quaint and humorous goings-on of the country-side.

"Her letters are as good as a comic paper," said Marise, sipping her wine.

"Translatable?" asked M. Vallery, "most of the comic things that happen in the French country-side aren't. But they're very funny for all of that." He laughed reminiscently and stroked his beard.

Memories of Jeanne and Isabelle, and what they considered comic stories rose blackly to Marise's mind. She turned a gay, laughing face to M. Vallery and translated for his benefit Aunt Hetty's latest story about what happened when a skunk got into the hen-house, and she and Agnes went to the rescue at midnight in their night-gowns and night-caps. It was as much to drown out what was going on inside her own mind, as to amuse the others that she did her liveliest best by the story, telling it with the gusto and brio which made her a favorite with people who liked youthful high spirits. It was broad farce, nothing else, and she did not draw back from the farcical color it needed to carry it off. It was a story, she told herself, that either made people laugh *aux éclats,* or it was a failure. Her audience was certainly laughing *aux éclats* when she finished the account of the homeric night-battle, laughing and wiping their eyes.

"That reminds me," said M. Vallery, his eyes glistening with mirth, "of a story about a love-sick dog that my uncle used to have."

"You're not going to tell that story here," announced his wife, with the calm accent of mastery, which once in a while slipped from her in an unguarded moment. He went through the form of protesting, claiming that it was nothing—now-a-days people were not prudish—but his wife settled the matter by taking the floor herself, turning to the girls, and saying laughingly, "That uncle of my husband's—he was one of the old school—out of a Balzac novel of the provinces. There aren't any more like him. It was through a to-the-death quarrel with him that Auguste and I met each other."

This slid her easily along into talk of early days, a quarter of a century before, when she was in one of the first lycées, at the time when lay-school teachers were an abomination and a hissing to the decent church-going bourgeois.

Dryly, with the inimitable terse picturesqueness of phrase which made her famous as a talker with people who demanded a great deal more than youthful high spirits, she took them back with her, twenty years, into the remote provincial city where she had encountered every narrowness possible to bigotry and reaction, and had wound it all around her little finger. Through her highly amusing recital of how she had played on the prejudices of those provincials, how adroitly she had employed against them their very vices, their jealousy and suspicion of each other, their grasping avarice, their utter dumb-beast ignorance of what modern education meant, through all this played, like a little sulphurous flame, her acrid scorn and contempt for them, her vitriolic satisfaction in having cheated and beaten them, in having turned them inside out and made fools of them, without their ever once suspecting it. Her husband's admiration of her powers was boundless.

"That is now one of the most properous and successful lycées in eastern France," he told the girls, "and every year they have a big dinner with my wife as guest of honor, with speeches and things, and somebody lays a wreath on her as though she were a statue. Quite a joke, hein?"

"Well, that must be an enjoyable occasion indeed," thought Marise, seeing the scene as though she had been there; the simple-minded provincials, trying simple-mindedly to honor the founder of their lycée; Mme. Vallery sitting at the right hand of their Mayor, with her mild air of deprecating the too-great honor done her—and her little sulphurous flame of vitriolic contempt playing over the convolutions of her brain. "Yes, it is a very pretty world we live in," thought Marise, laughing heartily at Mme. Vallery's satirical imitation of one of the clumsy speeches made in her honor on the last occasion.

She thought it still a prettier world, when in the cab as she was accompanying Eugenia back to Auteuil, Eugenia said, radiating satisfaction, "I'm to have my part in the fête-de-charité, too!"

"You *are!*" said Marise, "what are you going to do?"

"I'm going to give the money to pay for the appearance of a Russian dancer . . . the very newest thing. It will be the *clou* of the entire fête. And my name is going on the program!"

"Eh bien!" cried Marise in the liveliest surprise, "why, I didn't hear a word about all this."

"No, it was in talking with M. Vallery that the plan was made. He hadn't dreamed of their being able to afford such a thing. It was my own idea. He was quite carried away by it, couldn't see how I came to think of it."

Marise was silent, meditating profoundly on the prettiness of the world in which we are called upon to live. The more she meditated, the hotter grew her resentment. It was all very well to be cynical, and it was foolish and raw to be surprised at cynicism, but this was a little . . . really a *little* excessive! She flushed angrily as she went over in her mind the oiled exactitude with which each cog had slipped into the next, the casual invitation to Eugenia, M. Vallery's admiration of her beauty, the talk on the balcony . . . oh, poor Eugenia! what a fool she must have seemed, with her naïve impression that it was her own idea! And how that fatuous barber's model must have laughed with his wife after they had left! The shameless team-work with which they had turned the talk to something far-away, and kept it there . . . and, she flinched, her vanity cut to the quick, her own naïve blindness to the little game they were putting up on her. Well, she would know better next time. She had unpeeled one more layer from this pretty, pretty world of ours.

Speaking on impulse, she now said rather abruptly, to Eugenia, "I wouldn't have much to do with the Vallerys, if I were you. He's really an awful cad."

Eugenia looked at her with a knowing smile, "You're jealous," she said laughing, "he didn't take *you* off to show you the Luxembourg in spring!"

Marise was for an instant stricken so speechless by this idea that she could only stare. And by the time she could have spoken, she perceived that there was nothing to say, no comment on the prettiness of the world and the people who live in it, that began to be adequate.

At the great gates of the school-parc, Eugenia and her maid descended. Eugenia kissed Marise good-by, the correct kiss on each cheek this time. Nothing annoyed Eugenia more than any reference, intended or imaginary, to the time when she had gone about kissing her school-mates on the mouth.

After the other two had rung the clanging bell and been admitted, Marise stood for a moment, hesitating. Then she decided to walk home, although home was a long, long way from Auteuil. It would do her good, she thought, setting out at the powerful, swinging gait she had for the long walks which for her, as for the more energetic of her class-mates, had been the only form of out-door sport accessible.

She had decided to walk so that she could cool off, and think over the Vallerys' manœuver, and as she walked she had it out with herself, going deep. By the end of the first mile she knew it was foolish and futile to resent the afternoon's comedy. That was the sort of thing everybody tried to do, only few people were as successful as Mme. Vallery. She knew well enough what she would get, if she pelted right in on them now, as they sat laughing over their little triumph. They would never dream of denying it, any more than she or her father would deny being the author of a far-laid plan in chess, which led to an opponent's defeat.

It was all a part of the game, and she might as well make up her mind to it, and renew her determination to keep out of the game as far as she personally was concerned. They were no worse than other people, only more intelligent and more interesting. She could tell, to the very turn of the phrase, what Mme. Vallery would say to her if she should have the crassness to go in and make a scene.

"My dear child, no power on earth can protect naïveté! It is a lamb whose wool belongs to the best shearer. Let her sharpen her wits, your young friend. She'll need to, sooner or later. It ought to have been the best of practice for her, a little skirmish like the one we just furnished her. She would do well to practise before she gets into a serious skirmish with somebody who *really* wants something out of her. What is this fête-de-charité for? To please me? Not at all. To make some money for poor people, mothers and anæmic babies. Show me another woman in our circle who puts herself out as much as I do for the poor! Your pretty friend has more money than is good for her. I'm only securing a little of it for the needy."

That was true, too, thought Marise. Mme. Vallery really did a lot of good, and very unostentatiously. If people were only far enough beneath her in intelligence and social position and money, she would do anything for them, very simply, in the nicest sort of way. And if she took a rather horrid delight in making fools of people more pretentious, what had Marise to reproach her with—she who could not refrain from malicious teasing! It was part of the same thing. Everything was part of the same thing. And the same thing always turned out to be very much the same. Also, Mme. Vallery had really always been very kind to Marise, seemed really fond of her, had given her innumerable opportunities which otherwise she would never . . .

"What does she want to get out of *me?*" Marise suddenly asked herself, struck by a sudden suspicion and wondering why she had never thought of this before.

Pondering this, unpeeling another layer, an acrid odor in her nostrils, she struck out into a longer, swifter gait, at her old futile trick of trying to hurry away from what was inside her heart.

The tall, slim, lithe girl, walking swiftly through the sweet spring twilight looked like the personification of spring-time with her fresh young face, her dewy dark eyes, her sensitive mobile young mouth, red as a dark red rose. She looked like Youth itself, welcoming in the new season. Several people glanced after her, and smiled with sympathy for her freshness and bloom and untouched virginal candor.

CHAPTER XL

I

EUGENIA had been complaining that her new teacher in advanced French diction was very ill-natured and exacting, and had asked Marise to go with her to a lesson to back her up in a protest against his unreasonable demands.

The two girls drove up to the Français in Eugenia's inevitable cab, and leaving her inevitable maid to wait in it, passed through the dingy little side-door into an ill-lighted corridor and felt their way toilsomely up a stair-way not lighted at all. A dingy, stone-colored corridor with painted and numbered doors on each side, like a needy old-man's home or ill-kept reformatory. A knock at one of these, opened by a bald, pale, elderly man, with a knobby nose and several chins. A tiny, cluttered, stuffy room, with a lumpy sofa, two chairs, an easel and a window.

After her presentation to M. Vaudoyer, Marise sat down on one of the hard chairs to await developments. The actor was in a long, paint-stained blouse, and excused himself by saying that his pupil was a little ahead of time, "A real American," he said, smiling at both of them. He had been painting, he explained, waving a wrinkled old hand towards a canvas on an easel.

"Oh, you are twice an artist," remarked Marise, doing as she had been taught to do, automatically turning a pretty speech. As a matter of fact, she thought the sketch anything but artistic.

The old man's face clouded. "To be a painter, that was all I ever wanted," he said, looking with affection at the very mediocre landscape, and adding sadly, "All my life . . . all my life."

364

"But to have been—to be such an artist as you are on the stage—surely that ought to be enough," said Marise. This time she spoke sincerely, out of a very genuine admiration for his acting.

"One does what one can, what one can," said the old man, resignedly, unbuttoning his blouse and dragging it off, revealing snuffy and crumpled black garments. He looked, thought Marise, like the parish priest of a very poor and neglected parish. And he had been for years—why, for a life-time, one of the most solidly esteemed and admired actors in the finest theatrical company in the world. "What more does any man want?" Marise asked herself, wondering why his face in repose was so bitter and melancholy.

Before beginning his lesson, he gave a last look at his painting, "What do you think of it? What do you think of it?" he asked suddenly, turning on Marise, the question like a loaded revolver at her temple.

Much practice had steadied Marise's nerves against any sort of hold-up that could be practised in social relations. She said instantly, "I think it shows one of the most charming landscapes I ever saw. Where in the world is there such a delightful composition?"

She was dealing with some one infinitely more practised than she, who was not in the least taken in by her evasion. Sighing, he turned the canvas with its face to the easel, and told her over his shoulder, "It's in my own country, where I ought to have stayed and been a dumb-beast, and happy. Nowhere you ever heard of, a far corner of the Pyrenees. Saint-Sauveur is the name." And as if, in spite of himself, to pronounce the name moved him, he broke out, "It's the most beautiful place —a little heaven on earth—why should any one leave it to spend his life in this boulevard hell of malignity? Such noble lines in its mountains, such grand pacifying harmony in the valleys—enough to reconcile a man to being alive! Such details as it has too! There is a gorge there where the *gave de* Gavarnie rushes down. Always on the hottest, dustiest, most blinding summer day, it is cool there, the air green like Chartres stained-glass, and alive with the thunder of the water."

He frowned, shook his head, put his hand to a book on the
table, and said, dismissing his evocation with a shrug, "Eh
bien . . . eh bien . . . !"

The lesson began but Marise heard not a word of it, not a
word. She sat straight on the hard chair, her face a blank,
and walked up the street with Jeanne, seeing in the blue twilight, the pale face of Jean-Pierre Garnier approaching them.
The alcove curtains hung close before her, and Jeanne's voice
was on the other side. And then, the burst of men's laughter
from across the landing, cut short by Jeanne's closing the door;
and then the heavy, dragging step in the corridor, the loud,
harsh breathing. She waited, tense with fright, to see the curtains twitch open, and Jeanne's dreadful face appear . . .
some one was speaking to her, urgently, insistently, by
name. . . .

"Marise, Marise. . . ." It was Eugenia speaking to her,
"Help me explain to M. Vaudoyer that I haven't the least desire to become an actress, or to know every word of Molière
by heart! That I simply want lessons in how to pronounce
French correctly, the kind of lessons my English-diction teacher
gives me." She spoke with an impatient accent, and Marise
coming to herself saw the two facing each other with angry
looks.

M. Vaudoyer said indignantly, "It's not worth my while
to give instruction to a student who will not do the necessary
work."

"I will do any *necessary* work," Eugenia answered hotly,
"but what has reading a lot of deadly dull old books to do
with pronouncing French correctly? And if I'm not going
to be an actress or a singer, what *is* the use of all those idiotic
ah! ah! oh! oh! fee! fee! exercises?"

M. Vaudoyer sat down abruptly, and reaching for a large
red-and-white checked hankerchief, mopped his bald head
and perspiring face with it. He was evidently containing
himself with difficulty and waiting till he could be sure of
speaking with moderation before he opened his lips.

Eugenia explained to Marise with dignity, glad of the opportunity to state her case, "I come to M. Vaudoyer for lessons in diction. I don't come to study singing or seventeenth-century history. I hate history and all those dull studies. I don't see why everybody should always be trying to force me into them. M. Vaudoyer gets very angry because I will not practise singing lessons and because I cannot find the time to spend hours in the Bibliothèque Nationale reading all about everything that happened in Molière's time. What do I care what happened in Molière's time? What I want, what I am paying for, is a very simple thing. Instruction in French diction. I don't see that I am getting it."

Her accent showed that she considered her case unassailably good and reasonable.

M. Vaudoyer listened with attention, looking at her very hard, and when she had finished he nodded, "You are right, Miss Mills. I am not the teacher for you. I am a poor, old, impractical Frenchman, incapable of satisfying a practical American girl, who knows what she wants and has the money to buy it. You are the race of the future, you Americans, I of the past. There is no common ground between us." He spoke mildly. Eugenia stared. Marise winced.

"What do you mean, M. Vaudoyer?" asked Eugenia. "Are you sending me away?"

He said with a little smile, "You have sent me away, Miss Mills, far away. And as to what I mean, if you like, I will try to tell you. But you will not understand. I cannot talk the American language. I can only speak the French language." He paused, wiping his perspiring forehead again with his checked handkerchief. "There are two parts to every art. One is the thorough command of your medium; the other is the personality you express through your medium. Neither has the slightest value without the other. Neither is to be had without paying the price of all you have . . . *all*, all!

"You must have perfect command of your medium, just in itself, as a tool. Listen," he stood up, his heavily jowled face grim and stern, drew a long breath, as if he were about to speak, and then as at a sudden thought, paused, the expression of his face changing with comical suddenness to a broad smile, and began to laugh. The girls stared at him in amazement, wondering if he had taken leave of his senses. Apparently something very funny had popped into his mind, just as he was about to go on with his statement to them. It must have been really *very* funny indeed, for he could not stop his laughter, try as he might. It was too much for him. Both hands on his hips, throwing back his head, he pealed out an irresistible, "Ha! Ha!" as though he would burst if he did not laugh. Seeing their astonished faces, he tried to stop to tell them the joke, choked himself down to rich chuckles, opened his mouth to speak, and, the joke striking him afresh, went off again in a huge roar of mirth that made them both smile and then laugh outright in sympathy.

At this, his face instantly resumed its sad, stern expression, and he was looking at them severely as before, breathing quickly, it is true, as though he had been running, but without a trace of any feeling.

"There you see," he said drily. "That is an example of what I mean by command of a medium. To be master of *my* tool I must not only be able to laugh, when I feel like it, but whenever I need to laugh, whether I feel like it or not. And I assure you, young ladies, I do not feel in the least like laughing now, having had this glimpse of the future as it will be, shaped to the American mold, by the people of the future."

The girls were stricken silent by all this, their lips, frozen in astonishment, still curving in the set smile that was all that was left of their foolish, induced mirth. Marise was nettled and angry. He had no business playing tricks like that on them. She had been made to appear foolish, horribly foolish, and she resented it.

"Well, Miss Mills," he went on, addressing Eugenia, "you cannot get such a control of your medium, you cannot learn to speak any language beautifully, without long, long dull hours of the oh! oh! ah! ah! practice that you scorn. You cannot buy such a command of your medium, not for millions of your great round dollars. No, not the wealthiest, sharpest American who ever lived can possess European culture, by buying little pieces of it here and there, and hanging it up on his wall. By changing the very fibre of your being, that is the only way to become anything that is worth becoming. And you cannot change the fibre of your being without dying a thousand deaths and knowing a thousand births."

He puffed out a scornful breath and went on, "And for the other half, Miss Mills. You want to learn diction by reading to me. But what you read has sense. It is not just consonants and vowels. And to read it well, you must understand it. And to understand it, you must know something—do you understand me? You must *know* something. I soon found that you could not understand Molière, because you know no history, no literature, nor anything else you should have been learning. You cannot read with any over-tones in your voice, unless you understand the over-tones of what you are reading. You cannot read Molière, or anybody else, as if you were reading,

"'*Barbara; celarent; darii; ferio; baralipton.*'

"Or at least—" His carefully repressed indignation burst for a moment from his control; he said in a roar, "At least you cannot in *my* loge—not, not even an American, not even a representative of the people of the future!"

He had risen to his feet, trembling with his anger, a high-priest rebuking a blasphemy. The girls shrank back, startled.

At once he extinguished the flame, went for a moment to the window, and when he turned back, said quietly, "You must excuse an old man's bad temper, Miss Mills, and you must look for a politer, more practical teacher. I can give you the address of one who will suit you. I can, in fact," he said smoothly, "give you the addresses of several hundred who will suit you perfectly. I will send the addresses of several to you. Good-day, Miss Mills. Good-by, Miss . . ." He was vague as to Marise's name, but murmured something with an absent courtesy. He stepped to the door, opened it with an urbane inclination of the head.

Eugenia held in her hand the sealed envelope which contained the usual fee for a lesson, and now looked down at it, uncertain whether she dared offer it. He saw her glance at it, and relieved her of her uncertainty, "No, no fee to-day, Miss Mills. I have given you no lesson." As they passed before him, he added under his breath, "No lesson, that is, that will be of any value to you."

Marise glancing over her shoulder, saw him turn at once to the easel and reach for his palette and brushes. He had dropped them from his mind. It was the airy, finishing touch to their humiliation. She burned with anger and shame.

They groped their way down the darkened stairs in silence, neither trusting herself to speak, lest she burst into tears.

At the bottom Marise said neutrally, "I have a music lesson now. Would you like to come along?"

Eugenia said in a loud, quavering voice, "I should think not! I have had enough of their hatefulness for *one* day!" She went on, her voice shaken by suppressed sobs which did not at all fit what she was saying, "And I h-have an appointment w-with the hairdresser anyhow." She fumbled with a desperate haste in her little gold-beaded hand-bag, jerked out a lacy handkerchief and wiped her eyes angrily. But more tears came, a flood of nervous, excited tears, which ran down in big drops. She flung her arms around Marise's neck and hiding her face on her shoulder, cried out pitifully, "Oh, Marise, don't you ever just want to go back *home?*"

Marise's heart was very full of compassion, very barren of consolation. "I haven't any home to go back to, any more than you," she said in a whisper.

Eugenia reached up, pulled her head down and kissed her, still sobbing. Marise kept her cheek pressed against the other's tear-wet face, aching with her helplessness, burning to find some word of comfort, finding nothing but loving silence to express her tenderness and pity.

A door opened upstairs, laughing voices sounded on the landing above. The two girls drew apart and moved towards the door hand in hand.

II

Mme. de la Cueva had been crying and Marise guessed that she was getting ready to have a new husband. She seemed to have had bad luck in husbands. The one who had just been put to the door was the second Marise had known in the four years of her study with the pianist, and there had been at least two before that. It was a terrible grief to her always to find out that she no longer cared for the one she had; but she faced the facts with courage, allowing herself no dissembling, no bourgeoise timidity. The old one disappeared, and in a few months a new one was there.

"Good-day, my child," said the pianist affectionately, pulling Marise down to kiss her on both cheeks. "No lesson to-day nor to-morrow," she spoke solemnly, the tears in her eyes.

She began to cry openly.

Marise sat down by her, startled out of her own mood of resentment. "Why, dear Madame de la Cueva, why?" she asked, "What has happened?"

"I am going to America," said the older woman. "Georges Noel and I are booked for a concert tour of the world. We will be married in Australia."

The inevitable first thought of the magnificent egotism of youth was for itself, "Why, what shall *I* do?" cried Marise aggrieved.

Mme. de la Cueva did not resent this. She never resented anything which she recognized as natural. And this seemed to her pre-eminently natural and proper. She took Marise's hand in hers tenderly, maternally.

"It is for your good, my dear child, the change, though I know how you will miss me. You need some one else. A year with the old Visconti will be the making of you."

"The old Visconti!" cried Marise, "but he lives in Rome!"

"But it is perfectly possible for other people to live in Rome too! My dear child, a year in Rome at your age . . . it will be the making of you! You will always bless your poor old de la Cueva who secured it for you. Youth, talent, beauty,

Rome!" she drew the picture with envious admiration of its possibilities.

There was no use trying to reason with her, as one would with any one else, Marise knew that from experience— no use trying to show the material, practical obstacles in the way. What would her father say? How could she go alone to Rome to live? Not that Mme. de la Cueva would have hesitated at any age to go anywhere alone to live—but she would not long have remained alone! How like Mme. de la Cueva to dispose of her so calmly! Even as Marise said all this to herself she was aware by a sudden warm gush of pleasure and excitement in her heart that she was delighted beyond measure with the plan, that she had been longing for some change in her life, that she had been growing deathly stale in the same old round, the absurdly life-and-death consultations with Biron in the kitchen, the same old professors at the Sorbonne with the same old glass of sugar-and-water and the same high-keyed nasal delivery of the same old lectures, even Mme. de la Cueva with her same old clichés about mass and bulk in the bass. She felt no guilt about this last, for if there were one person in the world who understood entirely the fatigue at the recurrence of the same old things, it was Mme. de la Cueva! The pianist looking at her young disciple with discerning and experienced eyes, saw something of this and smiled sympathetically.

"You have been working, working, working, and now it is time to run a little free, my Marisette," she said, patting her hand, "you are . . . how old?"

"Twenty-one to-day," said Marise.

"Exactly! As though Fate had timed it. Very likely Fate did." She had a great faith in Fate provided one did not hang back before the doors Fate set open before one. Personally she had never hesitated to step through every one that had been even ajar.

"A year in Rome with the old Visconti, who has the most wonderful sense of rhythm of any man alive—the real, the living rhythm—the life, the personality of music! Make yourself a docile little pair of ears and nothing else when he talks to you of rhythm! And pay *no* attention, none, do you hear, to his fingering! It is *infecte, ignoble!* Then after a year, I shall be here again to see what else you need before I launch you—good old Maman de la Cueva will be thinking of you all the time. . . ."

"But I am not in the least sure I can manage a year in Rome," protested Marise, breaking in with a hurried protest against this taking-for-granted of everything, "I never dreamed of going to Rome! My father . . ."

"Oh, you can manage it," Madame de la Cueva assured her carelessly, "one can always manage whatever one really wants to do. Especially if it depends on a man."

She crossed the room now to pull at a bell-cord and to order tea of the stout, elderly maid who came. Such a cosmopolitan as Madame de la Cueva would of course have tea.

"We shall have tea together, my dear, to celebrate your birthday and my new plans, and to have a last talk together, the last talk before you grow up."

Her tears were forgotten. They had been shed, and that was the end of them. It was thus that one should live, she believed, crying heartily when one felt like it, and having it over with. She detested what she called the "brain-sickening Anglo-Saxon mania of bottling up emotion till it grows so intense you get no enjoyment out of it," and she was much given to cautioning against this mania those few of her pupils whom she took seriously and for whom she labored her valiant best, pouring out for them all her wisdom, musical and otherwise.

She came back now, and sat before the piano, her amplitude overflowing the stool as a mighty inflooding wave overflows a rock.

"While Giuseppina is making our tea, I'll play to you," she announced. She put her beautiful hands on the keys like a millionaire plunging his hands into a coffer of jewels and offering a choice between pearls and rubies, "What will you have? What do you feel like?"

Marise felt more like an earthquake in full activity than anything else, and chose accordingly, "If I'm going to Rome for a year, I feel like fireworks," she said with a rather breathless laugh, "something Hungarian . . . Liszt, perhaps."

Madame de la Cueva settled herself and was off, Marise's heart galloping beside her in the wild rush over the plain. The little lean, wiry, ewe-necked horse under her tore along, sure-footed, as carried away by the stampede as his rider. There was a lance in her hand, a lance with a little blood-red, ragged flag, fluttering loudly against the wind of their forward rush like a bird struggling to escape and fly. Marise heard its throbbing struggle above the rhythmic thunder of the hoofs and felt her heart fluttering like a caught bird in sympathy. And now, with a long, rending slide from bass to treble, it tore itself loose, the wind caught it and whirled it up high over their heads as they plunged along. There it rode among the clouds, like a scarlet storm-bird, sinking and falling and advancing to a longer, nobler, more ample rhythm than that of their many-hoofed clattering. Marise's heart soared up with it, soared out of the noisy clattering, up to the clouds, to the noble, long curves of the wind's soundless advance . . . soundless . . . the piano was silent. Madame de la Cueva had played the last half-heard, velvet note that was prolonged, prolonged by the sweep of that noble line. She and Marise floated with it for a moment, and then as it swept on and left them, they slowly eddied down to the ground like dry leaves.

Giuseppina came in with the tea. Madame de la Cueva turned round on the piano-stool, a fat, elderly woman with three chins.

"Not so bad for the old lady, hein?" she said, well-pleased with herself and with Marise's dazzled look.

Marise attempted no thanks, no comment. Silently, like a person hypnotized she took the proffered cup, nodding her desire for two lumps and lemon; and silently, like a person hypnotized she listened to Madame de la Cueva's monologue. The music like a rich wine had unloosed the musician's tongue. In a mood like this she "turned the faucet and it ran."

"My little one," she said fondly to Marise, "my little one, so here you are on the beach ready to take the plunge—

twenty-one to-day! And your poor old de la Cueva will not be here to advise you. Oh well, there's only one mistake that is worse than giving advice, and that is taking it. Never take anybody's advice, my darling, nobody's at all."

She drank the half of her cup of tea, not by any means noiselessly, wiped her mustache with the tiny, beautifully fine, embroidered tea-napkin, and hanging lovingly over the plate of patisseries, chose the fluffiest with a sigh of satisfaction.

"The only thing not to do, the only mistake possible to make, is to stand shivering on the beach, not to plunge in and breast the waves. Breast the waves!" she showed by a wide gesture of her powerful arm what she meant.

"And you can't swim with anything or anybody hanging around your neck. The moment they begin to weigh on you . . . p-f-f-t! off with them! Nothing you can do will help people who can't swim themselves. They'll only drag you down with them.

"My dear child, remember this, that if there is an element in life hateful to the free human soul it is what is called permanence. The only permanent thing any human being should recognize is his tomb. From everything else he must climb out and go on, go on.

"Above all, beware of permanence in love. It is a paradox ever to speak of love and permanence in the same breath. Life and death! They cannot exist together. Women as a rule, all women who are not artists, make their mistakes in that way. You are a woman now, and an artist, it is the duty of an older woman and an artist to warn you against it. The only way not to be a life-long victim of men is to take love as they it . . . for the pleasure. Men wish nothing from love but their pleasure. It is a vain and foolish striving to try and give them more, or to try and get more from them."

She took another éclair and said on a softer note, "I don't deny that women are more naturally given to the folly of seeking permanence in love than men. I myself have a weakness in that direction." Marise looked down into her cup to hide an involuntary smile at this. "Each time I love, the illusion is that it is now for eternity. Each time the wrench costs me tears. . . . You saw my tears, my dear!

"No, the only thing to do is to use it, as men do, to feed one's art. You heard how superbly I played that Liszt! That is Georges, that is the new flame leaping up from a lamp that was burning out!"

She poured another cup, and seasoned it with care. Marise ventured to say mildly, "I'm afraid I'm rather cold. I don't . . . I haven't ever cared much for men."

Madame de la Cueva shook her head, "Every unawakened girl thinks that. And once in a while there is a monster born, sometimes a man, more often a woman, who is born really cold—like a born half-wit or a two-headed cat. But any one of experience can feel them in the room, as you feel a snake. *You* are not cold, my darling. No one who can play The Tragica as you do, is cold. You are only a child. You Anglo-Saxons take so long to ripen. But all the better for your technique—that quaint prolongation of infancy. But *now*," she put down her cup and looked at Marise deeply and masterfully, "now your infancy has lasted long enough. In with you! Dive from the nearest rock! Head over heels! I shall hear the splash from across the world and rejoice."

Marise laughed a little nervously, partly because she was amused and partly because she was excited. That great mass of personality, radiating magnetism, would excite a statue on a tomb, she thought to herself, even though you didn't at all share her tastes, or like the things she did.

"And when I say, 'in with you,' I don't mean any of the sentimental slip-noose business of becoming a house-mother with children—oh, whatever else, my dear, no children. The only artists who can afford to have children are men, because men never really love their children and can abandon them at any time they need to. No woman can do that. Even *I* could never have done that!

"You see, carissima mea, in love a man always keeps most of himself for himself, as in everything else. You must do the same if you are not to be cheated in every bargain that life offers you. It is a hard lesson to learn. It will cost you many tears. But tears are valuable. You cannot live and be an artist, without tears. Shed them freely and you will see how you will grow."

She looked at her watch, "I expect Georges at five," she explained, and swept on to her peroration, "Remember, think of all I tell you when your wise old friend who knows life is far away. Remember! None of your Anglo-Saxon nonsense about trying to get along without sex-life. Take it, take all you need of it, but keep it separate from your real life as a man does, and it will never poison or embitter you." She laughed a little, triumphantly, "You will *do* all the embittering instead of enduring it. You have beauty. You can buy anything you want with it, if you learn how to use it. You have what will advance you more than any talent for music! You have a nice talent, but you will go ten times as far as a woman with a big nose and poor hair. Make your brain a little mint, my darling, coin your good looks into legal tender, and buy success."

She kissed the girl and dismissed her, with another look at her watch and then into the mirror.

Marise stumbled down the stairs, a little dizzied by the sudden removal of that pressing, urgent, magnetic personality. To step out suddenly from under it, was like stepping into a vacuum. Her ears rang.

At the street-door she paused, waiting for the mist to clear from before her eyes. She peered out into the quiet street, as if she were looking into life itself, the life that Madame de la Cueva had so magisterially set before her. And she loathed in anticipation everything that was waiting for her there.

There lay the world, grown-up life, Rome, her career, before her, and apparently there was nothing in it which she would not detest. Love . . . the love that Madame de la Cueva had shown her how to get . . . she shrank away from it with a proud, cold scorn, her nostrils quivering. Music . . . there was no music in that program, only an exploitation of music to buy personal success for her. And she loved music . . . fiercely she clung to that, as the one thing that would not betray her, the one thing she dared love with all her heart.

She stood on the threshold of the street-door, dreading to take even one step forward into it all, till the concierge looked at her hard, with a disagreeable smile, suspecting a rendez-vous with a lover. Marise saw the look, knew what it meant, felt it push her forward, knew in anticipation how that sort of look and what lay back of it would be always pushing her forward into what she hated.

With a long breath she stepped into the street, into the road that stretched before her. She held her head high, with an angry pride. The concierge-soul of the world must never know what was inside her life. The thing to do, the only thing she saw that was tolerable to do, was to take care that she was not being fooled. Well, she thought with a grave, still bitterness, she certainly ought to know something about that.

THE END OF ALL ROADS

CHAPTER XLI

1909

NEALE sat idly in front of the black-and-white façade of the Orvieto Cathedral, trying idly to make up his mind on a matter of no importance whatever and not getting on very fast. In his pocket was his ticket back to New York and his ship sailed in a week. But, of course, it did not sail from Orvieto. Should he go south to Naples where most of the passengers took ship? If he did, he could stop over four or five days in Rome. It might be interesting to revisit Rome. Or should he go north to Genoa, where the ship was due to stop the day after leaving Naples? He had not seen Genoa at all and he might be missing something worth while. It ought to stir any American's imagination to hang about the docks where a certain visionary, middle-aged sailor-man had gone up and down trying to raise the funds for a mad attempt to prove the world absolutely different from what everybody else had thought.

He sat there looking up at the Cathedral, deciding now for Genoa and now for Rome, and in between times forgetting all about the matter, so evenly balanced were the advantages, so unimportant was the whole business. When he finally stood up to go back to his inn, he remembered that he had still not settled which train to take.

He took a coin out of his pocket. He'd toss up. Heads for Naples, tails for Genoa.

The coin flashed up in the sun, and fell on the stone steps. In the intense, somnolent silence of the little provincial square its tinkle sounded loud and clear. All the loungers turned their heads quickly at the sound. Neale stooped over it.

Heads, Naples. All right. He'd inquire when he got to Rome if they didn't perhaps run a boat-train down, just before sailing time.

As he was unstrapping his suit-case that night in his room in

the Roman pension, it did not greatly surprise him to have
Livingstone knock at the door and step in. Livingstone had
been at that pension before, during Neale's first leisurely sauntering visit to Rome; Livingstone had turned up at the pension
in Florence before Neale left; he had run across Livingstone
in a Paris café sitting alone at a table, looking as much like an
attaché of the Embassy as he could manage. Livingstone
was no tourist but one of the professional inhabitants of
Europe; an American, that much he admitted, though neither
hints nor direct British questioning had ever extracted from
him his birthplace in the States. He was the sort of man who
had learned how to cross his long thin legs elegantly so that
the toe of one slim foot pointed downward. As at the
same time he was wont to fold his arms over his hollowed
chest, stoop his shoulders and droop his neck, and as he wore
gray gaiters and carried a walking stick he had good reason
to flatter himself that he had altogether the distinguished,
pinched, sickly, aristocratic look of the traditional promising
young-old diplomat. Neale was not surprised to see him in
Rome. He would not have been surprised to see him anywhere—except perhaps at work. It was Neale's guess that
three or four years from now he would have screwed up his
courage to wearing a monocle.

"Hello, Crittenden," he said, "it *is* you, is it? When Michele
told me you had turned up again, I was sure he must be
mistaken. I understood you were on the high seas, on your
way back to the land of the free and the home of bad cooking."

Without being invited, he sank down in a chair to watch
Neale unpack and wash, asking, "You were going back to
New York, weren't you?"

"Yes, I still am. I'm only in Rome for five days. But I
won't be long in the States. I'll be on my way to China
and the East."

Livingstone was mildly interested. "You don't say so!
Well, you might really get there by starting off to New York.
But I admit I don't see the connection. Why don't you take
a P. and O. for India?"

"A little business to attend to first. A small inheritance to cash in on."

"Inheritance!" cried Livingstone, sitting up straight. "The very word makes my mouth water. Why doesn't that ever happen to me?" The expression on his face was like that of the loungers in front of the Cathedral when they heard the coin drop.

Through the lather of soap-suds on his face, Neale laughed, "A very two-for-a-cent inheritance. An old great-uncle I hardly knew—never saw him but once or twice, years ago when I was a kid, left me his home and his little old-fashioned saw-mill and wood-working plant, back up at the end of no-where in Vermont."

"*No money!*" sympathized Livingstone. "But then of course you can sell all that for *some*thing. But no real money at all?"

"There's what he had in the savings bank—about four thousand dollars, the executor writes. Just enough to do nothing at all with."

Livingstone made a mental calculation. "I wouldn't wonder if you might get fifty dollars a month out of the whole thing. And that's enough. Ma foi! That's enough if you cut corners a little. *I* only have eighty-five. And then you can always give an occasional English lesson to piece out. You won't need ever to do a lick of work or ever live in the States. Mes felici-tations! That's the life! You'll be knowing Europe as well as I do, next. How soon will you be back?"

"I'm not coming back," said Neale, buttoning on a clean collar. "When I've cashed in and got what I can out of my uncle's business I'm going overland to San Francisco, and from there to the East."

Livingstone considered this, "Well, they do say that Chinese cooking is super-excellent once you get used to it."

"I'm not going for the cooking."

"No? What *are* you going for?"

"Oh, I don't know," said Neale rather sharply. "Because I feel like it. Why shouldn't I?"

Livingstone perceived that he had run on a hidden reef and

backed off. "Don't you want to come on into the salon and let me present you to the crowd?" he asked standing up and moving towards the door. "Since you were here some awfully nice people have come over from the Pension Alfierenti. Poor old Alfierenti died suddenly and his place is shut up for the present."

"No, thanks," said Neale. "I'm going up on the roof for a smoke before I go to bed."

"Oh, yes," Livingstone remembered, "you always did prefer the terrazza and your solitary pipe to the society of the ladies. Well, there is a nice view from up there; but between a view and a pretty girl who could hesitate?"

"Who, indeed?" said Neale dryly, going off up the stairs.

The plaster floor and low walls of the terrazza gleamed white and empty. As Neale had hoped there was not a soul there. Below him spread the roofs and domes and streets of Rome, richly-colored even in the white light of the moon, hanging like a great lamp over the city.

He took the corner that had been his favorite before, in the black shadow cast by a thick-leaved grape-vine, and perching on the edge of the wall, looked down meditatively on the city as he filled his pipe.

Well, so here he was in Rome—just as if something had pushed him here, where least of all places he had expected to find himself again. Odd that his year of travel should end with a second visit to the first European city that had stirred his imagination, that had given him a hint of what it was he had come to Europe to see. It was during his first stay in Rome that he stopped being a dumb, Baedecker-driven tourist, that he first got the idea of what Europe might teach him better than America could. It was here that he first thought of trying to get from Europe some idea of what men during a good many centuries had found worth doing.

For, unlike America, Europe was crammed full of objects little and big that men alone or in groups had devoted their lives to create. America had tried a number of experiments—once; but Europe had tried them all, so many times, at such different periods, in so many, so various centers of civilization! Such a crowded graveyard of human endeavor might perhaps suggest a satisfactory motive (if one existed) for going on living.

For a long time he had made no headway, had discovered no general underlying motive—indeed much of what he saw filled him with utter astonishment at the things men had cared for, even to the point of giving their lives to win them.

He still remembered that morning during his first stay, when he had stared with stupefaction at the rows of portrait-busts in the Capitoline Museum. So many men, most of them apparently intelligent had schemed and plotted through long years—and what for? To be the conventional head of an unworkable Empire, top-heavy with administration; to endure the hideous tedium of ceremony and pompous ritual which the office had imposed; to be forced to work through sycophants and grafters, to be exiled from healthy human life into a region where in the nature of things you could never hope to see one spontaneous sincere expression on any human face; where your life, your work, your reputation hung on the whim of the Prætorian Guard or the disgruntled legions on a distant frontier—why, if you lay awake nights you couldn't think of a more thankless job than being a Roman Emperor! And yet for centuries men had sacrificed their friends, their honor, their very lives to hold the office. Those old Romans, for all they looked so like ordinary every-day men you meet in the street, must have had a queer notion of what was worth-while in life!

Then he had left Rome and gone away without plan, anywhere the train would take him; and wherever he had gone he had walked about, silently attentive to what men had done with their lives. That was what he had been looking for as he walked around on battle-fields, or gazed up at Cathedrals or looked seriously at the statues thick-sown as the sands of the sea all over European cities; that was what he had been looking for as he sat alone in a pension bed-room reading a history or a biography that helped him fit together into some sort of a system all the diverse objects he had been considering.

Wherever he went, wherever he looked, he was like an archæologist raking over an inexhaustible kitchen-midden—he was surrounded by relics of innumerable generations crowding the long centuries during which men had lived and died on this old continent. Perhaps if he looked hard enough at what they had left behind them he might find out what men really wanted to do with their lives—perhaps he might get some hint of what he could do with his own life.

That was a subject he had never stopped to consider in America. Nothing in American life had suggested that you might have any choice except between different ways of earning your living. And yet he reflected it was rather an important question—at least as important as which baseball league you were going to root for.

It was so absolutely new to Neale to consider that question —any abstract question indeed—that for some months after he had shut down his desk in the office of the Gates Lumber Company, he felt his head whirl at the notion of trying to find an answer—an answer to any question, let alone so compendious a one as what it was that men wanted to do with their lives. The cogs and wheels of disinterested impersonal thought which had started to work in college, were stiff with disuse and refused to turn. All he had been able to do was to wonder, and stare, and read memoirs and histories, feeling like a strange cat in a very much cluttered garret. Was there anything in Europe that would really mean anything to him, to an American who was not esthetic, who refused to pretend, who frankly thought the average picture-gallery a dreary desert?

And then, very slowly, he had begun to make a guess that there was an arrangement in what looked so wildly hit-or-miss; as on the day when happening upon the little triumphal arch in Rheims he had at last got under his skin the idea of the Roman Empire, far-reaching, permeating with its law, customs, speech, the tiniest crevices of the provinces. To think of Romans living and governing and doing business in a little, one-horse, Gallic town like this! Maybe it hadn't been such a crazy aspiration to want to be Emperor—sort of like being President of the Standard Oil Company to-day. You knew in your heart that the job was too big for any man, but it was warming to your imagination even to pretend you were running a machine that covered the whole known world. And probably all of them had an illogical hunch that *they* would get away with it—and, by Jupiter, a lot of them had, and died peacefully in their beds. After all, so far as ordinary horse-sense went, wasn't devoting yourself to gathering together a great deal more money than you could possibly use, at least as odd a way of spending a human life as trying to hang on to the tail of the Roman Empire? And yet there were countless thousands of men all over Europe as well as in the United States who were hoping with all their souls that Fate would allow them to do just that. And a few did get away with it —just as some of the Emperors had. But it killed a great many—the Manager of the Gates Lumber Company, for instance. Every man knew that it might be the death of him, just as in the first century an Emperor knew he'd be lucky if he were killed quick. But nobody hung back for that in either century. Nobody really believed it would get *him!* Why, a year ago, Neale Crittenden himself had been tearing along towards it as hard as he could pelt.

Well, good God, you had to do *some*thing with yourself. You couldn't float along, your boneless tentacles rising and falling with the tides, like that jelly-fish of a Livingstone!

What was there for a man to do with himself? At all times evidently, some men had been satisfied in producing art of some kind or another—that wasn't any good for Neale. He hadn't an ounce of artistic feeling, wasn't even a craftsman, let alone an artist. And many men in every epoch had cared about fighting. That was more his sort—if you were sure you could find something worth fighting for! And many men had wanted to run things—not only for the feeling of personal power, but to straighten out the hopeless muddles humanity was always getting itself into. . . . He had lost the frail thread of his thought in a maze of speculations, comparisons, half-formulated ambitions.

But he had always come back to his problem. He did not

hurry. He had left the Gates Lumber Company so that he would not need to hurry! Sometimes he had caught a glimpse of the thread, lost it, felt it between his closing fingers, let it slip again. And whenever it escaped him and he found himself staring again at a jumbled confusion with no clue to its pattern, he had lit his pipe and smoked reflectively, his eyes fixed on whatever detail of European life chanced to be before them, a stained-glass window at Chartres, a crowded noisy café in Milan, the hydraulic cranes unloading cargoes from the Congo under the tower of Antwerp Cathedral. What men had left behind them looked from the outside like a heaped-up pile of heterogeneous junk, some good and some bad, and no way of guessing how any of it came to be. But Neale hung fast to that guess of his that there might be some meaning for him in it all, if he could only be patient enough and clear-headed enough to pick it out. He had never been an impatient temperament but he certainly had not of late years been especially clear-headed. During this reflective pause in his life, he felt his mind re-acquiring its capacity to do some abstract thinking. Released temporarily as he was from the necessity for immediate activity his head slowly cleared itself from the cloudy fumes given off by energy automatically rushing into action, blindly, planlessly. He began to perceive that he had been carried off his feet by the conviction of his time that activity, any activity at all, is all-sufficient, provided it is taken with speed, energy and decision. Neale had acquired speed, energy and decision in activity, but he'd be damned, he told himself once in a while, if he'd run his legs off any longer without seeing which way he was going.

As he sat now alone on the roof, overlooking the many, many monuments left as token of what men had wanted to do with their lives, he brought up and considered the few conclusions—the guesses at truth—the year had brought him. They didn't seem to amount to much, they were ridiculously slight as the sum-total of a year's earnest thought, but all this sort of thinking was so new and hard for him! At least such as they were, they were his own thoughts—he hadn't taken them on anybody else's say-so; and simple and inadequate as they seemed from the outside, they might be the first step towards understanding the truth—the truth for *him*.

To begin with, he hadn't in the least found out what men wanted or why they wanted it—all his classification had been like pressing wild-flowers and sticking them in a herbarium with the right Latin name tacked on—it cleared up some of the clutter, perhaps, but it left you mighty far from understanding life. All that he had learned from his classification was that men wanted a lot of contradictory things, and what one man would sell his soul to get, would break another one's heart to have. Well, wasn't that perhaps a clue? Wasn't it just that innate diversity which was at the root of a great many tragedies? Wasn't the trouble that men wouldn't let themselves act as individuals? Men were so hopelessly tied to the fashion of their century. Yes, men were fashion-ridden: they had no call to laugh at women's continuous-performance-vaudeville of big-sleeves, tight-lacing, hobble-skirts! Women cared about clothes, and every woman except a few dowds was out to look like every other woman, and just a little more so; men cared about the business of the world, and every man except a few freaks felt that he ought to outdo every one else at whatever all the men of his time were doing. And nobody wanted to be a freak. But the truth was that there were all sorts of men in the world all the time—who ought normally to do all sorts of different things. But did they? No, they didn't. No matter what you really wanted to do with your life, no matter what your particular life was best suited for, human tradition was always inflexibly insisting that you try to cut your life by the pattern considered fashionable at the time and in the place where you lived—try to be an Emperor in Imperial Rome, try to be a millionaire in twentieth century New York. People didn't seem able to consider even for a moment that there must be lots of men so made that they would prefer anything to the process of becoming an Emperor or a millionaire.

There rose before Neale now the restless, unhappy face of the young Frenchman he had come to know in Bourges, who one evening as they sat in the park near the Cathedral, poured out to him in a bitter flood his horrified sense of the closing in on him of bonds which he hated, which were being forged around him by the irresistible forces of social tradition and family affection. Fighting helplessly against overwhelming odds, he was slowly being shoved into becoming a *petit fonctionnaire* in Bourges for all his life. . . . *"Here,* in this *hole!"* he had cried looking around him with wild young eyes, like a rat in a trap. But there was his dear Maman's certainty that this feeling was mere youth, that he would soon settle down, and be contented in his office, and always, always be quite close to her; there was the relief of the family far and wide, now that he was *safe,* safe for life in a good little position with a nice little pension at the end! "Safe! How I loathe being safe!" he had cried. "Why wasn't I born three hundred years ago, so that I could have gone out with Champlain! Or later with Du Chaillou?"

In spite of all his sympathy for the poor kid, Neale hadn't seen then nor could he see now why anybody need wait for a Champlain or a Du Chaillou to come along. It looked as though the boy's grievance was because what he was meant to do didn't happen to be in fashion when he lived. Neale couldn't see what prevented him from getting right up on his feet from off the bench where he agonized, and marching off to the nearest port to work his way to Senegal, if that was where he thought he'd have the chance to use that latent stifled something in him which could never live in Bourges. Of course, it would give his mother a jolt, but if she was any kind of a mother, she'd want her son to have what was best for him. That was sure, if anything was. And as for the cousins and the aunts and uncles butting in . . . to hell with them! What business was it of theirs?

Neale had a suspicion that very likely the boy would be horrified by Senegal, not get on a bit better than in Bourges, and be mighty glad to come back to the safeness and comfort that irked him so now. If he had had pep enough to get on in Senegal, or anywhere else on his own, wouldn't he have had pep enough to cut loose from his leading-strings before this? Now was the time to do it, now or never, before he had acquired any personal responsibilities of his own choosing, that would *really* be an insuperable barrier to change. Neale felt nothing but the profoundest sympathy for people who found out they were in the wrong pigeon-hole after they had tied themselves up so they couldn't move. That was so awful a fate, that it did seem as though all grown-ups ought to league together in an impassioned effort to give youth as free a choice as possible. Instead of which—look what they'd done to this poor kid! Neale knew by the look of him how nervously sensitive he was. They'd trained nervous sensibility into him, instead of energy and combativeness. And then they brought to bear on him the thousand-pound-to-the-square-inch pressure of public opinion which provincial and family life in a small French town exerts on youth, to prevent its ever guessing at its essential freedom to seek out its own.

What sheep men were! . . . making long detours through open country to get around fences that had long since blown down.

In all the centuries of Roman Emperors had there been a single one of the misfits with good enough sense to see that he had got into the wrong job, and energy enough to pull out? Galba had declined the nomination a term or two, but in the end he'd accepted office—and got his throat cut inside a year. Even a high-class mind like Marcus Aurelius could think of no solution except, after office-hours, to write a book sympathizing with himself, like a fine-haired Corporation President solacing his soul by collecting cloisonné.

Of course the fashion of the country and the century was sure to fit some men. Old man Gates now: he *had* wanted to succeed in business, to be a millionaire, as much as Vespasian had wanted to be Emperor, and he had furiously enjoyed every hard-hitting moment of the life-and-death struggle which had carried him up from owning a small saw-mill in Connecticut to being the head of a rich and powerful company. He had died at eighty, as lusty and hard and sound an old condottiere as any other professional fighter who bestrode a bronze horse in an Italian piazza. But how about his son? What perhaps would the "young Mr. Gates" have liked to do with *his* life, if it had ever been suggested to him that he might do something else than go on making money by selling lumber for as much as possible above the price that had been paid for it?

What life-long mal-adjustment had resulted in that dreadful, twisted, weeping, elderly face which even now Neale could not forget?

Neale puffed a while silently, staring over at the Janiculum Hill, black with its dense trees beyond the moonlit city, until the distressing memory became less acute and he could go back calmly to his own problem. He was that much to the good anyhow. At least he'd found out what he did not want to do. He did not want to give his life to doing something simply because a lot of other men thought it was the only thing to do. At least he was sure that failure was certain along that road. And he was convinced that happiness—satisfaction, at least—was possible in human life. All his stored-up and accumulated health and strength and vitality made him sure that a sort of happiness was probable, even inevitable, if you had the good sense to get hold of the job you were intended to do. But what did he, Neale Crittenden, want to do? What was he intended for? He had asked himself that question a great many times and never had answered it yet. He looked again over at the Janiculum from which the beacon was flashing its message of red—white—green across Imperial Rome, across the Vatican. Over there stood the Garibaldi monument. There was a man who had known what to do with his life. He had created something. Oh, he was a product of his time, no doubt, and the busy little frock-coated Cavour had played a necessary part, but admitting all that, where would the Risorgimento have been without Garibaldi? In the fire and passion of his great heart, he had forged the sword of Italian Unity. Out of chaos he had created something with an ordered unity of its own. That was real creation. Was there any of it left to do—some little corner that an ordinary man could tackle?

Alone on the roof he pondered this, his hands clasped across his knees, his head tipped back, looking across the ancient city at the man who had kindled a fire in those old ashes.

And then, little by little, as the silence and beauty of the night spread out before his eyes in widening silver circles, he ceased pondering, ceased thinking even vaguely of himself, his life, other men's lives. He sat dreaming, his eyes as wide as a child's, his lips relaxed, his face absent and unconscious of self as that of one who listens absorbed and entranced to distant music. Moonlight—Italy!

Aware that he was no longer alone, he turned his head slowly and saw that a tall girl in white had come silently up the winding iron steps and was standing at the top looking at the sky. The moon shone full and soft upon her, from head to foot. He saw her as clearly as though it had been noon, and yet she looked as unearthly and mysterious as the night. She evidently thought herself alone. She stood perfectly motionless, her dark eyes fixed on a palely distant star. Neale thought he had never in his life seen anything more touching than the profound sadness of her young face.

He had not moved, had scarcely had time to draw breath; but she had felt him there. She turned her face toward where he sat, her head a little bent, searching the darkness of the corner from under long, finely-drawn brows. She saw him, looked straight into his eyes, her own shining deep and soft upon him. He was still too lost in his own enchanted dream to be able to move, to look away. He gazed at her as though she were part of the night, of the beauty.

Without a sound she turned back and sank like a dream from his sight.

CHAPTER XLII

THE next morning very early when he stepped out of his room, he saw at the end of the hall a little group of three people, the half-grown burly boy who carried water-pitchers and blacked shoes, the tall, aproned, black-moustached house-servant who swept the rooms and waited on the table, and the girl he had seen on the roof the night before. He knew her at once although she was in a street-dress now, and he saw only her back and the gleaming coils of her hair. He found that he had no intention of doing anything in the world but of going to speak to her, somehow; and turning down the tiled corridor he walked towards the three. They had their backs towards him and were all talking Italian with extreme rapidity. "Oh!" it came to Neale with a shock, "she was an Italian!" Of course, with those dark eyes and hair. It had not once occurred to him, during the night, that she might be an Italian. He felt hot with vexation. Damn it! He spoke so little Italian!

He stopped short in the passage-way irresolute, suffering that most wretched and miserable of human embarrassments, the one that began with the Tower of Babel. He wasn't going to make an idiot of himself trying to talk to her in that horrible broken tourist-Italian of his. His disappointment was so acute that he could not for an instant collect himself enough to turn away, and stood glowering at the three backs.

They were talking far too rapidly for him to understand what they said, but by their pantomime it was plain that the girl was moved by something which left the two men quite unaffected, that she was making a low-toned agitated appeal to them, which they received with the shrugged shoulders and uplifted eyebrows of reasonable men before an unreasonable idea. She was pointing out, leaning forward, shrinking back, she was saying, "Oh! oh! *oh!*" her low voice rising to a little

394

wail of distress that went to Neale's heart. He looked over their backs out of the window following the direction of the girl's hand, and saw at first only the beautiful, early-morning, myriad-winged swoop of the Roman swallows filling the bright air with their rhythmic wheelings. He had watched them for hours on his former visit, had thought them one of the most purely lovely elements of the city's charm.

"Oh!" cried the girl again, and covered her face with her hands.

Neale saw at last what she saw, a lean yellow cat crouching in ambush in a corner between a dormer window and a sky-light. As he looked the cat sprang up suddenly, a streak of murdering speed high into the air, and seized an incautious swallow swooping too low.

The two men at the window looked at the girl, shrugged their shoulders again and went back coolly to their work. The comedy was finished. What could any one do about it? Most evidently nothing. The man lifted his broom to sweep. The boy stooped to take up his water-pitcher. The girl took her hands from her face, and turned away from the window. Neale had expected to see her look agitated and excited; but her pale face was set in an expression of unsurprised endurance. It was evident that she too perceived that there was nothing to do about it.

"Well, there *was* something to do about it!" thought Neale wildly, feeling a fury of resentment at the two men. He'd show them!

He sprang past the girl with a great bound to the window and saw that, as he thought, a slope of tiled roof lay below it, the slope so gentle, the tiles so rough that it would be quite easy to keep his footing on it, although the drop to the court below would be dizzying if he stopped to look at it. But he did not stop to look at that, or anything but the cat, slinking slowly off across the roof beyond, the swallow in her mouth.

He took one long step out over the low window-sill and stood on the tiles. He heard the girl behind him give a cry, and it sped him forward. He ran along the narrow slope of tiles, one hand on the wall to steady himself till he could, with a leap, reach the roof where the cat was making off towards the ridge-pole with her prey. Here it was easier, a wide stretch of tiles over which he could really run.

The cat heard him, saw him, paused an instant, dazed by the suddenness of his appearance, turned her head and flattened herself for a leap forward. But his leap was quicker than hers. He reached her, and pounced on her with a swoop that was part of the forward rhythm of his running, pounced, seized her firmly, and forced open her jaws. The swallow dropped out on the tiles, wet and ruffled, its eyes closed, its poor, slim, gleaming head bent limply to one side as if its neck were broken.

Neale stooped and picked it up, stroking it pityingly and smoothing its pretty, rumpled plumes. He had been too late after all. But as it lay in his hand it seemed to him he felt its delicate body stir. Perhaps it was only half dead with fright. Did it move a little or had he imagined it? As he stood astride the ridge-pole of the roof, the level rays of the early sun shone straight into his eyes so that he could not see whether the bird's eyes had opened or not. He turned his back to the sun and held his hand, with the bird in it, closer to his face. Why, yes, the eyes were open, soft dark eyes that looked wildly and despairingly into his. The intensity of that sudden look gave him a start. He opened his fingers and the bird burst out of his hand with a loud beating flutter and soared up into the air. Neale threw back his head to watch it, moved almost to a shout of exultation as the twittering flock swooped past his head.

Then he saw that the cat was calmly making her way back to her ambush corner. "Hey, there!" he shouted gaily at her, and, sprinting along, snatched her up. "You're going back down cellar to catch rats, kitty mio," he told her aloud, laughing. He was astonished at his own high spirits. High up on the richly colored old roof, close to that glorious sun with the swallows dashing, twittering about his head, the rescued one among them, he could have flung his arms about and danced for sheer lightness of heart.

What he did was to tuck the protesting cat under his arm

and make his way back with considerably more caution than he had gone up. The passage along the narrow slope of tile below the window was worse than he had thought, made him a little sick to face. A damn-fool performance anyhow, he reflected, picking his steps, looking carefully away from the sheer black drop to the stone-paved courtyard below him. A very damn-fool performance for a serious-minded man of twenty-six to go careering over roofs like that.

With a short, quickly-taken breath of relief, he stepped over the window-sill back into the corridor. The men and the girl who had been leaning tensely out, watching him, stepped back respectfully to give him room.

Before he could turn to the girl, the servant had snatched the cat from under his arm, and with a fine air of virtuous indignation was cuffing her savagely over the head, pouring out on her a loud, highly-articulate flood of vituperation. The boy lifted his hand to join in the game, crying out, "Bestia del diavolo," "animaluzzo damnato!" and the like.

"Oh, good Lord!" thought Neale impatiently. "Isn't that just *like* them! Hey, *stop* that!" he cried aloud, and as the man paid no attention to this he seized him somewhat roughly by the shoulder in a grip that paralyzed the arm. He caught the cat as she fell and held her up over his head. He was so tall, so long-armed, that she now dangled high in the air, quite out of reach, yowling at the top of her voice, a ridiculous scene altogether!

He tried sternly to explain his feelings and issue his commands, but as was to be expected his Italian gave way under the strain: "Troppo in ritardo punire il gatto . . . it's too late to jump on the cat *now*, you poor chump; she wouldn't have any idea what it's for. Gatto non capisce . . . it's not her fault anyhow. She doesn't know any better. Take her down cellar, dans la cave; she's all right catching rats. That's what she's for! And look here," he stopped his pitiful attempt at Italian and ended fiercely, trusting to a grim eye and a set jaw to make his meaning plain, "Don't you try any funny business on the cat when I'm not around, or I'll knock your heads together till you can't see."

He heard the girl speak to the men in an Italian that was so rapid it made him dizzy and at the end caught the phrase, "do you understand?" The men nodded, by no means pleased at the rebuff, the boy motioned Neale to give him the cat, and carried her off carefully down the corridor.

"That was the very most splendid thing for you to do," the girl said to him, with a soft energy of accent.

He whirled about towards her, the immensity of his relief flooding his face. "Oh, you *do* speak English! You're *not* Italian!" he cried, the intonation of his phrase seeming to indicate that she had lifted from his mind an apprehension of infinitely long standing.

"Oh, yes," she said, smiling and looking directly at him, "of course I speak English. I'm an American girl. My name is Marise Allen."

Neale was so affected by the sweetness of her smile on him, by the softness of her shining dark eyes, that he felt himself blushing and stammering like a little boy. "M-mine is Neale Crittenden," he answered.

CHAPTER XLIII

THE dream-like Arabian Night unexpectedness which had descended on Neale the evening before, on the roof, continued shimmeringly to wrap everything in improbability. Instead of receiving his unfamiliar name with the vague, conventional smile of a new acquaintance, the girl raised her eyebrows high in a long, delicate arch and cried out, "You are! Really! The one who has inherited Crittenden's?" Seeing Neale's look of almost appalled amazement, she broke into a sudden laugh. Neale had never heard any one laugh like that, almost like some one singing, so clear and purely produced was its little trill. And yet it had been as sudden and spontaneous as a gush of water from a spring.

"I don't wonder you look astonished," she told him. "But you see when I was a little girl I used often to play in and out of old Mr. Crittenden's house and mill. I've never seen anything since in all my life that seemed as wonderful and mighty to me as the way the saw used to gnash its teeth at the great logs and slowly, shriekingly tear them apart into boards. Didn't you use to love the moss on the old water-wheel, too?"

"I never saw the mill or the house," he told her. "I never saw my great-uncle but once or twice in my life." He was too amazed to do anything but answer her literally and baldly.

"Why, how in the world . . . ?" she began to ask, and then as a bell from one of the innumerable church belfries outside began clangorously to strike the hour, she glanced at her wrist-watch, and shook her head. "It's breakfast-time," she said. She nodded, smiled and turned away, stepping down the corridor with a light, supple gait. Neale had never seen any one walk like that, as though every step were in time to music.

He went back to his room to wash his hands and brush

his clothes, which showed signs of contact with dusty Roman walls and roofs. When, ten minutes later, he went into the dining-room, five or six people were already at table, Livingstone among them. Miss Oldham, the head of the pension, introduced the newcomer to the others, mentioning names on both sides. To Neale's surprise, Miss Allen did not explain (as he had opened his mouth to do) that she had already seen and talked to Mr. Crittenden that morning. Instead, she now gave him the conventional smile he had expected ten minutes before, accepted the introduction as though she had never seen his face and went on drinking her café-au-lait.

More Arabian Nights. What did *this* mean? Neale swallowed the reference he had begun to their earlier meeting. Miss Oldham said to him with the wearily playful accent of the conscientious pension-keeper, fostering cheerful talk around her table, "I understand, Mr. Crittenden, that you and Miss Allen are in a way related, as I might say."

Livingstone joined in with his usual sprightliness: "Yes, Crittenden, why didn't you tell me you had a fellow-townswoman in Rome? Last evening when I went back into the salon and told the assembled company about you and your inheritance there was Mademoiselle Allaine, who had often, in her remote childhood, climbed on the respected knees of Monsieur your Great-uncle."

Miss Allen smiled quietly over her cup, remarked that it would have taken a bolder child than she had ever been to climb on the knees of old Mr. Crittenden, and, looking at her watch, rose to go. "Music, divine music?" inquired Livingstone.

"Yes, divine music," she answered lightly. "We are getting ready to play at a soirée at Donna Antonia Pierleoni's. I'm due there at half past nine to try out the piano in a new position in the room."

"Clear out there by half-past nine!" cried Livingstone, as if exhausted by the idea.

She did not seem to consider that this required any answer, made a graceful inclination of the head to the company at table and went off.

Neale was repeating to himself, in mortal terror of forgetting it, "Pierleoni. Pierleoni." He drank his coffee and ate his roll as though he had a train to catch, and, rushing back to his room, seized his hat and made off to the nearest café to consult the directory. With a sigh of relief he found that there was only one Pierleoni, and that the address was indeed as Livingstone had said, far away in the rich, new, fashionable quarter. He set off on foot, but before he had walked five minutes he was overcome with panic lest he be late, and hailed a rickety cab. Thinking of nothing but the precious address which he had committed to memory, he shouted it out to the cabman. Halfway there, he suddenly remembered that he had no possible business at that address. He had a horrid vision of driving up to the door, having the *portiere* ask him his errand, perhaps of having Miss Allen look out of the window and see the scene.

This threw him into such a fright that for an instant he could think of no escape and sat passive, borne along to his fate by the unconscious cabman. Then his wits came back to him, he called out to the cabman to drive to number seventy-five and not a hundred and twenty; and having thus snatched himself from destruction, perceived that they were even then turning into the street. At number seventy-five he descended, hastily paid the driver a good deal more than was due him, stepped into the house, inquired if a gentleman by the name of Robinson lived there, professed surprise and regret on hearing that he did not and walked on, settling his neck-tie nervously.

He told himself that he was acting like an imbecile, but he could not seem to consider that important fact seriously. Having started in to do anything, naturally he liked to put it through. Everybody did. And he really would like to know how under the sun a dark-eyed girl in Rome happened to know anything about his Great-uncle Burton. Any one would feel a natural human curiosity on that score. And he had only five days in Rome.

The idea that he had only five days in Rome fell on him like a thunderbolt, as though he had had no idea of it till that moment. Had he said he had only five days in Rome?

He walked along, looking up at the green waves of feathery foliage which foamed down over the fawn-colored walls from the verdure of the gardens inside. What a beautiful spot Rome was! He had not begun to appreciate it on his last visit. It was wonderful! Such light! He had never seen such sunlight anywhere.

Ah, here was number a hundred and twenty, a fine great doorway in the wall, with a gleaming brass plate, marked Pierleoni, at which Neale looked with pleasure. He walked on some distance, as far as he could go and keep the house in view, and, crossing over, walked slowly back. He was not now in the least ashamed of his conduct. By this time it seemed quite natural and suitable to him, just what any one would have done in his place. Of course he wanted to know about his great-uncle. Who would not?

He had made the trip to the end of the street and back perhaps a dozen times, his pulse beating more and more quickly, when from a distance he saw a little door beside the great one open, and a tall girl in a familiar light gray street-dress step out. But she was not alone. Beside her walked a man, a tall, stooped old man with a black coat and a wide-brimmed black felt hat. The girl's hand was on his arm. Neale felt as astonished and grieved as though he had caught his best friend cheating him at cards. It had never occurred to him that she might not be alone! And yet he now remembered that she had said "we."

He walked along behind them at a considerable distance, feeling for the first time rather foolish, a sensation which instantly took wings as he saw them, after turning into another street, stop at a door in the wall and ring. Perhaps she was going to leave him there. Neale gave a great start forward.

But perhaps she was going in with him? He halted where he stood, feeling very sick of himself and angrily resolving to turn his back on them and go off about his business. He had never played the born fool so in his life!

But he did not turn his back on them. He stood observing

them, while they went through a leave-taking which seemed to him very formal and long-drawn-out; and when the old man went in and the infernal gate actually shut behind him, Neale started forward with a bound.

But he reflected at once that it was too absurd to meet her here, in a quarter of Rome where no business of his could possibly have brought him at that hour. The cautious, adroit thing to do was to walk along behind her at a distance, till she had turned into a thoroughfare with shops, where he might conceivably be strolling. While he was making this sagacious plan, his feet bore him rapidly up beside her, where he took off his hat and said, "Good morning, Miss Allen," with a wide smile of satisfaction which he knew must look nothing less than imbecile.

Well, he had done what he had set out to do.

She gave him a "good morning, Mr. Crittenden," that showed no surprise, and with great tact began the talk on the only basis which gave him a reasonable claim on her time. "You want to hear how somebody in Rome knows about your great-uncle Burton, don't you? I'm afraid it's like so many other things that sound mysterious and interesting. It will only be quite flat and commonplace when you really know. It is no more than this. When I was a little girl in America, and then later when I was in college for a couple of years, I was sent to spend my summers in Ashley, visiting an old cousin of my father's." She looked at him from under her broad-brimmed blue hat, with a mock-regretful air, one eyebrow raised whimsically, and made a little apologetic gesture with her shoulders. "That's all," she said, smiling and shaking her head.

"Oh, *no*, it's not all!" Neale cried to himself with intense conviction.

Aloud he said, "But I want to hear more about what kind of a place it is. You see, to tell the truth, I'd forgotten that I had any Great-uncle Burton. And I never was in Ashley. Think of being in Florence and getting a letter saying that a saw mill in Vermont has suddenly become yours!"

"I should call it a most nice sort of surprise," remarked the girl with a quaintly un-English turn of phrase which he had already noticed and thought the most delightful thing in the world.

"And I'm on my way back to America now to see about it."

"What does that mean—to 'see about it'?" she inquired.

"Oh, sell it, of course."

She was horrified. *"Sell* it? To whom?"

"Oh, to anybody who'll buy it."

"Sell that darling old house, and those glorious elms. Sell that beautiful leaded-glass door, with the cool white marble steps leading up to it, and the big peony-bushes, and the syringas and that cold pure spring-water that runs all day and all night in the wooden trough. Sell that home! And to anybody!" She paused where she was, looking at him out of wide, shocked eyes. Neale was profoundly thankful for anything that would make her look straight at him like that.

"But, you see," he told her, "I hadn't the least idea about that darling old house, or the elms or the spring-water or anything. I never heard a word about it till this minute. I think the only thing is for you to start in and tell me everything."

As she hesitated, professing with an outward opening of her palms that she really didn't know exactly where to begin, he prompted her.

"Well, begin at the beginning. How in the world do you get there?"

"Oh, if you want to know from the beginning," she told him, "I must tell you at once that you change cars at Hoosick Junction. Always, always, no matter from which direction you approach, you must change cars at Hoosick Junction, and wait an hour or so there." Seeing on his face a rather strange expression, she feared that he had lost the point of her little pleasantry, and inquired, "But perhaps it is that you do not know Hoosick Junction."

"Oh, yes, I know Hoosick Junction all right." He said it with a long breath of wonder. *"I* changed cars at Hoosick Junction to get here!"

"Eh bien, and then a train finally takes you from Hoosick

Junction. You sit pressing your little nose against the window, waiting to see the mountains, and when the first one heaves up softly, all blue against the horizon, you feel a happy ache in your throat, and you look harder than ever. And by and by some one calls out 'Shley!' (you know he means Ashley) and you take your little satchel and stumble down the aisle, and the conductor lifts you down the steps and there is dear old Cousin Hetty with her wrinkled face shining on you. She only gives you a dry little peck on your lips, quick and hard, and says, 'Well, Marise, you got here, I see,' but you feel all over you, *warm*, how glad she is to see you. And you hug her a great deal till she says, 'there! there!' but you know she likes it very much."

She was talking as she walked, as if her words were set to music, her voice all little ripples, and bright upward and downward swoops like swallows flying, her hands and arms and shoulders and eyebrows acting a delicate pantomime of illustration, the pale, pure olive of her face flushed slightly with her animation. Every time she flashed a quick look up at him to make sure he was not bored, Neale caught his breath. He felt as though he were drinking the strongest kind of wine, he had the half-scared, half-enchanted feeling of a man who knows he is going to get very drunk, and has little idea of what will happen when he does.

"Yes, and then, and then?" he prompted her, eagerly.

"Well, and then you get into a phaeton. Oh, I don't suppose you have ever seen a phaeton!"

"Yes, I have," he contradicted her. "I've driven my grandfather miles in one when I was a little boy."

"Oh, you *know*, then, about this sort of—you have perhaps lived in a place like Ashley?" She was as eager as though it had been a question of finding that they were of the same family.

"I spent all my summers in West Adams, not so very far from Vermont."

"Ah then, you can understand what I tell you!" she said with satisfaction. "And in the phaeton you jog through the village, past the church, under the elms, with the white houses each under its thick green trees, and such green, green grass everywhere—not like Italy, all brown and parched; and then down the road till the turn-off for Crittenden's. For, you see, I also go to Crittenden's. My Cousin Hetty's home is one of the three or four houses that stand around your great-uncle's house and mill. And so up the road to Critten-den's between the mountains closer and higher, up into the quiet valley." Her voice deepened on the last words, and so did her eyes. She was silent a moment, looking out un-seeingly on the tropical palms and bright, huge flowers of the Pincian Gardens through which they were now walking.

"Eh bien, since it's you who are going home, you drive on a little farther than my Cousin Hetty's house, until up before you slopes a lovely meadow, smooth, bright, shining green, like the enamel green field in the Limbo where Dante puts Electra and Hector and Cæsar. At the top of the slope, a long line of splendid, splendid elms, like this, you know . . ." with her two hands and a free, upward gesture of her arms, she showed the airy opening-out of the wine-glass elms, "and back of them a long old house, ever so long, because everything is fastened along together, house, porch, woodshed, hay-barn, carriage-shed, horse-barn." She laughed at the recollection, turning to him. "You've seen those long New England farm-homes? I remember a city man said once that you could see the head of the lady of the house leaning from one window and the head of a cow from another. He thought that the most crushing thing that could be said, but *I* think those homes perfectly delightful, homely, with a *cachet* of their own, not copied from houses in other countries. And really, you know," she turned serious, thinking suddenly that per-haps he needed reassurance, "really, it's just as *clean* as any other way of living. You're just as far away from the animals as with any other barn, because you have so much woodshed and hay-barn and things between you."

To see her face with that quite new, housekeeping, matter-of-fact, practical look gave him the most absurd and illogical amusement. He laughed outright. "Oh, don't think for a moment that I would object," he cried gaily. "I'm not a bit fastidious. I wouldn't care *how* near the cows were—if they were nice cows!"

She thought for an instant he might be laughing at her, and peered keenly into his face, a more openly observing look than she had as yet given him. What she saw evidently reassured her, for she went on with a lighter tone, "Truly it has its own sort of architectural beauty. It doesn't have a bit of the packing-box, brought-in-and-dumped-down look that most dwelling-houses have, no matter how they're planned. It seems to have grown that way. The long, low old farm-house, weathered so beautifully, it looks like an outcrop of the very earth itself, like a ridge or rock or a fold in a field."

It was about at this time that Neale began to lose the capacity of listening to what she was saying. With the best will in the world he could not keep his mind on it. He found that he felt a giddy, dazzled uncertainty of where he was putting his feet and tried to pull himself together. He must really notice a little more what he was about. Her quick, rising and falling, articulate speech, her quick, flashing changes of expression, the play of her flexible hands and shoulders —no, how could he listen to what she was saying?

But she was asking him a question now. She was saying, "You're not really going to *sell* all that, to just *any*body?"

"But really," he answered, helplessly honest, "it sounds wonderful as you tell it, but what could *I* do with it? I couldn't very well go to *live* in Ashley, Vermont, could I?"

"Why not?" she asked. "A good many people have."

"Well! But . . ." he began, incapable of forming any an-swer, incapable of thinking of anything but the dark softness of her gaze on him. What was it they were talking about? Oh, yes, about selling out at Ashley. "Oh, but I have other plans. I am just about to go to China."

"China! Why to China?"

Neale lost his head entirely . . . "notice more what he was about?" He had not the least idea what he was about. He said to her rather wildly, "I hardly know myself why I am going to China. I'd like, if you will let me—I'd like ever so much to tell you—about it. And see what you think.

You know about Ashley, don't you see?" He was aware that
the last of what he had said had no shadow of connection
with the first, but that seemed of no importance whatever
to him.

They were standing now near a low wall, under some thick
dark ilex trees, a fountain dripping musically before them.
Mechanically they sat down, looking earnestly at each other.
"You see," began Neale, "I'm trying to find my way. I was
in business in the States, and getting along all right . . . 'getting on,' I mean, as they say. And then I got to wondering.
It seemed as though, as though . . . I wasn't sure it was what
I wanted to do with my life, just to buy low and sell high,
all my life long. Perhaps there was more to it than I could
make out. It certainly seemed to suit a lot of folks, fine.
But I couldn't seem to see it. I was all right. Nothing the
matter. Only I couldn't . . . why, I tell you, I felt like a
perfectly good torch that wouldn't catch on fire. I couldn't
seem to *care* enough about it to make it worth while to really
tear in and do it. And I thought maybe if I got off a little
way from it . . . sometimes you do see the sense of things
better that way. So I went away. I took a year off. I'd
saved a little money, enough for that. And I've been trying
to figure something out. Of course I've been enjoying the
traveling around, too. Perhaps that's the real reason why
I want to go to China, just to keep going, see new things,
get away, keep free. But I think about the other a good
deal . . . what can I do with my life . . . that's sort of
worth while, you know, if only in a very small way. I'm a
very ordinary man, no gifts, no talents, but I have lots of
energy and health. It seems as though there ought to be
*some*thing . . . doesn't it?"

He had stumbled on, breathlessly, involuntarily, hardly
aware that he was speaking at all, aware only that she was
listening. With her head bent, her eyes fixed on the ground,
the pure pale olive of her face like a pearl in the shadow
of her hat, she was listening intently. He knew, as he had
never known anything else, that she was listening to what he

really meant, not to what he was saying in those poor, plain,
broken words.

And yet, how could he go on?

The sudden plunge he had made, deep into an element
new to him, the utter strangeness of his having thus spoken
out what he had before but shyly glanced at, the awfulness
of having opened his heart to the day, his shut, shut heart. . . .
Good God, what was he doing?

At his silence, she raised her face towards him. To his
amazement her eyes were shining wet with tears. And yet
there was no sadness in her face. She was smiling at him,
a wavering, misty smile.

She stood up, made a little, flexible, eloquent gesture with
her hands and arms and shoulders, as if to explain to him
that she could not trust herself to speak, and, still smiling at
him, the tears still in her eyes, walked rapidly away.

CHAPTER XLIV

AFTER dinner that evening Miss Allen came up to where Mr. Livingstone and Mr. Crittenden stood together near the window and said to them, "Would it interest you at all to go to the soirée at Donna Antonia's to-morrow? She has been kind enough to offer me some cards of invitation, and it occurred to me—if you haven't anything better to do that evening—?"

Livingstone carried one hand to his heart, the other to his brow, and professed inability to recover from the shock. "My dear young lady, it's inhuman to shatter my nerves with a bomb-shell like that without a word of warning! You know well enough I'd gladly give one of my ears for an invitation to Donna Antonia's. Why then the false modesty, as who should say, 'If you've nothing more interesting on hand just step up and let me make you a Duke, do!'"

Miss Allen acknowledged the facetious intention of this with a suitable laugh and looked at Neale. He said, "Oh, of course I shall be glad to go."

"That's good then. I shall hope to see both of you."

When she had turned away to another group in the salon Livingstone put his head on one side and smiled down at his cigarette. "That's what comes of a little judicious attention bestowed in the right direction," he informed Neale. "I've been getting up at the unearthly hour that girl takes her breakfast for a fortnight now. Quite a charmer, isn't she?—though nothing to her friend Miss Mills. It's Miss Mills I'm interested in. Just wait till you see *that* joint production of American cash and European civilization! M-m-m! Hair like gold thread, and scads of money in her own right." He added seriously, "Miss Allen hasn't, you know—money, I mean, too bad, isn't it? Her father is only a salaried man—something or other for Paris for the something or other sewing-

410

machine company. Oh, no, I believe it's mowing machines, —or maybe twist drills—anyhow one of those missionaries from our own little home-paradise of cogs and gears. But of course the fair Allaine may make a lot herself if she really does get on the concert stage. Still you never can tell. There's an awful lot of interior wire-pulling to be done, managers and musical critics and so on, before anybody really is allowed to get to the bacon in the concert business, and is she really anywhere near professional skill, who knows? However, a pretty girl always stands enough sight better show than a plain one; or than a man. If she uses those dark eyes of hers to good account I should think 'most any manager or music critic would fall for her. *She* has a good skin, too; quite pleasant, that clear olive, though of course it's awfully common here in Italy. Just the same, a dark woman never has the *éclat* of a blonde. Wait till you see Miss Mills."

Neale broke in on his flow to remark in a suffocated voice that he had letters to write, and disappeared.

The soirée was horrible to Neale, a nightmare, a glittering wall through which he could by no means break to reach her, over which he could scarcely see at an immense distance her slim figure, dressed in yellow, a thin gold fillet binding her smooth dark head. She was talking, smiling, animated, at ease; and after she had played, much acclaimed. There was nothing surprising about *that*, thought Neale, applauding with all his might. Heavens, how beautifully she made music, how beautifully, how intelligently, with such a clear, sure certainty of her own powers! Of course everybody there admired her, paid court to her, made her the center of one group after another—always except the group where he stood! He felt heart-sick to be so cut off from her. As a matter of fact he was not in the least literally cut off from her. She kept relentlessly introducing him to one person after another whom he did not wish to meet. She kept coming up to him every time he had succeeded in shaking off a tiresome companion and was standing alone at last in a corner, looking everywhere over the curled, powdered, bobbing, restless, grin-

ning crowd to catch a glimpse of her. There she would be
at his elbow, gliding up from nowhere. He restrained an
impulse to snatch at her and hold her there, because each
time she melted away after she had said, "Won't you let me
take you to Donna Antonia Pierleoni," or "to Miss Mills," or
"to Signor Ambrogi," or to somebody or other with whom it was
necessary to talk and on whom it was necessary to try to keep
those wandering, seeking eyes of his. He took them in with
the top-layer of his consciousness, one after another of the
people with whom he was forced to talk. Donna Antonia Pierleoni, a haughty, elderly Roman lady who was, as Neale said
to himself, feeding her haughty Roman face as though she
scorned and despised lemon ice but *would* eat it since it seemed
to be her duty. It amused him greatly to observe that after
finishing one she took another at once.

Miss Mills—oh, yes, this must be the girl Livingstone
had been yarning about. Of course after praise from Livingstone it was to be expected that she'd look like a very
high-priced wax image in a hair-dresser's window; and yet
Neale's attention was caught for a moment by her pronuncia-
tion of a French phrase. Her inflection reminded him of
Marise Allen's, and he hung about her for some time in the
hope of hearing it again. Every time she repeated it, which
she often did, he smiled down broadly on her. She was a
pretty little thing. Livingstone was right. She was really
quite an object of art, if that was what you called them.

Signor Ambrogi turned out to be in politics, an assistant
Minister of Commerce or Industry or something. Why, he
looked for all the world like a New York business man—
might be old man Gates as he had been at forty-five. As
they tried to talk to each other in French that was not very
fluent on either side, Neale was reflecting that the Roman
governing type had changed very little. This strongly-marked,
clean-shaven, heavy-jowled head with its thick, hooked nose,
bold eyes, hard mouth and wrinkled forehead, could be put
without change in among the portraits of Roman Emperors.

They talked in their halting "lingua Franca" of business,
of railroads, of the use of commercial fertilizers on Italian

fields, of the conversion of water-power into electrical energy, and, finding Neale a good listener, the Italian told him about a power-plant in a volcanic region of Italy that ran its machinery by the steam escaping from the thin crust of earth over internal volcanic goings-on. For an instant Neale was quite stirred by this conception. It seemed a very neat idea, and it tickled him to have Italians turn such a traditionally American trick.

"Pretty good, pretty good!" he said applaudingly. "That's beating us at our own game."

"Pas si bête, en effet," said the other, well pleased by Neale's comment.

But this interlude was the only time when, even for a moment, Neale was delivered from his desolation at seeing her so far from his world, from any world he could possibly hope ever to make his own. That brilliant musician—how wonderful to be able to play the piano like that!—that beautiful young woman of the world, the center of this brilliant cosmopolitan crowd, friend of titled Roman ladies, and ministers—was it she whom he had followed in the street like any pushing, thick-skinned bumpkin, to whom he had poured out what he had never before breathed to any living being? What on earth could she think of him? For what kind of a flamboyant idiot did she take him? Well, the best thing to do—Great Scott, the *only* thing to do was to shut up and back out. As he walked home with Livingstone at midnight he had made up his mind to take the first train to Naples the next morning.

But he made no move whatever to do this, when the morning came. Dumb and stupid as a sheep, he made his way doggedly to the dining-room at the earliest hour, to see Miss Allen take her café-au-lait. As he went in at the door, he realized that his calculations were all wrong, that she had been up late the night before and would certainly sleep late that morning. But Livingstone had already seen him and hailed him. It was too late to go back and wait. He sat down, gloomily stirred the sugar into his coffee and listened to Livingstone fizz all over the place about the evening's entertainment which had uplifted him to exaltation. "You don't *realize*, Crittenden, what an opportunity that was to see exclusive Roman society, the kind that foreigners like us never meet, not the flashy, big-hotel, off-color crowd. Why, I was introduced to name after name that sounded like a page out of Roman history."

Neale thought with a passing grim irony that Livingstone's phrase was accurately turned—"introduced to names"— yea, verily. Well, names were what Livingstone was after.

"Oh, you up already, Miss Allen," said Livingstone, springing to seat her with an agility for which Neale hated him. He himself sat like a lump, incapable because of the sudden rush of blood to his head, of anything but nodding a silent answer to her greeting.

Livingstone needed no help in keeping up the conversation. He flowed on, delightedly passing in review every detail of the evening of which he had not missed a single one, apparently, from the way Donna Antonia's maid did her hair to the dandruff on the coat-collar of the old Visconti. "Of course I know he's a great musician and all that, but really if you will let your hair grow so long, you ought to have a pocket clothes-brush and *use* it, oughtn't you? Why don't you do it for him, Miss Allen? Every one says he is absolutely gone on you, that you could do anything with him!" He passed from this without transition to Miss Mills' toilette which had been, so it seemed, a veritable triumph.

"Yes, yes, wasn't it beautiful! Eugenia's clothes are simply wonderful." Miss Allen broke in to say enthusiastically, "She has the most never-failing taste."

"A never-failing pocket-book," corrected Livingstone. "You don't get far with mere taste *dans ce bas monde*."

Miss Allen finished her coffee, and, setting down her cup, remarked, "You two Americans seem to have made a most agreeable impression last evening. Donna Antonia called me back to say that Signor Ambrogi would be glad to see more of you. She wished me to ask you both if you couldn't come to have tea with her and with Signor Ambrogi this afternoon at five."

Livingstone fell back in his chair, dramatically. "The long struggle is over, Crittenden. Our fortunes are made!" he cried with his usual facetiousness, but by the expression on his face he was really moved and dazzled. "Kindly convey to Donna Antonia Pierleoni the assurance of our condescending regards and say that if we can spare the time from the press of other more important duties . . ."

Neale said plainly and bluntly, "I'm afraid I'd better excuse myself. I have a previous engagement."

The other two turned on him with faces of astonishment. "You're not *going?*" cried Livingstone, appalled.

"Why should I break an engagement?" said Neale.

"Why *should* you?" Livingstone gaped at him. "Only the trifling, insignificant reason that Donna Antonia is one of the greatest *grandes dames* in Rome, and Ambrogi one of *the* coming men in the government."

"Has that anything to do with me?" Neale asked with the sincerest incapacity to imagine any reason why it should. He was stricken with anticipatory boredom at the idea of having to make talk again with that disagreeable old woman.

Livingstone wondered if Crittenden had really understood from whom the invitation came. "Don't you remember meeting her? The one with the wonderfully high-bred type?"

"Oh, I remember her all right, the old lady with the predatory sharpness of beak and claw that's called aristocratic," said Neale, trying to get a rise out of Livingstone. That was usually easy enough, but he was now too genuinely concerned to defend his standards. "Now, Crittenden," he said, laying down his napkin and speaking from his heart, "to seem not to wish to continue the acquaintance of a lady who makes a civil advance—it simply *isn't done!*"

"Oh, go on!" said Neale, laughing at the idea. "Much she'd care what an impecunious American in a pension does or doesn't do!"

Livingstone had recovered himself enough to reflect that Neale's refusal would not at all hinder his own acceptance— in fact, on the contrary—"Well, well, no matter," he said with a change of manner, "perhaps you're right. Without a knowledge of the language, conversation in a small group *is* rather—Five o'clock, did you say, Miss Allen?"

"Yes, five," she answered. She went on, with a manner suddenly gay, "Perceive the difference in human fate. At five you will be taking tea with personages, and I shall be scurrying to take a belated music lesson."

"Why at *that* hour?" inquired Livingstone.

"I've put it off to help Eugenia get settled here. For she's coming over, bag and baggage, Joséphine and Mlle. Tollet, to live with us for a while. Isn't that jolly?"

Livingstone was visibly affected. He flushed a little, and cleared his throat before he asked with a careful reassumption of his usual airy manner, "Might I perhaps, if it is not indiscreet to ask, be permitted to breathe out upon the air a request to be informed what possible reason any one can have for leaving the golden bath-tubs (if I may so express myself) of the Grand Hotel, and sojourning at the respectable but hardly luxurious Pensione Oldham?"

"That's what I asked her last night when she told me. But it seems she's just tired of gilded bath-tubs (if I may borrow the expression) and wants a change."

"I might say without exaggeration that she would be reasonably sure of getting it," surmised Livingstone, looking around him.

Neale could think of nothing to add to the conversation. You never could get a word in edgeways when Livingstone was in the room, anyhow. His mind was full of something else too. "A music lesson at five." The name Visconti was as apt to be in the directory as Pierleoni had been.

At five he saw her go into the little gate in the wall from which during the next hour he did not take his eyes. He stood in the doorway of an apartment house across the street, and when the *portiere* came out responsibly to ask whom he wished to see, Neale told him in English, seriously with a long breath, "The girl I've lost my head over." As he accompanied this unintelligible information with a large tip, as his clothes were respectable, as he was evidently a foreigner, and had moreover a rather strange spark of excitement in his eyes, the *portiere* pocketed the tip, looked with respect at Neale's powerful proportions, and went discreetly back to his own affairs.

When she came out at six Neale was struck speechless. He had spent the entire hour thinking how she looked, remembering every detail of her beauty. And yet it was as though he saw for the first time that noble carriage of her head and shoulders, that heart-taking curve of her long fine brows, the smooth pale oval of her face, the touching wistfulness, the *seeking* look in her dark eyes. That was before she saw him. When he came up to her she broke at once into a laugh, her face sparkling and merry, a delicate malice in the mobile lines of her red lips.

"Oh, Mr. Crittenden, I've been wanting to see you! To share a joke with you! Such a joke! That invitation to tea, you know. You see, *you* were really the one Signor Ambrogi wants to see, you were the only one Donna Antonia spoke of. But I knew it would hurt Mr. Livingstone so, if he were left out. I made her understand that. So she said, 'Oh, well, if you insist, he can come too.' It's rather—don't you think it is?—rather a joke?" She began to laugh again. "Don't you see it, the scene when he walks in alone—the good Livingstone in his best clothes, so happy and so important, with his best brand of European conversation in the show-window—a comparison most likely of Caravaggio's theory of treating wall spaces with Correggio's. And what Ambrogi wants to discuss is American railroad terminal facilities! Ambrogi is a man of the people. He's made his own way up from the bottom. He has probably never heard of Correggio in his life. And doesn't see why he should," she finished with a peal of laughter.

Neale laughed, but he did not find it as comic as she. "I'd no idea of all that," he said uncomfortably. "Perhaps I ought to have gone. It rather looks like putting poor old Livingstone in a hole."

"Oh, no; oh, *no*," she reassured him. "They'll be good to him. They may look at each other once or twice. But nothing

more. He'll never know. He *doesn't*, Mr. Livingstone—
often he doesn't know."

"Not much, that's a fact," agreed Neale, reflecting that he
did not seem to either.

She asked him suddenly, "But really why *didn't* you accept?"

"Do you want to know?" he asked warningly.

"Yes, I really wonder."

"Simplest reason in the world. I didn't like Donna Antonia
Pierleoni very well. She seemed to me like a bad-tempered,
stupid old lady, mightily full of her own importance. Why
under the sun *should* I go and have tea with such a person?"

"Eh bien . . . !" she breathed out a long, soft ejaculation
of surprise, looking at him very queerly.

"You're thinking I'm very rude to say such a thing about
a friend of yours," he said, hanging his head.

"I'm thinking no such thing at all," she contradicted him.
"I don't believe you could *imagine* what I'm thinking."

"You never said a truer thing," Neale admitted ruefully.

"Well, I'll tell you," she said, "though it couldn't be interesting to anybody but me. I was thinking that I had never
heard anybody before who spoke the truth right out about
somebody who had wealth and position."

"You mustn't blame me for it!" Neale excused himself.
"I'm a regular outsider on all that sort of thing—you remember the Sioux Indian in the eighteenth century who was
taken to see the court at Versailles? How he strolled around
in his blanket and couldn't make out what all the bowing
and scraping was about? Well, he and I are about on a level
of blank ignorance of social distinctions."

"But you don't *wish* to know," the girl divined, "you don't
care if you *are* an outsider. Why, I believe," she said with
a little burst of astonishment, "I believe you'd rather be an
outsider."

He looked apologetic. "That's part of my dumbness, don't
you see? I just can't conceive why anybody should bother
his head about it. *I* tell you," he hit on the right phrase
of explanation, "I just don't know any better."

"Would you learn?" she pressed him more closely.

"Not if I could run faster than the person who was trying to teach me!" he confessed helplessly.

The girl broke into another laugh. There never was anybody who laughed like that, with her lips, and her gleaming, dancing eyes, and her eyebrows—even her hands had a droll little gesture of delightedly giving him up. What in the world had ever made him imagine that her expression was pensive or her eyes wistful?

"Do you mind?" he asked, rather uncertain what she was laughing at, and hoping it was not at him.

"Oh, I *like* it!" she told him, heartily. "But it's the very first time I ever ran into it. It makes me laugh, it's so unexpected."

"Well, it has its disadvantages," he broke in, seeing an opening to say something that had been on his conscience for two days. "It makes you do all sorts of unusual and unconventional things without meaning to at all. Like my talking to you yesterday morning, for instance, in the corridor of the pension, when I hadn't been introduced to you."

She stopped laughing, her face all blank with surprise. "Why, that was not unconventional! People at the same pension never wait for introductions. And anyhow I'm not a *jeune fille du monde*. I'm just a music-student. If you only knew how *some* people try to take advantage of that! Why, what in the world made you think it was not all right?"

"Well, when you didn't say anything about it at the breakfast table, when Miss Oldham introduced us, the way you looked as though you'd never seen me before. I thought you —I thought I—well, why *didn't* you mention we'd just been talking?"

"Oh—" She remembered the incident. "Why didn't I? Why *should* I? You always hide what you don't have to tell, don't you?"

Neale pondered this negligent axiom for a time, and then said hesitatingly, "But if the servants happened to mention it?"

"Oh," she explained quickly, as if mentioning something that went without saying, "oh, of course I told the servants not to speak of it."

"You did!" He felt that he was looking through what he had always thought was the opaque surface of things, and seeing a great deal more going on there than he had dreamed. "But can you count on them?"

She continued to be as surprised at his surprise as he at the whole manœuver. "Oh, of course you can never count on servants unless there's something in it for them. I gave them a little tip apiece."

"You *did!*" He could only stupidly repeat his exclamation. "What did they say?"

"Why, they found it perfectly natural. They won't mention it—not of course unless somebody else tips them more, and I don't see why anybody should, do you?"

Neale stood looking at her, a little consternation mingling with his astonishment. This was what it was to have been brought up in what people called a civilized way, this smooth mastery of concealment . . . how easy it had been for her, at the breakfast table yesterday, not to give the faintest hint she had just been talking animatedly with him; and this morning not the faintest hint to Livingstone that she was laughing at his expense. Why, that lovely face was just like a mask. You hadn't the least idea what was going on behind it.

There was a silence. She was looking up at him with a new expression, almost timidly. "You don't like my hiding things?" she asked him, coming to a stop. They were near the pension now, standing in the twilight on a deserted street.

He aroused himself to shrug his shoulders and answer evasively, "Oh, it's not in the least any business of mine."

"But you don't like it?" she insisted, looking straight at him with the deadly soft gaze that always made him lose his head entirely. "It's of no consequence—none," he murmured. But she still looked at him. He tried to think of some other evasive answer, but in the confusion of his mind he could not think at all. And he must say *something*. With alarm, with horror, he heard himself saying baldly, as he would to a man, to an intimate, the literal truth, "Well, no, not so very well, if you really want to know."

It was as though he had seen himself swinging an ax at an

angle that would bring the edge deep into his own flesh. He felt it cut deep and bleed. He dared not look at her. He wished to God he had gone on straight to Naples.

Somehow he *was* looking at her. Her face was deeply flushed. She looked as though he had struck her in the face. Well, now it was certainly all over. He might as well turn around and walk away and never look at her again.

He said blunderingly, in a trembling voice, "I'm *so* sorry! I didn't mean to say that. It's no business of mine. I'm awfully ashamed of myself. *Please* forget it. What do *you* care what I think? I'm nobody, nobody at all."

"Why did you say that?" she asked him in a low voice, with a driving intensity of accent, as though more than anything else she must have an answer from him.

"Well, you asked me," he said in abject misery, aware of the hideous, flat futility of such an answer. If only he were an expansive Italian now, he could think of some way openly to abase himself, instead of standing there callously and dully. "Oh, please don't think of it again," he implored her, wishing he could get down on his knees to beg her pardon.

She drew a long breath and put her hand to her heart. "It's the first time anybody ever told the truth to me, you see," she said faintly, with a strange accent. "I . . . I'll like it . . . I think . . . when I can get my breath."

To his amazement he saw that she was trying bravely to smile at him.

To his greater amazement he snatched up both her hands and carried them roughly and passionately to his lips.

CHAPTER XLV

DURING the interminable process of hanging the skirt of that yellow dress for Donna Antonia's soirée, Marise kept thinking of the Pantheon. The dressmaker's lodging was near there. If they could only be done with those draperies she would have time to step into the place which she loved best in Rome. She cast a look at herself in the cracked mirror which was all the inexpensive little dressmaker could afford. "I'm afraid it's higher on the right hip," she said, and settled with a sigh to endure more pinnings and unpinnings. "Strange, how important it is for the correct playing of Beethoven," she thought ironically, "that the drapery on one hip shall not be higher than on the other." She caught a glimpse of herself as she thought this, and frowned to see her lip curled in a cold, ugly line of distaste. Her thoughts were showing more and more on her face. She knew well enough what Mme. Vallery would say. She would say, "Don't pretend, dear child, that you don't know perfectly well that the kind of dress you wear has a great deal to do with everything that anybody cares about, and that the kind of people you must depend on to make your music profitable are the kind who care nothing about music and altogether about looks."

That was true, of course, but all the same it did make Marise sick to have people call a "soirée musicale" what really was a "sartorial evening." Of course it was understood that people were hypocritical about everything. She granted that they never called anything by its right name. But she did wish they would leave music alone! She *cared* about that!

"That's right now," she said aloud, looking intently from one hip to the other. "Perhaps a *little* more—no, it will do as it is."

She would have time for the Pantheon after all—ten minutes at least. Ten minutes for the Pantheon! She had been three-quarters of an hour with the dressmaker! That was her life! She walked in through the gray old portico, and, still fretting, her mouth still in the cold, ugly line, she stepped through the huge bronze doorway and stood under the vault . . . *"ah!"*

She always forgot how it affected her or she would come in every day as other people said their prayers. It was as though it had been made for her and had waited till she came, sore-hearted, to look at it and find a passing peace.

She lifted her face to the huge open circle at the center of the dome high over her head. Quiet strength came into her heart from those great gray stones. Century after century they had enclosed that lovely circle of open sky and sunlit cloud and swallow-flights. Every other ancient roof in Rome had gone down to heaps of rubbish, save only this, steadfast, enduring, letting in the innocent clear light of every day down to the heart of the old temple.

Daylight—that was what made the Pantheon a place apart for her—honest daylight. How cheap beside it was the theatrical yellow of the windows back of the altar in St. Peter's!

She looked about her for a place to sit, and, seeing no chair, took a prie-dieu and sank to her knees on it as though she were praying. She was praying in her way. She continued to look up at the heaped golden clouds, at the infinite depth of the blue, blue sky, at the ineffable clarity of the light, pouring in through the great round opening. It seemed to smile at her, an honest, loving, reassuring smile that flooded her vexed, somber heart as it flooded the somber, ancient building. What strength, what strength in those gray stones, to hold together where everything else had been broken and dispersed! How beautiful primitive things were! How consoling and healing—the hardness and strength of stones, the clarity of light, the transparency of the sky! If you could only somehow make your life up of such things—strength, sunshine, simplicity—and music!

She continued to gaze up, her hands clasped. Yes, she was praying, she was praying for a little share of all that.

What was that absurd Mr. Livingstone saying? Marise

glanced up sharply from her book and listened. Why, he was talking about Crittenden's—old Mr. Crittenden dead and had left that lovely old mountain home to some indifferent nephew? To make sure, she put her book down and asked a question or two. How strange that she should be talking about *Ashley* to people here in a Roman *pension!* Ashley! Crittenden's! Cousin Hetty!

She seemed to have gone again back to her book, but she was not reading. She was looking at a sunlit green valley, a white road winding through it, a glass-clear little river chanting under willows, low, friendly homes under tall elms, ugly old people with plain speech and honest, quiet eyes, smiling down lovingly on a skipping, frisking little girl.

> " . . . I see them shining plain,
> The happy highways where I went
> And may not go again."

After a time she closed her book and went up on the roof for a quiet moment alone, to go back to Ashley, to look at those blue, remembered hills.

But there was some one else on the terrazza. She made out a man's figure under the grapevine. Being a girl, she thought impatiently, she was obliged to turn back and shut herself up in her stuffy room. It continued to be exactly as it had been in Bayonne. The world was one great Jeanne, with a nose twitching for scandal. Ashley was far away!

She had watched the horrid little tragedy of the swallow with such intensity that when the catastrophe came she almost felt those curved claws sink into her own flesh . . . *bon Dieu!* What was that man doing climbing out of the window—a madman! No, *he* had seen the cat, too! What a leap! And now how he ran—like a *prestissimo alla forte* passage! *Ah!* He had caught that wretched cat. But the swallow was dead. He was too late! How gently he picked it up. Did *men* ever feel compassion for things hurt?

Oh! *oh!* the swallow had flown out of his hands! How it soared up and up! Who would not soar, saved by a strong, kind hand from such terror!

He had turned to come back. It was a good face—but after she had seen the expression of the deep-set, steady eyes she could see nothing but that. Eyes that looked kind, but not weak. In the world about Marise it had been an understood axiom that only weak people were kind.

And what now—eh *bien!* To defend the cat! What did he care about a cat?

Yet she saw it at once. What he wanted was justice. Think of any one's wanting justice for anything—let alone a *cat!*

No—how quaint, how amusing—one unexpected thing after another!—he wasn't a bit conceited about what he'd done —how *funny* that he was embarrassed and shy! Why, no man with Latin blood could have restrained himself by any effort of self-control from a little flourish of self-satisfaction after such a dashing exploit. He wasn't thinking how she must be admiring him. He wasn't thinking of himself at all. How—how *nice*—to see him blushing and stammering like a nice, nice boy. She could scarcely keep back the laugh of touched and pleased amusement that came to her lips.

Eh bien, he might blush easily and be shy, but he knew as well as any Latin how to catch at a chance indication from a woman, and how to be at the right place at the right hour. When she and il Maestro came out of Donna Antonia's door, she saw his tall figure at the end of the street. Ridiculous, what a start it gave her! And as soon as Visconti had left her there he was beside her with one long bound. Now she would really look at him enumeratingly and see what sort of face he had.

But when she looked at him she saw that his eyes were smiling down at her, and she went no further than the eyes again.

She began to tell him about Ashley, of which she had dreamed the night before, the first time in so long. It had been a good dream, all about going home to Cousin Hetty and playing dolls up in the attic again. And it was good, how good, to talk to some one about it, the first time—why, since she had left Ashley! He seemed like—like what Americans

meant when they spoke of their "own home folks." Marise
had never had any such. There was a real reason to give
herself the fun of telling about Crittenden's too, since this
Crittenden was soon to be there. She would just let herself
go for once!

But how she did run on when she let herself go! She
hardly knew herself, chattering like this, as fast as her tongue
could wag. Chattering and laughing and gesticulating—and
not able to stop—the foolish way people do who have drunk
too much champagne, the foolish way a canary does when you
take the dark cloth from his cage and he sees that the sun
is shining, the way silly girls do the first time they have
a conversation with a young man. Yes, that was the way
her voice sounded. Why could she not stop chattering and
laughing? What must he be thinking of her? She would
stop. She would change the subject. She would look at her
watch and say that she was late for an engagement and must
take a tram-car and leave him.

Forming this plan, she led him rapidly through the gate into
the Borghese Gardens where there are no tram-cars, through
which lay the longest possible way home. She thought glanc-
ingly of this inconsistency, but it did not seem very important
to her, because she began to be aware of something that startled
her a little. She was now taking him all over the old house
at Crittenden's. Yes, it was as though she had taken his
hand and were leading him through those fine old rooms.
She was aware of him—like that—as though their hands really
did touch, warmly and actually touch—and she liked it!
She who detested above everything else the slightest physical
contact with another human body—who hated men for only
looking at her bare arm as if they would like to touch it.

Oh, well, oh, well, it was nothing—she brushed it aside,
it was gone. She told herself hastily in a phrase she had
heard Mme. Vallery use, that a very fine physical specimen
of a man exercises a sort of unconscious magnetism on every
one near him, that has no more real human significance than
the way a pebble naturally rolls down hill and not up. And
he certainly was what any one would call a fine physical

specimen, so tall, so solidly, vigorously built, with such a long, swinging step—she glanced at him as she talked—but it wasn't his strength that gave him his individuality—it was his *quiet* look.

They had come out from the Pincian now, stopped and were looking at each other, under the ilex trees. From the way he had answered her astonished question about China she had known that he was going to say something to her, really something that he meant, as people never do, something from far underneath the surface. But she had never dreamed that he would so throw open the doors of his heart and let her look in to see something she had never thought was in any one's heart,—the honest desire to do something with his life beyond getting out of it all he could for himself. It was like daylight shining down, clear, into dark shadows.

Marise dreaded Donna Antonia's musical entertainments. They were nightmares, at least for a girl with no recognized definite rung on the social ladder as her own, at least for a paid entertainer who was paid not only to play a Beethoven sonata, but to look well, to add to the social brilliancy of the evening, to make up for Donna Antonia's prodigious inertia by rushing about, seeing that everything went smoothly, that the servants did not sequester half the ices, that each guest had some one to talk to. If she could only come in, play her Beethoven and go away again!—That was really all she was paid for. No, of course the pay for the rest of what she did was Donna Antonia's "taking her up," her familiarity in the great house, those occasional condescending "cards for her personal friends," all that Donna Antonia could do for a young pianist's future. Every one told her that her fortunes were made, now that Donna Antonia had taken a fancy to her, every one expected her as a matter of course to make the most of her great opportunity, to flatter Donna Antonia, to run briskly on her errands, to accept with apparent pleasure the amused, patronizing friendliness of a capricious great lady who on some days was caressing and petting, like a person with a pet cat, and on others was cold and distant, like a person who has no use for cats. She was not only to play for Donna Antonia whenever she was asked, but sit on a cushion, let her hair be stroked and talk intimately with Donna Antonia of things Marise would much prefer not to know about; or on another day to be willing to dash out in a cab to get a delayed dress from the dressmaker's because the maid was busy with hair-dressing; or, as on this evening, act the part of helpful daughter of the house, when her real position (which all the guests knew perfectly well how to make her feel) was that of temporary toy and amusement. What really underlay all that advice to make the most of this great opportunity was a doubt whether she was genuinely gifted enough to make her own way by her talent, was the feeling that the best way to make up for deficiencies in her musical equipment was by accumulating personal influences of social importance on her side. The "great opportunity" which Visconti's other pupils so envied her was nothing more or less than making the acquaintance of these wealthy, important, unmusical people, and being more adroit in making use of them than they of her. This was perfectly understood all around—especially by the men watching to find a weak spot, who looked at her admiringly and found graceful things to say about her playing and her arms and her hands and her hair and everything else they dared mention; especially by the old Ambrogi, with his brutal certainty that as long as he was mounting in power, any woman—oh, they made her *sick!*—Donna Antonia and Ambrogi! Such *old* people, with bags under their eyes and flabby necks! And they really didn't care a sou about each other—he wanted only to make use of the position that Donna Antonia's birth gave her, and she only wanted to have the prestige of owning a politician; or perhaps the prestige of showing that in spite of bags under her eyes she was still not too old for that sort of thing.

Before she ran up to make sure that no guests were stranded in the library without being served with ices, Marise looked cautiously into the dark corner on the landing to make sure that Ambrogi was not there. Horrid—an old man like that who could not keep his hands off women thirty years younger than he! But as for that, the old Visconti himself could not keep his off women fifty years younger than he! As she sped swiftly along the upper hall, a crocus-colored Atalanta in her pale-yellow dress, she was saying to herself, "Oh, well, that's the way men are, none of them can keep their hands off women"—all except self-conscious posing marionettes like that absurd Livingstone, or men like her father, who took it out in caring about what they ate and drank. How harmless that was—in comparison! How *nice* it was in comparison! Had she ever been impatient with Father because he cared so much about what he ate and drank? She felt a little wave of affection for him. She really must try to get back to Paris for a few days, and make sure that Biron was keeping up to the mark.

There, the last person was served. And everybody had somebody to talk to. Oh, how tired she was, how sick of all this! This was a soirée musicale! These were the people on whom she was to count for musical success. She was supposed to be here to play Beethoven! She broke into a nervous laugh at the idea.

Of course she had known that Mr. Livingstone would be enchanted at the invitation from Donna Antonia. And of course Mr. Crittenden would be too. Anybody would. To have made such an impression on Ambrogi—it was remarkable!

But he wasn't enchanted. He said he wasn't going. What under the sun did that mean? Did he think he could get an invitation to dinner if he held off from this one to tea? Yes, probably that was it. Well, she wasn't sure, that was the way to work Ambrogi. Still you never could tell. Perhaps the boldness of it might take Ambrogi's fancy.

How funny, funny, funny, the head Ambrogi would show at the tea-table when poor Livingstone turned up alone with that self-conscious, naïvely-sophisticated manner of his, so proud of seeming a man of the world. And Ambrogi despising men of the world for imbeciles! She would tell Mr. Crittenden about it, when she next saw him, and make him laugh too.

But when she told him he did not laugh—not so very heartily. He seemed concerned about Livingstone—of all people! Was it possible that he *liked* Mr. Livingstone? Could it be he was standing up for him whether he liked him or not, as he had for the cat?

And now what a queer question he was asking her—about why she had said nothing at the breakfast table about having already met him. Why, how naïve that would have been! Why should you? And he kept on talking about it as though he saw something in it she did not. He was looking at her very queerly, not at all admiringly. How strange it seemed to have any man look at a woman and not pretend at least to be admiring her—strange—and rude—and uncomfortable! She must make him *say* something. He'd be forced then to smile and turn it off—whatever it was, with a pretty phrase that pretended to be admiring.

Oh—horrible! How could any one be so rude! Why, it was as though he had struck a blow at her! Brutal! And why? Why? What harm had she done him? Why did he want to hurt her? He was cruel! She had not known any one could be so cruel and hard—hard as a stone (where was it she lately had seen great hard stones?).

What could you do when some one was rude to you? What did any one do who was so affronted?

Beyond the dark fury of her amazement, her resentment, her anger, her bewilderment, a light began to break slowly like a distant dawn. As she looked at him, stammering, remorseful, horribly unhappy, aghast at what he had said, but never once dreaming that he might simply unsay it, she became aware of what had really happened:

She had asked him a question and he had told her the truth.

CHAPTER XLVI

"This is the life!" thought Livingstone many times during the next weeks. He had not enjoyed himself so thoroughly since he came to Europe to live. He was now provided, as he expressed it, with all the cultural advantages of Europe and all the social atmosphere of an American summer-resort; for Miss Mills seemed to wish to try, along with pension life, the unchaperoned familiarity of real American girl-life. Mlle. Vallet, her old school-teacher, companion-dragon was unceremoniously left behind, or sent out by herself to do the conscientious sight-seeing which took all her evenings to record in her diary.

Miss Mills did sight-seeing too. The tacit understanding which grew up at once was that they were all four seriously to see Rome and to make up for the very haphazard way in which heretofore they had been profiting by their situation. It was certainly, thought Livingstone, a most agreeable way to do sight-seeing, in the company of two such good-looking girls, one of them with money to burn. Of course he could have wished, they all would have preferred, some one less lumpish than that great, grim Crittenden to complete their quartet. But not every American is capable, thought Livingstone, tying his necktie in the morning and looking at himself in the glass, not every American is *capable* of taking on European polish. And of an American business-man what could you expect? Livingstone admired and did his best to imitate the exquisite good-breeding of the two young ladies, which kept them from ever showing the slightest impatience with Crittenden. As far as they were concerned it would have been impossible for Crittenden to guess that he was not in the same class with the other three. An occasional quick look of astonishment from Miss Allen when Crittenden made

one of those crude speeches of his, and a recurring expression
of quiet fatigue on Miss Mills's face when they had had a
little too large a dose of Crittenden were the only traces of
their real feelings which showed on the surface.

That famous soirée at Donna Antonia Pierleoni's had seemed
to be the start of all this agreeable new period of sociability.
Livingstone abhorred fatuous men, but it really was rather a
remarkable coincidence that after seeing him for the first long
talk they had ever had, Miss Mills should at once have
decided to come to the *pension* where he was staying. She
had never had a real opportunity to know him before that,
Mlle. Vallet always shadowing her around, the conversation
always stiffly in French in deference to Mlle. Vallet's feelings.
That, after her first real impression of him, she should immediately have moved into a room three doors down the corridor
from his—any man might be pardoned for considering it
marked, really marked. It quite fluttered Livingstone with
the idea of the possibilities involved—although he scorned
fortune-hunters above all other men. It was not her fortune,
it was her wonderful little person that he admired, the perfection of the finish of every detail of her body and mind.
Livingstone often felt a sincere reverence as he looked at her
beautiful hair and skin and clothes and hands and feet that
had cost—oh, nobody knew how much to bring them to that
condition. And her accomplishments, her exquisite French
and pure Italian, her knowledge of art-critics, and which
Luini was considered authentic and which spurious! The
harmonious way she sat down or stood or sat at table! There
was a product of European civilization at its finest! How
crude and coarse-grained the usual striding, arm-swinging
American girl would seem beside her, like a rough, splintery
board beside a finished piece of marquetry. Even Miss Allen,
who was, one might say, carelessly and indifferently European
simply because she happened to have been brought up in
France, often seemed rough and abrupt compared to her.
There was nothing of the deliberate, finished self-consciousness
about Miss Allen's manners, which Livingstone had learned
to admire as the finest flower of sophistication. It was true

she really did play the piano very brilliantly. But still she had to make her living somehow! One could be reasonably sure with her good looks that she was counting on using the concert platform, if indeed she got to it, as an angling station from which to fish for wealthy eligibles. Crittenden needn't fool himself that she would ever look at *him*, with that ridiculous little inheritance he had played up so, on his arrival in Rome!

Not that Crittenden seemed to be trying to make an impression! Quite the contrary. Was there anybody who, more than that poor fellow, seemed possessed to put his worst foot foremost? If they hadn't been pitiable, Livingstone could have laughed at the breaks Crittenden constantly made, at the way he was everlastingly showing himself up as entirely an outsider to their world.

That evening, when they fell to talking of their favorite dishes, was a sample. As a parlor amusement they had been challenging each other to construct imaginary meals such as would be perfection if you could only get them together,—sole frite from the Ambassadeurs; roast duck with the inimitable sauce of Foyot's; Asti Spumanti, the *real;* Brie straight from the only farm in the Seine-et-Marne that made it right . . . all that sort of mouth-watering, exquisite imaginings. When Crittenden's turn came, had he risen to the occasion? Had he made the slightest effort to make a decent appearance? No, he had said, "Oh, count me out on this. I have a regular hired-man's appetite, and if it begins to fail, I go out and run a mile and then I can eat anything!"

Livingstone tried his best to cover up such breaks with hasty, tactful improvisations of talk, but he had noticed the amazed stare with which Miss Allen had received this partticular revelation of Crittenden's crudity.

Miss Mills had stared, too, or as near to it as she ever came, over in the Capitoline, when she had asked Crittenden if he happened to know anything about Constantius Chlorus, at whose ugly face they were just then looking. Crittenden had answered in that coarse, would-be comic jargon he occasionally affected, that he didn't remember reading a thing about him, but if there was anything in physiognomy he must have been a ward-heeler who had sandbagged his way to the head of the machine. Miss Allen had not been able to avoid laughing at him outright then, and Miss Mills's look had been all too eloquent.

But the worst was the pig-headed provinciality of his attitude about picture-galleries, his avowal of a regular commercial-traveler's ignorance of paintings and his refusal to try to learn to appreciate them. "There are only, so far as I can make out," he said, "about a dozen canvases in all Europe that I really *like* to look at. And you don't catch me trailing around till my feet drop off, looking at all the thousands of second-raters that give me a pain. Why should I?"

Livingstone was so shocked and grieved by the crassness of such a statement that he really longed to take Crittenden in hand. He knew so well how to learn to like pictures, because (although he would not have admitted it to any one) he had begun as crassly as Crittenden. He *knew* what to do; he could tell Crittenden step by step how to pull himself up to a higher level, because he had done it himself. You read esthetic books, lots of them, and all the descriptions of paintings you could lay your hands on, and all the stories you could find in Vasari or any one else about the lives of the painters (Livingstone had a whole shelf of books of that sort that were *fascinating* reading—as amusing as La Vie Parisienne)—and you read what Ruskin and Symonds had thought about this or that canvas, and what Berenson's researches had proved about its authenticity. If you could, you took the book right along with you to the gallery, reading about the picture as you looked at it; and you kept at it till you *did* see in it what people said was there. That was the way to form your taste! Even Crittenden could get somewhere along those lines if he tried.

But he seemed to have no interest in anything but history and Michael Angelo; Crittenden was perversely fond of dragging them over to the Sistine Chapel till their heads were ready to drop off with the neck-breaking fatigue of staring up at those sprawling figures.

There was, however, one advantage about the expedition to the Sistine Chapel. They were always so fearfully tired afterwards that they took a cab back to the Piazza Venezia and had ices together at a café. It was the first time since he had lived in Europe that Livingstone had been able to walk into a café with a handsome woman and watch the other men stare. That was a European manœuver which he had not somehow been able to accomplish, a tailor-suited, low-heeled, sailor-hatted American girl-tourist with her Baedecker in her ungloved hand, being by no means a figure to make other men stare. Of course it was perfectly evident that Miss Mills and Miss Allen were only nice girls (he hoped it was not *too* apparent that they were only Americans), but they were handsome and Miss Mills was always stunningly dressed. It was next best to what Livingstone had always secretly longed to do, as, eating his frugal demi-glace, he had watched a medaled Italian officer or monocled, heavy-eyed man-about-town sitting opposite a conspicuous woman-de-luxe with high-heeled slippers, a provocative gown, and a huge hat shading her black-rimmed, roving eyes, the only movable feature of her spectacular face, painted and powdered to a hierarchic immobility.

That was the life! That was what Livingstone would love to do! Thus to *afficher* yourself with a really bad woman, how deliciously un-American and cosmopolitan! On the other hand, those women were said to be very expensive and hard to handle, rapacious, without the slightest scruple as to how they emptied your pockets. Livingstone was in mortal terror of letting one of them get any hold on him and his tiny resources. He knew he would be no match for her. And anyhow all he wanted of one was to sit, jeweled and painted and conspicuously non-respectable, across a table from him at a café, so that other men would look at him as he now looked at other men. He often wished he could hire one just to do that.

However, in the meantime, it was a very pleasant pastime (and might, by George, *lead* to something, who knew!) to sit across the table from two merely nice but really very good-looking and well-dressed girls and listen to their innocent prattle.

And although they were Americans, they had lived abroad so much that they had many European ways which Livingstone found very fascinating and superior. For instance, they were quite at home in Roman churches, and whenever they went to listen to special music in some chapel the girls had a quick, easy capacity for dropping to their knees in a quite un-self-conscious way that made them to Livingstone's eyes fit right in with the picture. If it had not been for Crittenden, whose stiff provincial American joints never dreamed of bending, he would have knelt beside the girls. Not that he *believed* in any of the religious part of it! But it was so European to go down on your knees in public. If he did, he was sure that people around them would think that he was a member of one of those ultra-smart English Catholic families.

Crittenden always was the great, hulking obstacle in the way of any flexible and gracious Europeanizing of their lives. Livingstone had seen the two girls recoil time and time again, shocked by his bruskness. And it was not only to women that he was brusk. He had occasionally an insufferable way of treating any one who approached him with a civil question, as when Livingstone on a sudden recollection had said to him, "Oh, but by the way, Crittenden, how about your being only five days in Rome?"

"*How* about it?" Crittenden had repeated as though he'd never heard of it before.

"Why, you said you had to return at once—that inheritance, you know—you said you had only five days."

Crittenden had had the impertinence to stare at him hard and say coolly, "Oh, you must be mistaken about that."

Civilized people didn't have such manners!

And that other time, the evening when he had stayed up late on the terrazza to smoke with Crittenden, when he had asked, "But all men of the world agree that nothing is so full of flavor as an affair with a married woman. You, no doubt, Crittenden, have also had your experiences, eh?"

What sort of an answer did Crittenden consider it, to burst

out with that sudden great horse-laugh as though Livingstone had been telling him a funny story?   The man simply had no experience or understanding—a raw, crude, bumptious provincial, that's what *he* was!   One who had not even sense enough to know how pitifully narrow his life was.

CHAPTER XLVII

COMING to know a new acquaintance was, thought Marise, as though you stood back of a painter, watching him stroke by stroke paint the portrait of a sitter whom you could not see.

Of course Mr. Neale Crittenden, like every one else, was physically quite visible, and, like every one else, entirely hidden by this apparent visibility. What you saw of people's surfaces and what was really there were two very different matters—Marise had learned this axiom if no other. What she saw of the newcomer was quite startlingly, disturbingly attractive to her. All the more reason to draw back warily and look carefully before she took a step forward. When on seeing him for the first time in the morning, or coming on him unexpectedly towering up above the crowd in some narrow, dark Roman street, she felt the ridiculous impulse to run to meet him like a child, she told herself impatiently that it was due to mere physical elements—his health, the great strength which made itself felt in his quietest movements, and a certain expression of his deep-set eyes which might very well not have the slightest connection with his personality, which might be a mere trick of bone-structure, the way his eyes were set in his head perhaps. They chose the show priests for the great festivals at Lourdes for some such casual gifts of physical magnetism.

No, there was nothing whatever to be known from surfaces, Marise told herself. The subject of the portrait was always really quite invisible behind the thick, thick screen of his physical presence. All that was safe to do was to watch the strokes by which one by one he himself painted his own portrait.

Marise often told herself all this as she was hurrying down the corridor to be the first person in the breakfast room— the first, that is, after Mr. Crittenden, who was a very early riser.

438

I

To begin with there was the dashing outline sketch of the first two or three days when, in a few bold lines, he had seemed to set up the figure on the canvas; the rescue of the swallow; justice for the cat; that first walk and homesick talk about Ashley, and at the end those stammering words of his which had seemed to show—Oh, that had now turned unreal to Marise! He couldn't have said that—and meant it!

Then the soirée, the impression of force and originality he had made on the people he had met there, her natural certainty that he must of course have calculated that impression in order to profit by it—and then—at this recollection, Marise always laughed silently at her own astonishment when he had called Donna Antonia "a bad-tempered, stupid old woman." Donna Antonia certainly was that, and every one knew it. But nobody else would dream of saying it out loud, any more than they would give their honest impression of the ritual of a secret society.

II

And then, just when she had been so drawn towards him by his strength and kindness—that brusk blow in the face. Marise had felt many times before this a thin, keen blade slipped into her back by a hand that took care to be invisible. But never before had she encountered open roughness. It was staggering! Breath-taking! Always, as she remembered it, her first thought was, as it had been then, a horrified wonder why any one should wish to hurt her. Always afterward with the memory of his dreadful, stammering distress, his remorseful kissing of her hands, his helpless inability to unsay what he had said, she knew once more, as she had known then, that she had encountered something new, something altogether different from any human relationship she had ever known, a relationship where you did not say things in order to please or displease people, or to make this or that impression, but because you thought they were true. That was fine—oh, yes, that was fine. But it was like dashing yourself against hard stones—it hurt! And it made her fear the hand that had hurt her. She watched it, and sometimes all but put out her fingers to touch it, to see if it were really so strong and hard as it looked. She feared it. She envied its strength.

III

That had been a stroke of the portrait-painting brush which frightened her to remember. But there were others that made her laugh, like the time, off in a hill-village in the Roman country-side, when he stepped into a little shop to buy a box of cigarettes, and came back with a great paper-bag of the villainous, hay-like tobacco issued to the Italian army, unsmokable by any but an Italian private soldier. To their amazed laughter, he had replied sheepishly, with a boy's grin of embarrassment that the little daughter of the shop-keeper, ambitiously doing her best to wait on a customer, had misunderstood his order and had weighed it out and tied it up before he realized what she was doing. "I was afraid if I let them know she'd made a mistake her father would jump on her. Fathers do seem to do such a tall amount of scolding anyhow. And she was so set up over having made a sale all by herself."

Marise had laughed with the others over that, and laughed when she thought of it—but her laugh often ended abruptly in bewilderment—how was it he could be so kind, so tenderly kind to an Italian child he had never seen before, and so sternly rough with her? That rankled; and then, when she had had time to think, she recognized it, all over again, with the same start of astonishment, for the truth-telling she had never encountered.

IV

Mr. Livingstone had said something sentimental about man's love being based on the instinct to cherish and protect, and woman's on the desire to be cherished and protected. Eugenia had acquiesced; Marise, who hated talk, sentimental or otherwise, about love, had said nothing. But Mr. Crittenden had protested, "Oh, Livingstone, you've got that twisted. That's the basis of love between group-ups and children. You don't insult your equals trying to 'protect them'! Nothing would get me more up in the air than to have somebody 'protect' me from life. Why should I want to do it to anybody else? Protect your grandmother! A woman wants to be let alone to take her chances in life as much as a man!"

V

They were crossing the Forum, on their way to a stroll in the shady walks of the Palatine. From the battered, shapeless ruins of what had been the throbbing center of the world rose suffocatingly to Marise's senses the effluvium of weariness and decay. She always felt that Rome's antiquity breathed out upon her a cold, dusty *tædium vitæ*.

She thought of this, turning an attentive face and inattentive ear to Mr. Livingstone, who was trying to make out from his guide-book where the Temple of Mars had stood.

"You're holding that map wrong end to," said Mr. Crittenden.

"It's too hot to stand here in the sun," said Eugenia very sensibly.

They passed on, over heaps of ancient refuse, into the ruins of the myriad-celled palace of the Cæsars, silent now, not an echo left of all the humming, poisonous intrigues that had filled it full.

"Here," said Mr. Livingstone, stopping in a vaulted, half-wrecked chamber, ostensibly to comment on things, really to get his breath after the climb, "here in such a room, only lined and paved with priceless marbles, and hung with Asiatic silks, here you lay at ease in an embroidered toga on a gold-mounted couch, and clapped your hands for a slave to bring you your Falernian wine, cooled with snow from Monte Cavo, —that was the life!"

"I thought it was in the Arabian Nights you clapped your hands for a slave," said Eugenia.

"In Rome you probably cracked a whip," suggested Mr. Crittenden. "But I bet you a nickel it didn't make any difference *what* you did, your slave came when he got good and ready and brought you another kind of wine from the one you ordered—and lukewarm at that. They'd probably used up all the Monte Cavo snow to cool the wine down in the slaves' hall."

"What possible basis have you for saying all *that?*" cried Mr. Livingstone, exasperated.

"That's the way things are! Folks that try to use slave labor always get what's coming to them in the way of poor service."

"Oh, but in Rome you had the right to kill him!" cried Mr. Livingstone, jealous of his rights.

"Sure you could kill him—and in New York you can fire your stenographer. What good would that do you? You couldn't get intelligent service out of the next slave either, unless you had him educated to be intelligent, and if you did that he'd be such a rare bird that you'd save him for something better than standing around waiting for you to clap your hands at him. He'd be running your business for you."

"Oh, pshaw, Crittenden, why be so heavy-handed and literal! Why wet-blanket *every* imaginative fancy?"

"Oh, I didn't realize you were imaginatively fancying," said Mr. Crittenden, laughing. "I thought you were trying imaginatively to reconstruct the life of ancient Rome. And I was trying to do my share."

They passed through dusky, ill-smelling passages, clambered over a pile of rubble and stood in twilight at the foot of a long, steep, vaulted stairway. Far up, like a bright roof to its obscurity, were green leaves, blue sky, bright sunshine. All that sparkling, clear radiance seemed to heighten the boyish fit of high spirits that had entered into the usually rather silent Mr. Crittenden. He pointed up to the stairway and cried, "From antiquity to the present! I'll meet you at the

top!" and off he went, bounding up the high, steep steps two
at a time, as if his vitality had suddenly swept him away
in the need for violent exertion.

When the two girls emerged later, "Ladies, allow me to
introduce to you the present day," he said, calling to their
attention with a sweep of his hat the dark, sumptuous green
of the cypresses and pines, the splendor of the golden-blue sky,
the fresh sprinkled smell of the earth on the shady paths.
"Not so bad for poor little old actuality, is it?"

The girls sank breathlessly on a bench. Livingstone appeared, slowly hoisting himself up the steps, one at a time,
and puffing. Mr. Crittenden walked around and around restlessly, as though that upward swoop had been but an appetizer
to his desire to let out the superabundance of his strength.
He looked, Marise thought, like a race-horse fretting and
pawing and stepping sideways. How could he have that eager
look in this dusty cemetery of human strength and eagerness?

Glancing up at his face, she saw it lighted and shining
with amusement—what seemed like tender, touched amusement. He was looking at something down the path. Marise
looked with him and saw a workingman, one of the gardeners,
digging in the earth of a rose-bed. Beside him capered and
staggered a little puppy, a nondescript little brown cur with
neither good looks nor distinction, but so enchanted with life,
with itself, with the soft, good earth over which it pranced
that to see it was, thought Marise, like playing Weber's "Per-
petual Motion." As she looked it tried to run in a wavering
circle around its master, tripped over its own feet, tumbled
head over heels in a soft ball, clumsily struggled up and sat
down to draw breath, a pink tongue hanging out of its wide,
laughing mouth, its soft young eyes beaming with mirth at
its own adventures. Its master glanced down and addressed
some clucking, friendly greeting to it, which threw it into an
agony of joy. Wagging its tail till its whole body wagged,
it flung itself adoringly at its master's trousers, pawing and
wriggling in ecstasy.

Mr. Crittenden caught Marise's eye, and shared with her
in a silent smile his delighted sense of the little animal's

absurdity. "Perhaps if we looked down from this height and got a bird's-eye view we could settle that point," said Eugenia to Mr. Livingstone, who was still concerned about the location of the Temple of Mars. "There's a fine view from the wall at the end of this path."

They strolled together to the wall, and Mr. Livingstone spread out on it his plan of the Forum.

Marise looked down dispiritedly at the mutilated pillars and broken pieces of carved marble, and most of all at the bits of old Roman flagged paving. Nothing gave her a more acrid sense of futility than those old, old flag-stones over which so many thousands of human feet had eagerly, blindly sought their journey's end. Had any of them ever found what they sought? She murmured under her breath, "Isn't it all horribly, horribly depressing? Doesn't it make you feel all those endless centuries bowing your shoulders down to the earth—why not now as well as later?"

She had stated it as she felt it, a truism, what every one must feel. Eugenia and Livingstone accepted it as such. "Yes, I often feel as ancient as the stones," said Eugenia pensively.

Mr. Crittenden put in hastily, "Not on your life, it doesn't depress me! Why should it? You don't seem to realize, Miss Allen, what an immense difference there is between us! I never really took it in before myself—not until this visit to Rome. But it's immense! Enormous! Let me tell you about it. They're dead and we are alive! Alive!"

Marise looked up at him, thinking that in truth she had never felt any one so alive. He bent his eyes to hers as Livingstone, with a little gesture of giving him up, drew Eugenia to the corner of the wall and traced lines on his map.

Mr. Crittenden went on whimsically, "I don't believe you ever fully considered the great importance of that point, Miss Allen. It came home to me all over again as I was looking at that puppy. Millions of dogs have lived and died before him; but by some amazing miracle life is just as fresh a wonder to him as if he were the first puppy ever born into the world! It's incredible! I never realized it till I struck all these relics of dead-and-gone men—it's incredible how none of them, not all the millions of them, can tarnish the newness of my own life for me! I can go my own new path over those old paving-stones—me and the puppy—and you— and all of us!"

Marise laughed a little, still looking at him, listening to something he was not saying, which played about his bold, clear face like sunlight and shone on her as warmly.

Now a spark of wildness came into his eyes, half laughingly reckless, half desperately in earnest. "You saw what happened to the puppy when its master threw it a kind word? Well, I haven't the gift of wriggling all over so wonderfully as that, and I haven't any tail to wag, but when you look at me like that, Miss Allen, I . . ."

"We *think* the third line of pillar-stumps is the side wall of the Basilica Julia," said Eugenia, stepping towards them, the guide-book in her hand.

<h1 style="text-align:center">VI</h1>

They were standing under the great gray dome of the Pantheon, innocent clear daylight flooding all the great gray building.

"Oh, isn't it beautiful, their idea of leaving the circle open to the sky?" Marise burst out. "Doesn't it make our dark, modern churches with their imitation Gothic stained-glass seem cheap and affected? Every church all over the world ought to be like this, and then we human beings might be fit to live with."

Livingstone put in a horrified protest, "What! Miss all that exquisite twilight that makes a church a church? I was just thinking how fiercely, literally bright this noonday sun is. Daylight leaves no mystery, nothing to your imagination."

Marise turned confidently to Mr. Crittenden as an ally. She was sure, as sure of anything in the world, that he must be on her side. But he hedged and said neutrally, "Oh, great Scott! It would be a horrible act of tyranny to

have *every* church like this. There are lots of folks who'd
hate it. They have a right to have some things their way,
haven't they?"

"Oh, I *didn't* think *you'd* take that side," said Marise,
feeling betrayed and longing for a sweeping, exclusive affirma-
tion to match her own. He so often hedged, it seemed to
her, wanted to qualify statements. Oh—it came to her with
a start—that was another form of truth-telling! He was
trying to make his statements express the truth, rather than
his feelings!

He now said, judicially, "As far as I personally go, it depends what I'm looking at. If I'm looking at a very fine statue
or something that seems really beautiful to me, I want as
good a light as possible to see it in. If—if I should ever
have any personal happiness in my life, I'd want daylight
to see it by. But when it's a question of looking at the
interior decoration of the average modern church, why, the
more mystery and twilight the better."

This made Marise laugh. He often made her laugh, more
than she had ever laughed before. And yet he never told
funny stories.

He now went on, "I suppose it depends on your opinion
of what there is to see. If you think your imagination can
do better for you than reality, of course you want a lot left
to it, and plenty of dark corners for it to work in. Just now,
it seems to me that reality is so much beyond anything my
poor, starved imagination could have done. . . ."

He did not look at Marise as he spoke. His tone was
perfectly matter of fact. She wondered what the other two
made out of it. She knew very well what she made out of it.

VII

They were sitting on the terrazza in the evening, with several
other people from the *pension*, having their coffee sociably
around the big round table and looking out over the roofs
and domes and church-towers of Rome. The conversation
had been chit-chat, as was usual during meal-times, and Mr.

Crittenden had contributed little to it. His massive capacity for silence when he had nothing special to say was a constant source of wonder to Marise. Not to "make talk," even very commonplace talk, was a betrayal of a tacitly accepted code as much as calling Donna Antonia a "bad-tempered, stupid old woman." She had been taught that it was one of the pretenses which must be kept up under penalty of the ruin of all civilized intercourse. She envied and resented his freedom from it.

She addressed herself directly to him now to force him out of his reflective taciturnity. "Do you agree to that, Mr. Crittenden?"

"To what?" he asked, making no decent pretense of being abashed because he had not been following the conversation.

"Why, Mr. Livingstone was saying that artists are the only human beings to be envied, the only human beings who really *live*, intensely."

"They're the only ones who talk about it," he offered as his variation on the dictum. "That's what an artist *is*, isn't he? Somebody who happens to be put together so that it kills him to keep anything to himself. He just goes up in smoke, if he can't run and tell the world what he has seen, or tasted, or handled, or got hit by, and the way it made him feel. I admire and revere artists. They certainly do a lot for the rest of us. But I don't see any reason to think that they feel things any more intensely than anybody else, and I don't see anything so terribly enviable in their lot. There seems to be a lot of hard work about it, if you judge by the way they carry on. I don't see why you can't enjoy beauty and feel tragedy, even if you keep your mouth shut. You can feel it just the same, can't you? I'm sure I've felt things about a million times more intensely than anything that ever got into a book. And I can't say I'm any less satisfied with my fate because I'm not thriftily trying to use those same feelings as raw material for an art."

Marise was laughing outrageously by the time he had finished, partly at what he said, partly at Mr. Livingstone's scandalized expression. She was ashamed of the way she laughed over Mr. Crittenden's teasing of poor unconscious Mr. Livingstone.

"You don't understand, Crittenden, you don't get my point at all. There's something—something—" Livingstone brought it out with a remnant of the provincial self-consciousness before fine phrases which he so deplored, "there's something god-like, divine, in being an artist, *creating* something."

Mr. Crittenden moved from his negligent pose, tightened up a little. "Oh, if you mean by 'artist' a class broad enough to take in everybody who creates something, yes, of course, they're the only ones who really live. That's what most of us are trying to get a chance to do, trying to create a little order out of chaos. But that's pretty nearly the whole ant-heap of the human race, isn't it? Except the leisure classes."

Mr. Livingstone was in despair of making the Philistine understand. "It's something we have so little of in America, it's hard for an American to recognize its existence," he murmured to the company in extenuation of his compatriot's denseness.

Mr. Crittenden sat up straighter. "I used to make my living buying and selling lumber in the New England states," he said, addressing himself for once to the company, "and on one of my trips I met a man in a narrow mountain valley up there who was a creator if there ever was one. He had started life as a mechanic, left school and went to work at sixteen, in a shop filled with soulless cogs and bolts and screws and springs. And his creative instinct rose up and seized on those things as the appointed raw stuff for his creation. When I saw him he was the head of one of the biggest metal-working factories in the country, a good many hundred men working for him, and devoted to him, turning out tools that have simplified the tasks of mechanics the world around. I never saw a happier man. I never saw a human life more completely fulfilled. Yes, you're right, Livingstone. The creators are the enviable ones."

"That wasn't in the least what I said, or meant!" protested Mr. Livingstone warmly.

"It happens to be fresh in my mind," said Mr. Crittenden,

half apologizing for his unusual loquacity, "because to-day, walking on the Due Macelli, I happened to see a case of his tools, and outside, just glued to the window, a young Italian mechanic, gazing in at them, his face on fire with his admiration and appreciation. Quite a long way, isn't it, for a Yankee creator to reach out a helpful and stimulating hand? But he's a first-rater, of course, a genius. The rest of us can't hope to do that."

Later, as they all went down the stairs together, Marise asked him, "But there isn't anything . . . is there? . . . that the rest of us, not creative geniuses, can hope to do that's creative?"

She had not the faintest idea what he could find to answer. She herself could conceive of no answer possible. With all the intelligent people she had ever known, it had been axiomatic that there *was* no answer.

He did not speak at once. She had noticed that he often took time to reflect seriously on what you had said before he replied. Marise had never seen any one before who seemed to give so much more care to understanding what you said than to concocting something that would sound well to say in answer. There were times when, incredible as it seemed, Mr. Crittenden seemed really to use language to express what he meant rather than to attain his ends. She waited now, and as she waited she was aware of the erectness and vigor of the tall body stepping beside her. In the corridor he halted for a moment, facing her, his head bent thoughtfully, his eyes shadowed by his broad brow, his hand, that powerful athlete's hand of his, meditatively over his mouth as he considered.

He had given her question a good deal of thought, and yet when he took his hand down to speak he said abruptly, impulsively, as though the words had broken up through what he had been meaning to say, "Couldn't we . . . any of us . . . couldn't we hope to create a beautiful human relationship? Beautiful and enduring?"

CHAPTER XLVIII

Neale was in despair at his dumb helplessness before the inert resistance of social relations. A man with any adroitness would not submit passively to this sprung-up-from-nowhere tradition that he and Livingstone and Marise Allen and Eugenia Mills formed an indissoluble foursome, never to advance or retreat save in a solid bloc, like a French family, with all the uncles and cousins and aunts. How had it started? *He* certainly had had nothing to do with it. That's what you got for being stiff-jointed and literal as he was about personal relations. The practised old hands ran circles around you, and had things all their own way.

Such at least was the color of Neale's meditations when he was alone in his own room. When, as one of the quartet, he set off on a new expedition, he could think of nothing but his light-headed pleasure at being there at all, walking beside her, catching sidelong glimpses of her when he was supposed to be looking at a statue or a fresco, talking to her over the others' heads, trying to say something to *her*, through the infernally "general" conversation which Livingstone kept up as though his tongue were hung in the middle.

And there was a certain advantage too—he was not flexible-minded enough to label it, but he recognized and was quick to profit by it—this parading around in a group gave the most intoxicating quality of intimacy to the brief, snatched occasions when he did manage to see her alone; even though a good many of these few precious moments were, as a matter of actual fact, passed on a noisy street-corner, waiting for a tram-car to come and carry her off, or on a narrow Roman sidewalk, trying to keep abreast of her as she stepped quickly through the dense, sauntering Italian crowd, stopping five deep to stare at something in a window, or holding noisy and affectionate family reunions on the sidewalk. None of that mattered. The noise, the clatter of tongues, the pressing and shoving of the crowd, the ear-piercing yells of the street-vendors—it was all essential silence to Neale because none of it was directed at keeping him apart from Marise, as was the low-toned urbane conversation of the sight-seeing quartet.

He let himself go like a boy—as indeed he never had as a boy—on the few occasions when he waylaid her in the street, without Eugenia Mills, who seemed to have as great a passion for her society as he had. He was really a little out of his head with suspense, after an hour of anxious waiting about, smoking nervous cigarettes, his eyes on both ends of the street at once, his heart leaping up when he thought he saw her tall, nobly borne figure in the distance, dying down sickly when it turned out to be some other dark-haired girl. When finally she was really there he was too elated for pretense, swooping down on her, his hat in his hand, grinning—he knew it—like an idiot. He saw people in the street turn and look after him meaningly and smile to each other—and what did he care how big a fool he looked to them!

They fostered, for these queer, unprivate, intimate moments, a little tradition of their own, a tacit understanding that they would save up for them the things they specially wanted to talk about, the questions they wanted to ask each other that were no business of other people. They talked as fast as they could, sometimes Marise, sometimes Neale, as though they could never get caught up on what they had to tell each other. Neale was astounded to hear himself chattering, fairly chattering. They talked a good deal about Ashley, a great deal about their personal likes and dislikes, a good deal about what Neale was trying to get out of Europe. This seemed to interest Marise, curiously to interest her. She was always bringing him back to it. He was, she told him, new in her experience of Americans-in-Europe. She had seen so many, all her life, and thought she had them all sorted and labeled ". . . the kind, like my father, who find themselves just in their element at last in the religious seriousness of Europe about eating and drinking. Sometimes I think they're the ones who get the most out of it. No, oh, no, there's another sort, the ones I specially love. The middle-aged school-teacher who saves up her money and comes just once comes at forty-five with a ripe mind and fresh, fresh eyes, such as no European can have. I'll never forget what I heard one of them say in Paris. I was tearing along, trying to get to the market and back before I had to go to a class, my mind full of nothing but the price of new potatoes and a terribly hard set of velocity exercises I'd just begun. I came up behind two such dear, dear American tourists, and heard one of them say, so happily, with a long breath of satisfaction, 'I've waited all my life to see that.' I looked around wildly to see what she was talking about. And there stood Notre Dame! Had I seen it? No, too many picayune cares on my mind. But I looked at it then, looked as though it were the first time I'd ever seen it.

"And then there are the rich Americans who want to buy everything and do buy everything, and go away empty-handed. And the kind who want to be what they think is sophisticated, who feel it's really worth spending your life learning how to order a meal with the right manner in the most expensive restaurants in every city, and to know how to find the horridest café-chantants that don't dare advertise in the papers, and that the people of the country never go to see.

"And then the other kind, who come over, the whole family of them, and go to register at the New York Herald—you know the sort, 'Mr. Jehoshaphat Jones, President of the J. Jones Farm Implement Company of Broken Ridge, Indiana, together with Mrs. Jones, Miss Elizabeth Jones, Miss Margaret Jones and Master J. Jones Jr. are stopping at the Hotel Vouillemont. They will shortly start on a tour of the Chateau Country, and after that expect to travel in Switzerland.' You can see Mrs. Jones cutting that notice out and sending it home to Broken Ridge. They're *nice,* I like that kind, when they don't get too tired and begin to snap at each other. I always feel such a deep sympathy for Jehoshaphat when I see him dragging his sore feet around over a hard, hard museum floor; and such a sympathy for Mrs. Jones, when he makes them all stand around at an Alpine railway station while he delightedly figures out and explains how the funicular works."

There were times when she ran on, mirthful, flashing, keen, droll, amusing herself and making him laugh as nothing had ever made him laugh before, out of sheer, light-hearted hilarity. As he watched her, talking animatedly in her beautiful, clearly articulated English, her plastic face a comic mask, fooling and bantering till she had him shouting, and yet with that core of shrewd observation and real intelligence underlying all she said, sometimes he remembered with a start his first sight of her up there on the roof—what was the meaning of that unearthly sadness the moon had shown him?

She was not, it is true, by any means always gay on these stolen talks together. She could be stern and brief, as when he asked her challengingly, one day, "Well, you've been in Europe all your life, nearly. What have *you* got out of it?" She answered, "To work hard and not to expect much from anything—except from music."

Her face that was sometimes as meltingly soft as a Correggio girl-saint, looked dark and set. He had been so disconcerted by her look and accent, that like the lump he was, he had found nothing to say before she hailed her tram-car and left him.

Often she made him talk, talk as he had never dreamed of talking to any one, leading him on to flight of wordy self-expression, such as he blushed afterwards to remember, sure that he must have bored and wearied her. And yet there never was such a listener as she, attentive, silent, except for just the occasional comment that launched him off on further talk, when his self-consciousness coming warningly forward bade him stop before he seemed a solemn ass. She made him intensely desire to share with her everything that was in his mind. Helpless before the compelling personal look with which she listened to him, he poured it all out pell-mell, what he had been struggling to lay hold of, ever since he had left Hoosick Junction.

"One of the things that keeps coming over me, is the various-ness of folks. We don't begin to take enough account of that. Plants now, they're various too—sure they are. An Alpine harebell is as different from an oleander as I am from a natural-born artist. But everybody that has any sense knows that an oleander would freeze and starve to death if you planted it up near a glacier. You can tell that much, just by looking at it. But you can't tell a thing, not a doggoned *thing* about a human being just by looking at him, can you?"

Marise agreed with intense conviction that you can tell less than nothing by looking at a human being.

"And then the human race has got itself so mixed up. There isn't the slightest chance, not one in a million, that a harebell will spring up in a Roman garden, and be burned to a crisp by sunlight that just makes an oleander feel good and comfortable. But that's what happens the whole enduring time with folks."

"Why, I wonder," cried Marise, with a startled look, "if that is what happened to me."

"I know it's what happened to me," said Neale. "I believe it happens to lots more folks than have any idea of it. They blame it on the climate, so to speak. But the climate's all right for some one else. It's not *their* climate, that's all. Let's start out on a hunt for our climate, will you?"

"I'm afraid it's very hard to make a guess at it," said Marise soberly but making no comment on the "our."

"It surely is. It's terribly hard. The point is that nobody but the person himself can make any sort of a guess at it. And it's awfully hard for *him*. Wouldn't you think, when it is so hard under the best of circumstances, that folks would try to teach every youngster to make the best sort of guess possible as to where he really belongs? But they never give you any hint of that, in any of the 'education' you get in school or out of it. They seem to be in mortal terror for fear you will find it out yourself. They jam your beak down on the chalk-line and hope to goodness you'll never look up long enough to see that only your own foolishness keeps you there. Or they keep you there till you've tied yourself up with responsibilities, so you *can't* get out. Whatever is the

fashion of your country and of your century, that's the thing
for you to do, whether or not.

"I believe that's what Europe has done for me, made me
realize that our present fashion isn't foreordained, nor the only
one natural to men.   Think of all the centuries after the
Roman bridges went down, when people got along without
bridges, because no provision was made to keep alive the minds
that happened to be born with latent constructive powers.
No, no, there must be no fooling around with godless abstract
mathematical ideas, nor fiddling with compasses.   A crucifix
or a sword must be in every man's hand.   Every man must be
a fighter or a saint, if he was to be allowed by public opinion
to have his necessary share of esteem and self-respect.   And
there are so many kinds of folks besides fighters and saints!
Century after century they died without having lived, and we're
walking around over their dust this minute.   And yet even
the fighters and the saints needed bridges!   And here we are
in the twentieth century, jumping the life out of anybody who
isn't interested in building bridges, and hooting at him if he
feels the impulse to try to be a saint.   It's enough to make
you tear your hair out by handfuls, isn't it?"

Another day Marise launched him off on the same theme by
asking him skeptically, "Well, suppose you could have your
own way about things, what would you do to help people find
their own right group and work and climate and surroundings?
I don't see how there is the faintest possibility of helping
them."

"I'd start in," said Neale, "by suggesting to them, all through
their youth, in every way possible, the idea that folks could
and should move freely from the life they're born to, to another one that suits their natures.   They have to do it while
they're young and footfree, don't they?   I wouldn't start in
by hammering them over the head with the idea that there
are only one or two classes that anybody wants to belong to.
I'd jump with all my weight on that idiotic notion that one
class is better than another, as if any class was any good at
all for you, if it's not the one you belong to naturally!   I'd
grease the ways to get from one to another, instead of building

fences, especially if the change would mean making less money. Just think of all the natural-born carpenters and mechanics that fall by chance into professors' families, or millionaires' homes. They never get any chance in life. Just look at the hullaballo that was made about poor old Tolstoi's wanting the simplicity of a working-man's life. Just look at the fiendishly ingenious obstacles that are put in the way of any working-man's son who wants the culture and fineness and harmonious living that got so on Tolstoi's nerves. And look, even Tolstoi was just as bad as the rest. Because *he* happened to want simplicity and a hardy open life, didn't he start on the warpath to drive everybody else to it. Good Lord, why try to hold up one ideal as the only one for millions of men, who have a million various capacities and ideals and tastes? They'd enrich the world like a garden, with their lives, if public opinion only allowed them to be lived."

"Do you know Rabelais," asked Marise, "and his motto, *'Fay ce que vouldras?'* Everybody in his day thought it fearfully immoral."

"Oh, I suppose that every wise man since the beginning of the world has found it out in his way before now. But they're not allowed to tell the rest of us plain folks so we understand. Or maybe you don't understand anything till you find it out for yourself. I don't believe I do. Do you?"

"I'm sure," said Marise with a quiet bitterness in her tone that burned like a drop of acid in Neale's mind, "I'm sure that I personally haven't found out anything, nor do I understand anything whatever. Nor, till this minute did anybody ever suggest to me that there was really something worth while to find out. Nobody—nobody but you—ever dreamed of asking me to go on a quest to understand. That's why I —go on, go on with it. Why do you stop?"

But that day Neale had been too much startled by the glimpse of a somber discontent under her keen bright intelligence, and too much moved by her speaking of his bringing something different into her life to "go on."

He tried desperately to think of some way to ask her about it, to offer to help her, to implore her to open her heart as he

was opening his. But he was stricken with shyness, with a
fear lest he had misunderstood, lest he say the wrong thing.
He could only look at her hopelessly. What a clumsy, heavy-
handed china-smasher he was, anyhow!

But such glimpses of what lay beneath the surface did not
come often, though he thought about them a great deal. He
wondered if there was any connection between them and her
evident habit of not talking seriously, of bantering keenly
about superficial things, rather than giving any idea of what
she was really thinking. Perhaps she did not trust people
enough to give them any idea of what she was really thinking.
Perhaps she fell into that grim mood when she thought seriously. Why should she? And yet she was always making him
talk seriously, about ideas he really cared about.

Once he said to her clumsily, "I must bore you to death,
with all these half-baked ideas of mine, when you're used
to such brilliant talkers."

She startled him with the energy and vivacity of her answer,
"Oh, I *hate* what you call brilliant talkers. I'm so sick of
them! You can't imagine what it is to me, like a long drink
of clear water, to hear somebody trying to say what he really
thinks."

He asked, sincerely and naïvely at a loss, "Why, why does
anybody talk at all, if not to say what he thinks?"

She answered, with a certain smile of hers which always made
him uneasy, a dry, ugly smile, "Don't you realize that the real
purpose of talk is to pull the wool over the eyes of the person
you are talking to, to make him think you are more clever than
you are, and to get something out of him for yourself that he
would not let you have if he knew you were taking it?"

Then with one of her lightning changes to that melting look
and smile before which he always succumbed wholly, she went
on, "The truth is that I hope all the time that in your thinking
over and over there may be a hint for me, who was never taught
to do the least bit of thinking for myself. So go on, let me see
it all, just as it comes. Let me pick out for myself what will be
of use to me."

Well, if she wanted that, she should have it—or anything

else he could give her. It was part of the reeling, glamorous intoxication into which she cast him, to hear himself going on like a stump-speaker. And she was adroit at hitting on subjects that made him talk. One day as they were amusing each other by describing their school-life, his as different from hers as if they had been brought up on different planets, football was mentioned. In no time she had him helplessly loquacious, explaining football to her. Think of having to explain football to anybody! He explained how you played it, and some of the rules, and how terribly you cared about it. And suddenly found that he had explained it to himself, that he really understood it for the first time.

"It's a kind of education that America has worked out for herself unconsciously, I believe, the American college idea of sports. No American undergraduate dreams of playing to amuse himself. He'd scorn to. *He plays to win.* That's the American idea. And it's a splendid one. To give every ounce in you to do what you set out to do—no lackadaisical dilettantism—your whole heart in it—and *go to it!* That's the way for men to live."

He was aware that Marise looked at him surprised by his fire. He was surprised by it, himself. He guessed perhaps he was ready to go back to work; perhaps he'd had enough of sauntering around. "That's what you learn in college athletics —how to give yourself to some aim and not to keep anything back for yourself. That's great, you know," he told her imperatively. "It is! It takes the personal littleness out of a boy to give his all to reach a goal. It makes a man out of a boy. But, oh, Lord!" he burst out with a great swing of his arm, "When that *has* made you a man, why don't they let you know that you have more goals to choose from than just different ways of making your living, most of them just buying and selling different sorts of things? You're trained in athletics to put your very heart and all of it, into what you do. That's *fine!* But why don't they train you just as hard to put your whole intelligence into being sure that what you're putting your heart into is worth doing, and is what you're meant to do? They don't train you for that, they won't even let you have a quiet minute to think of it yourself. They keep you up in the air all the time, whooping it up about your duty to 'win out!' to win the game! Sure, any man that's got blood in his veins wants to win the game. But *which* game? It's all very well, turning a boy into a grown-up human being, but you've got to . . ."

"I wonder," broke in Marise thoughtfully, "I wonder what might turn a girl into a grown-up human being?" And then before Neale could open his lips she blushed, shook her head as if at a slip on her part, and said quickly, "Oh, there's my car, now."

She ran out to take it. Neale stood on the corner, cursing the whole race of tram-cars.

When it passed him, close to him in the narrow street, he caught sight of her face. It was bent downward as if to hide it from the other people in the car. He saw that there was a very faint smile on her lips as if she could not keep it back, a little sweet, secret, happy smile. Her whole face was softly shimmering with it.

Good heavens! why hadn't he gone on with her! He leaped forward and sprinted after the rapidly disappearing car.

And stopped short in the midst of the traffic. You can't make love in a *street-car!* What an imbecile he was!

Often, after she had left him, he pelted off into the Campagna, walking for miles "like a madman," said the leisurely Italian countrymen, slowly stepping about their work. Neale felt himself rather mad, as though the steady foundations of his life had been rent and shattered, as by a blast of dynamite.

Dynamite? What was it somebody had said to him once, about dynamite? He tried to think, but could not remember. Perhaps it was something he had read in a book.

Once, after such a headlong tramp, he came in and wrote a long letter to his mother, telling her all about Marise; a strange thing for him to do, he thought, as he dropped the letter in the box. But everything he did now seemed strange to him. Strange and yet irresistibly natural.

CHAPTER XLIX

If only Marise would go away, would go *away* and give her a chance, thought Eugenia despairingly, coming slowly into her sitting-room where Mlle. Vallet sat writing in her journal. Joséphine heard the door close and hurried in with her quick silent step to take off her mistress' wraps.

"Mademoiselle looks so *tired* after these long walks!" she said solicitously, scrutinizing with a professional expertness the color of the young face. "I don't think they agree with Mademoiselle at all. This climate is too soft to walk about so. Nobody does. Mademoiselle might—without presuming to advise—Mademoiselle might be wiser to go in cabs."

Eugenia held out her arms as Joséphine slipped off her pretty, fawn-colored silk coat and then let them fall at her sides. She was thinking, *"Cabs!* What would he say to some one who went everywhere in cabs!"

"Oh!" cried Joséphine. "Those abominable ruins! Mademoiselle's dear little bronze shoes! Cut to pieces! Oh, Mlle. Vallet, just look at our poor Mademoiselle's shoes, the beautiful bronze ones. And there's no replacing them in the shops of *this* country!"

Mlle. Vallet tipped her head forward to look seriously over her steel-rimmed spectacles, agreed seriously that there was certainly very little left of the pretty bronze shoes, and went seriously back to writing with her sharp steel pen a detailed description of her expedition to the Catacombs. Mlle. Vallet was a very happy woman in those days. To be in Rome, after years of grinding drudgery in the class-room, to be free to look and wander and observe at her leisure for so much of the day—she often told Eugenia that she had never in her wildest dreams supposed she would have such an opportunity! She studied and sight-saw with conscientious and absorbed exactitude, and wrote down voluminous accounts of every day's sights and the thoughts they aroused in her. "It will be the treasure-book of my old age!" she said. "I shall take it down from the shelf when I am old, and live myself back into this wonderful experience!"

"Her old age!" Eugenia wondered when she thought old age would begin. She looked a thousand years old already to Eugenia. Heavens! Think of ever being old like that, yourself. What use *could* there be in living if you were old and reduced for your amusement to writing down dates and things in a journal!

"If Mademoiselle will step into her own room," said Joséphine. Eugenia came to herself with a start. She had been standing in the middle of the room staring at Mlle. Vallet's back. But she had been thinking about Neale Crittenden, about those deep-set eyes of his, and how his face was lighted up when he smiled. When he smiled at her, Eugenia felt like moving from wherever she was and going to stand close beside him. What made her feel so? It was like a black-art. There was that girl at school who had been bewitched by the Breton mission-priest,—bewitched so that she fell into a fever if she could not see him every day.

"There! Sit there!" said Joséphine, pressing her competently into an easy chair, and beginning to undo her hooks and eyes. "I haven't much time. Mademoiselle is so late in coming in. Just a little cold-cream—this horrible southern sun burns so! Oh, I can feel this awful Roman dust thick on every hair! I do wish—without seeming to presume—I do *wish* that Mademoiselle would consent to wear a veil— everybody does."

Eugenia moved her head from one side to the other wearily. How Joséphine did chatter! She never had a quiet moment, *never*, and she was so *tired*. Feeling the supple, smooth professional fingers beginning to put on the cold cream, she held her head still and thought.

Very bitter thoughts and bewildered . . . of a person betrayed. She *was* betrayed! She had done everything . . . everything that she had known how to do. She had spared neither time nor money nor effort. She had worked (and she

hated to work) she had *worked* to learn all the things she
should know. She had beaten Marise at her own game. She
talked better French than she, so her diction teacher said;
and ever so much more distinguished English—she *never*
made those slips into Americanisms or Gallicisms that Marise
did. At least not in conversation, sometimes she still thought
in American. She knew ever so much more about dressing than
Marise, and about lace, and about manners. She had come to
the point at last of being sure of her manners, of being able
to sit down, instinctively composing herself so that she would
look well from all angles, of not having to think of how to shake
hands or leave a room, any more than she thought of the adjustment of a gown that Joséphine had put on her. Whereas
Marise still fumbled at the back of her neck at times to make
sure of a hook, or had that common trick of feeling her hair
to see if it were in order. Marise had stood still in all that,
and she had gone forward to the goal. But as she reached
it . . . !

How could she have thought for a moment that she cared a
thing about him—he was horrible and rough and as American as—as—a typewriter! What *made* her care about such
a man? She wouldn't have, if it had not been for Marise.
It was Marise's fault. She never would have dreamed of
looking at him if she hadn't seen that first evening at Donna
Antonia Pierleoni's soirée that Marise had lost her head
over him. That made her curious about him of course, and
somehow before she knew it something about his eyes or smile
—oh, it *was* as if she were bewitched that he should make
her feel so, make her want and want and want till she ached,
to have him look at her—and all the time he never looked
away from Marise.

"There," said Joséphine, slipping out the hairpins, and taking up a handful of the bright hair to inspect it, "I believe—I
believe," she pondered the matter profoundly, her dark,
sharp intelligent face selflessly focussed on the problem, "I
wonder if we ought to wash it a little oftener here than in
Paris? There is more dust. But washing it takes the oil

out so. Perhaps a little more of the Meylan dressing. That has a little fine oil in it. I know the recipe."

Joséphine knew everything there was to know about toilet-preparations, and about how to use them. She adored her profession and adored Mlle. Mills for being such a beautiful subject. There were times, when she had pinned the last shining curl in place, put the last breath of invisible powder on the rounded young white neck, fastened the last hook in the exquisitely fitting gown, and got down on her knees to straighten the gleaming silk of the fine silk stockings, when she wondered what she had done to deserve such good fortune.

She often watched Eugenia out of the door, as tenderly, impersonally proud of her as a painter of his canvas, as a patissier of his tart; and then feeling somewhat worn with activity and emotion, stepped back, took off her corsets, got into the rumpled untidy wrapper which was her personal favorite, put carpet slippers on her tired feet, and sat down with a novel of high-life to rest.

Eugenia occasionally thought seeing her thus, that *she* never was allowed to relax in unpicturesque ease. It seemed to her that Mlle. Vallet and Joséphine were the ones who were *really* enjoying Rome! She worked so hard, she had paid the full price—and somehow the coin was of no value in this new country to which she was now transported, where she had not wanted to come, from which she would give anything to get away. She did not *like* Mr. Crittenden—she never had liked him—oh, why wouldn't he just once look at her and see what was there, instead of talking over her head that queer talk of his? She put on her loveliest toilettes, things that made Joséphine almost weep for pleasure, while Marise wore that same old gray dress day after day—she ruined her bronze shoes for him, stumbling around on foot over those horrible old ruins—how she loathed ruins! Why on earth did any one want to *pretend* to like to look at them!

History! That was what he was always talking about—history that she had always hated. Here it was again to plague her! How could she have guessed that he would care about history? She sat up now till all hours reading it, till Mlle. Vallet was afraid for her eyes, and yet he didn't seem to notice when she said something about it. He just took it for granted, as if she were a man.

What did Marise *want* of him anyhow? She couldn't possibly expect to *marry* him . . . neither of them had a cent of money. She ought to think of that, to think what was best for him. It was selfish, self-centered of Marise. A man like Neale ought of course to marry money. When she thought what *she* could do for him! Married to her he could have exactly the life he was meant for—travel, leisure, ease—! What was it about Marise that he liked? She could do everything better than Marise now, except play the piano, and it evidently wasn't *that* he cared for in her, because the afternoon they had all gone to the Visconti recital, he had listened just as intently to the men students and the other girls as to Marise. And when Marise asked him afterwards what music he liked best he told her bluntly the Bach that Professor Visconti himself had played, and Marise had said she did too. She hadn't seemed to realize what an affront to her that was. *Why* did Marise care so much about him? Why did anybody? Eugenia couldn't understand. She couldn't understand. Her throat had a hard aching lump in it because she couldn't understand.

"A loose soft coiffure for to-night," murmured Joséphine dreamily to herself, happily twisting together the beautiful golden strands, "and the pale-blue mousseline de soie—not the evening-dress!" she was shocked at the idea, though nobody had suggested it, "the high-necked one with the little myosotis embroidered on the ruffles." Joséphine worshipped that dress.

Her strong dark flexible fingers hovered around the golden head as though she were calling down blessings on it. As a matter of fact she was. She slipped off the silk peignoir, washed with almond-scented water the white arms and neck, and the white tired feet. She dried them with a fine linen towel by gentle pattings, not to coarsen the skin. She put on the white silk stockings and white high-heeled slippers, and a white satin underslip. She stood a moment to be sure she had thought of everything. Then carefully, carefully she slipped on the pale blue mousseline-de-soie. "A-ah!" it *was* as sweet as she remembered it!

Eugenia had submitted to all this with a forlorn patience. That was all the good it would do. He would look at her as if she were dressed in a meal-sack, never even notice that she had changed her dress. What *else* could she do, could any one do? What more did he want? She was betrayed; somehow life had played her false, a callous heartless dishonest trick! Why *should* she care so much? She didn't want to care. Why did she long to have him look kindly at her, till her heart ached? Why every day, every day, should the disappointment *hurt* her so? She hadn't done anything wrong to deserve to be hurt so. If she could only stop caring. If only Marise would go away.

Eugenia sat very still, while Joséphine set a jeweled comb at exactly the right angle in the golden hair. One lovely little hand was at her heart as if by pressing hard on it she could stop the ache, the other held the fresh, scented handkerchief clutched tightly, in case this time she could not keep back the tears. She mustn't cry. She mustn't cry, because Joséphine would have to do her face all over.

CHAPTER L

ONE night Marise woke up with a start, staring into the darkness, feeling very cold and sick. She knew what had happened. She had come to her senses in time. She had almost slipped into the trap, the trap set for her by life, which she had so mortally feared. She had been playing a foolish, reckless game of hide-and-seek with herself, pretending that she did not know what was happening. She knew perfectly well what was happening. Neale Crittenden was in love with her. And she was falling in love with him. She wanted him.

Oh, this was the way it must always happen. This was the way all women were caught in the trap . . . these dizzying moments of joy, this causeless singing of your heart, this blind, rapturous rushing forward with outstretched arms to clasp all life to your heart . . . treacherous deadly life that only sought to debase you.

She had always wondered how women could go on, go on to the fatal moment from which there was no drawing back. Now she knew. You were poisoned, you were made mad till you longed for that moment with all your being.

But she had come to her senses in time to draw back. She would save herself, defend herself, since there was no one to help her, now more than ever. First of all, she knew passionately, she must not think of him for a moment or she would not draw back. She must not remember how he looked or spoke or moved, not even the sound of his voice. She must concentrate her thoughts on the one fact that she had almost been caught in that great dreadful trap, that she, Marise, who knew so much better, had almost fallen in love . . . love!

She drew the covers about her, as she sat bolt-upright in the dark, her teeth chattering. Love! She sickened at the sound. The gray cat . . . Jeanne . . . Isabelle . . . the pictures in one of the hidden books at school . . . the passages in her mother's novels . . . her mother . . . Madame Vallery . . . Madame de la Cueva . . . they were all of them looking at her out of the dark, pointing at her, shaming her, exulting over her . . . "You too . . . you have come to it."

The gray cat! She was like the gray cat! She began to sob hysterically and thrust the covers into her mouth to smother the sound.

What could she do? What could she do? She had no strength left. She did not know how to defend herself! She did not want to defend herself!

She could run away. Even poor defenseless things could run away. She stopped sobbing, and sprang out of bed, lighting her candle with trembling fingers. Her watch showed three in the morning. There was a railroad time-table down in the dining room. She huddled on her wrapper, thrust her feet into slippers and, shading her candle-flame, crept downstairs.

At five, hatted and cloaked, she was gently shaking Eugenia and saying, "I'm so sorry to bother you, but do you happen to have some money on hand? I've been worrying about Father for some time. It's so long since I've been back to straighten out the household for him. I've just decided to get off on the early morning train. I ought to go to see Jeanne too. It's past my regular time for making her a visit. If you could just loan me enough to buy the ticket to Paris? I've almost enough as it is, but I must leave some for Miss Oldham and my *pension*."

How kind Eugenia had been! How discreet and uninquisitive! She reached under her pillow, pulled out her gold-meshed purse with the ridiculously large sum in cash she always carried with her, and gave her a five-hundred-lira note together with a kiss on each cheek. "When will you be back, Marise?"

"Oh, I don't know. I don't know. Quite a long time. I may—I shall probably not come back at all. It won't be worth while. Mme. de la Cueva will soon be in Paris again. Good-by, Eugenia dear. You'll be soon coming north, too, won't you?"

"Oh, I dare say," said Eugenia, "if it gets too hot here."

Going down the hall, silent and empty in the dawn, Marise stopped for an instant before his door. For an instant she was forced to think of him, the thought like a weakening potion. She stared hard at his door, her hands pressed tightly together, trembling from head to foot. She was going away. She would never see him again. She turned back towards her own room. She could not go. She ran desperately down the stairs, sick at the idea of what love is. She had almost been caught. She heard the steel jaws snap shut as she fled.

CHAPTER LI

"Yes," said Eugenia at the breakfast table, "Marise was suddenly called back to France by family matters. She is her widowed father's housekeeper, you know; and then too, there is an old servant somewhere who brought her up, whom she feels it her duty to go to see every once in a while."

"What's her address in Paris?" asked Mr. Crittenden urgently.

"I can give that to you, but if you're thinking of writing her a card it wouldn't reach her, for she was to go directly on to the south, and I haven't the least idea what *that* address is. Some tiny village on the sea-coast, I believe. Or is it in the Pyrenees? But she will be back very soon, almost any day. It's hardly worth while trying to write her. She'll be here before a card could follow her around."

Mr. Crittenden got up, leaving his coffee untouched, and left the breakfast-room in his unceremonious American way, without a sign of decent civility.

Mr. Livingstone looked at Miss Mills eloquently, with a shrug which meant, "What can you expect?"

Eugenia waited till every one, except herself and Mr. Livingstone had left the room, and then said hesitatingly, "Mr. Livingstone, I wonder . . ." He was on the alert in an instant, surprised at her personal manner. "It's an outrageously big favor to ask of you, but I don't know any one else adroit enough to manage it." She paused, reflected and drew back shaking her head, "Oh, no; no! what am I thinking of?"

By this time Mr. Livingstone was in the chair beside her, assuring her warmly that if there was anything, *any*thing he could do to be of service—"I shall consider it an honor, Miss Mills, I assure you, an *honor!*"

Miss Mills let her blue eyes rest on his deeply, as if sounding the depths of his sincerity, and then, with a yielding gesture of abandon, decided to trust him, "I've been foolish, and I'm so afraid I shall have trouble unless you can help me. Promise me you won't tell Mlle. Vallet. Or *any* one."

Impassioned protestations from Mr. Livingstone.

She looked over her shoulder to be sure they were alone, "You know the rule of the Italian government about taking out of Italy any valuable antiquities. They are so afraid that tourists of means will carry off some of the fragments of Greek and Roman sculpture. I *knew* about it of course, but I'd no idea it was really enforced—those things so seldom are in Europe. And I bought a lovely little antique bas-relief to go over a mantel-piece in my Paris apartment. I had it sent yesterday, up by the Simplon route; it's too late to get it back and now I'm in mortal terror of what may happen at the Italian frontier. I heard last night the most dreadful tales of what they do to any one who tries to smuggle out such things— not only fines, you know, but lawsuits, lawyers to frighten you —*publicity!*"

She looked very pale and anxious as she explained all this so that Livingstone was deeply touched. But he wondered what she thought he could do about it.

"I'm really ashamed, now I've come to the point, to ask you what I thought. But I *will*—and if you think it too preposterous—more than I have any right to—it's this. To take a pocket full of money (I don't care *what* it costs) and go up to the frontier station and when it comes along, bribe it through the inspectors. You see, Mr. Livingstone, it's something that not everybody could manage, even with ever so much money. But you understand the European mentality so perfectly. It would need to be done with just the right manner. . . . Oh, no, *no*," she broke off abruptly, getting up from her chair. "What a thing to dream of asking any one to do! What claim have I on your . . . ?"

Livingstone, blinking joyfully, sprang up too, protesting that nothing would amuse and interest him more than such a mission. And for *her*, any mission would be his joy!

"Well, think it over. Let me know to-night. I'm ashamed to have mentioned it," she said in confusion. "I don't know how I dared. But oh Mr. Livingstone, I am so troubled

about it. And I am so alone! No one on whom to . . ."
She had gone, murmuring apologies, touched by his instant
response, leaving Livingstone as much moved and agitated
as she.

She went through into her own rooms and told Joséphine,
"Put those manicure things away for the time being. I must
go out to do a bit of shopping. But you can have them ready
at ten. I'll be back by that time. It won't take me long."

Neale stood, frowning and looking at his watch, waiting
for Eugenia to come down from the ladies' dressing-room and
have dinner. As he fidgeted about, looking glumly at the
brilliant scene about him, he was wondering with inward
oaths of exasperation what in hell could be the matter with
anybody's clothes and hair after the slight exertion of sitting
perfectly still in a cab from the door of the pension to the
door of the restaurant. It was not, God knew, that he was
impatient to have her join him. It was because he was in
a steady fever of impatience to have everything over, the
evening, the day, the night—to put back of him another of
those endless, endless days—to be one day nearer to the time
when Marise would return.

"*What?*" he said irritably to the smooth-voiced waiter who
now approached him with an intimate manner. "Oh, *I* don't
care which table!"

"Here, sir, is one right by the edge of the terrace, where
the view is finest," said the waiter in excellent English.
"Perhaps the lady would like a screen. There is occasionally
a draught from below."

He hastened to set a small screen, to rearrange fussily the
handsome silver and linen on the daintily-set table, to slant
the single fine rose in the vase at another angle.

Another waiter, also impeccably polyglot, with gleaming
hair, admirably cut clothes, and an insinuating manner, now
murmured in Neale's ear, "What wine, sir?"

Neale answered on a mounting note of irritation, "Oh, I
don't *care* what wine!"

"We have an excellent Frascati, sir, that is our specialty.

Not found everywhere, sir. The ladies usually like it.
Or . . ."

"All right, serve that," said Neale, adding to himself un-
reasonably, "If you knew so well, why bother me about it?"

The real waiter in charge of his table now arrived in all his
majesty, the first one having been but an aide. Neale saw
by the earnest expression in his eyes that he intended to
make their conference a serious one, and cut him short as
he began to call over the possibilities of the menu by a repeated,
"All right, that'll do," before he had had time to do more
than mention one sort of fish or one entree, or one variety
of fowl.

"There, *that's* over!" he said to himself with a long breath
of relief as the pained waiter turned away to carry into exe-
cution that brutally impromptu order.

Eugenia arrived now, followed by a little stir all over the
restaurant, as people turned to pay tribute to her beauty and
her toilette. "He can't help noticing *that!*" she thought
happily, her pride and satisfaction showing itself only in an
increase of the perfectly unconscious naturalness with which
she took her seat.

"Oh, what a beautiful view!" she said in a low tone to
Neale, looking down over the cypresses of the Palatine to the
city, like a heap of uncut jewels, dully, deeply colored, under
the light of the setting sun. "You know how to choose a
table, I see!" she added admiringly, in an intimate tone. She
wondered if perhaps he had come out in the afternoon to
reserve it. She noticed the screen now, and looked at him
gratefully, really touched.

The waiter arrived with the soup.

"Yes, it is a fine view," said Neale, rousing himself. "A
very fine view indeed. That's the Colosseum over there, isn't
it?"

"Yes," said Eugenia, "and that's the Arch of Titus."

"That's the one with the awfully bad bas-reliefs, isn't it?"
said Neale.

"Oh, *no*," corrected Eugenia, "the one with the poor sculptures is the arch of Septimius Severus. The arch of Titus

is the *good* one, you know, with the bas-reliefs of the Hebrews."

"Oh, yes, of course. You're right," admitted Neale.

Eugenia thought to herself triumphantly, "Ah, it's not only Marise who can talk history with him!"

She was very happy, happier than she ever remembered feeling. Everything had played into her hands. Everything was going perfectly. She had succeeded in getting him into just the sort of restaurant where she could show to the best advantage.

She was eating her soup with a lively appreciation of its excellence and found herself perfectly able to keep up an artistic and historic conversation with Neale; but she was also acutely aware through the pores of her skin that every woman around her was jealously scrutinizing her costume. She expanded joyously, like a cut flower set in water. How *well* everything was going! Certainly Neale must be aware how he was being envied.

She made a remark about the style of the gigantic statues on St. John Lateran, visible in the distance, and turned her arm slightly so that her sleeve would hang better.

Neale answered the remark about the statues on St. John Lateran and continued to look in that direction as though he were thinking about them.

He was saying to himself, "Five days since she left! Only five days! God! How am I going to live through any more of them. How many more sleepless nights! Will she ever get back!"

"Yes, isn't it warm to-night?" said Eugenia, seeing that he was wiping his wet forehead with his handkerchief.

"Unseasonable, very," agreed Neale. He had turned sick with his recurrent panic lest she *never* come back. He ought to have taken that next train and gone right after her, as he wanted to.

The waiter brought the fish. It was not what Neale had ordered, but a more expensive variety. He looked somewhat apprehensively at the gentleman as he offered it, but the gentleman did not seem to notice. On this the waiter disappeared and brought back a bottle of wine, not the variety Neale had bargained for.

"Have you any news from Miss Allen?" asked Neale.

"Oh, no," said Eugenia, slightly surprised. "When she's coming back so soon, she probably doesn't see there's any need to write."

She began on the fish. After the first mouthful she said to Neale with enthusiasm, "You know how to order a dinner as well as to choose a table, that's evident."

"It was the first fish he proposed," said Neale.

Eugenia thought, "How much better breeding he has, after all, than Mr. Livingstone, always boasting of his savoir-faire."

Neale's thoughts were jumping incoherently from one thing to another. "Funny place Rome is, to be planning how to run a woodworking plant in Vermont. Funny change of direction, from planning to go out to China and the East, about-face to planning to settle down and take root. You wouldn't think that would appeal to a man who had had the idea of ranging the world a while longer, to tie himself . . ." This attempt at reasonable consideration of things vanished in an explosion of emotion, as if a spark had fallen into gunpowder. "Oh, if she *will!* If she *will!* Why didn't I make a chance to see her alone before she went away?"

Eugenia was talking about traveling. She had noticed Neale's interest in travels. "I'm thinking, Mr. Crittenden, of making a leisurely trip around the world—not one of those detestable, herded, conducted tours. And yet how else can I go about it? What would *you* do? I'm so ignorant of anything outside of Europe. I *wish* I had some one intelligent and enlightened to go with me. It's so forlorn to travel alone!"

"Why, you'll *like* traveling alone!" said Neale reassuringly, thinking of his own past year. "It's great not to have to bother with some one's else tastes and notions and foolishness and limitations."

"Oh, but," said Eugenia, looking down at her wineglass pensively, "of course it's better to be alone than with some one whose tastes and interests are nothing to you. But to have with you some one you really *care* for . . ."

Neale thought suddenly what the past year would have been

if he had had Marise with him, and cried out fervently, "Oh, of course, *that* would be the ideal!"

The waiter brought the roast and the Frascati. And still the gentleman made no objection. Well, he would bring a cordial with the coffee, ordered or not. The gentleman didn't seem to know what he had ordered or what he was eating. And no wonder, with such a beautiful girl across the table. The waiter shot an experienced, appraising eye at Eugenia's clothes. "He ought to be good for a big tip," he reflected hopefully.

Eugenia thought best to leave a thoughtful silence after the remarks on companionship in travel, and sipped her wine with downcast eyes.

Neale was trying again to think things over reasonably, trying to do as he had always done about everything, to get things clear and straight and sure in his head. There must be no possibility of a mistake where Marise was concerned. "How *about* this now? I've gone stale on other things. How do I know I won't have a slump some time later? A human being is so full of such damn unexpected things—I must be *sure* for Marise's sake. How can any man be . . ." At this he was shaken by so terrible a throe of desire, of longing for Marise that he was frightened. He sat pale, breathless, helpless before it; suffering, tortured, exalted.

When he could breathe he wiped his forehead again. His fingers were shaking. He would go out of his mind if she didn't come back soon. His need for her was like a man's need for air and food and water and sleep. Think reasonably about such essential needs as that! A man cannot live without them. He could not live without Marise. He had not lived before he knew her.

"How moved he is," thought Eugenia, seeing his pale, shaken look. "But he doesn't dare speak. He will to-morrow. Or the day afterwards."

The waiter brought the dessert. Also coffee with the unordered cordial.

CHAPTER LII

FATHER had grown stouter. He always did. But he looked very well. And his shirts and socks seemed to be all right. Mélanie had seen to them, although the dust was thick all over the furniture, and the windows were semi-opaque with smoke. Father was glad to see her, said she was looking very pretty and asked her kindly if she didn't need some more money; but he was not in the least enthusiastic over her reforms in the housekeeping. "Who cares about dust!" he told her. "And as for smoke on the windows, I'm never here in the daytime anyhow except for lunch—and I don't want to look out of the windows then." And as for getting hold of Biron to keep him up to the mark, Marise found that it was trying to put your finger between the tree and the bark, to get between Biron and her father. Every evening after they had both earnestly finished the serious business of eating dinner, Biron left Mélanie to the mere brute labor of cleaning up and washing dishes while he put on a clean apron and came into the salon to consult with his employer about the two meals of the morrow. Marise was astonished at the learning and acumen displayed by both of them in the matter. However had her father learned so intimately all the resources of Les Halles in all the seasons? He subscribed to a newspaper which gave a complete report of the arrivals at the market from both sea-shore and countryside, over which he and Biron pored intently, putting on round spectacles and bending their portly frames over the page. And there was a wine-sellers' journal too, the news items of which were brought up for consideration once a week.

"When it fails, I go out and run a mile, and then I can eat anything."

Mélanie was no longer allowed to serve the meals thus prayerfully planned and created. It was Biron himself who

476

brought in the *plat*, set it down and waited anxiously till it had been tasted and the verdict pronounced. He did not sit down opposite his master and share the meal . . . not yet! But Marise had an intuition that it would not be long before he would. Why not? He was the only other person capable of appreciating that meal. He and her father were bound together by a common passion: they completed and rounded out each other's lives. Where else could Mr. Allen find such another cook? Where else could Biron find another such employer? They were blood-brothers, fellow-priests of a common cult. They might be thankful that somehow they had found each other in the world.

When, after a few days of sharing this ménage, she told her father she thought she would go down to see Jeanne, he said, sure, that was all right if she felt like it, and was she sure she didn't need any more money?

Under the thick green shade of pollarded sycamores sat old Jeanne in the wheeled-chair Marise and her father had given her. The young girl, whom Marise and her father paid to take care of Jeanne, came running to unlock the gate and let the visitor in.

There was old Jeanne, her head tied up in the black coif, just as Marise had seen her a thousand times, her face all twisted to one side just as she had seen her that one time she could not forget. And how glad she was to see Marise, pulling her down to kiss her on both cheeks, crying a little for joy and wiping away the tears with her one active hand; for although she had recovered somewhat, so that she could eat and talk a little if she formed the words very slowly and was not excited, she had never been able to use her paralyzed arm or leg again.

Marise must sit beside her, and let old Jeanne look into her face closely with her loving old eyes, and stroke her white young hand with her gnarled fingers that had worked so hard for the child Marise. And when her first agitation was over, and she was calm enough to try to talk, the questions, the loving, anxious questions: Was she well, the darling, darling

girl? And was she happy? And did that Parisian slut of a
maid look out for her decently? And who did the marketing?
And who did her hair, her beautiful, beautiful hair? Jeanne's
brown hand rested lightly on the shining dark head. No one
had hair like her Marise. She must let it down so that Jeanne
could see it again as in the old days. And how about her
linen? Jeanne was troubled on this point. Linen was not
what it had been and the way it was washed in Paris was a
crime. A Parisian family were staying near by, and Jeanne's
daughter-in-law did their washing. Such grimy, gray linen—
it made Jeanne sick to think that perhaps her darling was
no better cared for. Marise must needs open her valise there
and then, and take out a chemise to show Jeanne, who handled
it, held it close to her one good eye, touched the tip of her
tongue to it, and gave it back, saying, with an attempt at tolerance, "Oh, well, it's as good as a laundress can do nowadays,
I dare say," and possessed herself of Marise's hand again,
holding it to her heart fondly.

Marise found the tears were in her eyes. How sweet it
was to be loved! She clung to the old hand as she had when
she was a child and Jeanne's had been the only hand held
out to her.

The old, crafty wrinkles came around Jeanne's eyes. She
pulled Marise's head close to her and whispered, "You've
never told? Nobody at all?"

"No, no," said Marise hastily. "No one." She felt the
old sickness rise to her throat as she said it.

"And you're not . . . no man . . . you're not engaged
or . . ."

"No, oh, no!" said Marise, still more hastily.

Jeanne's face quieted. She drew a long breath and stroked
Marise's hand. "That's right! That's right! They're all
alike, my darling. Don't forget that. They're all alike when
it comes to women."

Next morning Marise was amazed to have Jeanne greet her
all over again, as though she had not seen her, with fresh
surprise and joy, the same questions, the same trembling stroking of her hair. Only why was her hair up on her head?

That must be just a joke. She must be playing being a lady. And was she sure she knew her catechism? Her white veil was ready, finer than any other little girl's veil. How lovely she would look in it!

"Yes," whispered the young caretaker, in answer to Marise's look of bewilderment, "she doesn't remember you were here yesterday. She often imagines you are with her when she is quite alone. We hear her talking happily to you. And now she does not know the difference between you and her own daughter who died. No, she will never know if you just slip away now. She will never know that you came or that you are not still here."

When Marise went quietly out at the gate she left Jeanne dozing in her chair under the plane-trees, dozing, and waking to talk lovingly to the two little girls who had both died so long ago.

She had learned in the village that Mlle. Hasparren was no longer teaching in Bayonne, had gone back to her own little hill-town in the Pyrenees. Marise knew the way there very well, having spent many a week-end and vacation with Mlle. Hasparren in the old days. The boy from the farm where Jeanne was living chanced to have an errand that took him over the pass and down into that valley. On an impulse Marise asked to go with him. She stowed her valise away under the plank seat and scrambled up beside the bullet-headed boy in the blue béret. How it all took her back to her childhood! The little two-wheeled cart flew off behind the swift small horse, rattling and jolting up hill and down, just as when she and Mlle. Hasparren had gone off together.

At the beginning of the long steep road up to the divide, she and the boy go out and walked, her shoes soon powdered white with dust. How dusty Mlle. Hasparren's shoes had been the day they stood waiting in the station . . . !

They plunged down the other side into the green, poplar-planted valley with every home, every turn of the road as it had been. They stopped at the tiny, white-washed cabin, with its leafy atrium of sycamores. As the boy drove away and the sound of his rattling wheels died to silence, Marise heard from within the first notes of the Sonata in G, the one she had first studied with Mlle. Hasparren.

She went in without knocking, sure that the little home contained no servant, and there sat Mlle. Hasparren, her hair several shades whiter, her black dress several degrees shabbier, her quiet worn face and steady eyes bent lovingly over the keys. The music was like the very sound of her voice.

They sat up late that night talking—Marise must tell all about Rome and the old Visconti, as legendary a figure to Mlle. Hasparren as Paganini; and Mlle. Hasparren must tell how she came to leave her city-school and go back to the little mountaineers in the rough, plain village class-room. "I seemed to feel nearer to them," she said, not knowing very well how to tell why she had, "and I felt a great longing for my mountains and my own old home. And they need music here. Do you remember Father Armandariz?"

"Oh, yes," Marise nodded. She had never forgotten the lean young priest who led the open-air singing of his improvised chorus in front of his fortress-like old church. "Oh, yes, don't you remember we used to drive over just to hear his choir sing here and in another parish too?"

"He is doing wonderful work. We work together a great deal."

"You! With a curé!" Marise was astounded.

Mlle. Hasparren laughed. "Oh, yes, yes, those radical ideas of mine. Of course I still have them. But they don't seem so important as they did. Father Armandariz and I are good friends. We both love music. That's enough. He puts cotton in his ears when I let fall a heresy, and I dip my fingers in the holy-water font and cross myself when I go to play the organ in church. Those are little things, and little things mustn't be allowed to interfere with great ones."

That evening Marise watched a choir rehearsal, Mlle. Hasparren at her piano, Father Armandariz, bony, threadbare, hollow-cheeked, his eyes gleaming with ardor, leading now the group of serious-faced Basque girls in black mantillas, now the great-chested, burly Basque men whose resonant basses shook the little house. One of them (Mlle. Hasparren had said he was the village shoemaker) was given a bass solo and practised it over several times, while the others listened. He held his head high, drew in a great breath and sang as though it were the meaning of his life he were singing out, "Magnificat anima mea Dominum!" And then all the others with him, "My soul magnifies God!" Father Armandariz stopped them. "No, the altos were too slow on coming in. Once more." And then again, "Once more."

They all kept their eyes on him earnestly; they began again unfalteringly as many times as was necessary; before the evening was over they looked tired; but it was a good fatigue, and when they finally finished and turned to smile at each other and fold their music sheets together, their faces wore a quiet, purified serenity which Marise envied them. This was music. Not one of them was thinking of himself nor how the music had made him appear to advantage nor how he could use music as a tool to get ahead of other people, or get himself talked about.

The memory of Donna Antonia's soirées, of Mme. de la Cueva's good advice came into her mind. People called that sort of thing "art-atmosphere," didn't they? It was the cemetery of art, that's what it was, with the egotism of the performer dancing on the grave. One evening here, such an evening as this—there was more music in it than in months of chatter about the clothes and hair and morals and incomes of the people who make it on the platform.

At the piano Mlle. Hasparren and Father Armandariz were talking together of the next evening's rehearsal, Mlle. Hasparren occasionally illustrating with one hand what she was saying. How deeply human was the look of intimate confidence they bent on each other, the ugly young priest and the ugly old school-teacher. They might well be thankful that they had found each other in the world.

Mlle. Hasparren turned around now and asked Marise if she would not play for them. "I would be so proud to show my friends what an old pupil of mine has come to be," she said fondly.

It seemed to Marise that she had never in her life felt so like playing. What should it be? She swerved on her way to the piano to stoop to kiss Mlle. Hasparren's swarthy cheek, and, sitting down, with an affectionate smile at her, began the Toccata in D minor, just as Mlle. Hasparren had taught it to her, with all she had learned since then. She had never played to such an audience; when she turned around Father Armandariz was looking beatific and Mlle. Hasparren exalted with pride. She had never played so well. She had, she felt, just begun to know what music was.

Mlle. Hasparren had set up for her a folding cot in her own room, since there was no other bedroom in the tiny house. They slept side by side, near enough so that they could have reached out and clasped each other's hands as on that night so long ago when Mlle. Hasparren had pulled Marise out of the black pit. Marise could not go to sleep. Long after Mlle. Hasparren lay breathing deep, her dark face relaxed in a selfless quiet that was not more selfless than her waking look, Marise lay looking out at the stars and the mountains, thinking, trembling, sometimes feeling hot bitter tears in her eyes, sometimes feeling her heart swell high with strange, unearthly aspiration.

Mlle. Hasparren was right. She had always been right. To keep clear of all troubling, maddening, personal relations that were sure to end by poisoning you, not to want anything for yourself, to give all for music—how *safe* you would be, to live like that. And how sweet it would be to feel safe! She never had. She was so *tired* of feeling afraid. Why *not* live like that? When you knew it was the only safe way! When you knew that if you did not, you would fall headlong into that dreadful mire that splashed up such indelible stains upon your mind at even the few chance contacts with it which life brought to a girl. Yes, that was the only safe way. Never to go back to Rome at all. Somehow to devise a life all devotion to music, with the miserable personal affections burned up in that greater ardor. Yes, that, Marise decided, that was the only tolerable, the only endurable future she could see.

People began to stand up, to put on their wraps and collect their valises. The train was passing the outskirts of Rome. It would be in the station in a few minutes.

Marise tied on her veil over a piteous white face. She had said she would not go back to Rome at all. She had scarcely been ten days away. She had come back. Like any other woman she had come back to the trap.

CHAPTER LIII

SHE had not seen him yet. She had had her breakfast sent to her room when she heard he was still at the pension. She had thought certainly he would be gone away by this time.

She knew he would not have gone away!

She stood now with Eugenia at the entrance to the Pincian, up on the hill, by the fountain, under the ilex trees looking down over the city.

This was where their first walk together had ended.

"I think I see Mr. Crittenden just come up the Trinità steps and turning this way," remarked Eugenia, looking in that direction.

If Marise could have stirred, she would have run away. She turned her head and saw him coming. Although he was still so far away that she could not make out his face, she knew by the sudden tautness of his figure, by the spring forward of his step that he had seen her.

There he came, striding strongly towards her, as he had come to seek her out, across the world, across all time. He looked infinitely familiar to her, and yet infinitely different from all she had been thinking of him. She had forgotten! What had she been imagining him?

When he drew near enough to be sure it was she, he snatched off his hat and swung it around his head with a bright, boyish gesture of joy. The wind ruffled his hair, the sun shone full on his bold, clear face, on his deep eyes, on his tender, full-lipped mouth.

He was smiling at her, all his heart in his smile. He was welcoming her back.

Marise felt a warm gush all over her body, as though her heart had suddenly begun to beat again, as though he had welcomed her back into life. Why, this was Neale! This was no monster to dread. If she had seen him, only seen his face that morning, only had one look from his eyes that both smiled and were steady . . . she would never have run away.

She was not hurt at all, only frightened half to death! She was not just a woman in love, ready to give herself up to a man. She was Marise in love with Neale.

He had come up to them now, his breath coming fast as though he had been running. For an instant he did not speak, taking her hand silently in his. All that life had made of him looked out on her from his clear eyes.

With a beating flutter, her heart sprang up from its numb torpor of fright and spread its wings.

"Well, we certainly have missed you!" was what he finally said.

"I'm very glad to be back in Rome," she answered.

CHAPTER LIV

HE had stood this gregarious flocking around just all he was going to, Neale decided that morning, up under the ilex trees, exchanging commonplaces with the two girls, unable to say or even to look what he felt, because Eugenia was there. And he'd had plenty of Eugenia during the last ten days.

What a nightmare those ten days had been to him! What a hideous block-head he had been to let Marise slip away from him, even for a time, before he had made a chance to see her, *really* to see her, in a quiet place where they could hear themselves think—with none of those third and fourth persons hanging around. What had he been thinking of, drifting along like a man in a dream, with no sense of time?

But that absence of hers had waked him up. Yes, it had waked him up! He had not had one consecutive night's sleep since she had been gone, starting up continually from a doze with his arms empty when he had dreamed she was lying in them. How had he ever lived through that suspense and uncertainty without losing his mind? He was very grateful to Eugenia for having kept him from making an awful fool of himself and getting into a blind mess of confusion. She had kept him in Rome by telling him that Marise would be back any day. If it hadn't been for that—where would *he* have been? Looking for a needle in a haystack all over Southern France, and Marise back in Rome.

Well, she was back and he had been too frightened not to have learned a little sense. He'd manage a walk with her alone, just the two of them before the day was out or— How could he?

How did you do anything? You just went and did it.

He went boldly to her room and knocked on the door. When Marise came to open it, he said, "To celebrate your return, won't you let me show you a specially lovely spot on the Campagna I've found? I've been taking some long, solitary walks while you were away." He added firmly, "No, not Miss Mills and Mr. Livingstone because they don't like to tramp, and this is 'cross country."

There! It had been no harder than that. Why in the name of heaven hadn't he thought of the simple, obvious way to get the thing done? He went back to his room and sat down, staring at the wall, to wait till afternoon came and to try to plan what he would say when it came. He hoped a great deal that she had read Browning.

But she hadn't. As they passed through the city walls and came out, just the two of them, under the wide sky he asked her about it, timidly; for he was horribly frightened and moved, now that he had her to himself. And she said that she was sorry, she was very ignorant of English and American poetry, having been so little in an English-speaking country. Neale sighed. No luck! She went on to suggest apologetically that she ought some time to go back to America and take a course in English Literature, or at least gather the books about her and read. "My old Cousin Hetty's front porch wouldn't be a bad place," she said thoughtfully.

"I'm going to see that front porch before so very long, you know," said Neale, springing one of his surprises, with a rapidly beating heart and an impassive face.

She darted one of her swallow-swift glances at him.

"Yes, you've persuaded me. I've persuaded myself. I'm not going to sell the Ashley property right away, not without going up to look at it at least. I've been thinking a great deal about what you said that first day. I've been thinking a great deal anyway—can't—can't we sit down some-where?" He flung away any pretense of having a special place to show her. She too had apparently forgotten it. They sat down on the short grass, their backs against a low heap of stones, part of the ruins of a very ancient aqueduct. Far in the distance a flock of sheep roamed with a solitary shepherd leaning on his staff.

"You know—you know what we've been talking about, trying to find one's way, know what you were meant to do. Well, my guess about myself is that I'm a maker by birth, not a buyer or seller. The more I think of it the better it looks to me, like something I'd like to put my heart into doing as well as I could—taking raw material, you know, that's of no special value in itself and helping other men to make it worth more by adding work and intelligence to it. You know what somebody said about the ounce of iron that's of no use, and the hundred hair-springs the watchmaker makes out of it. I don't see why I didn't think of it at once when I knew Uncle Burton had left me the mill. But I'd never have thought of it if you hadn't helped me. It takes me so *long* to get around to anything anyhow. And you are so quick! You see, I know a lot about the lumber-business, and quite a bit about saw mills, and I can get on fine with workmen. I *like* them, and I *love* working in the woods. And—and—" he brought out the second of his carefully planned points, "it would be a home too. You said it was a home. Everybody wants a home, Marise."

He sat silent, listening to the word as it echoed over their two homeless heads. And then he took his courage in his two hands and turned towards Marise. What he saw in her face so shocked and startled him that every carefully planned word dropped from his mind. He forgot everything except that the dark, set look was on her face and all that tragic sadness he could not forget.

"Marise, Marise—what is it?" he cried, frightened. What could he have said?

With her shoulders and eyebrows she made an ugly, dry little gesture of dismissing the subject, and said ironically, "What makes you so sure everybody wants a home?"

He stared at her stupidly, not able to think of anything to say, till she went on impatiently, irritably, "It's just sentimental to talk like that. I never heard you say a sentimental word before. You know what homes are like,—places where people either lie to each other or quarrel."

Neale was startled by the quivering, low-toned violence of

her accent. Why should she wince and shrink back as if he had struck on an intolerably sensitive bruise—at the word, *home?*

"Why, let me tell you about my home," he said eagerly to her, in answer to the tragic challenge he felt in her look, her tone. "I don't believe I ever told you about what my home was like; just the usual kind, of course, what any child has, I suppose, but—let me *tell* you about it."

He began anywhere, the first thing that came into his mind, what the house was like, and where the library was, and how he liked his own room, and the security of it; his free play with little boys on the street that was his great world, and how he felt back of him, as a sure refuge from the uncertainties of that or any other great world, the certainties of what he found when he ran up the steps every afternoon, opened the door, his door, and stepped into his home, where he was sure of being loved and cared for, and yet not fettered or shut in. "Father and Mother always let me alone, let me grow."

He told of the meal-times and his boy's raging appetite, and his mother's delight in it. He told of the evenings when Father and Mother sat reading together; of the free-flowing tide of trust and affection between his parents, changing with their changes, never the same, never different; trust and affection of which he had never been really conscious but which had always been the background of his life. He remembered even to his father's tone as he said, "Oh, Mary," and her instant, "Yes, dear, what is it?"

He had not thought of it for years, he had never before thought consciously of it, had always taken it for granted as he took daylight, or his own good health. But there in that foreign land it all stood up before him, clear in its own quiet colors, visible to him for the first time against the other worlds he had been seeing and divining. He thought of foolish little gay things to tell her—he could not have guessed why they came into his mind—about the house smelling "trunky" when it was time to go to West Adams, and Mother, who could never get the trunk packed, and Father's joking her about it. And the long trip over to the city; Father always waiting to let him see how the ferry-boat was tied up. And in the train how Father kissed Mother good-by and then Neale, and then Mother again, and put his cheek for an instant against hers. This time Neale looked back through the years straight into his father's face, proudly, and held his head high.

He found himself telling things that he himself had never thought of till then—his parents' tolerant patience with his boy's fits and starts, with his egotism and absurdities, with his periods of causeless and violent energy, his other periods of causeless, violent indolence.

And West Adams, he had always till this moment taken for granted the stability of that second home of his, that had been his father's before him, like a rock to which his tossing little boat was moored whenever he wished. Grandfather and Grandmother, plain old people—like Marise's old Cousin Hetty perhaps—grown as much alike as an old brother and sister, who still went off blue-berrying on the mountain together every summer.

And then, when he had needed his home no longer, the adventuring-forth of his father and mother, and his guessing for the first time how they had tamed their self-centered youth to be parents; the moment when he and Father stood together under the old maple-tree and understood each other so deeply, with no words, all the years of affection and trust rising up and standing there with them; and how Father and Mother had driven away as if for an Indian Summer honeymoon, Mother's face smiling through her tears. He told— yes, even that—how for an instant he had felt hurt and left out, and Mother had known it and come running back to say a last loving good-by to the little boy he had been.

Marise had not said a word as he brought this all up for her to see, nor did she when he had finished and was silent. But he could see that her hands, folded together in her lap, were shaking. He waited for her to speak. He knew there was something ominous in her silence, like gathering thunder. His heart was heavy with it. He was afraid of what might be coming. But he longed to have it come, to have it tear down the barrier between them.

"So that's what you have known—what every child has, you suppose!" she said passionately, her voice quivering and breaking. She stopped herself abruptly. She could scarcely breathe, her agitation was so great. She knew what she would do if she opened her lips again. But she would die of suffocation if she did not speak. It rose within her like a devouring flood, all that old, ever-new bitterness; and beat her down.

She heard herself, in a desperate, stammering voice, telling him . . . *telling* him!

The words that passed her lips did not seem words but bleeding, living, tortured things. She was mortally sick and faint, but she could not stop. Once as in a flicker of lightning she knew what she was doing, and tried to stop—but she had torn it loose from those fibers that had grown so close and hard around it, she had wrenched it away—bloody and raw—it was too late to stop.

When she finished she leaned her face on her hands and was silent, feeling as though she had died. When she finally looked up at him she saw that the tears stood thick in his eyes. She had never dreamed that for good or ill one human being could feel so close to another. It was as though she could not tell whether those tears were his, or had come healingly into her own dry eyes.

She saw the anguish of his yearning sympathy—and yet what was it he said? Something she had not dreamed any one could say, "Oh, the poor little girl you were! Wasn't there *any one* to help you to get it straight, to understand it?"

"Understand it!" she said harshly. "I understood it only too well."

He looked away from her, across the plain, and kept a thoughtful silence. Then he said, "I don't believe you understood it in the least. Is it likely that any fourteen-year-old little girl could understand anything like that, anything that must have begun, had its real causes back before you were born—and why should you take the point of view of an ignorant old woman who certainly had the ignorant old woman's appetite for scandal? You probably didn't even get straight what really happened then—it sounds fearfully mixed up, you know, as though there must be more than that to it. Let alone its *real* meaning, its human meaning, that you couldn't possibly have understood at fourteen, if you had known all the facts—and there certainly were lots more facts than what you saw and what that old woman put into your head.

"And, anyhow—oh, Marise, no matter *what* it was, it has nothing to do with your life *now!* Why do you let it mean so much to you? Just think how long ago it happened! It hasn't a thing to do with *you.* How can it?"

She flushed a deep, shamed red, and asked in a whisper, "You don't think that I . . . that I would be like that?"

He cried out furiously, "No, no, *no!* What an idea! It's nothing to you—nothing, I tell you. It's been nothing to you for years. You ought to have stopped thinking of it ever so long ago. Everybody starts all over again. You're yourself. You don't have to keep carrying that around with you. It doesn't belong to you. Let it fall. Leave it here!" he commanded abruptly, springing to his feet and holding out his hand to help her rise. "Leave it here! And walk off into your own life."

She stood up beside him now, so giddy with a strange new lightness that she laid her hand on his arm to steady herself.

At her touch he flushed hot with the desire to put his arms about her and hold her passionately close. The desire was so intense that he had for an instant the hallucination that he had done it, that she leaned her head against his breast. But he had been so harrowed by sympathy for her poor bruised heart, had been so touched by the revelation of the delicacy and fineness of fiber which had but served to deepen the dreadful, unhealed hurt with which she had lived helplessly, he was so moved by her white, drawn face, lifted to his own with a childlike faith in what he said, he was so wrung with his thankfulness to see on that pale face a sensitive reflection of his own certainty . . . oh, now was no time to burst out on her with the flame of his passion, now when she was so weak, so defenseless. He put aside his passion with a strong hand, resolutely.

Looking at him, she saw his face flush darkly with his desire, and felt herself as safe from a touch as though she looked down on him from a high tower. Had she ever felt safe before?

She leaned on his arm like a convalescent. She walked off beside him quietly, into her own life.

The walk back to the city walls was as full of a comforting, silent sense of each other's presence as though they had lived their lives together.

Once in a while they spoke together as simply and naturally as children, of small, everyday things, of little changes he would need to make in his house, an old cistern to be drained and filled in, the half-rotten maple which darkened the living-room cut down to let the sunlight in.

In one of the quiet silences, full to the brim with their nearness to each other, Neale remembered what he had meant to do with this afternoon, what he had so self-consciously planned to say. The thought made him abashed and humble. How infinitely deeper life was than you could ever know till you began to live. He had thought he loved Marise as much as a man could love a woman. He saw that he had only begun to guess what love could be, that it is a tie between two struggling human beings, as well as between a man and a woman, and that it is not to be had without effort and growth. It was something that would take all there was in him to live up to.

As he walked beside her, he was dedicating all there was in him to loving her.

II

She was tired, heavenly tired, when she reached her room that late afternoon. She had not been tired like that since she was a little girl; relaxed, abandoned before the soft-footed advance of sleep. She could scarcely think coherently enough to remember to send word that she would not appear at dinner, before she was undressed and in her bed. There was nothing in her mind but this exquisite fatigue, from which presently, even now, as she thought of it, sleep would drift her away. She laid her tired head on the pillow with a long breath. Some weak tears gathered in her eyes and ran slowly down, but they were sweet tears, not bitter. And so she fell asleep.

It was late, when she woke, well on into the next day, and the room was filled with the crystal clarity of daylight. As she opened her eyes, she was thinking as though it were the continuation of a dream, that if she ever had children she would . . . she would take *care* of them! She would learn how always to be close to them, so that she would be there, ready to help them when . . . She wouldn't leave them helplessly to think that the evil was in life itself and not in coarse and evil minds. She wouldn't leave them for years to think that the poor, mean joking of sniggering servants is all there is to life and love. She would stand up for them, look out for them! Marise stood fiercely on her guard for them now, up in arms against what threatened them.

It had never before in her life, not even fleetingly, not once, occurred to her that she might ever have children. She knew now that she wanted them. That was the second step into her own life.

CHAPTER LV

NEALE could not sleep. Of course he could not sleep. Sleep was for fools with nothing to think about. But Neale had . . . such things to think about!

She had let him in. She had let him in. He stood in the holy of holies and knew that he was welcome.

Now he knew the meaning of her look that first evening on the roof. Now he knew why, up there under the ilex trees that morning, her dear eyes had been for an instant wild as if with fright when he drew near. And yet, even before she had let him in, her eyes had softened from fright to quiet trust as he looked down at her, had softened to that look, *her* look, which thrust him through and through with love for her.

He turned impatiently back and forth on his bed, seeing, everywhere he looked, those liquid dark eyes, that sweet, sweet mouth, till he held his empty arms out longingly in the dark. His desire was like a fire. He knew such pain as he had not dreamed of, and he would not for any price have lost an instant of that pain. Had he ever said he was an unlighted torch? He was flaming now, to his last fiber.

Presently he got up, lighted his candle and dressed. It was impossible to lie still with this fire of life blazing in him. He would be beside himself by dawn, if he had not worked some of it off. He let himself out carefully into the corridor, and walked down to her door. There, before it were her shoes, her little, dusty shoes which had brought her back to him. He picked one up and held it in his hand. He stroked it like something alive. The dust on it was dear to him.

When he stepped out into the silent, deserted piazza a church clock struck two, boomingly. The night air was cool on his cheek. The great, starlit dusky sky, spacious over his head, was none too large to hold the greatness in his heart that night. It filled all space to the last dim, shining star. He set off at random, anywhere, not noticing where his feet took him, up one street and down another—blindly, as he had lived. And yet somehow he had found his goal.

The splash of water struck on his ear. He saw in the starlight the dim sheen and sparkle of a fountain—Trevi. He stood still to think of what it reminded him—Madison Square and Martha.

His heart went out to Martha as he stood there. He thought of her not with embarrassment, as the woman he had loved before he met Marise. He had not loved her. He thought of Martha tenderly, calmly, with deep gratitude. He owed all this to her. She had saved him from the second-rate, dingy life he had been so dingily ready to accept. She had somehow divined that there must be something else. Something else! Neale was shaken at the thought! Why, now, this instant, if some one struck him down dead as he stood there, he would have lived more, known more of the joy and sacredness of love than after forty years with Martha. He wished he knew how to pray, so that he could pray that Martha too might know it.

And then, with a rush, Martha was gone from his mind, and Marise stood there, Marise, looking up at him with piteous, frightened eyes that softened to trust, to quiet trust.

He set off swiftly, swinging his arms and talking to himself. How could he be worthy of such a trust! He *would* be worthy of it. By God, he would give her a square deal. A square deal such as no other woman ever had! The whole of his heart, his respect, his honor. He would share his life with her loyally, as with an equal . . . no hidden thoughts, no half-way openness, no dark corners of compromise, no secret chambers kept for himself. All the great gates flung open to welcome her into her own home.

He flung his arms wide, and looked up at the stars, which were beginning faintly to grow dim against the whitening sky.

His passion seized on him now and shook him till he was faint with it.

When it passed for a little, he turned back towards the

east, towards the Pincian hill where he had so often walked with her, where he had seen her that morning. The shade of the ilex trees was full of her presence to him. He was far from there, half across the city. As if it were a goal he had set himself, he began to hasten, to lengthen his stride, to let out some of the strength that boiled up in him like a geyser.

It did him good to walk furiously fast, to tire himself a little. His thoughts grew less wild, his heart stopped leaping and pounding. She had looked frightened because she was afraid of love, poor darling, as she was of life. He would show her what love could be. He would wash all that old poison of doubt and distrust and fear out of her life with the ocean of his love. They would live together so openly, so honestly, so naturally, that she could forget wholly all the sick, morbid impressions that her life had left on her, that she would come to trust and love life and love and nature, with its serene progression of birth, growth, death, even the decay which is only preparation for another birth.

Why, that was something he could *do* for her! He had something to give her, something she needed, something to match a little the golden treasure she poured out on him with her every glance. It was incredible good fortune! How under the sun could a man, a poor, plain, ordinary human being, live so that he might be worthy of such transcendent good fortune?

He was swinging up the long steps now, the dawn white and clear about him. Here was where he had turned that morning and saw her standing afar off, bright under the black shade, come back to him! Here was where he had been near enough to see her face, her brows drawn together, the seeking look in her eyes. He had always thought Marise's eyes seemed to be looking for something. Here was where he had seen that they looked frightened. And now he stood on the very spot where she had stood, and he saw again her eyes soften into quiet trust.

If somehow she might find in him what she was looking for! His heart stood still in awe.

He looked out over the sleeping city, its roofs and domes and towers coming palely into the new day; and he saw her dark eyes soften from fright to quiet trust.

God! Suppose he had never lived, never known Marise! The sweat stood out on him at the thought.

If she could . . . if she could look into his face and find that life had put there what she sought.

The sun rose magnificently and cast over all the world a flood of golden light.

Neale stood in it, praising and magnifying God, who had sent him into life.

CHAPTER LVI

THEY were on their way to hear a Palestrina mass in a chapel at St. Peter's, and stopped beside one of the great fountains rushing with a leap into the brilliant air and falling in white clouds of spray.

"I've heard," said Livingstone, "that if you get at the right angle to the sun, you can see a million little rainbows."

They began to walk here and there over the wet, moss-grown paving-stones around the base of the fountain, looking up at the glittering splendor of the upward plunging water, their ears filled with the liquid silver plashing and dripping of its fall. "Perhaps this isn't the right fountain, with the sun where it is," suggested Livingstone. He and Eugenia walked off across the wide piazza towards the other fountain. Neale turned towards Marise. She was standing on the other side of the basin, and as he looked at her the wind flung the huge white veil of spray over her. She stood in its midst like a novice in her white robes . . . or like a bride. Her eyes were lifted to the great plume of the leaping water.

He sprang toward her, crying jealously, "What do you think of when you look like that?" He raised his voice to drown out the shouting uproar of the water.

The wind caught the spray and cast it away to the other side.

She answered him, dreamily, "I was wondering how we could ever know what we are made for?"

The wind shifted and for an instant cast the white veil over them both. Through it he called to her, "*I* know! I know what I was made for! To love you all the days of my life."

The wind whirled away the sparkling curtain of water. They stood in the quiet golden sunshine. His ears rang in the silence. Had he really at last cried it out to her? Or was it only one more of the thousand times when he had cried it soundlessly to his own heart? Eugenia and Livingstone had come back, were beside them now, between them; carrying them along up the endless steps to the church door. It was like walking in a dream. Neale tried to see Marise's face, but it was hidden by the broad-brimmed droop of her hat. Only the sweet, sweet lines of her lips. . . .

No, it could not be that he had spoken. It had been only another of those blinding moments when his heart flung itself up, shouting, into the sunshine of her look.

They stepped silently into the dusky, incense-perfumed chapel. Mass had begun. Eugenia and Marise sank to their knees, Livingstone standing on one side, Neale on the other, the crowd pressing thick and close about them.

From the choir came a long, sonorous chant, and then a silence, in which Neale's thoughts, pounding and hammering in his head, were stilled to one great, solemn petition.

The priest turned and passed from one side of the altar to the other. He raised his hands over the heads of the kneeling people and chanted the "Pax vobiscum."

"Et cum spiritu tuo," responded the choir, on three long, sighing notes that brought peace with them.

Standing there, upright, looking over the heads of the densely packed crowd, his eyes fixed on the steady yellow flame of the altar-candles, Neale felt a touch on his hand. His heart stopped beating. He knew the lightest touch of that hand, as he knew the lightest sound of that voice.

He stood motionless, not breathing . . . waiting.

He felt Marise slip her hand into his, and hold it fast in a close, close clasp. But not so firm as his own on hers. Through the dear flesh of that dear hand he felt her pulse beating against his own, as if he held her in his arms.

The yellow flames of the altar-candles flickered and blurred before his eyes.

A great "Hosanna!" burst from the choir. Or was it in his heart?

CHAPTER LVII

How suddenly it had all broken up, Livingstone thought forlornly, their pleasant little quartet of walks and talks. He had the sensation of being left stranded by the ebbing of a tide which had seemed to buoy him up on great depths. With the disappearance of Miss Mills back to her Paris apartment, the very light had gone out of everything. Miss Allen never had had the social grace and ease of Miss Mills, and now she ate her meals silently and vanished immediately, and Crittenden, not being a social light on any occasion, was of less than no use in saving the situation.

Livingstone was reduced to solitary mornings spent in museums, with a book of art criticism in his hand; or on Sunday mornings, when admission was free, on a bench in the park on the Palatine. The benches were very comfortable there, not mere backless slabs of stone, and when you felt like sight-seeing you could get up and lean over the wall and look down into the Forum and pick out where the different buildings had stood.

He stood thus, his back to the long, cypress-shaded path, trying to be archeological, his guide-book open on the wall. Which of the battered rows of stumps of pillars had been the Temple of Vesta and which the Fornix Fabianus?

He heard voices back of him. To be exact he heard Miss Allen's voice back of him. Livingstone was so paralyzed by the quality of it that, gentleman though he tried to be to the marrow of his bones, he was for an instant incapable of stirring and announcing his presence. *That*, Miss Allen's voice! She sounded as though she had come into a fortune. But what under the sun was she saying?

"Here, exactly here, is where we stood when you said you were like the puppy, and when you rolled the dusty weight of all those centuries off my shoulders. And now come along. The next place in the pilgrimage is St. John Lateran, where you said, you brutal Prussian, that nothing would induce you to protect a woman!"

"Come, come, this is eavesdropping. Something must be done!" said Livingstone to himself. He shut his guide-book with a slam to give them warning, and faced about resolutely. But they had paid no attention to his warning. They stood with their backs to him, and, oh! hand in hand like rustics at a country fair. But she had called him a brutal Prussian! And a puppy!

"Ahem!" said Mr. Livingstone, loudly, not knowing what else to say.

They turned about, and saw him, and seemed neither surprised nor ashamed. Miss Allen stepped quickly towards him, smiling and saying, "Oh, Mr. Livingstone, we were meaning to tell you anyhow. . . . Mr. Crittenden and I are going to be married."

She smiled at him dazzlingly as she spoke, but Livingstone was not at all sure from the expression of her eyes that she saw him. It crossed his mind that she would have smiled as dazzlingly as that if a lamp-post had stood in his place.

"Married!" he cried, really aghast for both of them. That sensitive, imaginative girl tied for life to that unfeeling, rough, hard fellow. What on earth did she, even for a moment, see in him? And as for Crittenden . . . any man with a little money of his own, personable enough to marry advantageously, throwing himself away on a girl without a penny either now or in prospect! To what a wretched, cramped life he was dooming himself and her . . . back rooms in greasy, third-rate pensions, never any margin for decent clothes. . . .

"Yes, and we're going to live in Ashley, Vermont."

Livingstone sank down on his bench, appalled. Worse than third-rate pensions! Worse than the human mind could conceive!

"Oh, no! No! No!" he cried to her as though he were clutching at her as she sank to ruin. "No! Don't say that! You've no idea . . . my dear young lady, you haven't the faintest idea what an impossible life that would be. You mustn't consider it for a moment. Crittenden, you mustn't let her consider it. An American country village. Good God! You don't know what it is, what the people are!"

"Yes, I do, too," she told him gaily, giving the effect, though she stood quite still, of executing a twirling pirouette of high spirits. "I've lived there. It's really going back home for both of us."

"Home! Why, Crittenden certainly told me he'd never been there in his life!"

"Oh, pshaw, Livingstone, don't be so heavy-handed and literal. Why wet-blanket *every* imaginative fancy?" said Crittenden, laughing loudly as though some one had made a joke. He might, for the impression he made on Livingstone, have joined hands with the girl to dance madly around him in a circle. But this was no laughing matter. This was terrible! Tragic! They had simply lost their heads, both of them, lost their heads and had no idea what they were doing. You could tell that by the wild glitter in their eyes. They were infatuated, that was it, infatuated. He must try to recall them to their senses. He turned imploringly to the girl. "But . . . but . . . but . . ." He was so agitated that he could not bring out his words. He stopped, drew a long breath, and passed his hand over his forehead. Then, very solemnly, "Do you know," he said to her, warningly, "do you know that you will probably have to *do your own work?*"

At this, she burst into an inexplicable, foolish shout of laughter, opening her eyes very wide at him and saying, "Appalling!"

She looked up at Crittenden, who for his part never took his eyes an instant from her.

How foolishly she talked! How foolishly she laughed! Why, they were acting as sentimentally as . . . Mr. Livingstone could not think of any comparison adequate to their foolishness.

They were moving away now, nodding good-by to him and smiling at each other. At the top of the dark steps leading down through the Palace of the Cæsars to the Forum they turned and cast a backward glance at him, who stood stock-still where they had left him, staring after them, dumfounded. Miss Allen looked at him and then came flying back, running, her light dress fluttering. What did she want? What was she going to do, with that shining, tremulous, mirthful face? Livingstone felt afraid of her, as if, like a swift bolt of summer lightning, she might strike him through and through.

What she did was to take his face in her two hands and give him a hearty kiss on each cheek. *"Dear* Mr. Livingstone!" she said (or was it *"poor"?*)

Livingstone had the impression, from the expression of her face, that she would have kissed a cab-man with equal fervor, and that Crittenden would have watched her do it with the same fatuous look he had now.

They went down together into the vaulted darkness and desolation of the ruined palace. Livingstone, leaning on the wall high above, saw them emerge together into the Forum and step off over the ancient flagged paving. And still hand in hand! Mr. Livingstone had by this time thought of an adequate comparison. They were as sentimental as a couple of Rogers statuettes!

Looking up, they saw him leaning there. They waved their hands and called up some laughing greeting to him. But he could not understand what they said, because they were too far away from him.

Hand in hand in the fierce, literal brightness of the noonday sun, they trod their new path over the ancient stones.

THE END